OCTOPUS ALIBI

Octopus Alibi

Tom Corcoran

THOMAS DUNNE BOOKS
ST. MARTIN'S MINOTAUR ✖ NEW YORK

THOMAS DUNNE BOOKS.
An imprint of St. Martin's Press.

OCTOPUS ALIBI. Copyright © 2003 by Tom Corcoran. All rights reserved. Printed in the United States of America. No part of this book may be used or reproduced in any manner whatsoever without written permission except in the case of brief quotations embodied in critical articles or reviews. For information, address St. Martin's Press, 175 Fifth Avenue, New York, N.Y. 10010.

www.minotaurbooks.com

Book design by Jonathan Bennett

Library of Congress Cataloging-in-Publication Data

Corcoran, Tom.
    Octopus alibi / Tom Corcoran.
      p. cm.
    ISBN 0-312-29127-2
      1. Rutledge, Alex (Fictitious character)—Fiction.   2. Key West (Fla.)—Fiction.
3. Photographers—Fiction.   I. Title.

PS3553.O6444 O28 2003
813'.54—dc21

                                                                          2002032504

First Edition: February 2003

10   9   8   7   6   5   4   3   2   1

ACKNOWLEDGMENTS

Heartfelt thanks must go to Franette Ansel Abercrombie, Carolyn Ferguson, David Sayre, Sandie Herron, Richard Badolato, Cherie Binger, Wendy L. Nelson, Teresa Murphy Clark, Jay Gewin, Marty Corcoran, and Dinah George.

Again I thank all the booksellers who "hand sell" my Alex Rutledge novels. And special thanks to all the book reviewers who don't spoil readers' surprises by revealing plot twists.

As the circle of light increases,
so does its circumference of darkness.

—Albert Einstein

Greed is a fat demon with a small mouth
and whatever you feed it is never enough.

—the commissaris, in *Just a Corpse at Twilight*
by Janwillem van de Wetering

OCTOPUS ALIBI

1

THE AIR INSIDE THE taxi could have fertilized a Glades County cane field. Secondhand curry and clove gum fought the driver's sour odor, and a thick nicotine haze on the windows gave the sky a sickly mustard tint, blurring the five electric towers south of us. I wished I was back in Key West, inhaling salt breezes through screens, packing for my photo job on Grand Cayman Island. My southbound flight was forty-eight hours away. I had let too many pre-trip details slide.

My wish to be elsewhere passed quickly. Sam Wheeler had done me a lifetime of favors in recent years, favors hard to pay back. This was a chance to chip away at my debt. I needed to be right where I was, in the backseat of a taxi in a stamp-sized parking lot near Fort Lauderdale. Sam, too, was doing what he had to do. In the room where he stood, it was fifty degrees colder than anywhere else in South Florida just before noon.

Unnerved by our proximity to the morgue, the cabbie kept checking his mirrors, twisting to scout the upscale mobile homes across the street. After a county van departed, he moved his taxi from open sunlight to the shade of a bottlebrush tree. He left his engine running and turned up a small orange radio he had taped to the dashboard. The box was tuned to a talk show, a meeting ground for people whose opinions and mouths outran their smarts. He had stuck an old religious icon, a feathered crucifix, to the dash below the radio. I wanted to invoke its powers to make my day end better than it had begun. I doubted that I was tuned to its wavelength.

After several minutes of stale air and radio talk, the man tapped his finger on a gauge. "We lose this cold air, mon, or I got to go."

He was wise to worry on a hot April day. Most cars that old, idling with the air conditioner cranked full blast, would boil radiators in ten minutes. I leaned forward, checked his temp needle. It rested a hair above normal.

Engine heat was not his problem.

Sam had been inside the innocuous, sand-colored building for only seven minutes. I had no idea how long he would be in there. I slid the man twenty bucks—a third of it tip. I would rather sweat in ninety-degree open air than be force-fed drivel while I stuck to cheap vinyl seat covers. We could call another cab when Sam was free.

Harsh brightness hit me as I walked from the taxi. The driver backed, spun his steering wheel, and launched forward at full throttle. He fishtailed, braked for an instant, and almost hit a sheriff's cruiser at the apron. The deputy shook his head and drove to the vacated shady slot as if near misses happened all the time. He got out, gazed up the road, kick-closed the county car's door. He was about five-eight, with a crewcut, huge muscles, a thick neck, and broad chest. He wore a red polo shirt, had a gold badge clipped to his belt, a weapon in a hip holster. He ignored me as he strode to the building. He was a lawman on a mission. I could've been dancing on stilts, juggling kittens and hand grenades. He would have ignored me.

Broward County's a tough beat.

Sam had shown up on Dredgers Lane at seven-thirty that morning. My head was half under a pillow, but I recognized the single knock, his soft two-note whistle through the porch screen door. Strange way to start a

Monday. It was too early for a social call, and Sam never came by without phoning first.

Sam looked whipped and puzzled. He fixed his eyes on the kitchen wall and skipped the salutations. "You got a busy day?"

I thought about the legal-pad list, chores I had put off, bills I hadn't paid, quotes I should have mailed days ago. I pictured my last-minute scramble, from the house to the airport, two days away. Then I thought about everything Sam had done for me.

"I mean, if you're busy, Alex . . ."

"Nothing I can't ignore," I said.

"I need to be in Broward for a couple hours. I bought two tickets for a turnaround. I'll buy us a good lunch. We'll be back here by five."

With the constant easterlies, the past couple weeks of twenty- to twenty-five-knot winds abating, I'd have guessed that Sam would want to spend his day on the water, catching up with regular customers. He was dressed for work. He'd become sensitive to sunlight in recent years, and always wore lightweight long-sleeved shirts and long trousers. But I noticed that he wore sneakers instead of his leather boat shoes. I couldn't imagine a fishing guide and Vietnam vet needing a traveling companion. I decided to let him explain when he was ready.

Teresa walked out of the bathroom, wrapped in a large towel with a smaller towel around her head. She nodded hello, but looked displeased to find Sam in the house.

"Is there time to brush my teeth?" I said.

"Take a shower. The flight's not till eight-twenty. I'll make coffee."

Sam spoke softly as he drove his old Ford Bronco to the airport. "Not really my business, but is Teresa that unpleasant every morning?"

"She does her major thinking when she wakes up. That brain whips up to speed before the coffee hits. Plus, she worked late last night."

We crossed Garrison Bight. Sam didn't glance at his boat slip or check which guides were still at the dock. He moved his cup to his left hand so he could shift gears. "She doesn't like dawn distractions?"

"Especially when she clocks out at midnight. I keep my distance."

"The woman in the bubble?"

"With me outside, looking in," I said.

"Tell me again that apartment deal."

"Her landlord went to monthly rentals, on short notice. He jacked up the rent and drove out four different tenants. It's gone from an apartment to a condo, then a residential atrium. They never trim that dime-sized yard. They'll probably advertise it as a two-bed, two-bath estate with mature foliage."

"So, you got a roomie?"

"Hell, the past eight months we've lived together in two different places. This cuts our commute by ten blocks."

"Okay so far?"

"Three days. She has her moods. It's too soon to decide."

Sam drove across to Flagler. "I got a call at six from a deputy medical examiner in Broward. They found a dead woman up there, beat up bad, dumped on a tree lawn in a ritzy subdivision. They say it's my sister, Lorie. They want me to do the formalities, sign the piece of paper."

"The sister you'd lost track of?"

"Since the mid-Eighties." Sam paused, then said, "The same month the Challenger blew up, Lorie went poof, too. She'd sent me a photograph; she was holding a snook she'd caught in Chokoloskee. I called a few days later, but the phone was disconnected. I never heard from her again. My sisters up north, Flora and Ida, they never did either." Sam went silent a moment, then added, "Lorie had a few problems back then with abusive boyfriends. Strange, she was still in Lauderdale."

"How did they track you down?"

"An old picture of me in her wallet. I mailed one to each sister from Fort Benning during Jump School. Lorie probably couldn't read yet. Flora was about to start school. Little Ida, come to think of it, I don't know if she was born. I signed the backs of the photos, 'Love, Brother

Sam,' with my service number under my name. I was one gung ho son of a bitch."

Sam was quiet on the flight. It's not easy to talk on a droning commuter plane, anyway. This one was full of sunburned spring breakers, leaving the party, flying back to reality. We'd bought the *Key West Citizen* and the *Miami Herald* before boarding and swapped sections during the flight. Several front-section articles normally would have drawn comment from Sam. He'd had nothing to say. Not even a wisecrack about toasted college kids. Our friendship had endured because we could survive silence in each other's company. This deflated mood was not reflective or pissed-off quiet. In the years I had known Sam, I had never seen a silence of absolute sadness.

He nudged me, pointed as we descended over the Everglades on final glide into Lauderdale. Months ago he'd described the huge highway cloverleaf below us. The Interstate had wiped out Andytown, the crossroad where Sam had been a teenager. He still could claim Muncie, Indiana, as his real hometown. But his sisters, born in Florida, at home, had lost their roots to road planners, graders, and cement mixers. The interchange was larger than the town that preceded it.

After we touched down, Sam said, "Lorie was so damned stubborn, like my old man. She and the old man were going at it in the car one time, back when 441 was in the Everglades. He was snarling and she was snapping, arguing over nothing. He pulled to the shoulder and told her he wasn't going to have her damned sass. She could change her tone or walk home. She got out and closed the door. A mile down the highway I realized he wasn't going to stop. He was going to let a nine-year-old girl hike ten miles on a rural two-lane. I told him to let me out, too. He did, and drove away. I'd walked maybe two minutes back in her direction. The next thing I knew a big Oldsmobile sedan pulled over to pick me up. Lorie had thumbed herself a ride. We damn near beat the old man home."

"How did he react to that?"

"He never said a thing. She never did, either."

"Tough little girl."

"I guess not tough enough."

The sun stared down as if I were on trial. I looked away as if guilty, stood next to a drainage culvert under a tree hung with flaming crimson blossoms. I checked my watch, then told myself to quit checking my watch. The cabbie was halfway back to the airport hack line. I still smelled of clove gum and curry.

The Broward Medical Examiner Lab looked like thousands of other single-story Florida office buildings. I had to think that some county architect in a hurry to start happy hour had whipped out the plans on a Friday afternoon. A landscaper had tried to save his ass with sweet viburnum, live oak, dwarf poinciana, and wax myrtle. I found it strange that Broward had set the laboratory in a Dania Beach section of upscale mobile-home parks and midscale condos. A trump of all flags at half-mast, an empty flagpole, stood near the entrance. Its ropes fluttered in the breeze, and heavy hooks slapped the hollow pole. The setting brought to mind the conflict in my career, the extremes of beautiful and gruesome, of fulfilling jobs and those that were draining and dangerous.

Three years ago I had thought that part-time forensic work would boost my cash flow and fill slack time. I had started with the Key West Police, jobs that didn't require science or complex procedures. My name got talked up. Within months, Monroe County's detectives were calling when their full-timers were overworked or on vacation. The only good thing about my sideline was extra bucks toward my bills. The bad part was how close I came to tragedy, how crime jobs had dragged me into a realm I'd avoided most of my life. I still worked regularly, mostly out of town, doing light journalism, ad-agency shoots, and magazine features. But those gigs promised me no great future. Within the past few months, two ad clients had been bought out. Their choice assignments had vanished along with their corporate names. Even with the Grand Cayman job, my fiscal year could be as hollow as the empty flagpole. Unless I hit a surprise jackpot, a windfall out of the blue, I faced seven more years of mortgage payments. My short-notice, one-shot forensic jobs could make the difference between eating and going hungry.

Sam once wisecracked, "If you or I ever go broke, we can blame domestic taxes and imported beer."

His one-liner was going south. Along with my bank balance.

At ten after twelve a white cab rolled into the morgue's parking lot. The woman at the wheel yelled, "Yo, you Rutledge?"

I nodded.

"We waitin' on somebody?"

I nodded again.

"Man inside saw your cab leave. Happens a lot, they call for another one, they call for me. Your friend got a relative in there?"

"That's what they told him."

"You're on the clock, honey. Damn, you're a tall one." She shut off her motor, dropped the keys in her shirt pocket, pulled out a box of Benson & Hedges. She had yanked her hair into a ponytail and was dressed twenty years younger than her face, fighting time. She had spent a few years on the beach, or smoking had parched her skin. Probably both.

"Cross your fingers," she said. She fired a cigarette, held it high so the smoke wouldn't blow my way. In her other hand she held the cigarette box and a Bic pinched between her thumb and two fingers. She waved that hand toward the building. "They've been wrong in there before."

"You don't look as nervous as the man who brought us here."

"Black man?"

"Yes."

"They're immigrants from the voodoo league of nations. They're afraid that their spirits will escape to the morgue, or their souls will be ravaged to the sound of a hundred batá drums. Or, worse yet, dead people walking—zombies and fire hags—will dance a *rada* in their rearview mirrors. This is the tissues-and-sympathy hack. I get sent here a lot."

"You deal with it okay?"

She waved again, toward the flagpole. "I used to work inside a door that's inside that door. I saw what came through the back, the sad messes they off-loaded. I never got used to it, but it didn't weird me out. When I was inside, I taught myself not to react, not to have feelings. I don't know how I did that, I really don't. Looking back, I worry about that part of me. I worry about it more than ghosts or bad luck or whatever."

"So it's immigrants fighting their imaginations?"

She nodded and inhaled hard, sucked smoke down to her knees, then picked a nonexistent tobacco flake off her tongue. Old habits hang in.

"Imagination can be more powerful than reality," I said.

"They'd be shitless for sure if they ever saw the real thing." The smoke leaked from her lungs as she spoke. She patted the taxi's roof. "The heat of the day, in nutso Gold Coast traffic, this job is heaven. Take my word."

"Heaven?"

"Well, raw heaven."

Sam stepped out of the building, flinched, and put on his sunglasses. He walked toward us without expression. His walk carried more resolve, as if he had reached a decision, promised himself a course of action.

"You hungry?" he said.

The question surprised me. "Are you?"

"It was somebody's sister, but not mine. Fish sandwich okay?"

I shrugged.

Sam asked our driver to take us to Ernie's Restaurant.

"Eighteen-hundred block of South Federal," she said, then looked me in the eye. She had told me that people behind those doors sometimes got it wrong. She wanted to win her point.

I nodded, and silently gave it to her.

2

TWENTY MINUTES LATER OUR cabdriver pulled into the restaurant lot. She turned to Sam, pulled an unlit cigarette from above her right ear. "Be careful, buddy," she said. "I used to work in that county lab. Six years, and I seen it all. The news you got sounds good, but you didn't win no lottery. I'll tell you why. Unless you're one in a thousand, you went into the grieving process, and coming out unscathed isn't automatic."

Wheeler pulled out his wallet. "I don't feel this way because I skipped breakfast?"

"Was your sister's ID on the body? Current ID, photo of the victim?"

"Nothing current. Her Social Security card, a copy of her birth certificate, a few photos, personal papers. Stuff no one ever carries around."

"No valid driver's license, no unexpired credit cards?"

He shook his head.

The woman bit her upper lip and nodded. "You look like the kind of guy, you can handle straight talk. Take it from an old hand, for what it's worth. This ain't scientific, but it's up here." She tapped her forehead. "The doctors call it empirical evidence. Better than fifty-fifty, your grieving might be right on. You follow me?"

Sam paid our fare, opened his door, then turned and looked her in the eye. "You mind if I ask your name?"

She pointed to the license on the passenger-side visor. "Irene Jones. Unique handle, eh? The assholes at the morgue used to call me 'Goodnight Irene.' I guess that's not the most sensitive thing to say to you right now."

Sam waved it off. She asked his name and he told her.

We walked past a military-straight row of newspaper, real-estate-flyer, and coupon-pamphlet boxes. Sam said, "Let's hope the place smells like grease. I want this stench out of my nose."

Inside the restaurant's door, a dozen people waited for tables. Sam gave the greeter his name. She ignored the line, led us to a remote booth, and took our drink order. Sam ordered us two beers apiece.

"Preferential treatment?" I said.

Sam said, "We've got a meeting when the local fuzz gets here. Macho boy, said he'd buy our food, which is unlike a cop. I have no idea what he wants. He said to try the conch chowder."

"Local knowledge is good," I said.

We watched a server spritz a vacant glass-top table as if he owned stock in Windex. The mist floated our way, made us grateful our drinks and food hadn't arrived yet. I let Sam have his quiet, his time to consider what might come next. I figured he was pondering the "straight talk" from the woman in the taxi.

Detective Odin Marlow showed up four minutes later. I spotted the red polo shirt and muscular build immediately. He was the deputy I had seen in the morgue lot. He clutched a box of Benson & Hedges in his left hand. The pack and a Bic, just like Goodnight Irene Jones. Sliding a breath mint into his mouth, Marlow introduced himself as "BSO, CIU," as if the initials meant big stuff to us. He wore a badge. That said it all. The greeter appeared with an iced tea, made special with two straws and two lemon slices on the rim. She put the glass down, gave the deputy a flirtatious sneer.

Marlow took his tea, then said, "Mr. Rutledge, you mind sitting over there? I'm a lefty. I'll bump your arm fifty times while I'm eating."

He didn't give a crap about arm bumping. He wanted to face us and not worry about his gun being next to my hand. Sam slid over so I could fit on his bench. Marlow placed his cigarettes and lighter on the table as if they were ceremonial objects and settled into the booth. He smelled like a sniff sample in a fancy magazine. He wore a diamond pinky ring and an antique Gubelin watch on a leather strap. One more piece of jewelry and his department's internal team would be on his butt. The men at the top don't like to see their boys display wealth. Perhaps Marlow had shown his supervisor a receipt for zirconium. Maybe that's how they all dress in Lauderdale.

The server took our food order, and Marlow started right in. "We found her out in District Eight, in what we call the I-75 Corridor, the extension of 595. You got your housing developments popping up like palmettos, your wealthy folk from south of the Gulf Stream, most of them from south of the equator. Where they come from, you know, they're kidnap targets, they can't shop, can't spend their money. It's low profile for survival. This is the comfort life. They got their Expeditions, their cable TV, slate tile floors, the built-in vacuum cleaner systems, pools, the malls, red tile roofs. They also got public schools, no more political strife, no more family security guards."

Sam said, "This has to do with a dumped murder victim?"

"The last thing they want in their new neighborhood is a body. I got no proof, but I say no way this was Latino connected . . ."

Neither Sam nor I had suggested such a connection.

". . . and that improves our chances of solving this thing. Bumps it up from one percent to, say, three percent. So we know it's not your sister. All we got is fingerprints and a dental imprint, which, with women, who are less often in jail and rarely in the military, drops our chances back to two percent. Take into account, women change their names when they get married, we're back below the one percent chance."

"That relates to the victim," said Sam. "Let's go sideways. What're the odds my sister's alive?"

"I hate to use the word 'zilch,' but here's how it works. Criminals working credit scams swipe names from the living. People who want new identities grab names from the dead."

"And here we've got . . ."

"New identities go to people hiding from the law, or hiding from partners they've screwed over, or hiding from abusive spouses."

"So, if I found old dental records for my sister . . ."

"Don't even think about it. It's bad enough looking for a name to match a body. Working backward don't cut it."

"You don't call a slim chance better than none?" said Sam.

"I know where you're coming from. The M.E.'s investigators called you in, got you jacked up, put you on a mission. Before you knew it wasn't her, you were thinking 'eye for an eye' to even the score. Call it a private retribution. You figured you owed your dead sister that much. Am I correct?"

"Was it a robbery?" said Sam.

Marlow shook his head. "You'd find high-end clothing. Tan lines where the watch and the rings are gone. This victim, she was a WalMart customer. She was small change. She was a poor target. I'd guess revenge, or she knew too much about bad people. Or, like I said, spousal abuse."

Sam shrugged, wandered off in his thoughts.

No one spoke as our food arrived. We began to eat. Marlow shifted gears. "Tell me about that island of yours," he said. "You really like Key West?"

Sam didn't look up from his food. "Other than the military, not many people live there because they're forced to."

"It's been years since I've been south of Florida City. Key West was full of gays and people smoking dope on the beach. That still the deal?"

"It's strange down there," said Sam. "And loud. Chain saws, cockatoos, straight pipes, roosters, and sirens. You'd probably hate it, Officer Marlow. Don't waste your gas money."

The detective gave Sam a minute of silence, then said, "It's *Detective* Marlow, and I'm reading your mind."

"It's blank," said Sam.

"You were thinking of ways, and don't tell me it ain't true. You're riding revenge energy. Nine times out of ten we appreciate that type of reaction. It reduces our job load. Ten times out of ten we bust you for it."

"I'm not the violent type."

"You may not be the type, but you were a paratrooper. You're the right age, you pulled a tour in Southeast Asia. It's my guess you were trained for . . . what did they call them, contingencies? So you find out it ain't her. You shift your mission, you try some freelance snooping. We like that about the same as two-bit vigilante work."

"Think what you want."

Marlow pulled a ballpoint and a tiny Spiral pad from his trouser pocket. "When's the last time you saw her?"

" 'Eighty-six."

The detective stared at Sam. "All these years, could she have found you? How long you lived in the same place?"

"Since 'eighty-one, the same place. My number's in the book."

Marlow stared at his pen, then began to snap it back and forth between the two bottles in front of Sam. The pen was not for writing. It was a prop, and the cop had taken notice of Sam's desire for two beers. "So if she had gone online, clicked 'People Search,' typed your name, you'd have popped up on her screen?"

Sam nodded, shrugged again.

He said, "You got pictures of her?"

"Nope."

The pen went to the edge of the table, its use as a prop expended. "We wanted to let you know, ask your cooperation. We're gonna run a squib in the *Sun-Sentinel*, announce that the body was ID'd as your sister. It could work for both of us. I'll maybe learn something about the victim, and you'll maybe connect with a lost relative. The squib won't show up in Miami. It won't show in the Keys. We plan to keep it strictly local."

Marlow went to a vacant expression, waited for Sam's reaction. I didn't look at Sam, but I knew he wasn't showing emotion, either.

Marlow found another prop, a subtle distraction. He used a french fry to trace designs in his remaining ketchup. "Your own sister," he said, "and not a single photo? Can I ask why?"

Sam looked him in the eye. "You have your methods. I have my limits."

"Nifty answer. What's it mean?"

"You want to blow her out of the weeds. I'd like to coax her out."

"Look at it this way," said Marlow. "Her fifteen years to find you goes the other way. You've had fifteen years to find her. I take it you haven't tried."

Sam shrugged.

"And you're worried about her picture in the paper?"

Sam nudged me. "What do you think, Alex?"

"There's more to gain than lose," I said. "But if she's alive, could it put her in danger?"

Marlow leaned toward Wheeler. "This guy your roadie?"

Sam said, "No, my witness."

"You got a business card?"

Sam pulled out his wallet and handed one to the man.

The detective read the card, stood, snatched his cigarettes. "Do yourself a favor, Captain Wheeler. Do like you've been doing since Ron and Nancy were in Washington. Wait for her to call. Thanks for the club sandwich. You'll find a taxi out front in five minutes."

Marlow sucked in air, tensed the muscles in his chest, then walked from the table. Ten feet away he hesitated, then looked back at me. "The watch was my father's," he said. "Right to the day he died, he was police chief in Greenwich, Connecticut."

Marlow exchanged patter with two waitresses on his way out.

"Real sweetie," said Sam.

"His next smoke was more important than our talk," I said. "He neglected to ask if you had other brothers or sisters."

"Right. The type who promises what he wants you to hear and delivers what he wants you to believe. Finish your beer."

We walked outside to find Marlow still there, leaning against his county car, smoking a cigarette. He said, "I'm curious, Mr. Wheeler. How's fishing in the lower Keys this month?"

Sam shook his head. "Constant east wind, just like here. Messed things up good."

Marlow agreed, "When the wind blows, fishing sucks."

"Let me put it this way," said Sam. "Yesterday and the day before were my first all-day charters since mid-March. The weather kicked up the water. The bay-side shallows look like milky green soup."

Marlow had a distracted look in his eyes, as if he'd gotten smoke in one of them. "I was thinking of running my Fountain down there this weekend. It's been months since I ran that Yamaha 225. I need to run it more often."

"If the sea bottom's riled, the fish can't see your bait," said Sam. "The wind's an ugly enemy. Like I said before, don't waste your gas money."

Marlow nodded, still distracted. "Speaking of not setting your hook, you decide to snoop around up here, this is not a quaint beach town anymore. You'll get yourself in a world of hurt. Hire yourself a private eye. We got 'em for all budgets and needs. You want to go that way, give me a call."

Sam didn't talk in the cab. He stared at sprawl, fast-food joints and tire stores, and reacted to none of it. At the airport, he called Marnie from a pay booth. I heard him say, "False alarm. I'd rather see Lorie dead than looking like that woman must've looked when she was alive."

The flight back to Key West was bouncy. Late-afternoon heat played hell with the air mass above heated land and the cooling sea. A salt mist lay on the Keys, reflecting sunlight, obscuring the horizon. North of us, a single-cell cumulonimbus had drifted off the mainland and vertical arrows of lightning danced inside it. If the pattern held, it would be seven months before the cool, dry breezes of tropical winter returned.

Sam remained quiet, consumed by another man's jargon and his own frustration. Throughout our fifteen-year acquaintance, the past six or seven in close friendship, Sam and I had come to know each other well. Even in his worst moods, Sam never had failed to express himself.

The engines' buzzing zoned me out. I fled to a half-hour nap. I dreamed about my father chasing me into the house, in a rage. I don't remember why we argued—something about a friend's loud muffler in our driveway—but I recall my mother screaming his name as he caught me in the kitchen and hauled off to slug me. I ducked, and the dent in the freezer door couldn't be repaired. My mother got a new fridge. My father's hand was in a cast for two months, but he got off my case for the rest of the school year.

I woke and filed my dream under "the past," then thought about the next forty hours of my future. I needed to squeeze in five days' errands before I escaped to an island where I knew no one, where I would welcome solid, income-producing work. The Keys' incessant wind had chipped away at my sanity. I damn sure would wallow in Grand Cayman's perfect weather.

Sam stared out the aircraft's window.

I said, "You ever wish your father was still alive?"

"Yep, twice," he said, "but only for two reasons. He would unplug my radio whenever he heard 'What'd I Say?' or anything by Buddy Holly. I wish he'd been around to see Ray Charles perform at the White House. I'd have loved to stuff that in his racist face. And I wish he could've attended that football game in Lubbock, Texas, when forty-nine thousand people made the Guinness Book of Records by singing 'Peggy Sue' in unison."

The pilot made his seat-backs speech. Sam poked me with his elbow. "Before I hung up, I asked Marnie to fetch us at the airport."

"Your Bronco's at the airport."

"Yep, it is. Somehow that fact departed my mind while I was talking. So we won't tell her it's there, and we'll hope maybe she won't see it. I can't have her worrying about me. She gets neurotic."

"What's happened to your memory?" I said.

"I keep forgetting to take my ginkgo biloba."

"Can I ask the main distraction?"

"Marlow bothers me. What detective would ask if he could plant a phony squib in the paper? What cop would sit down to talk about immigrants? And how, on his salary, does this guy own a boat big enough for a Yamaha 225? Did he inherit that, too?"

"Why lunch?" I said. "He thinks you know the dead woman? He suspects you of something? Doesn't make sense."

"That's his cop job coming through. He thinks, 'Arrest them all, let the courts sort it out.'"

I heard a Vietnam echo in the phrase. "Arrest for what?"

His grim expression had frozen as if he would never again laugh or speak in jest. "He'll find something."

"What's that look in your eye?"

"I'll find something, too. With Detective Odin Marlow attached."

3

OUR COMMUTER PLANE ANGLED above a twenty-story cruise ship standing off from Key West Harbor, drew attention from flocks of pastel-draped sightseers on the redesigned Mallory Pier, then chased its cruciform shadow past a hundred bed-and-breakfasts, the bright tin rooftops of Old Town. It flew high above the ghosts of old turtle butchers, shrimpers, long-liners, career whores, chandlers, cockfighters, spongers, ice chippers, shipwrights, dock jockeys, mechanics, and stevedores.

Sam checked without comment the charter wharf as we descended past Garrison Bight. Air turbulence bounced us above the Salt Ponds, mild wind sheer, an edgy end to our hollow trip. We touched down into what I guessed was a twenty-knot headwind, back on the rock, battle-weary, Sam no better off for his round-trip. After he'd had time to reflect, I'd tell him my theory. There is no such thing as a good phone call between three A.M. and sunup.

Marnie Dunwoody had hung back by the Avis lot to save the short-term parking fee. We walked outside, saw her orange Jeep Wrangler, and waited as she pulled from the distant curb and drove toward us.

"What was our cabdriver's name?" said Sam.

"Goodnight Irene Jones."

Under a long-brimmed ball cap, Marnie had a wary look, trying to guess Sam's frame of mind. I clambered into the rear seat as he walked around to the driver's side to give her a hug. In a blue cotton shirt, khaki slacks, and walking shoes, Marnie was dressed for her ten-hour day, searching stories for the *Key West Citizen*. Her light brown hair was shorter than I'd ever seen it. Even after the hug her wariness remained; without words, she knew Sam's mood, knew she would have to adjust to it.

The scramble began around us. Taxi drivers threw down their smokes, popped trunk lids, solicited the first ones out the door. Marnie finessed the confusion of vehicles, then rolled between parallel rows of palms toward South Roosevelt. She said one or two things to Sam, raising her voice above the wind noise. He nodded but kept silent. I focused on an enormous anvil-shaped cloud to the south that expanded upward like a slow explosion of cotton. Three minutes later we stopped for the light across from the Grand Way Luncheonette. It hadn't been open for business since I had lived in Key West. Every few years someone repainted the building and sign but never opened the doors. I didn't know why, but that was okay. The place offered an aesthetic opposite to endemic tear-downs and remodeling jobs.

"I need to stop by the boat," said Sam. "Check a couple things."

"You want me to come back for you? I'll drop Alex and—"

Sam patted her on the thigh. "I'll get a ride from Turk, or I'll walk."

We followed two kids on motor scooters down First Street. They jacked around, wove back and forth, aimed at each other. They wore no helmets or shirts. If they tumbled they'd be scarred like barber poles—if they lived. We trailed their oily exhaust to North Roosevelt. They ran the light as it went red. Marnie stopped.

Fifty feet away, Captain Turk, who kept a guide skiff next to Sam's *Fancy Fool* in Garrison Bight, walked out of the Union 76 convenience store.

Sam said, "See you at home. Let's call for a Thai supper." He stepped out of the Jeep, slugged my knee—a nonverbal "thank you"—and ducked traffic to cross the street. I moved up front before the light changed. Marnie had a small metallic sticker on her dashboard: SIT DOWN, BUCKLE UP, HOLD ON, SHUT UP.

As we crossed the boulevard and started up the Bight bridge, I looked back. Turk reached into a sack and handed over a Miller Lite. Sam twisted the cap, tilted back the cold beer.

Marnie stopped for the light at the Naval Station Annex. "Shall I assume that he needs time alone?"

I felt the thirst that I knew Sam was quenching. "Between the MEs, the cops, and a woman cabdriver, he got his head twisted in six directions."

"Which direction did it send him, going forward?"

"You'd better let Sam explain," I said. "I saw it from my point of view. His take, I might get wrong."

"I've never seen him so . . . detached."

"He used the word 'distracted,' but yes."

"He was too embarrassed to tell me that his Bronco was right there in airport parking."

"You were good not to mention it. You look like you've had a long day yourself."

"Long for fifteen reasons, Alex." A minute later she turned onto Fleming. "How's your new living arrangement?"

"Remains to be seen."

"The remains of what?" She grinned. "Shouldn't it be perfect?"

A loaded question. But Marnie and I had been friends since before I had met Teresa Barga. Marnie never had tattled or betrayed a conversation.

"I've seen her four times in three days," I said. "Two of those were in bed while one of us was ninety percent asleep. Our affair has turned into April weather: cloudy, windy, and eighty."

"As opposed to . . . ?"

"Sunny and hot."

"I get the picture." She turned down Dredgers Lane, stopped near my porch, shut off her motor. She turned to face me and look me in the eye. "Look, Alex. I've got bad news. I wish I didn't have to say this. I wish I didn't have to tell anyone. Besides worrying about Sam, this was a big part of my long day. Naomi Douglas died in her sleep last night."

I felt as if she had slugged me. I felt as if I'd dropped through a hole in the car floor, through a crack in the crust of the earth, into a dark cavern where nothing goes right or makes sense. I managed to say, "I didn't know she'd been sick."

Marnie shook her head. "She plum wore out, is all I can figure. It gets us all, eventually. I know you've been her friend the past few years."

"But . . . damn. You saw her. She was healthy, perfectly alive."

"Some people reach old age before others," she said. "Most of the time you can't tell by the outside what the inside is doing."

"How old was she? After all this time, I don't even know."

"She was only sixty-eight," said Marnie.

"She acted half that."

"Right, she did. But in this town age is relative. Some people come to Key West to get a new life. Some people come here to die. Naomi did both."

"With flair," I said, "and a happy attitude. Is this her reward?"

Marnie was quiet a moment, then said, "She probably looked young because she didn't hang out in bars."

"Does Teresa know?"

Marnie squinted, looked away. "I have no idea."

Naomi Douglas had come to Florida in the mid-Eighties from the upper Midwest. Widowed, she had used her late husband's insurance proceeds to resettle herself far from reminders of old contentment and new heartbreak. She had bought an attractive two-story home on Grinnell, two blocks from my place on Dredgers Lane. I knew that she'd invested in stocks after the market's mini-crash in 'eighty-seven. The boom of the Nineties had allowed her to remodel her home and yard and become a supporter of numerous Key West causes and charities. She had asked me several times to donate my photo expertise to promote historic restoration projects. Her charming manner had made it impossible to turn her down. She had paid me back by touting my name for several lucrative jobs, and by purchasing two of my photographs and displaying them in her home. She never remarried. I had seen her many times in the company of the island's older, wealthy men, gay and straight. I'd never had the impression that any of them might be a love interest. More than once I had wondered about my feelings toward her. I had always found her attractive, never worried that she was of my parents' generation. I had been in other relationships throughout the time I'd known her. Nothing had come of my feelings, or the attraction.

I said, "How old would Sam's sister be?"

"Lorie'd be close to forty. You think she didn't make it?"

"I don't think Sam's holding much hope."

Marnie hadn't moved in two minutes. She finally turned, looked toward the porch. "Your phone's ringing."

I don't know why I hurried, but I did. Perhaps to run from the fact of my friend's death. The front door was unlocked, wide open. I caught it before the answering service clicked in. Key West Police Detective Dexter Hayes Jr. monotoned, "Oh. You're *not* dead."

I took a moment to think through his words, then said, "They won't have me in the club."

"I haven't seen you in a while. I assumed the worst."

"Was I supposed to be calling you? I thought our deal worked the other way around. I hoped it did."

"Too true," he said. "There's only one reason I'm calling."

"You got told to call me."

"Not in so many words, Rutledge. Please say you're too busy . . ."

"I'm too busy . . ."

". . . to snap photos of a suicide victim."

"I've pledged my late afternoon to a special project."

"That piece-of-crap Mustang you got?"

"It's a Shelby."

"Once again I'm right?"

"No. I'm redoing my Weber grill. They should use me in ads. Like people who drive cars for a half-million miles. This is an early-Eighties model."

"Lotta value in those relics," said Hayes.

"I paid to have the grate sandblasted. I bought heat-resistant paint for the outside of it."

"This guy took himself out with a shotgun on his canal bulkhead."

"What did he do?" I said. "Ricochet the shot off the sidewalk?"

"He did a Hemingway, put the barrel in his mouth."

"So, it wasn't a question of aim?"

"There isn't much left from the earlobes back. It's all in the canal. He was facing the house. He blew brain salad into the mangroves."

"I'm photographing a void? Pictures won't show a damn thing."

"I was hoping you'd say that. It reaffirms my opinion of your attitude."

"Anybody we know?" I said.

"Mayor Steve Gomez."

"Oh, shit."

"That's what a lot of people are saying," said Hayes. "City Hall will echo with the sentiments come morning."

"What happened to the 'Happiest Man in Politics'?"

"Steve cashed it in."

"Cootie Ortega's not an option?"

"He's grieving."

Cootie was the city's full-time forensic photographer and lab man. Over the past ten years he'd built a reputation for screwing up but had kept his job thanks to the century-old Conch tradition of nepotism.

"Is Cootie grieving over Uncle Steve, or his soon-to-go patronage gig?"

"Let's say fifty-fifty," said Hayes. "He started to document the scene, went maybe ten minutes, but he lost it. Broke down and wept. I have to admit it looked like genuine anguish. Maybe the guy has human emotions. Took me by surprise."

Hayes went silent. I stayed silent.

He blinked first: "Okay, I'll beg. Just this once? Out of respect for Ortega's mourning?'"

"If it's open-and-shut suicide, why pictures?"

"Butt-covering one-oh-one. In case any little thing comes up—down the road, couple of months, couple of years. It'll look like I followed procedures, went through the motions."

"I've had a long day. You're sweet to call."

"That's the kind of guy I am. Trouble is," he said, "you turn me down, they'll tell me to lose your number. You've come to the attention of my boss, the lieutenant, the bureau commander. He wants me to find someone more dependable."

"I've always liked the odd dollar or two. You sound like you're on your cell."

"Like there's a phone booth in the mayor's yard?"

"They'll be able to tell by your phone records that we talked."

"You better come on over."

"What's his wife's name?" I said. "I met her once."

"Yvonne's a wreck. Her boss at City Electric broke the news to her. She heaved her lunch into a computer. A four-grand puke. You probably don't know they separated a year ago."

"News to me."

"Maybe it's what brought this on. I hear he's been into the bottle for a few months, hiding it like most alcoholics. But, yes, she's in the house with a dozen Cuban relatives, sisters, cousins—including Cootie, who happens to be the only male relative—and two aunts. Sometimes I think it's worse when people are divorced or split up. The ones left behind are thinking 'What if' and feeling guilty. Anyway, she's audibly upset."

"Gotcha. Gomez wasn't a Conch, was he?"

"Nope. First time I met him was when I got back to town last September. You know the house?"

"I think so. Two big sago palms, Riviera Drive?"

"Forty-one twenty-four," said Hayes. "Hurry. Don't wear shorts."

I walked outside, wondering why Teresa had neglected to lock the house. Marnie Dunwoody sat sideways in the driver's seat, her legs dangling to the Jeep's small running board, her cell phone to her ear. I stood back to give her privacy, watched a half-dozen palm warblers maneuver crazily around the yard's trees and shrubs. They looked drunk, almost colliding with each other and with tree limbs. I guessed they had copped a buzz off ripe berries in the trees. Warblers are more common in October, rarely stopping in the Keys on spring migration. I'd heard that this year's constant easterlies had forced them to land.

Something made me look back at Marnie. Her face was fixed, ashen, her gaze unfocused. A moment later she clicked off.

She read the same look on my face. She said, "Gomez?"

"Dexter just hired me."

"Two in one day. Get your stuff. I'll give you a ride."

"You look like you just lost a relative."

Marnie nodded. "Maybe the same way you feel about Naomi. A year before I started with the *Citizen*, a friend of mine volunteered me to help with Steve's first campaign, when he ran for city commissioner that one term before he ran for mayor. I went into it two-faced, like a cynical bitch, looking to get the goods on a wily politician." She stopped to take a deep breath. "For the life of me, I couldn't find anything wrong with the guy. He had good ideas, he treated people fairly. If he said he'd do something, he did it, or he tried. He was a dork, socially, around women. I guess he was one of 'the guys.' He liked to have a few drinks and hang out. But he never chased groupies. As a politician, he fascinated me."

"So, you kept up with him?"

"I've kept a file on him since my first week at the paper. He was my silent specialty, my pet project. I saw him as a man with a future. I kept track of his career and his decisions. Every two years I studied his campaigns. All this time, I hoped it would form a pattern—where he was coming from, who might own him, what he might do in the future. I thought I knew how he ticked. If he'd gotten into state or national politics, he was my story. If he'd gotten into a scandal, he was my story."

I said, "How does suicide fit the picture?"

She shook her head. "Too many important things going on. Most of them good for the island. It's like the city's lost its last fragment of a conscience."

In spite of Marnie's admiration, I knew that, in recent years, Steve Gomez had been tagged the "absentee mayor." He'd missed commission meetings because he'd gone to hunt deer with friends in Texas or near the Everglades, or to shoot birds in Wyoming and Nebraska. He'd gone to out-of-town expos to promote industry for a tourist-trap island that needed new industry like Duval Street needed more T-shirt stores. He'd been zipped by the media for distant conferences on the public's nickel. Mayor Gomez had ignored his critics. He'd let them have their say, refused to explain himself, and refused comment. He'd let his voting record speak for itself. He'd won each election with an overwhelming majority.

For some reason, victory hadn't been enough.

"Maybe he had a health problem," I said. "Depression, or indicators of Alzheimer's. Maybe cancer that he'd kept secret."

Marnie looked at Fleming Street as if an answer might appear next to the stop sign. "Why do I have a feeling this town's going to change because he died? I mean change big, and not for the better. I always thought the whole country got skewed after JFK was killed. Same idea, different scale."

"Teresa's in for it," I said. "This'll be a PR nightmare."

"Hey, that's why the police department calls her a media liaison. She's a spokesperson, she's got a business card, and she's got to deal with the likes of me. It's what she wants on her résumé, and it's what they pay her for."

27

Tough summation, I thought. No sympathy, either.

"It'll be more of everything," I said. "Emotion, the bullshit. No fun."

"She was having fun at lunch today."

"Do I want to know about this?"

"I shouldn't have said that," she said.

"We don't keep tabs on each other."

Marnie nodded. "I know. Sam and I thrive on trust, too. I apologize."

"You were thinking about my 'April weather' remark."

"Cloudy, windy, and eighty." She almost smiled. "That's actually funny."

"This has been a long one for all of us. It's about to start up again."

She agreed. "Go get your cameras. If you've got any crackers or bananas in there, my stomach's crying for help."

As I turned back to the house, my mind spun. Two in one day? Naomi, just like that?

Who else was crying for help?

I needed a long nap. I needed to keep my eyes wide open.

4

RIVIERA DRIVE IS A mix of luxury homes, cement-block Florida specials, and dumps disguised by vegetation. By Key West standards, it's an upscale neighborhood. Houses to the north have back-fence neighbors. Southside homes, like Steve Gomez's, back up to a deep canal and a shallow salt pond bordered by twisted, bug-filled mangroves.

Marnie and I didn't need an address. Four unmarked Crown Vics had jammed to within fifty feet of Gomez's twin sago palms. Spotlights, beefed shocks, window tint dark enough to win civilians a love note from city hall. Not exactly unmarked. The house looked new, from what I could see beyond the wall. I had heard that Gomez had knocked down an eyesore to build before he ran for office, had turned his double-lot yard into a showplace.

Marnie wedged her Jeep into the last spot in sight, snug behind Teresa's blue Shimano motor scooter. A blowsy middle-aged woman in a huge denim shirt and strained cutoffs marched to the edge of her sparse lawn. She stood guard, made sure the Jeep's tires didn't dig up her turf.

Marnie faced forward, reached behind my seat to grab her briefcase. "The old bag has eight toilets out behind her house," she said quietly. "She turned them into yard planters. She called the paper and asked us to do a story on her. She's a chatter. Let's move fast."

We saw no one out front. Except for a fifteen-by-fifteen-foot square of turf for the palms, only a two-car garage was open to the street. Key West's Crime Scene van sat on a short, peach-colored apron in front of the garage.

Riding across town I had recalled the last time I had seen Naomi Douglas. She had been sitting on the deck at Louie's Backyard, smirking in the late-day sun, not quite enjoying a ribald joke. I had wanted to capture the life in her eyes, the mischief and goodwill that matched her smile, but I hadn't brought my camera. Now, two weeks later, I would have to focus on the shredded remains of a man's head, details of nature I didn't want to know. I felt as if I had reversed my priorities in life. I took peace in the idea that a week on Grand Cayman might fix my brain as well as my wallet.

"No sheriff's car," said Marnie. "Not even his fancy-ass Lexus."

"He must have caught a ride with someone else."

Four years ago Fred "Chicken Neck" Liska had waggled money in my face. I blamed him for drawing me into my grim sideline. He had been a detective with the KWPD and had asked me to photograph evidence. Before he turned in his city badge, then won last year's election to become Monroe County's sheriff, he had worked six years under Mayor Gomez. I recalled times when Liska had spoken of the mayor. His tone had shown respect for the way the man did business. From Fred Liska, those words had amounted to effusive praise. If this had been murder rather than a suicide, he could have opted to take jurisdiction. I knew he would be shaken by the mayor's suicide. I was equally certain of his relief at not having to take the case.

The Crime Scene van began to roll down the apron. The driver spotted Marnie, recognized her, and shook his head. He drove east a half block, then turned north toward Flagler.

"What the hell was that?" said Marnie. "He's going to Stock Island. They can't be taking Gomez away."

"Hayes wouldn't call me to shoot scenery."

"They keep that van downtown all the time, on Angela."

"So he's rolling empty," I said. "He got another call."

"More important than the mayor?"

Set into the bordering wall, seven feet from the street pavement, was an opaque door and an access keypad. I nudged the door and bumped a uniformed officer who'd been posted guard. After a beat or two of posturing, he recognized us. He did a double take on Marnie's height, waved me in, then held up his hand to stop her. "Identification."

"Get fucking real," said Marnie.

"Rules," he said.

"You want me to run a story about your wife's beaver shots on the Web?"

The cop went stone-faced. Marnie barged past him and beelined for Teresa.

I hung back and scoped the scene. Teresa stood twenty yards away, next to a tall traveler's palm. She wore the white blouse and navy slacks that she had worn before Sam and I left the house that morning. She had added two cell phones, a notebook, silver bracelets, and silver earrings. At five-ten, her height matched Marnie's. Her brown hair touched her shoulders. Reporters from the *Herald*, the *News-Barometer*, and *Solares Hill* listened to her speech, took notes. She stood with perfect posture, gazed above their foreheads, and held their attention.

Two dozen people stood around in clusters. This was Key West behind the scenes, the straight-faced parlays, the spin of island power, the roles that needed to be reshuffled with a major player dead. The mayor's assistant, a young man I knew only as Jay, chatted with the city manager, a tyrant in her forties. Two city commissioners—a hardware store owner and a retired Navy captain—powwowed with a judge and an Aqueduct Authority honcho. The common uniform among the mourners was dark suits and grief. The fixers were identical to Steve Gomez's brokenhearted colleagues. An outsider like me couldn't guess their political intents and agendas. But I knew that adjustments were in the air.

I scanned the cream-colored house, its pillars, its red tile roof. Then

I saw him. Down a walkway, under a portico, Detective Sergeant Dexter Hayes Jr. stood alone, staring at the canal.

I approached him from behind. "You called?"

"Why don't I get the cut-and-dried cases?" He kept his eyes on the canal. "Why can't this be a simple overdose, sleeping pills, with a plastic bag over his head? Where's his suicide note, his videotaped explanation?"

"What's your worry?" I said. "You've got nothing to solve, and you've got Teresa Barga. Your efficient press-liaison person will explain to the world why a normal man checks himself out for the long run."

"She's been great," said Hayes. "I don't know what you've been doing or saying to her, but the past few days she's been a tornado."

"I've seen her in motion. I call it a tropical storm."

He looked at me sideways, not knowing whether to laugh or disagree. He said, "I don't want to know."

Dexter Hayes had grown up in Key West, but he had worked for the city for only six months. He had come from Boynton Beach SWAT to fill the detective slot vacated when Fred Liska ran for sheriff. Dexter was the only son of "Big Dex" Hayes, a large-sized, low-level manipulator who, for years, had run victimless rackets in Key West's black section. Big Dex had made no secret of his work. Even a newcomer like me knew his legend within months of arriving on the island. Folks assumed that white men controlled Big Dex's puppet strings. In the mid-Nineties, Big Dex made cash demands, acted too big for his britches, and his protection blew away. Deputies knocked on his door one morning before dawn. He spent two years reconsidering his leverage at Union Correctional.

Dexito, as young Dexter was called, had left for college within weeks of his high school graduation. Except for rare visits to his parents' home, he hadn't returned until he'd accepted this new job. Many old locals wondered if he hadn't come back to rectify the bad his father had done in the Sixties and Seventies. A few wondered aloud if his job was a ruse, if he was setting himself up to follow in the big man's footsteps.

Dexter dumped his coffee dregs into a crown-of-thorns shrub. "You can thank me now or later. Technically, we have a crime scene, a violent death with no witnesses. You, on the other hand, have a skate gig. You don't have a body, and you don't have to hurry, except I don't want you to take all night."

"He was in that van I saw go?"

"He was in it. Go around back, be a genius. Give me up and down, frontward and backward. You're here to shoot scenery."

Had I heard an echo? "You don't trust me with real evidence?"

"I had to call in our marine recovery team, to collect . . . you know, brain and hair in the canal. I needed to get the remains out quick, due to gawkers in boats and because of the family. I shot two rolls of Polaroids myself. One boat team guy had a camera. I had him shoot the juicy ones."

"What kind of camera?" I said.

"A yellow waterproof job."

Wide-angle hell, I thought.

"Waterborne gawkers," I said. "No wonder it upset the next of kin."

Hayes turned away from me, stifled a yawn. "Some family members *were* the gawkers. Like they wanted a jump on the eleven o'clock news. Anyway, go run a couple rolls. Do a nature tour, catch some rays. It's pretty back there. Gomez put the same care into his garden that he gave to the city."

"Tell me again. What am I supposed to shoot?"

"It's your job to be clairvoyant. Think of a few pictures we haven't taken yet. And do me two favors: Don't touch the shotgun; it's in my custody, but I don't feel like toting it around. After you're done, draw me a scene diagram, like you learned to do in your correspondence course."

Dexter had ordered me to boost my forensic skills if I wanted to keep working for the city. I had never signed up for the course.

He let my mind fumble, then said, "Just kidding."

"Come steer me around," I said. "Help me document the air."

"What, I should hold your hand? I'd rather stand in the shade, save my energy so I can authorize your paycheck."

I exited the walkway. The police marine recovery team—four men the size of Mark McGwire with skin the color of Sammy Sosa's—had blocked the canal with "Crime Scene" tape. They wore wet suit vests and shorts, rubber shoes, belts cluttered with penlights, clippers, and other tools. They looked bored, sleepwalking through the motions. Two sifted surface water with scoop nets. I thought it unlikely that splatter had stayed afloat, that hungry fish had ignored it. An officer in a stubby gray Avon argued with a boatload of irate residents who wanted to get home for supper.

Winding paths split Gomez's yard into three sections, two filled with Barbados cherry, sugar apple, and mango trees. In the third section, a sea grape loomed above a teak rack that held potted bromeliad. Gomez had built a brick and stainless steel barbecue at the yard's west end and disguised a large equipment shed as a grass shack. I had never seen so many orchids.

Had he built himself a paradise, then shot himself to celebrate?

I found his body's outline painted parallel to the seawall, next to a small bloodstain. Someone had chalked lines and arrows around the outline. Tiny numerals noted distances from the mayor's hands to the shotgun, from his feet to the seawall's edge. Nothing about the scene looked right. If the gunshot had gone south, over the canal, why had he fallen sideways? Wouldn't the force have knocked him backward? How had he depressed the trigger, and why hadn't the shotgun slid farther away with its recoil?

I decided to stop asking myself questions. I had no expertise, no way to answer them. That was Dexter's job, anyway, and he wasn't busting his ass to gather evidence.

I looked over at him. He stared back and I knew that he'd been following my eyes, reading my thoughts. I canted my head to beckon him closer to me, to see things from my angle. Hayes shook his head, started back toward the walkway.

"I guess I'm through," I said loudly.

He stopped walking, tilted his head, but didn't turn to face me. "Is that, like, you quit?"

"Why should I be interested? You sure the fuck aren't."

Now he turned, began to walk closer, but kept his eyes on his marine recovery team. From fifteen feet away: "Did you kill the mayor, Rutledge?" Then, a twist of his head to check my response.

I read his conjecture on the spot. I pulled a boarding pass stub from my pocket, fluttered it at him. "I was out of town, Dex. I flew to the big city and back. But you force me to ask, do you think *anyone* killed him?"

"No, I sure don't," he said. "I'd bet you my car that Steve killed himself. But if he didn't, and I'm out a car, I'll bet you two more cars that his killer's out front, part of that political melee we both have no time for. Since your alibi's airtight, I'd just as soon go where the action is, to do my phony-baloney job. Is that okay with you?"

I nodded.

"I liked the man," he said. "He dealt square and played fair. I don't trust a single other member of the city commission. What I'm saying is: My job is going to change, somehow or other, and not for the good. I will miss him. If he didn't pull that trigger, I will find the man or woman who did."

He didn't wait for my answer. He turned and left the patio.

Vegetation blocked line-of-sight for most of my scene-setting photos. I shot one roll eastward from the barbecue, another from the opposite end of the seawall. In several photos I included the home's Florida room with its old-fashioned jalousie windows.

I focused on the jalousies and a short woman inside, whom I assumed to be Yvonne Gomez, the estranged wife. She wore a black slacks and white blouse combo, which, over the past thirty years, had become the uniform of Conch women working at the city, county, or local utilities. Cootie Ortega stood next to her, patted her shoulder, looked to be speaking calmly, comforting her. He glanced in my direction, then toward the police boat team, and then back to me. I was glad not to be in his shoes.

Do estranged wives become unestranged widows?

Another question I couldn't answer.

I wanted to limit my detail shots to the area near the painted outline. I placed my compass and short ruler next to a chalk line, took a close-up, and backed off for two that included the seawall. I ran three to show scrapes on the concrete, then noticed similar marks the length of the walkway. Gomez had moved yard furniture, or had loaded a boat for a cruise. I didn't want to spend all evening documenting gouges. I ran a poor man's panorama, eight overlapping frames, to show the canal and the hammock on the far bank. Without stepping on the softball-sized bloodstain, I got five wide angles from the point of view of a man about to die.

I repacked my cameras, took a last look. I couldn't imagine having time to create such a garden, or finding the time to appreciate it. Ten years ago a boatload of Cuban refugees had found its way into this canal. Sunburned, destitute, they had appealed to a resident for help. They had no way to know that their benefactor, the man who had given them Cokes and snacks, chairs on a shady porch on dry land, was Jimmy Buffett. I wondered what they had thought of his home, his hospitality. Or what they would have thought of Gomez's equipment shed, a structure that could house a family of four.

I listened to a jet goose its engines at the airport, a half mile distant.

We fly on with our lives. Except for Steve Gomez and Naomi Douglas.

"Hey, bubba." Cootie Ortega waved me to the Florida room. He held the door to allow me inside, into the shade. "How you be, amigo?"

"Be tired of dead people."

Ortega agreed. "Always, I'm that way, bubba. I hate these dead-people jobs, but this one, you know . . . I just couldn't. Lemme ask, you shoot that Olympus brand, right? You wanta buy some used camera stuff?"

The man saw the handwriting on the wall. He knew that his ace had been played, that his city job was in jeopardy.

I played dumb. "You trading up to digital, Cootie?"

"I'm going to that medium format, Rutledge. I like those *como se llamas*, those Hasselblad deals. I want to shoot art photos out by Marvin and the Snipe Keys."

"Birds and fish, Cootie? Cormorants?"

"No way, bubba. I can't do nature crap." He walked to the door. His footsteps echoed off the floor tiles. He waved southward as if the Snipe Keys had mysteriously appeared on the Salt Flats. "Gonna take some tourist girls out there for beauty work. Little tan titties, butt-floss bathing suits. I'm gonna enter me some art shows, win me a bunch of prize money. Once I lay in my reputation, I sell sunset pictures to big corporations to hang in their meeting rooms, you know what I'm saying? Bucks."

Grief takes odd forms. "That's a concept, Cootie."

He said, "So . . . how about it?"

"I've got everything I need. I'm not feeling all that rich."

"I'll do you right," he said.

"See if you have an Olympus eighty-five lens, Cootie. I can always use a backup. Or maybe a forty lens. You could sell me an OM-4 camera body, if the price was right."

"I'll have to look," he said.

"You do that. Bring the gear by the house, but call first, okay?"

Yvonne Gomez came onto the patio, pain-faced, deflated. I didn't know the woman, but I nodded hello. She stared at me as if I were a wood post. She was having a bad day, but she also looked like a woman who could make any occasion unpleasant. I turned to leave the sunroom and noticed two glass-front cases on the side wall. One held a dozen kelly-green ribbons. The one that read FIRST PLACE—CARAMBOLA was from last year's Florida Keys Tropical Fruit Fiesta, and FIRST PLACE— LONGAN was from the year before that. I didn't read the others, but I was sure that Gomez had competed well, for years, in multiple categories.

The other glass case was designed to hold four shotguns. Two sets of pegs were empty.

I found Detective Hayes alone on the painted driveway. No city officials, no media people in sight. He handed me the keys to Teresa's motor scooter. "Marnie had to leave," he said. "Ms. Barga needed to get to her office for a few press releases. She rode with the city commissioners. She said you're invited to dinner on somebody else's nickel. An old friend or something."

"That's what I hear."

"She asked if you'd call her personal cell number."

I said, "Who found the body?"

"Next-door neighbor. The man heard a boom, thought a gas can on his boat had exploded. He came out to the seawall and saw the truth. He was still heaving in the canal when I got here."

"Two guns in the glass case, back there in the sunroom."

"I saw," he said.

"Gun number three was out by the canal."

"I know your next question," said Hayes. "Go on home."

"You need me to drop off your film?" I said.

Hayes handed me two rolls of Kodacolor. "We'll split the chore. You drop 'em off, I'll have the prints picked up tomorrow."

"Did Gomez have a part-time caretaker for this place?"

Hayes looked disgusted. "How the hell should I know crappy details like that? You want me to go in there and ask his grieving wife about plants and trees? I'd like to be home right now, drinking a beer like you're going to be in fifteen minutes. But I've got to document exit procedures. I've got to dictate a report, tell how a self-inflicted gunshot snuffed a damned good mayor. You have fun at supper. I'll grab a midnight snack."

"Don't choke on your fat self-pity, Dexter. You might snuff a damned good martyr."

5

DUFFY LEE HALL WORKED out of a large two-story house on Olivia, where I stopped to drop off the death-scene film for processing. The warm smells of his neighbors' suppers filled the street. He came to his broad, shaded porch with two cold Corona Lights and offered me a cushioned Adirondack chair.

I had bolted two cups of coffee, skipped breakfast, barely touched lunch in Lauderdale, and passed on a banana when Marnie borrowed one of mine. Dexter Hayes's midnight snack remark hadn't helped, and beer was not what I needed.

Hell, I thought, if it keeps my stomach from imploding . . .

"You don't look so hot," said Hall. "This one get to you?"

"Other things." I tilted back the beer. "Hunger and heartbreak."

"You had a thing for the mayor?"

"Remember those eleven-by-fourteen prints?"

"You sold to Naomi Douglas? The start of your fine art career?"

"She died in her sleep," I said.

"She had taste."

I agreed. "She had everything."

Hall promised to guard my negatives, to not release them to anyone else.

Sucking suds on a breezy veranda was an improvement on an ugly day, but I needed quick bulk intake, token nutrition before stomach acid ate its way to daylight. I chugged the Corona, thanked Hall, and drove the motor scooter to Dorothy's Deli on Simonton. My belly growled while I read the newspaper and waited for a smoked ham and provolone on whole wheat. Three *Solares Hill* articles in a row made me think of Naomi. An art opening, a Paradise Big Band concert, a garden seminar. I felt pissed off that she had died, more pissed that I had nowhere to direct my anger. I told myself to be grateful for the time she had been in my life. Small consolation. I walked out to the soft evening light, my hand in the sack, clutching ham and cheese. I found Teresa waiting next to her parked scooter. She had changed out of her work outfit, wore a black cocktail dress and extra blush to fake a tan. Passersby might have mistaken her grimace for sun squint.

"Dexter dropped the ball?" she said. "You didn't get told?"

"Sorry," I said. "I heard about dinner. I was too hungry to wait."

"I thought gourmet might be a welcome change, Alex. An old friend of mine is in town. It's a free meal."

The fun at lunch that Marnie had mentioned. "Friend from childhood?"

"We worked together at Chili's in Gainesville. I think my junior year."

I played naive: "She must be doing well these days, to roll into town and treat a guy like me to supper."

"He's a he, and he's that kind of person. People said he came from a wealthy family on the West Coast. I always had the impression he didn't have to work, but he took jobs to kill boredom."

"He get here today?"

"I ran into him the night before last, in the Waterfront Market. He bought me a beer at Schooner Wharf, and we played 'What happened to . . . ' for an hour or so. He's been in town a few days and he might stick around another week. This morning he called the office and asked me to lunch, so I went. I told him about you, and he offered us dinner tonight."

40

"It's been a long day," I said.

"A nice meal will improve your outlook."

"A good night's sleep will make me better company at breakfast. I don't want to be in a shit mood tomorrow like you were this morning."

"Oh. The direct shot." She looked away, then back at me. "It was those mosquitoes in the shower. And I saw a scorpion yesterday, thank goodness *after* I was dry. At six-thirty it's a rude, cold wake-up."

"The price of luxury. It'll get better in summer."

"Your sarcasm is not reading well. Who's shitty now?"

"It wasn't your first time in the outdoor shower," I said. "You knew what you were getting into."

"Like I had a choice."

"You were forced into sharing my home?"

"You want me gone?" she said.

"I wasn't saying that."

"You weren't reading a recipe for key lime pie."

"And you weren't complaining about mosquitoes and scorpions."

"You're right," she said. "It's the end of a long day, Alex. Are you joining me and Whit?" She waved her hand at a small yellow car parked a few yards up Petronia. My eye followed her gesture. I hadn't noticed the man in the BMW Z-3. He tilted his head to drink from a clear plastic water bottle.

"Whit?" I said.

"His name's Whitney Randolph. People call him Whit, which is ten times better than Whitney. You want to meet him now?"

"No. Just tell me where and what time."

They were headed for drinks at Louie's Backyard, then an eight-thirty reservation at Camille's on Simonton. I told her I would try to make it.

She stepped aside and relinquished possession of the scooter. She said, "I don't think Steve Gomez was suicide."

Was this neurosis or the judgment of a criminologist? "Did you voice your opinion?"

She considered her answer. "Not in so many words."

"Like, 'no'?"

"Like, no one wanted to hear it."

"I do," I said.

Her eyes bored into mine. "No matter what happens tonight, let's have coffee on the porch in the morning."

I told her that was a splendid idea. I wondered what would happen tonight that would qualify as "no matter." The BMW drove away. I stayed at the curb and ate the whole sandwich before I started home.

Three messages waited at the house. One for a photo job that conflicted with my trip to Grand Cayman. One from Sam asking me to call when I got home, to wake him from a nap. Marnie must've gone to her office to write the Gomez story. Jack Spottswood's law office also called—no reason given—but his office closed at five, and I couldn't respond until morning.

I called Sam. He caught the second ring and said, "Nothing like Añejo rum and a heavy nap."

I asked him to call me on Teresa's cell phone in forty-five minutes. His call would give me the option of faking an excuse and bailing out of dinner. He said I was a whiz at contingency planning. I laughed, but it made me think of Detective Marlow's remark about Sam's military training. Marlow had hit the nail on the head. I had seen several occasions when Sam had confronted danger, thought ahead, considered all possible actions and reactions. Each time he had prevailed. He was one of the lucky ones for whom time slowed in moments of peril.

I showered and caught myself stupidly worrying about which brand of shampoo to use. I chose the one closest to hand, neglected to shave, put on shorts and a long-sleeved shirt, and rode my bike to Camille's. The night had brought a chill; there would be cooler, clear weather in the morning.

I reminded myself to take the high road. Whit Randolph was a friend of a friend. He was in town for a short time and, I needed to presume, had not come just to connect with Teresa. If I were to cause a scene, make a big deal of the man's presence, it might self-fulfill and throw me a situation I didn't want. He wasn't a threat to my status quo, I thought, then wondered why "status quo" had come to mind rather than "happiness."

At the Truman light I stopped behind a bunch of young people in a funky old hearse. The bumper sticker on its back door read, FRIENDS HELP YOU MOVE. REAL FRIENDS HELP YOU MOVE BODIES.

Teresa introduced her friend as Whitney, then called him Whit after that. We shook hands like opposing captains at midfield, though his grip was limp fish. Randolph, up close, was not what I had expected. I had imagined some square-jawed buff stud with a beaming smile and Devo hair. I found myself shaking hands with a slender man with a receding hairline, a pressed sport shirt and a plain Seiko watch. His face showed more intelligence than guile, his mannerisms more awkwardness than cool. It would take fewer than ten minutes for me to revise that first impression.

A server arrived and placed a wineglass in front of me. Someone began moving things to make room for a bread basket, then made a commotion out of pouring olive oil into a jelly dish and grinding pepper.

"I watched you lock your Cannondale out there," said Randolph. "Nice wheels. What is it, an F600?"

"Right, Mavic rims, clipless pedals . . ."

"With a Super Fatty HeadShok front post," he said. He poured wine for me, them for himself. A glance at Teresa's glass told him she didn't need more. He turned back to the window. "Why that bike on a flat island?"

"Rough pavement. The shock absorber's for chuckholes. I hate surprises in the dark."

Whit agreed. "Damage that thing, the repairs'll set you back. What's that expensive-looking seat?"

"It's a Bell."

"Must've gone a couple hundred . . ."

"Eighteen ninety-five at Kmart. For day-to-day, it's more crotch-friendly than the CODA that came with it."

"Gotcha. I hope you sealed the original seat in a Ziploc. I'd hate to see mildew . . ."

"Done," I said.

"Cool."

Perhaps "cool" wasn't the word for it. Whit Randolph hadn't added wine to Teresa's glass. He had left her out of the conversation, and I had fueled the fire. I looked and saw the squinty eyes I had seen at Dorothy's Deli. I'd told myself to take the high road . . .

"What brings you to Key West, Whit? Vacation?"

"A couple business deals have been driving me nuts. I had to get out of Fort Myers, come down here to kick back, duck the lawyers and real-estate sharks. I'm shopping for a boat, like a twenty-three-foot twin outboard, and I've got a couple investors down here I need to talk to."

"Your deal in the Keys?"

"Not here, no. But this isn't a bad place for the future. I've got four or five things in the works . . . Savannah, Fort Myers, St. Augustine, Tarpon Springs. I play around." He rethought his flip words, and qualified them: "I mean, I make deals that work for everyone, but it's game-playing for me. It keeps my mind fresh. You know what I'm alluding to?"

Alluding? Was this a vocabulary test? I knew who he was deluding. The slitty-eyed look on Teresa's face had blossomed into admiration.

"And you're a photographer?" he said. "With the police department?"

I shook my head. "The city work is minor income. I do advertising and magazine articles."

"And fine art, I understand."

Yes, I thought. Except that Naomi wasn't around anymore to encourage me. "That's my version of game-playing, I suspect."

"So, like, you live on an island. Do you own a car?"

This guy was either an equipment freak or a smokescreen artist.

"It's a 'sixty-six Shelby GT-350H. I keep it garaged, mostly use the bike." Pour on the gear, I thought. "There's also a 1970 Triumph Bonneville, a T120R. It's a first-kicker and a ball."

"Must have cost you your ass."

I suspected that Butler Dunwoody, Marnie's brother, had spent a strong dollar on it. "It was given to me," I said. "I ruined an old Kawasaki doing this guy a favor last winter, so he—"

Teresa said, "His Kawasaki was burned by a man on a killing spree."

Randolph wasn't impressed. "Was he murdering machines? I hope he got burned, too."

"He took his exit with multiple wounds. He took out several people first."

"At least you're still here," he said. "Better your bike than your ass."

Teresa's cell phone rang. She feigned embarrassment at disturbing other diners, then answered and handed it to me. "It's Sam. Invite him to join us."

Sam said, "You want out of there, amigo?"

I made my "Yes" sound tentative, listened to dead air for a moment. I leaned toward Teresa, "He's outside."

"Invite him in."

"He doesn't want to intrude, but he needs to talk with me."

"Fine. We'll be right here."

I worry about the word "fine." I finished the ounce or two in my wineglass, grabbed a dinner roll as if I needed something to carry me through a quick chat. I assured them I'd be back as quickly as I could.

An unmarked county car sat across the street in the First State Bank's drive-thru lane. Dark paint, tinted windows, facing the wrong way, with a clear view of the street and the restaurant. An odd spot for surveillance, especially with Camille's full of locals.

I couldn't be nosy on my bicycle, so I walked toward the vehicle. From fifteen feet away I recognized Deputy Billy "No Jokes" Bohner. I hated the idea that my least favorite officer had jumped the ranks to civilian-clothing stakeouts. Bohner knew that I had recognized him. As I walked past his door he lowered the window and said, "Howzit goin'?" in a tone that spoke, "Go shit in your shoes."

I said, "Doing great, Deputy."

"You gotta be, eatin' in a place like that." The window began to rise.

I said, "How's that badge life treating you?"

The last words I heard from Bohner were, "High-ticket stuff."

My lost meal or his promotion?

I left my bike locked at the restaurant and walked to Sam's eighty-year-old house on Elizabeth between United and South. He had retrieved his car. The Bronco sat out front, and the entranceway door was ajar. I let myself into the yard, and found Sam sitting back on his screened front porch.

"Was the dude a dude?" he said.

"He was a used car with fresh paint."

"A walking warning?"

"He looked like a puppy with attack training. I need to watch my wallet as well as my roommate."

"Clouds of hustle in the air?"

"Thick ones." I passed on the hard-seat rocker, picked a cushioned chair. "But that's my perspective. No way to tell how Teresa's reading it."

Sam handed me an open beer, then looked into his dark yard. I could tell his mind was churning, so I didn't interrupt. A minute or so later he said, "I got to thinking, that dog-and-pony deal at the morgue, our flaky sit-down with Detective Odin Marlow . . ." He paused, took a slug. "This is strange territory for me. I did a lot of deep thinking after Nam. I came home, my friends didn't. It took me awhile to sort it out. Good war or not—you ask me in a hundred years, maybe I'll know— but I answered my country's call. And I promised myself I would stop thinking, stop talking about it, and get on with my life. I took a long vacation from deep thought. I'm not saying I wanted to be numb in the gray room, but I wanted to deal with questions that really had answers. Questions from today with answers no later than tomorrow."

"Sounds like the road to sanity," I said.

"So here's what I came up with. If the dead woman can lead me to Lorie, and Lorie's dead, okay. But if Lorie's alive, in some kind of danger, and I'm here in Key West ignoring warning signs, I could never forgive myself."

"Okay."

"Can I count on you?"

"That's why I'm here."

"You promise not to use the 'C' word?" he said.

"Closure?"

"That's it. The better word is . . ."

"Revenge?"

"No," said Sam. "Satisfaction."

I let that one sit, figured it matched Sam's personality.

He said, "Do we know any Gold Coast attorneys?"

"No name pops into my head."

Sam pondered it a moment. "Is your old girlfriend still in West Palm?"

I nodded. Annie Minnette had lived with me for three years. Our only interactions since we had split had been e-mails about friends' marriages, deaths, and births. "I haven't heard from her since her Christmas card," I said. "She was still with that law firm in Pompano."

"Here's the plan. I don't know what I'm going to do, who I'll meet, who I might piss off. I want to report to you once a day, preferably close to six P.M. I'll talk to you or your machine, tell you where I am. If I don't call, I probably need help. If I don't tell you where I am, I definitely need help."

"I leave for Grand Cayman the day after tomorrow."

"Shit, I forgot that." Sam sat back in his chair, thought for a minute, then pulled a fat envelope out from under a stack of magazines. He tossed it onto the table and it fell open. Hundred-dollar bills fanned out. "How much you going to earn down there?"

"About that much," I said.

"That's ten grand."

"About half that."

"Good," he said. "I just hired you away."

"And you'll be . . ."

"In Lauderdale."

I drank beer and raced my brain. I knew Sam Wheeler as well as I had known anyone in my life, his calm, his laid-back habits. But this version was an irrational stranger, fixed on a crusade, trying to buy my services. This was a headstrong Sam, on a quest that promised an unhappy ending.

"It's not just this job," I said. "I kiss off this one, I lose a client. It's a lot of jobs and money in the next few years."

Sam nodded and sat back. "I'm an asshole for asking."

"I feel like an asshole for turning you down."

"Can you check for messages?"

Truth time. "I don't like the sound of it. What happened to questions with answers?"

He ignored me. "If I have to be found, I want someone to know my last location. That would be you."

"They use 'found' when a body's discovered."

"Whatever," he said. "How you fixed for cash?"

"A couple grand in checking."

Sam pointed to the envelope. "It's my personal bail-bond fund."

"I can't carry this to Grand Cayman."

"Leave it here. You got a bank box?"

I nodded.

"Perfect. If I thought I needed you on six-hour notice, I wouldn't do it. It's good enough that we keep a regular link, same time of day, every day."

"Where you going first?"

"I called my sisters. They remember old photos of Lorie with friends in bars where she hung out. I think I still have the last couple of letters she sent. Maybe I can dig through some boxes, pull 'em out, find a lead or two. I'll go up there, check into a motel, rent a post office box so my sisters can send me pictures and addresses and names of roommates."

"Can I ask, as a sympathetic friend, why you're doing this?"

"Detective Marlow wasn't there to talk about fishing or boat motors or newspaper pictures. He was sounding me out, sizing me up. He wouldn't do that unless he had some kind of follow-up. I don't know why he asked me not to snoop, and that troubles me. Also, I think my sisters and I are guilty of neglect. We didn't owe Lorie much more than keeping in touch and, most of the time, with her moving place to place, she made that a task. Most of the time she made friendship a task. Even so, we weren't much good for it when we knew how to find her. Since she vanished, none of us has put much effort into tracking her down. We let it slide. Lorie was her own kid and had some goofy ideas about sibling rivalry and parental neglect, so there was always the chance she disappeared on purpose. Maybe we figured that chasing after her would amount to invading privacy, going places it wasn't our business to go. Now it's a different deal."

"Seeing the dead stranger multiplied the guilt?"

"Getting that call this morning jacked the guilt. The dead stranger made me promise my sister better treatment. You want another beer?"

"Still working this one."

We sat on the porch another fifteen minutes without speaking. It was a perfect night for open windows, a breeze, low humidity, but a neighbor's air conditioner cycled on and off every few minutes. A gaggle of bicyclists on South gabbed loudly, one exclaiming, "Oh, my Gawd," four times before they rode out of earshot.

Sam said, "I don't want to be rude, but I hear my bed calling. You want to sit here and relax, I'll give you another free beer."

"My bed calls, too," I said.

I snapped Sam's gate and started back to Camille's for my bike. I had a million things to do, with thirty hours before my flight south. I patted my pocket to make sure I still had Sam's ten grand.

One message waited at the house. Duffy Lee Hall, on a problem with two of the film rolls. "It doesn't look like your work, Alex. It looks like a mild wide-angle lens, with a light leak. I can salvage most of these, but they're fogged and it won't be pretty."

The boat team member would be disappointed to learn that his waterproof camera wasn't anything proof. I didn't want to be attached to that problem. I decided to let Duffy Lee break the news to Dexter Hayes in the morning.

6

I WAS AWAKE MOST of the night, wide awake after five A.M. with my head in an old Elmore Leonard book. I worried for Teresa's safety, and fought an urge to bike around town looking for the yellow BMW. My gut analysis was that I didn't trust Whitney Randolph, so I didn't trust Teresa in his company. But I feared if I found her and all was innocent, she would end our relationship out of embarrassment on short notice. My consoling thought was that there had been dozens of nights in past months when we hadn't slept together. If she had seen other men, I never would've known. I had never felt betrayed, and after all that time, she had moved in with me. Common sense said that, if she had other interests, she'd have found a place of her own. Yet another voice warned that Randolph was a fresh interest who had shown up just as Teresa became my housemate.

The rising sun grayed the sky. I knew I'd be worthless for the day ahead. I closed my book and began a must-do list, including stashing Sam's "king" grand and pulling my passport from the safe-deposit box. I wanted to buy a new backpack-style tote and a tripod carrying case. I needed two or three decent dinner shirts.

My brain stumbled when I attempted to prioritize the list.

She arrived in a cab a few minutes after six, in unwrinkled clothing. She walked in sober, bleary-eyed, biting her upper lip, looking defiant and guilty. She wanted to have the first word, but it wouldn't come. All she could do was shrug, look sheepish, show me the hint of a teardrop, and disappear into the bathroom.

I waited in the rocker. My mind stayed blank out of fatigue. I sensed no inner guidance. I didn't know whether to be patient or defiant myself. She came out wrapped in a beach towel, carrying her soap and brush.

Eye to eye, we shared a moment of silence.

I said, "This is a guy you used to work with?"

"Not exactly."

I had phrased my question to nudge her toward the truth. I'd hoped for a different answer. It was my turn not to respond. I walked to the kitchen and began the coffee ritual that had kicked off many more pleasant mornings. I liked equal amounts of Folgers, Bustelo Cuban, and Starbucks. The blend offered flavor, kick, and geography. Just like Key West.

Teresa stood just outside the kitchen. Her defiance had returned. "Alex, if you can't handle answers, don't ask questions. What am I supposed to say, Whit and I have a 'past,' or some other word for it?"

"I could've stood the truth the first time through."

"Think about your friend Buffett's song. What is it, 'Pre-You' that talks about the people we used to date?"

"Date?" I said. "How about 'boink,' or some other useless euphemism, some other word for it?"

"I think the lyrics suggested that previous lovers were stepping-stones to where we are now."

"How previous are we talking? I thought you majored in communications in college."

"We are not talking, we're arguing," she said. "I didn't major in fucking, if that's what you mean."

"No, I meant what I said. Timely info, without circular talk."

"Your directness is not reading well. And I wasn't fucking all night.

I was talking and listening, and if we don't drop it now, we'll be very sorry."

"If we drop it now, other arguments will take its place."

"Okay, I'll get a condo. I don't need charity. I don't need free rent. I make my own money." She started for the backyard shower.

"You need some rest?"

"I'll clean up and go to work. I'll be fine."

"We were going to have coffee on the porch this morning."

She closed her eyes and took a deep breath. "Yes," she said. She looked at the porch, through the screens at the quiet lane. "I still want to do that. I've wanted to do that every morning."

Ten minutes later, again wrapped in the beach towel, she combed out her wet hair.

I poured two cups. "Last night you thought it might be murder."

She lifted her brush and nodded. "It's too simple. Something's not right."

"But you didn't say that to Dexter?"

"Or to anyone else, either. They've all got their heads set on suicide. But I swear, the vibes inside that house were way off tune."

"When did you go in?"

"After the *Herald* left," she said. "One of the commissioners wanted to console Yvonne. I went in, too, to express my sympathy."

"Had you met Yvonne before?"

"No. And she sure wasn't what I'd expected."

"What was wrong?"

"She acted like she didn't need consoling. She kept looking outside, at the officers in the mangroves, like she was afraid they were going to find something. I don't know what, his scalp or something. I mean, how would you find anything? There's so much crap in there, dead branches, leaves, who knows what. But that's how she looked. Like they were bothering her, she didn't want them to find a thing. She wanted them to go away. You were out there taking pictures, and she looked like she wanted you to leave, too. I finally decided she wanted me to go away, too."

"So you left?"

Teresa shook her head. "I asked if she had a place to go, or someone to stay with her for a few days. I was thinking she didn't want to hang around the scene of her husband's bloody suicide, which I thought made sense."

"And she said . . ."

"She said, 'Hell no. This was always my house, and I'm moving back in.'"

"People grieve in different ways," I said. "Maybe she hated the guy. Maybe she's happy he's gone. It doesn't mean foul play."

Teresa stared at me. I felt as if she were looking through my eyes, into my thoughts, to judge me the way she had judged Yvonne Gomez. "You're a man," she finally said. "You're allowed to think like a man." She took a long brush stroke through her hair. The towel fell away from her breasts, the cold air touched her nipples. She covered herself, then said, "Let me call this one, okay? It was worse than strange. She can't move in, anyway. It's still a crime scene, without a crime."

"Are you going to say something to Dexter today? You want me to give you a little boost, advice on how to phrase it?"

She shook her head. "I was hoping you'd ask around, see if anybody had a problem with the man. I mean, you've done things in the past year or two, figured out those scams, those other murders. You've helped the police find some evil bastards."

"It's not my job to fight for truth, justice, and the American way."

"It was when you were in the Navy," she said.

Where had that come from? I couldn't recall ever discussing my Navy years with Teresa. "That was my job description then," I said. "I'm not in the service now. I'm not a cop, and I don't have to carry the crimes of Monroe County on my back. I'm worn out from the past couple of years of getting sucked into one shit storm after another. What do cops call burnout?"

"Burnout. When nobody's around they call it dirtbag overload."

"I'm suffering their occupational depression, and it's not my career. For a dead friend, like Naomi, if she had died that way, I might feel compelled to dig. I don't know why Steve Gomez shot himself, and I don't know if anyone else shot him. He had friends, and I wasn't one of them. I didn't dislike him, or anything like that. I simply didn't know him well. If I ever drank a beer with him, it was only because he and I were in a bar at the same time. We never met to have a few. He wasn't a tight part of my life. He was mayor of a place where I pay taxes."

She stood and tightened the towel around her, as if now not wishing to have me see any part of her unclothed. "I was afraid you'd say that."

So much for coffee every morning.

"Look," I said, "just because I'm not into it doesn't mean I won't help. If you've got a hunch, turn yourself into a steel trap. Keep your eyes open and notice everything. Remember it all, but don't write it down at work. If you want help, okay. But I'm going to be your admin assistant, not your deputy."

Teresa didn't loosen her grip on the towel, but her mouth twitched. "If I need help, you're going to be in Grand Cayman. Thanks for the offer. And have a nice trip."

She went to work, I finished the coffee, and I wondered why I had blown off her suspicions. A week earlier I would have taken them as gospel. I would have marched to Dex Hayes, embellished her argument with a theory or two of my own, and pitched evidence no matter how circumstantial. To advance my bullheaded cause, I would have challenged Dexter's abilities as a detective and a human being. I hadn't done any of that.

Instead, I had found fault with Teresa's behavior of the past fifteen hours. I had ignored the stresses of her past few days. She had vacated her condo, stored her furniture, moved her belongings to my house, and dealt with a media crush because of Steve Gomez's position in the community. She had capped it by doing a poor job of juggling her gentleman friends. A charitable person would anticipate and forgive her neurotic impulses and views.

An objective and selfish person would ignore her.

The half gallon of straight caffeine failed me. I reclined on my bed to think out my day ahead, fell asleep, and was wakened by pounding rain. Thousands of ball peen hammers pounded my tin roof while someone slapped the yard with flat rubber paddles. There was no lightning, no thunder. Only percussion. I leaned off the mattress to look out the bedroom door. Slivers of sun shone through the living room blinds. I threw off my sheet, went to the main room, watched pouring rain form puddles and reflect sunlight. When it stopped, the humidity would skyrocket, and the air would weigh more than wet towels. Unwaxed cars and corroded tin shingles would look fresher. It would be a three-T-shirt day.

In that short nap, dreams had bounced in my head. I had been in Naomi Douglas's bedroom only once, to help hang a framed watercolor above her headboard. I had hoped several times that she had shown me the room as a subtle invitation. I'd never acted on those hopes. In my dream a woman's body lay in repose, in that room. Her face had been Julia Balbuena's, a former lover who'd been murdered up the Keys two years ago. In the dream her face had been blue, as it had been when I had arrived to take photos for the sheriff at Bahia Honda. Unsuspecting and unwarned, I had recognized her corpse, had identified her to the deputies.

Not a nightmare, but the beginning of one.

I fled to my backyard shower where I searched for tokens, figments of reality. I noted the beginnings of a wasp's nest. One more thrill for my new roomie. I found her pastel-handled shaver hung on a teak peg. I would have to inform Teresa that a razor left outside in Key West would grow hair of its own, would rust in minutes to a glistening copper-hued wedge of iron oxide. It was time for WD-40 on the door hinges. Time to clean the showerhead so its spray would go to the pits and not the eye-balls. I made mental plans to scrub the floor slats and varnish the inside of the door, and find a new soap holder . . .

But I couldn't get my mind off Naomi Douglas, our ten-year friend-ship, the levels of our friendship.

At times I had put her on a pedestal, viewed her as a grand angel who had come to bless the island. Other times we were equals, co-conspirators, planning how my photos or some new promo approach would best benefit the cause, the charity of the moment. She possessed a liveliness, depth, a unique air, a sharp sense of business. Her cantan-kerous moments were few, and taken for regality. She had showed few eccentricities, though one was her unwillingness to dwell in the past. She once told me that she loved the future as a concept, but worked to live each day for itself.

Naomi always wore light cotton, never denim, and expensive walk-ing shoes, not just sneaks. She had worn minimal, distinctive jewelry—two rings, a bracelet, a shirt pin, earrings with an artsy flair. Either her hair never grew, which I doubt, or she was careful to have it trimmed often to a length that spoke of comfort and elegance. I had come to count on the constancy of her appearance, her outlook, and her cheer.

Eight or nine years ago Naomi gave me the swelled head. My housemate then, Annie Minnette, had always pointed out her favorite photographs, had told me which ones were "good," and which images didn't work well. Naomi had gone beyond one-word critiques, had told me that she liked where I had placed my horizon, or the picture's offset balance, the play of tone, the war between colors. She had urged me to take myself more seriously, or at least express myself without an ama-teur's cynical mask of uncertainty. Naomi claimed to see art in my workaday photos. I still recall the exact spot where I stood, in the San Carlos Theater lobby, when she said to me, "I need to ask two favors."

"I'll say yes twice."

"Don't be so hasty. I want to buy two of your photographs."

"The brochure's got—"

"The brochure's at the printer," she had said. "It's behind us, and thank you. But I see something in your pictures that's higher than illustrating a darned brochure. I want two prints"—she indicated the ones she liked—"matted and framed. And signed, of course. You name the price, and don't think for a minute that I'll accept them for free."

When she paid me for the two framed prints, she also gave me a book of Walker Evans's photos from the 1930s. She ordered me to keep up my habit of taking pictures as often as possible, told me that I could become the next Walker Evans. Most of her flattery had bounced off, but her words had been pleasant to hear.

Several years ago I had helped her construct a display kiosk for a charity function, and we had gotten sweaty and dusty in the yard behind her house. We'd stopped for a break, some bottled green tea. Something about the afternoon light, or the perspiration on her upper lip, or her different look with her hair tucked behind her ears . . .

My gaze must have given me away.

She'd said, "You look at me like that, I wonder about your thoughts. You know that I'm broad in the beam and light of sail. I'm not shaped like your girlfriend."

"I've always been a sucker for eyes and smiles."

She had laughed. "Then you better watch yourself, buster."

Nothing ever came of it. I suppose I didn't want to change the nature of our friendship. She was honorable enough not to cause problems in my then-current relationship. Our social and business friendships had brought me pleasure. I had a girlfriend who made me happy.

Yet I wished I'd spent more time with her. There must have been many days when I rode my bicycle across Grinnell, past her house, and hadn't stopped. Perhaps I had pressing appointments, or didn't want to socialize just then. There'd always be time, I had figured. There'd always be another chance to catch up on chat, to show off new pictures, to have a quiet glass of green tea on her screened porch.

Naomi Douglas had helped other artists besides me. She had been a visionary, a volunteer, and a person who smiled more than she frowned. The world needs more like that. As of right then, it was short one and I was minus one fine friend.

I was inside shaving when the brass bell clanged. Marnie stood at the door, dressed for a day in the "home office": running shorts, a tank top, a ball cap on backward. I waved her in, invited her to make more coffee, and finished getting dressed.

"He left at seven-thirty, driving."

"Will the Bronco make it past Tavernier?"

"I dropped him at the airport. He reserved a car."

"Here's to dependable transportation," I said. "I didn't see you at the house last night. I was on the front porch with Sam for almost an hour."

"Here's to Dinner Party Sam. I wasn't home until midnight. I was out on the dark city streets, playing journalist detective, getting the low-down on Yvonne Gomez."

"And?"

"Steve Gomez was brokenhearted. A friend told him that Yvonne was screwing around. Her thing was to go to motels with tourists during city commission meetings. She would turn on the TV while they did their thing. As long as the mayor was right there in his official chair, in grainy black-and-white, he never could catch her. But secrets don't last long on this island. I guess he confronted her. She told him she wanted out of the marriage. She wasn't after money, either, because she had her own. She didn't care what she got, as long as she got rid of him. She moved out and rented a cottage on Love Lane, of all places. She called it her Love Shack."

"Cold woman," I said.

"Broke his heart. It explains a lot. Of course, somebody might argue that this constant east wind drove him crazy."

"Why 'Dinner Party Sam'?"

"You know how he is. He's always got to rise to the occasion, answer the call, do the right thing. His one big flaw, living out his macho self-image. We had a dinner party going last year for people I work with and their spouses or partners. Sam got a phone call. Captain Turk's motor had died out by the Snipe Keys. It was a half hour before sunset, and we had eight guests sitting down to dinner. Sam didn't think twice. He went to his boat, powered out to the Snipes, and towed Turk in. He got home, smelling of sweat and beer, just as our last guests left."

"It's the rule of the sea . . ."

"The rule of the house was that he did all the dishes. Anyway, back to last night, Sam went to bed early. This morning he woke me up before the sun came up. He was, let's say, amorous and vigorous. So if I look like I'm walking bowlegged . . ."

"You look like a woman on a mission of her own."

"As did your girlfriend yesterday afternoon. Sam said he pulled you out of dinner at Camille's."

"She got home after the garbage trucks," I said.

"I guess we all learn things about our housemates."

"Why does my life have to be this rolling sine wave of information?" I said. "It's good news, bad news, and I'm not begging for a boring straight line . . ."

"She moves into your home, then doesn't come home . . ."

"Last week I watched Teresa do a wonderful thing. I didn't know she spoke French, never heard her say a word of it. She knows French as well as we know English. We were in Fausto's, in the checkout line. This woman barged to the front feigning bewilderment, excusing her-self in French and pointing to the baby she held in her arm. I assumed a diaper emergency. Teresa said something in French and the woman butted back out and went to the rear of the line. Outside on the sidewalk I asked Teresa what she'd said. She'd told the lady that her child didn't smell like caca, but the lady's breath smelled like beer. She told her she'd call the police on child-abuse charges if she didn't wait her turn."

"Maybe she should've been a cop instead of a news liaison."

We both quit talking, and thought about what we'd been saying. An idea came to mind. "Marnie, who found Naomi?"

"I asked that question, too. The police weren't sure. The call came from Naomi's home. The officer I talked to figured that a neighbor found her. He said that a lot of people didn't want to get caught up in legalities. Maybe she had a housekeeper."

I shook my head. "No woman as active as Naomi Douglas would need a housekeeper."

Marnie shrugged and stood to leave. "She was always on the go, maybe she didn't want to spend time cleaning. Knowing Naomi, we also could guess that she employed someone who needed the money."

"Was it a woman's voice or a man's that called?"

"You're not going to believe this. The call came through on a line that wasn't recorded. The dispatcher who took it couldn't recall if the voice was male or female."

I was unlocking my bike when I heard the phone ring. If I waited three more rings my answering service would pick up. I had eighteen seconds to decide: win big or lose big. I got it just in time.

Jack Spottswood, attorney-at-law. "Alex, have you ever been executor of an estate?"

"I've been called some bad-ass things, but never that."

"Guess what. You're up to bat. Naomi Douglas named you in her will."

"Why would she leave me money?"

"That's a minor part of it. What I'm getting to is that she asked that you handle her estate, the financial details. As executor, you'll get a set fee. But don't go ordering a new car."

"Don't executors get asked or warned in advance?"

"Most of the time, yes. Not this time."

"When do I execute?"

He asked if I still lived on Dredgers Lane.

I told him I did.

"Can you come down to the office about three o'clock? We can go over the papers."

I said, "Tell me about the time factor."

"You got a conflict?"

"I leave tomorrow for a seven-day job in the Caymans."

"Come down here and sign papers, I can put this in motion. Some of this can take weeks and months. The sooner I start it, the better. The rest, we'll do it when you get back."

She had planned it, and I had to laugh. Naomi would be part of my life, and I would stay part of hers. Amazing woman.

7

I RECALLED THE WORK crew in 1998, tossing chunks of drywall and flooring into a Dumpster at the Fleming Street curb near Duval. The West Key Bar had been one of the classic wood-floor saloons on the island, but there is a huge difference between classic and classy. It's amazing what plans, paint, glass and cement will do. The first level is now a glitzy clothing store. The Spottswood law offices are upstairs. A lot of old woodwork remains in salute to the structure's history. Today's pale walls, mahogany furniture, and office art would baffle the old bar crowd.

I sat in Jack Spottswood's office while he finished two calls and rejected a third. He asked a woman named Robin not to interrupt unless his daughter called. He sat back in his leather chair and took a deep breath.

"There won't be a funeral, Alex."

"We could pack a church," I said.

"That was Naomi's decision. She left a directive letter with her will. The only thing she wanted was a gathering on Louie's Afterdeck. There'll be a jazz group, champagne, and six tables of hors d'oeuvres. Anyone who cries has to donate a hundred bucks to AIDS Help and leave the party."

Perfect, I thought. "Her sense of style plays on."

"It does. She had fun on this island. She put a lot into it, too, but I don't have to tell you that." He checked a file. "Her body's at the funeral home on Simonton. They'll cremate. We didn't want to taint the directive, so she gave me verbal instructions. She wanted her ashes scattered at Woman Key."

"This is a case where we don't ask permission?"

Jack cracked a smile. "I can't advise you on that."

I smiled, too. "Ah, but you did."

"Anyway," said Jack, "our first problem is finding her older brother, one Ernest Bramblett. He'll get the bulk of the estate. Ever met him?"

"Never heard of him," I said. Odd that she'd never mentioned his name.

"The will is only three years old, but the guy's address is history. Robin went looking on the Internet but found nothing. I remember Naomi saying recently that she had been in touch with him. He's out there somewhere."

"Can I look through her papers?"

"Or maybe go on her computer. I was hoping you'd take care of that."

"Where did they grow up?"

Jack flipped through some pages. "Akron, Iowa. She's leaving money to the Akron-Westfield School. I never knew there was more than one Akron."

"There's one in New York State, too."

"You get to all the hot spots, Alex. Anyway, we contacted the *Akron Register* and Northwestern Bell. Mr. Bramblett had previous accounts, but he left no forwarding info. If you don't have one, I've got a house key here."

"I never had a key."

Jack told me I was free to enter Naomi's home. Her household items could be given to friends or charity. I would make those decisions. She had specified sums for the Red Cross and a half-dozen local causes. I would determine sources for that money, from the sale of stocks and bonds, cashing certificates of deposit, or tapping bank and brokerage accounts. Jack agreed to help me set up an escrow account for handling estate costs. He wished me luck, told me to call anytime.

"When I asked why she would leave me money, you said it was a minor part of it. How minor?"

"I will be the trustee of a small amount to, quote, 'further the fine-art career of Alex Rutledge.' It's twenty grand, for camera gear, film supplies, printing, framing, and so on."

"Not too damned minor," I said.

"She must have believed in you."

Our meeting had been quick. I sensed that Jack had other business on his desk, so I stood to leave. "Shame about Steve Gomez."

"Crazy, what he did." Jack tilted his chair, inhaled, looked away. "Steve was another one. He put a lot of himself into this town. Some people live for today. He could see the future. His last margin of victory was a landslide, a fine job review from the voters. Today's front page did him right. They got a positive quote from every important person in the Lower Keys. I guess, if he killed himself, Steve didn't agree with the mandate."

Jack thought for a moment then said, "You watch. There's going to be a mad scramble at the city. Steve left some real estate deals blowing in the wind. The commission's voting could go haywire. There's no telling what they'll pass or reject."

"Dexter Hayes got me out to photograph the scene."

"I'm glad you saw it rather than me."

"Nothing to see," I said. "They took him away as I got there."

"Why'd you have to take pictures?"

"Only Dex Hayes knows that. I got garden shots. Botany one-oh-one."

Jack sneered. "The almost-ex-wife won't keep it up. I know her people. They buy everything they see. Boats, pickup trucks, cars, vacant lots, you name it. They let it all go to hell. Six months from now that garden will look like any overgrown yard. Shame about that." Jack gazed through his oak blinds. "Bigger than that, it's a damned shame about

Steve. I once saw him snipping dead leaves off a peace lily in city hall. He liked his plants."

I walked outside to blustery weather. A thin comfort line splits the rough northeast wind from the island's prevailing southeast breeze. You didn't see salt mist unless you gazed a few blocks down a street, and you might mistake it for dust blown from Key West's nonstop sewer digs and road repairs. You felt it on your skin, in your eyes, on anything you touched, then you tasted salt on your lips.

Grand Cayman's weather pattern was separate from the southern Gulf of Mexico's. I would be gone in twenty-four hours.

I stared at Fleming and Duval. The Holiday Inn, Fast Buck Freddie's, two fancy clothing shops. There once had been the La Concha Hotel, B.O.'s Fish Wagon, Kress, and a pharmacy. Nothing is as sure as change, especially in the tropics. The death of Naomi Douglas was large in my life but had little impact on the island and its history. I would think about Naomi long after I had forgotten buildings and businesses. And the more I heard about Steve Gomez, the more I wished I had known him better.

Plastic bags and dead sea grape leaves skittered down Fleming. I fought the wind east to Grinnell. I began to lock my bike in front of Naomi's house, then changed my mind. I rode two more blocks to my house to get a camera and my mini-cassette recorder.

A phone message greeted me, from Teresa. "I'm paying for my lack of sleep, like riding a roller-coaster. I've been doing office things, filing that I've put off for weeks. Alex, if I tell you I'm horny, will you please believe I'm thinking of you and no one else? Call me if you get a chance."

The phone rang as I switched off the answering machine.

Sam Wheeler: "Glad I caught you, so we could talk one-to-one."

"How you making out?"

"Bad. I drove through Islamorada this morning, which I hate. The locals are militant slowpokes. I stopped for gas in Tavernier, that Circle K between the north- and southbound lanes at mile marker ninety-three. I'm in such a snarl over this shit, I pulled out of the place, went ripping up the road. I was back in Islamorada before I knew that I had fucking U-turned."

"You're a distracted man."

"Then I get behind some drizzle-dick in a beater Falcon wagon covered with decals, with painted coconuts hanging from what's left of the bumpers. It's his civic duty to do twenty, so everyone lives a safer life at his turtle pace. I about went nuts before I got to Florida City."

"Get anything done?"

"Marnie advised me to research Detective Marlow in the library up here. It took me an hour to find the right branch and another half hour to find the right desk. Then the clerks gave me a runaround. Something about microfiche files sent out for scanning. They told me that media credentials might improve my luck. I'll have to bounce that one back to Marnie. Tell her, if you see her, but I'll leave a message, too."

"So that's it?"

"I bagged the post office box and checked into a hotel so my sisters can FedEx me stuff. I ate a chicken Philly cheesesteak, whatever the fuck that is. Then, get this, I went to buy beer in a 7-Eleven, and I ran into our cab driver, Goodnight Irene Jones. She wanted to meet me for a drink later tonight, told me she hung out in a joint called Cheers."

"And you said . . ."

"I told her not to count on me. Meanwhile, I can't figure out how to tune the rental car's radio, and I wish I'd bought two six-packs instead of one. That about sums me up."

Sam gave me a Hampton Inn's address and phone number, told me the room he was in. He advised me to buy stock in Amstel Beer.

Ten minutes later I chained my bike inside Naomi's picket fence. I let myself into her house, then locked the door behind me. Someone had shut down the air-conditioning. I was hit with musty smells from drains and air baked by attic heat. The house looked clean, though, with mahogany tables waxed, rugs vacuumed, wood flooring swept. I opened the four living room windows, a first-floor bathroom window, and the back door. Then I flipped on a ceiling paddle fan. The breeze began to blow papers off the tables. I closed three of the windows, sat a moment, and observed.

Naomi had filled her main room with tropical and nautical artifacts. Two old solid rattan rockers and a rattan love seat. Crab-trap tables, driftwood posts in a corner, under a hanging plant. A framed 1940s-era postcard packet with eight images of "quaint" Key West connected vertically. A table made of two antique louvered window shutters under thick glass. Four small prints of hundred-year-old Winslow Homer ocean scenes hung on the rear wall.

I spent twenty minutes taking photos of furnishings, framed art, and the contents of cupboards. I wanted a visual record for her brother and proof of value for the tax people. I made audio notes to myself about what I had done, things I needed to do. I felt a traitor to my grief, going about my task, my manner so similar to procedures at crime scenes. I consoled myself with grand cliché: It was what she had wanted me to do. She had named me in her directive, wanted me in her home, dealing with her possessions, closing out her life, her accounts. I still felt unease as if something was wrong, missing, misplaced.

I thought about Spottswood's words. "She must have believed in you."

I entered the small pine-paneled room that Naomi used as her office. With my arms extended, swung in an arc, I could almost touch all four walls. The room was a perfect hideout for someone privately proud but modest in public. Above me was an old Hunter ceiling fan with oak blades. An antique table served as her desk, an antique chest her filing cabinet. She'd placed a cotton print-covered pillow on her oak office tilt-chair on rollers. A white Bose Wave Radio/CD sat on top of the chest. The room was a compact statement of elegance and function. Pure Naomi.

I sat in her chair and studied items hung on the north wall. An Honorary Conch declaration signed by Wilhelmina Harvey in 1996. A pilot's license issued in 1967. A diploma and a Master of Fine Arts certificate, both from the University of Wisconsin. A citation from the Illinois chapter of the American Red Cross. A signed Jeff MacNelly print called *Personal Trainer*, in which a dog riding a bicycle leads a woman in jogging clothes down a street in Old Town. A valuable collection of framed signed letters and notes from Twain, Hawthorne, Welty, and Faulkner. There was no room in the office to use my flash. I would have to photograph each item elsewhere.

Next to the window was a photo of Arthur Douglas, Naomi's late husband. Barrel-chested, a crewcut, not much of a smile. She had told me about going with him to business social functions. She'd said that his fellow executives' wives all had too much jewelry, too many homes, cars, memberships, pets, and vacations. They had been wealthy so long that they'd run out of ways to spend their husbands' money. So the women had gone to the knife for retrofits. Naomi guessed that many of them had been trying to compete with their daughters' youth. The oddest result of the face-lifts and tucks was smiles. All permanent and identical. When she told me of this, Naomi had folded her arms across her belly and said, "I don't care if my jowls droop to my waist like my boobs. I will never join the Smile Club for Women."

I opened the chest's top drawer and caught her scent. The faint smell took me to an image of Naomi's face, laughing, looking me in the eye. She changed her expression to speak softly, to tell me something important. I wished I could have heard her voice, known her mind at that moment. Her purse and a small pouch were in the drawer. The pouch held three watches, eight or ten jeweled pins, several gold necklaces, earrings, and bracelets. I pocketed the pouch. It needed safer storage, elsewhere.

I looked through a stack of utility bills, bank statements, ATM receipts, and coupons. A recent bill from Dr. Lysak's office, a basic visit. I had met Lysak at a charity party several years ago. Young, buffed-out, pleasant guy. Under the stack was an old photo of Naomi. She stood with three other women in a large yard. Red and yellow maple leaves filled trees and covered the ground. By the date on the back, she had been thirty, give or take a few. Her smile was identical to the one I knew.

I tilted back in the chair and started her computer. As the hard drive spun up to speed I checked my watch. I thought about all the things I needed to do before flying out at noon the next day. I hadn't packed, hadn't withdrawn cash from the bank. I decided to take Jack Spottswood at his word, to postpone my executor duties until I had returned from Grand Cayman. I shut down her computer and returned to the living room.

I had found nothing of Iowa. Naomi had adopted Key West and divorced her past. I wondered again what had bothered me about the decor. The easiest answer was no fresh flowers. She always kept blossoms in a tall vase on the large table. Some had come from her yard, most from the grocery store.

Then it struck me. My photographs, the two that Naomi had considered "fine art" and had bought from me, were not above the sofa. The wall was empty. I looked into the bedroom. A navigational chart was on one wall, a vintage Caribbean watercolor on the other. The room looked exactly as I had seen it when Naomi had asked me to help hang the watercolor. She had died in her bed, and I found it odd that the bed wasn't stripped of its blankets and sheets. The bed looked enticing, as if waiting in the day's dimming sunlight for Naomi to slide in for another night's rest.

I shut off the fan, closed the window, went to lock the back door. Just outside were two garbage cans in a wood rack. Trash pickup was twelve hours off. The first one I opened was empty. Inside the second can was the sucker punch. In a crush of broken glass, bent frames, and curled mat paper were the two photos that I had sold to Naomi years ago.

8

I WALKED OUT OF Fausto's with a six-pack and two bottles of wine. I downed a beer as I rode home, finished one while I locked my bike to the mango tree, started another while I peed the neighbor's hedge. I was going to do a righteous job of packing my duffel bag. I would forget sun lotion, underwear, and extra ball caps.

Four beers plus a snifter of Merlot sent me to bed without my supper. Teresa woke me around ten-thirty and tried to snuggle. I later learned that I fell back asleep. She rubbed my back at six-thirty, a sign that specific attention was desired. That time she had better luck, as did I. I tried to keep my face averted so I wouldn't vaporize her eyelashes with halitosis. At one point, with her on top and flushed and lovely, we took a break.

"This is not just to relieve inner tensions, Alex, so you'll know. And it's not so I won't stray while you're gone. You might recall that we haven't done it since I moved here."

"You've been busy."

"I know." She looked up as if to count tongue-in-groove wall slats behind the bedposts. "I'm starting to think maybe I should become a cop, quit this spin-doctor crapola. My office hours are undefined."

"They'd be worse if you were a cop."

"Maybe I can be a bagger at Publix."

Change the subject. I said, "I'm not going to see you for eight days."

She looked into my eyes, into my blurred thoughts. "Let's put one in the bank," she said. She squeezed, lifted, and reached down to fit us together. I tasted her sweet breasts and resumed our lovemaking. It worked for Teresa twice, the second with a loud, unladylike curse at release. After ten minutes I proved unbankable.

I blamed my substitution of beer for basic food groups.

"I don't think that's it," she said. "You're sad about Naomi, which I understand, and you're nervous about this faraway photo job, or something else is gnawing at you. I hope it's not Whit."

"I'm enjoying the view. Baby-thumb nipples, these bare, pastel knees, and your half-in and half-out belly button. I'm worried about this stubble down here, these tan line ingrowns. I could have done without hearing his name."

"If he was your problem," she said, "you'd be different. You'd be pissy and distant and short with me. Don't ask me how, I just know. You wouldn't talk about knees. You wouldn't want to look at my muff. Or my stubble, whichever has your attention."

"Both."

"I knew that." She rubbed my forehead. "What else is in there?"

I told her about my new role as Naomi's executor, about documenting the house on Grinnell, my shock at finding the framed photos in Naomi's trash can.

"So, we're talking grief and disappointment, not worry?"

"Disappointed," I said, "but I'm baffled, too."

"It makes no sense. She would trust you with her estate but toss your work in the garbage? No way. Who's been in that house?"

I shrugged against the pillow. "Somebody was in there. It was spotless. The bed was made." I thought back to what Jack Spottswood had said about Steve Gomez's landslide election victory. "You think somebody gave my fine art a bad review?"

She looked at the light starting through the blinds, then at the clock. "If I had time, I'd give you a killer massage." She moved her

hand to where we blended, tangled, our damp crushed skin, reassur-
ance for the moment. "Or any massage you'd like."

"But you have to go to work, and I still have yesterday's errands."

She got out of bed, stood naked before the mirror above the bureau,
and inspected the skin on her face. "When you come back from Grand
Cayman," she said, "are you going to be more romantic?"

I admired the view, then noticed an old scratch on the skin of her
right buttock. I hadn't scratched her during our lovemaking. I said,
"Only if you're my roommate."

An hour later I had finished coffee, showered, repacked the duffel, and
checklisted my camera bag. I had decided that my old tripod carrying
case could make one last trip. I took a bowl of cereal salad to the porch:
equal portions of Cinnamon Life, Toasted Oatmeal Squares, Cranberry
Almond Crunch, and Smart Start. Like blending coffee, one of my small
indulgences.

Rule of life: If cereal's in your plans, the phone always rings after
you've poured milk. Marnie spoke the instant I picked up. "Check out
the 'Opinion' page in the *Citizen* before you go."

"You can't read it to me?"

She grunted.

I said, "Naomi named me her executor. She wanted a going-away
party at Louie's."

Marnie told me to plan it soon and to have a good trip. She hung up
before my cereal went soggy.

It wasn't a good morning for cereal.

I heard a hissing muffler in the lane. It took me a moment to recognize the deep-discount Taurus that Cootie Ortega had lowballed at a
fixed city auction. Its window-tint film had peeled. The white paint had
oxidized to a dull blue-gray. Corrosion pocked the hood, trunk, and
roof. I doubted that any water but rain had touched the sedan during
Ortega's tenancy. Cootie kicked his door shut, carried a small paper

sack and a frayed tote toward my door. I went outside to intercept. I wanted our meeting to take place on my porch, not in my house. Exhaust smoke lingered in the lane, threatened to drift toward the screening. I could count on the fact that Ortega had never changed his car's oil.

He wore a thin cotton V-neck T-shirt, shiny suit trousers, and a pair of antique Hush Puppies. His cat's-eye sunglasses looked like a prop Jayne Mansfield might have worn in a B-minus movie. Ortega was buffoon enough without promoting the fact. I couldn't wait to hear his sales pitch. I didn't need equipment. The cameras would have to be giveaways for me to bite.

"Brought you some Conch fritters, bubba," he said.

Sure as hell, grease oozed through the brown paper bag. I'd packed my Tums in my Dopp kit. I couldn't figure why Cootie wanted to re-exercise the old Conch political method of buttering-up, offering bollos from the vendor's stand by the aquarium. I was going to buy camera gear, or decline. I wasn't going to do the man any favors. Gut bombs would not sway my decision. I thanked my stars that he had brought fritters rather than bollos.

"Sweet of you, Cootie." I pointed at my unfinished cereal. "Can I simply admire them, or do I have to eat?"

"Eat. You got some paper towels?"

Cootie followed me into the kitchen, took care to check out my house for anything with salvage value. He looked too long at my broiler oven. Ironic. I had never seen him notice details at a crime scene.

"How are things at the city?" I found a new roll of towels, led him to the porch table. "Any changes going down? Or will they show some respect for Steve's memory a day or two?"

He spread eight fritters on two towels. "You mean, like . . ."

"Right. Anybody want your job to vanish, and mine with it?"

"I don't think so, bubba. The idiots adjust to everything down there. I mean, what could happen? Worse is they'd fire me, and that might be the best thing. I been kicking serious money on eBay."

I asked what he was buying and selling.

"This and that, whatever's moving."

I tried to pin him down. "Lately?"

He wouldn't budge. Shook his head. "You don't remember me, do you?"

"Cootie, I've worked the same crime scene as you eight or ten times in the past three years. What's that mean, I don't remember you?"

"I mean, not now, bubba. I mean in the 1970s. That coffee window next to the El Sol coin laundry on Duval. That place was my mama's, you know that? She have me runnin' her window seven days, all year, selling plastic cups of Cuban coffee, seven cents back then. You ride up there every day, ten-thirty, on that gold three-speed English racer with the high handlebars, put your elbow into my buche window. You order two little cups, pay your fourteen cents, tip me eleven. You toss 'em back, the sweat come out your forehead, you ride away high as a blimp."

I never had paid a moment's attention to the man who had served me Cuban coffee for years. He had always been yakking in rapid-fire Spanish with people inside the kitchen, always treated me like any other customer, another lazy newcomer to his island. I had never connected the young man from back then with the one I now knew. I smiled at Ortega, shook my head.

He tossed a fritter into his mouth and pointed to another, then at my mouth. "You one of the few hippies then, one of the few who had a regular wire bike basket instead of a stolen blue MacArthur milk crate tied to your handlebar. One day you know, you wore a tourist-looking T-shirt, a sailfish jumping each side of your ribs, crossed fishing poles in the middle, I told you that day that's the stupidest shirt I ever saw. You laughed, and you told me that's why you bought it. You said you paid three dollars at McCrory's at Eaton and Duval."

His sales pitch was better than I had expected.

I took a bite of conch fritter to placate him, tasted bell pepper and onion and hot sauce. Amazing how little we know about people we see and work with. I couldn't believe that he recalled more about my early days in town than I did, details that long ago escaped my brain. If he had paid that much attention to professional details, he might have made a decent crime photographer and darkroom technician. But he'd failed that gig. I couldn't believe that Cootie Ortega had ever been observant, ever given a half a damn about anything except getting by on the cheap.

"I've got a noon plane to catch, Cootie. Show me what's for sale."

"Lenses, including a twenty-eight, and this OM-1 body for a low price, bubba. Don't worry about instant cash, you know?"

I reminded myself to visit an ATM.

Cootie picked up on my worried expression. "You ain't got lots of loose money, maybe you got stuff to sell. You're talking to a collector, here, buyin' and sellin' Beanie Babies, old worthless stock certificates, pre-1990 NASCAR items. The list goes on, brother, however you want. You tell me. I know you ain't got Barbies, but certificates, racing collectibles, old Hot Wheels—lots of guys got that stuff. You pay me anytime. We'll work it out."

I had assumed he'd want instant dollars. And I hadn't expected to buy a thing. Four lenses were priced so low I'd be a fool not to get them. I also bought the OM-1 camera body and an old T-20 flash unit. I passed on the twenty-eight lens; I had one that I used rarely. I gave Ortega two hundred, told him I'd write him a check for the balance when I returned from Grand Cayman. He took his fritters to his Taurus. I called a taxi.

For a moment I stood on the porch and appreciated for the thousandth time the morning sunlight washing through my screens. I searched my mind, imagined the shoulder-height coffee window, the man in that window. The man had no features, no face. I couldn't change my memory. My opinion of Cootie Ortega, however, had shifted. Not so much upward as sideways, to account for his memory and the fact that he'd cut me a deal on the lenses.

I was dumping out cereal mush when the phone rang.

Sam said, "Glad I caught you before you dusted off to the airport. Get a pencil while I piss and moan about you, down in Grand Cayman this evening, knocking back tall rum, staring at bare-breasted beach lovelies. I can almost hear the reggae music from here, you bastard."

He'd read my mind, but I didn't want to rub it in. "I got a pen in my hand. Paper, too."

"Okay, I'll quit the crap. I need some favors. I don't know how you'll do them on quick notice, but you've got sources in that graft-ridden city of ours, and the newspaper frowns on Marnie doing this stuff. Write down Florida tag XSW-252, on a puke-green Chevy Cavalier. I need full info on that one. This guy likes to play tag, likes to follow people, but I turned the tables. It's a long story for another day. Next is MJC-547, a recent Toyota Camry, dark green or black. This dude was a fellow-followee, near as I could tell. Call Marnie if you get a hit on either one and give her what you learn. I'll get it from her. You got those numbers okay?"

I told him I had them.

"New subject. These pictures my sister overnighted could've been taken any time from the late Seventies until Lorie disappeared. One's a group shot. I've found people here who don't recognize Lorie, but they say it looks like the crowd that hung at the Parrot, maybe in 'eighty-three or 'eighty-four. So I need names of bartenders who worked there, and anybody you can think of who might have been in Lauderdale then."

"Nobody right off, but I'll put my mind to it."

"Damn," he said. "Where is my head? Captain Turk used to bop back and forth, and I'll bet he hung at the Parrot. He used to chase Gold Coast rich girls so he could get a sugar mama to be his ticket out of fishing. I'll call him at the dock. You think of anything, tell Marnie and I'll get it from her. Slurp a Cayman toddy for us working stiffs, bubba."

I copied the tag numbers onto another scrap of paper and put them in my wallet.

A benefit of having a roommate was that I didn't have to close up my house. I took one safety precaution: I left a note for my neighbor and close friend, Carmen Sosa. I told her that I'd be gone, but Teresa would be around. I also copied the tag numbers for Carmen, and asked her to get Marnie any info she could.

The cab showed, and I was out of there with a half hour to pick up my passport and hit the ATM. A stress-free exit.

I asked the cabbie to wait in a loading zone on Southard. I was inside the bank, lifting my passport from the lock box when I realized I had left Sam's ten thousand stashed in my house. Whose memory was thinning in times of stress? I withdrew eight hundred for travel cash and decided Sam's money was safe enough where I'd hidden it.

I hurried back outside. Whit Randolph had angled his yellow BMW to the curb, just ahead of the cab. He was at the money machine. I wanted to dodge him, tiptoe to the taxi.

"Rutledge, thank God it's you, just in time to save my ass. I can never make these things work. These damned arrows point between two buttons to push, they got language choices, and Christ! I want my money, and this bastard's asking me how much I want to deposit."

"I've used this one a few times," I said.

"Here, hold this." He handed me a plastic water bottle and glanced at my face. "Take a hit if you want."

I sniffed. Straight vodka. The constant cocktail before lunch.

Randolph read me. "Every journey begins with a first stagger, Rutledge. Especially on this island." He poked the buttons, ran the prompts one more time. The machine beeped and spit back his card.

I said, "Let me show you . . ."

"Good, good. My PIN's four-nine-oh-five. See if you can get me a hundred bucks."

I wasn't comfortable with his telling me his secret number, but what the hell. I wasn't going to steal his debit card. I handed the plastic bottle back to him, pressed a few buttons, watched the twenties spit out. I showed him how to close out the transaction and forgo the receipt.

He put the five twenties in his sport shirt pocket. "You've saved my day, Alex. Let me tell you, man, I love your fine cottage. I love that brass bell out front, your different-colored croton bushes, all that art on your walls."

"Thanks for saying . . ."

"I mean it. It's a great funky hideaway. You've got a yard for puttering, the perfect porch for rum drinks. If I wanted a treasure like that today, I'd have to shell out big money."

I had zoned out the fact that Randolph had picked up Teresa for dinner. I felt invaded, upset more by his being inside my home than my knowledge of his PIN.

"Thanks," I said. "It's a quiet lane, and it was cheap by today's prices. Call it a lucky pick a long time ago."

He looked at the damp stains on his sport shirt. "You sure sweat a lot down here, don't you?"

"Me, or people in general?"

He chuckled. "Do you sweat anything? The way Teresa talks, I doubt you do. I meant people in general, but mainly me. Right now, I can't fucking stand myself." He looked toward Duval Street. "Buy you a beer?"

"No thanks," I said.

"What's the matter, man? I rub you wrong?"

"Nope. It's just that everybody's new in town."

"You get a lot of beer offers?"

"That's not it. Once you're here for a while, you don't have that much time for midday drinking. You follow?"

"Sorry if I offended you."

I started back to my taxi. "You caught me in a hurry and a weird mood."

"Are those legal in Key West?"

"This is a place without many rules," I said. "Don't ask permission, and you know the rest."

"I like that setup. If I don't get forgiven, what do I do, change my name?"

"That won't work. You'll have to leave town."

He grinned but didn't look at me. "Once you're here for a while, that's harder to do."

9

MY TURN TO LEAVE town. Not a minute too soon.

Years ago, five times a day, a twin-prop commuter would land, swap milk bottles for Hershey Bars, and depart. Two dozen people came and went, and foot traffic vanished, leaving the airport quiet as an empty church until the next turnaround. These days you still see pale skin inbound, sunburns outbound, but activity in the airport never stops.

I fought the crowd to check in for my flight.

I felt a welcome mental departure forty minutes before takeoff, a weight off my shoulders. I was going to Grand Cayman to work, but also for reasons people came to Key West: fewer reminders, better vibes. I needed to escape day-to-day crap, realign my priorities. My first moment of peace came when I told myself not to worry about having a housemate when I returned. There wasn't much I could do about it, even if I stayed.

I bought a *Key West Citizen*, but couldn't find a wall to lean against. Too many racks of brochures, weekly papers, dining guides, real estate tabloids. The vinyl chairs in the small lounge were taken. I walked outside to sit on a park-style bench, but the Lower Keys Smoke-Out Squad had picked the zone for a bull session. I went back in, stood near baggage claim, and found the editorial that Marnie had mentioned.

IN MEMORY OF A WORKER AND A GIVER

The death of Steve Gomez touches everyone on this island. The man brought goodness when he arrived here twelve years ago. He passed it around freely. The man did not have a selfish bone in his body. He did things for Key West and its residents that most of us never noticed, many of us will never know about.

Key Westers will remember Steve's quick smile and laugh, and his sense of fairness. He made a difference in local politics, and never allowed his campaigns to lean to the negative. His votes in commission meetings showed no favorites and took into account the welfare of longtime, less fortunate residents. We have many lessons to learn from examples he set. We suggest a short prayer, an expression of thanks, a moment to reflect on the life of Steve Gomez.

A generous tribute. I guessed that Marnie had written the piece. I also guessed that someone had edited it. Under it was another eulogy.

IN MEMORY OF A GIVER AND A WORKER

Key West suffered a double loss yesterday. It makes sense that more of us knew Mayor Gomez, but those who had come to know Naomi Douglas will miss her smile and energy. A "freshwater" Conch, she, too, gave freely of her time and resources for the betterment of this island. Naomi had an eye for spotting the needs of the town and a talent for recruiting citizens who could cure problems and obviate challenges before they became our problems. She set examples for us all to believe in the arts, trust our best instincts, and honor our culture.

Naomi Douglas helped many individuals and causes, sought no recognition, made friends and no enemies. The later years of her life were a fine celebration of the best aspects of Key West.

A bit generic, I thought, but a great gesture. Another Marnie Dunwoody touch. I flipped to the Crime Report but got sidetracked by the obituaries.

STEVEN WEBB GOMEZ

Steven Webb Gomez, 46, beloved husband of Yvonne, passed away on April 19, in Key West. Steve had been mayor of Key West for the past six years. Born in Iowa, Gomez moved to the Keys in the late 1980s to "leave the snow shovel behind and reinvent my life." A former Peace Corps volunteer, an avid sailor, and a master electrician, Steve worked with Exotic and Wild Bird Rescue of the Florida Keys, the Habitat for Humanity, the American Red Cross, and other charities.

In addition to his wife of ten years, Steve is survived by a sister, Elizabeth Ann Hamper, and a brother, Dennis Gomez, both of Akron, Iowa.

A service in celebration of Steve Gomez's life will be . . .

Both of Akron, Iowa?

Outside, at a pay box, it took thirty-five cents to screw up my plans for the day. I dialed Marnie Dunwoody's cell phone. On the third ring she said, "Yes?"

Cagey woman. Her caller ID had come up blank. I said, "Hey."

"Alex, I thought you'd be gone by now."

"Do you know of any link between Naomi Douglas and Steve Gomez?"

She was quiet a moment. "I don't think they were friends. In all the time I've known Steve, I've never seen him with Mrs. Douglas."

"Today's obituary says his brother and sister live in Akron, Iowa. Naomi's brother's last address is that same town. It's not like it's Miami or Chicago. Two people from a small town in the Midwest die the same day on a Florida island? I think date of death takes on new meaning."

A long silence at the other end. "Oh, crap."

"I don't suppose anyone at the paper suggested he might have been . . ."

"Murdered? I haven't heard a thing like that."

"Do your research like a true sleuth, Marnie. You admired the man. He deserves a fair shake after the fact."

"He deserved that ahead of time."

We promised to stay in touch.

I dropped a couple more coins and began to dial Dexter Hayes's number. I quit, knowing his view on Gomez's death, his disinterest in Naomi Douglas. I got through to Sheriff Liska, found him in his office. I pitched my discovery, my suspicion, my reluctance to call Hayes.

I said, "You want to look around, I got a house key from Spottswood. She named me her executor."

"Okay, we don't need a warrant. Can you meet a deputy in ten minutes?"

I had already half formed my decision to stay, the minute I had caught the Akron link. Maybe I wanted Liska to force me into it. "I'm at the airport, about to fly off to a job. I need the money."

"Tough rats, bubba. You just stepped in it."

I said, "You going to pick up the case?"

"You think it's automatic? I can't take on 'suspicion' cases inside the city limits. If the newspapers ever found out, I'd never hear the end of it. On the other hand, if the city wants to show me that a murder or two took place, I'll make a decision. No way I'm going to grab jurisdiction on a 'maybe.'"

"Then why am I meeting a deputy?"

"I'm cautious. I'm not stupid."

"Can your deputy pick me up here at the airport?"

"Be on the curb by the Conch Flyer Restaurant. I'll send all your best friends to get you." He clicked off.

I would be a day late to Grand Cayman.

I got myself bumped off the flight by a friend behind the counter. I asked her to pull my bags from the outbound luggage and to hold them for a day. I dialed Teresa's office and got her voice mail. I said, "Your hunch we talked about? It might be right on. What I said about a steel trap? Play your cards close at the office. I'm here for another day."

I worked up the cojones to call the ad agency that had booked me into the Cayman job. I begged the account executive to bump the gig a day. He waffled. I knew he was being lazy, knew the deadline was bogus. The delay would cause logistical problems. That was my fault, and the agency would be embarrassed. I offered to work at two-thirds my day rate. The underpaid young man in Sarasota put pained reluctance in his voice, then said okay.

My escape from the rock had lost its traction.

10

THE WHITE FORD EXPLORER carried a green and gold paint scheme, a roof-mount light bar, and ten years' worth of dent and rust repairs. Detective Sergeant Bobbi Lewis unlatched the right side door, moved a leather gear belt and a belly-pack from the passenger seat to the floor behind it, motioned me in. She wore khaki slacks, a white polo shirt with an imprinted badge, and new running shoes. She flashed a bored "wild goose chase" expression, offered me no greeting, tilted back a can of Mountain Dew. Her face looked flushed, and she smelled of bath soap and hair conditioner. She tapped a dash decal, an official reminder to fasten my seat belt. Once I got past the good odors, the SUV's interior smelled like all police vehicles. Sweat, spilled coffee, the sour residue of aftershave and boot polish. The steering wheel was red, but the top of it had faded to grayish pink.

Bobbi Lewis does a fine job for the county. She's smart and deliberate, tough behind her femininity. Plenty of people have misjudged her five-eight size, attractive presence, her ability to use force. I'd worked with her twice. We had shared success, and I felt comfortable with our rapport.

She blew past taxis to the airport exit. "So, what is it?" she said. "The original sidewalk sleuth speculates that a shaky link between deaths, this hometown commonality, gives us proof of multiple foul play?"

Commonality? Foul play? I had never heard Lewis use cop jargon.

"I didn't claim 'proof,' detective. I told your boss there was a chance that two crimes had been committed."

"Liska said you were the woman's executor. That your only interest?"

"I reported a possible crime. Problem?"

Lewis kept her eyes dead ahead. "Right. You made a nine-one-one call direct to the top man. You like that kind of power?"

She'd always been friendly before. So much for rapport. I smelled toothpaste breath and assumed she was on a late-shift, late-sleep schedule.

"He thought enough of my reasoning to send you here."

She nodded. "The mayor takes himself out. The elderly woman dies in her sleep. They kicked the bucket the same day for a reason?"

"Hell of a coincidence."

"Coincidence happens," she said.

"If we found a reason, we might find crimes."

"We?"

I couldn't play verbal Ping-Pong with a pro. I could tell no answer would satisfy her. She had been ordered by Sheriff Liska to check out my tip. I wanted that to happen without prejudice. I shut up.

She said, "Why the airport?"

I told her about Grand Cayman.

"Tough life," she said.

"Did you know the mayor?"

She checked her mirrors, then turned my way for an instant. "Yeah."

Her tone told me shut up again. We drove over the Bight, toward Eaton.

"Been out to Stock Island lately?" she said.

"Not since that murder." A few months back, she and I had worked an ugly one that was linked to several others. The killer had tried to warn me away. He had torched my old Kawasaki. "Not that it's ever on my regular rounds," I said.

We turned onto Grinnell. She backed into the only vacant spot in sight. RESIDENTIAL PARKING was painted on the pavement. "I hate to do this," she said. "My good friend lives on Catherine. There aren't any meters or special spaces, and she hasn't parked within a block of her house since Christmas."

We climbed out, she popped the back hatch, and removed a tool-box and a large towel. "Good thing that wind died down," she said. "It was about to drive me nuts."

I snapped out of my world, into the real one. For the first time in three weeks the thrashing of fronds and treetops had ceased. I heard Skil saws, distant sirens, Harley-Davidsons, packs of mopeds. Key West's soundtrack had resumed.

"You've been in the house?" she said.

"Last night, maybe twenty minutes. Maybe a half hour."

"I need to know what you did, what you touched."

I described my wandering through the house.

"You've touched the computer, so it's contaminated by your prints?"

I nodded. "I used the front and back doors, the windows in the living room. I walked through the kitchen, checked out the refrigerator for spoiled food."

"And?"

"Trash pickup was yesterday. I figured the outdated chilled items could wait a few days. I could deal with it when I got back from down south. Better than garbage sitting in the hot sun getting ripe."

"Good. Don't touch anything in the refrigerator. Did you use her toilet? Take a pee in there?"

"No."

"Wonderful. Don't touch anything this time, even if you touched it before. Doors, windows, the kitchen, whatever."

"You're going in with all these precautions," I said. "But you're not tuned in to my theory."

Detective Lewis took a step back, held her hands like a coach explaining strategy to a rookie. "She died in her bed, but her 'sudden and unexpected demise' was unattended. State law requires that such deaths be followed by autopsy. You with me so far?"

I said I was.

"The elderly in Florida skew the mortality rate. And autopsies run up huge expenses. They aren't ordered as often as they should be, and this county isn't blessed with fine facilities. If there'd been body bruises, the funeral home people would've informed us. Or they would have called the state attorney's office. I've seen their list of red flags. They're all trained to spot petechiae, signs of strangulation, punctures, bruising, other tip-offs to murder. We got no reports. Where does that leave us?"

I shrugged, shook my head.

"Did you see broken windows or marks on the doors? Signs of forced entry? Things askew, to indicate a struggle?"

I kept shaking my head. I wanted to suggest that Naomi had been killed somewhere else and placed in her bed. I let Lewis ramble.

"I got no report of an ice pick in the eardrum," she said. "We have no signs of foul play. Are we thinking gas inhalation or electrocution? Are we looking for arsenic in the Ovaltine? Poisoning would give us clues."

I stared at her. She had built an argument before the facts.

She said, "We're down to natural causes. A part of her body gave out. Maybe she died of a broken heart. Let's go have a look around."

Maybe Naomi knew that a man from her hometown was going to shoot himself. Maybe that's what broke her heart.

Lewis scanned Naomi's front porch. She checked out the front window perimeters and the door frame, looking for pry marks or security sensors. She took in the wooden furniture, the cushion fabrics, dark green shutters. She studied the house number in gold leaf on the glass transom, the mailbox, a woven, lidded basket. I was struck with the same feeling I'd had when Cootie Ortega was in my home. Lewis was sizing up the porch, putting value to objects.

Finally she stooped, spread the towel on the floor, and placed her toolbox on it. It looked to me like a homemade evidence-gathering kit. She pulled out cloth socks to be worn over our shoes, two pair of rubber gloves. I saw a Polaroid camera, a small autofocus camera, a thirty-foot measuring tape, and a digital voice recorder.

We put on our socks and gloves, and she pointed at the lock. I let us in. She took her box and towel inside, made room for me, then stopped. If we didn't open a window quickly, we would croak from the heat.

She asked me not to move for a minute or two. She looked around, saw what she needed. She removed a small telephone from her box and plugged its jack into a port in the living room's front wall. She connected the digital recorder to the phone, and pushed the TALK button. From where I stood, I heard the staccato tones that indicate messages.

"Bingo," she said. "Have you got BellSouth's message service?"

I told her the access number.

She clicked the recorder and dialed the number. "This didn't happen this way," she said. "You dialed the number. You wrote down what you heard."

"I was going to do that, anyway."

"Right," she said. "You dialed star-sixty-nine, too. You wanted to know where her last call came from."

I felt goose bumps on my arms, the kind I got for brilliant lyrics, great music licks and solos. I followed her orders, stayed put. When she had finished noting the last incoming call, she left her gear hooked up. I assumed that she wanted to catch calls that rang while we were in the house, do the caller ID routine each time.

Lewis moved back to our position near the door. She stood still, moving only her eyes. It looked as if she wanted to get a feel for the house in which a woman had died, wanted to find another dimension, a higher level of focus. I didn't say a word.

I had been in the house twenty hours earlier. This time I looked at each piece of furniture differently. I wondered what I might have touched, what evidence I might have fouled or ignored. I felt a different longing for Naomi. I studied her bookshelves, her tattered paperback copy of *For Whom the Bell Tolls,* and Gene Lyon's *Search for the Atocha* in hardcover. I'd given her *The Sibley Guide to Birds*. Odors dug deep into my memory. The room held her cologne, the potting soil in her table plants, the Cuban coffee that she and I enjoyed. The room smelled of loss.

"Liska said you're the executor. Who gets all this?" Lewis didn't look at me for an answer. She continued her observations.

"Her older brother, Ernest Bramblett," I said.

"How did he react to her death?"

"I haven't found him to tell him. That's my first chore."

She said, "Is he from Akron, Iowa, too?"

"That's what Jack Spottswood thought. But Jack's secretary tried to contact Bramblett. She learned that he's not there anymore."

"So he's dead, too," she said, "or the killer."

"Is that how these cases work?"

"We look at the families. How you going to find him?"

"Pick through her correspondence, spend time in her computer."

Lewis looked around the living room, used her hand to fan her face. "She got a Mac or a PC?"

"Macintosh."

"Shit. I can't find my way around Macs. I'll let you do that. You can spend the afternoon in Iowa, long distance. And see if she's got her check ledger in there. You know Quicken and Excel?"

I nodded.

"This place is squeaky clean. See who she's paying to keep house. Give me a call later."

"So, this is it?"

"You want me to declare it a crime scene? Bring in forensics, string the yellow tape? You won't be able to track down her brother, do the business you have to do."

She had been off to a good start. Something had snuffed her interest. I said, "How do you test for poisoning?"

"You hope she's not cremated. At this point, it takes a court order."

"Can I use your cell phone?"

Lewis stared out a window. "I'll use it first," she said. "I'll tell Liska I'm not convinced there's been a crime."

"He'll be glad to hear that. I'll have to make another power call to him."

"To say what?"

"To tell him you've got a chunk of driftwood up your ass. And the next time he makes me cancel a flight reservation, he should send over a real investigator."

Lewis looked away. I half expected her to come around with a right hook, to settle my hash and shut me up. Instead, I saw deep hurt in her eyes. The same rule applied as before. I kept my mouth shut.

"You enjoy your crime-photo cameos?" she said.

Be careful, I thought. "The financial part helps."

"You also helped us with closing a couple bad ones."

"That type of result is not my goal. I try to shoot good pictures."

"I beg to differ, comrade. That one with your buddy the banker, and the Stock Island murder, you got like a dog on a scent. You went balls to the wall. You made those cases your own personal vendettas."

"That doesn't mean they fulfilled my ambitions. I need to have a life, too. It's that part that gets away from me."

She stared out the window. "Same dog bit me."

Quiet, Rutledge. Quiet.

She turned to face me. As her head swung, her light brown hair brushed her cheek. "You asked if I knew the mayor?"

"Right."

"We had a fling two years ago. It lasted eight months. Is that the 'know' you meant?"

Shit. I had stepped in it again. Four inches of duct tape would close my mouth. Her admission explained her attitude.

"He wouldn't leave his wife," she said. "He was too much in love with her. Who can explain it? I was a dumbass for starting up with a married guy in the first place. After we split up, I found out she was screwing around, too. Multiple partners. I couldn't tell him. I couldn't break his heart that badly. Somebody needed to do it. Coming from me, it would have sounded like sour grapes. Or come off like I was trying to rekindle our deal, which I was not."

My mouth was shut, lips sealed. I wanted her to stop.

She didn't. "You're the first person I've told. Don't feel obligated to pass it along. Especially to your friend Dunwoody from the *Citizen*. She's always been a Gomez groupie. Most likely she still is, and she does a good job. So it's our secret. I needed to say it to someone. Now it's off my chest."

Goodnight Irene Jones had warned Sam about the grieving process. "It's hard to lose friends," I said.

"It makes you relive history, for a few days at least. I didn't think missing him was in the program. I was wrong."

"Do you think he was capable of . . ."

Lewis glanced at me again. "Yes, Rutledge. I think he committed suicide. He talked about it twice while I was seeing him. That kind of talk is a big fat warning. It was part of the reason I went away. Hell, it was the main reason. I knew that our affair wasn't helping his sanity. Some men, their dicks turn off their brains, but not Steve. Our romance chewed at his conscience. We were together, but he was always somewhere else. For a while I blamed the fact that he was a politician. For another while I blamed my job. Before I was over it, I blamed everything but the Russians." She walked to the window. "You know the neighbor?"

I looked into the yard next door, saw a woman in her late thirties or early forties. "I've seen her at Fausto's. I can't put a name to her face."

Lewis hurried out to the porch, peeled off her booties and gloves. I took off my stuff and caught up as she was saying, "Did Ms. Douglas have a lot of visitors?"

"I seen this man here," said the woman. "And that lady that runs a fancy gift shop on Greene Street. She'd come by, I don't know, once a week, late in the day."

"Do you know the woman's name?"

She shook her head. "They'd sit on that porch, drink their high-priced wine. They opened it with a corkscrew. Their first sips, they always clicked their glasses. Like every day was a damn celebration."

"Did you see anyone else?"

"That lady who talks to bugs."

"I see," said Lewis. "The woman who talks to bugs."

"Right. She's an exterminator who, well, I don't know what she does. It looks like she has a prayer session with herself, telling the bugs to stay away from Mrs. Douglas's house. I think that's why I have so many over here. They all leave next door and come to me."

Lewis said, "Is that your phone ringing?"

The woman laughed. "It's my bird. It imitates more than words. It does the phone, the microwave beep, garbage truck brakes, you name it. I've had that bird for years. It does a great flushing toilet."

Lewis bit inward on her lips, held back her reaction. "Let me ask you this. Did you see anyone who, say, looked like a domestic?"

"You mean, like a local person?"

"Someone who cleans houses."

"Oh, that's right. That black woman. I don't know that woman's name. Maybe I'm better off. She was not a friendly person. I'm not saying she was mean. I saw her feed stray cats. She'd wave to that old black man that rides the bike with American flags on it. He would wave back at her, and they'd smile like teenagers. She'd look at me, wouldn't say hello, wouldn't say boo. Like I was a damn stop sign."

"So, no one else?" said Lewis.

"One other man, and this is how I knew that lady was so important. She worked on charities and all. I'd read in the paper that she met all the time with people from the Arts Council. But this one other person came by a lot. That good-looking mayor, bless his soul. I got to admit, I voted for his face."

Lewis's eyes caught mine for an instant as she looked to the tree-tops. A few seconds later she turned and thanked the woman, then led me back to Naomi's porch. She had something to say, but couldn't form her words. She went inside, gathered up her phone gear and tool-box, stared again at the walls. She finally said, "Naomi must have had a wallet and jewelry."

"They're locked up at my house. I found them yesterday afternoon and took them home."

"Did she own a car?"

"I never knew of one," I said.

Lewis nodded, went back to staring. "This is still a city case, you follow?"

"So I get to jump the political fence?"

"You get to bear bad tidings. Other than that, you don't do anything."

"So you confirm the shaky commonality, as you called it, then you sit on the sidelines?"

She gave me a "so what" shrug. "I'll tell Liska I'm spooked. You stop the cremation, if it's not too late. You track down the cleaning woman. Do what you can to find the brother. Play it out, however you need to. Bear in mind, though, you come back in here, you might foul evidence."

"That cell number you gave a few months ago. Will it still get to you?"

Lewis shook her head. "My week off starts tomorrow. This is a break I need now more than ever. With what I just told you, you can under-stand. I need to get out on the water, wash the cobwebs. Put all the drudge work behind me. Get some windburn instead of this pallor. I called your friend Sam Wheeler to book a couple days of fishing. He said he'd be out of town for a few days."

"Try his pal Captain Turk."

"That's what Sam told me to do. Maybe I can find a place up the Keys to veg out and sleep late. Anything on the water with no phone. With any luck, I can stay away until all this is over."

"You don't feel compelled to question two deaths?"

She shook her head. "I am a worn-out woman, and I'm part of a large team. No single case has to be tattooed on my shoulders. Anyway, why do you need my help? I've seen that look in your eyes, Alex. You're on another quest. You won't let up until the big prize is in your bag."

"This vendetta stuff was your concept, not mine."

She nodded. "I just have to wonder if, this time around, you'll get your ass kicked all to hell."

11

I HOPED BOBBI LEWIS felt great altruistic renewal. She had vacated the Residential Parking spot that had troubled her conscience. Little matter that she had ditched a potential murder investigation, willed it from her caseload, let it fall into the heap of good intentions gone slack.

I sat in Naomi Douglas's compact, pine-paneled office, again pondered the woman I had known. Naomi had come to Key West to live out her life, had made friends quickly, shown style and energy. She had cultivated the island art scene, the preservation and cultural groups. Her checkbook had helped people find their visions, live their dreams. She had charmed and helped me as well, boosted my self-worth when I needed it. I saw her as a flower in the rock garden, and I owed her my best efforts to ensure that my "speculation of hometown commonality" was mere paranoia.

I called the funeral home. I wasn't sure whom to ask for, but learned that the man who'd answered was the only person in the building. I told him my name. He introduced himself as Roger Fading. He had a nasal Conch accent.

"You're calling about Mrs. Douglas? I saw your name on the forms."

I asked if she'd been cremated yet.

"Sir, we have a backlog this week. Two kidney failures, a scuba-diving accident, and two cancerous livers. And, of course, our dear mayor. I was told there was no service planned, so I changed her priority."

"You've put Naomi to the back of the line?"

His tone went defensive: "Yes, well . . ."

"That's fine, Mr. Fading. What are the chances she could stay there for a few more days?"

A shift to formality: "Is there a problem with payment, sir?"

Fading and I got what we wanted. He would get quick cash and he would delay his work. He had no questions. I had one less problem.

I called Jack Spottswood's office to ask about autopsy. He was not at his desk, and I didn't want to leave a confusing message. I asked his assistant to send a check to the funeral home.

I hung up, turned on Naomi's Macintosh, found her Excel program, and went straight to her financial stats. She had built a schedule of upcoming bills versus expected income. She had maintained a stock-portfolio-tracking sheet. Blue chips anchored her holdings. She had played with a few small cap stocks. I figured that she had gambled no more than three grand. I found her check ledger, but it listed no checks written to individuals. They all were to companies: utilities, insurance, a broker, and two funds.

I used the finder function to search for files that had "Ernest," "family," "Bramblett," "Akron," or "brother" in their names. No hits, except for notes on One Human Family. I spent five minutes dreaming up alternative categories. My brain finally shifted into gear. I found her address book, phone numbers, and e-mail addresses, printed them, and shut down the Mac. I could use my phone for the drudge work.

I walked to Naomi's living room, wishing I had a better feel for her mind, her secrets, and her fears. I also needed to sort my own thoughts, reexamine my motives. Had I let the Akron, Iowa, connection drag my logic too far? Had I turned a hometown into a bogus assumption? Was I crying wolf, whispering murder and hollering bullshit? The next door neighbor's linking of Naomi and Gomez had boosted my theory, at least to me. It hadn't affected Bobbi Lewis the same way. Something had turned her off, maybe during her concentration. Lewis was conflicted, but she was sharp and a pro. I couldn't believe that she would torpedo a case to save herself a few bad memories.

I closed up Naomi's home. The outside air was moist and smelled of faint mildew in the porch chair cushions, moss under the concrete steps, and beyond the porch, turned dirt and fertilizer. The neighbor was still working in her yard.

I waited until she looked up, then said, "Can I ask you one more thing?"

She rubbed her nose with a knuckle. "They think she was killed, don't they? I know who you are. My nephew develops your crime pictures. They aren't letting that woman die in peace."

"You said the gift shop owner came by at a regular time."

"That's right, I did."

"How about the mayor? Any particular time of day?"

She leaned on her rake, worked a finger into her ear. "I seen him come midday. He'd be just before lunch, or just after it."

"He never came by any other time? Or at night?"

She checked her fingertip. "Not that I recall. But what do I know?"

By the time I arrived home, I thought I understood Bobbi Lewis's quick departure. She had sensed what I had deduced. Steve Gomez had not been in love with his wife. He had been in love with Naomi Douglas. Lewis had left the Grinnell house consumed by grief, falsehood, and the reminders of a ruined love affair.

My mind clicked on a zinger, and its clarity surprised me. I had started my day making love with Teresa, but wary of her feelings for Whit Randolph, fearful of her desire to create a secret lovers' triangle. I was ending the day juggling three other names. Bobbi Lewis felt jealous of Naomi Douglas. I felt affection toward Naomi and, with that, jealousy toward Steve Gomez. Was I guilty of building a secret quadrangle?

No wonder I felt tired.

I checked my phone, found one saved message. I was treated to a lovely English accent. "Hello, Alex Rutledge. This is Jennifer Royce-Cooper at the Island of Calm Resort and Bath Club. We were so disappointed that you weren't on your scheduled flight. We sent our van to Owen Roberts Airport for the day's last arrival, to no success. So sorry you can't join crew for our reception supper and midnight greeter. We will look for you on tomorrow's high-noon flight. Bye, now."

Oh, Jennifer.

I was uncapping a beer when the phone rang. Monty Aghajanian, my old Key West cop friend, now with the FBI in New Jersey.

"Good of you to call," I said. "You once saved my life. By Native American tradition, you're always responsible for me."

"Again it needs saving? What are you begging for now?"

"I'm in what you Feebs call 'high gear.'"

"Tell me about it," he said. "I'll tell you about my last ten months."

"I've got twenty-four hours before I catch a plane. My bank account needs this job to happen. I need some fast info."

"No can do."

"I know, I know. Rules, more rules, eyes in the ceiling, ears in the wall. Are you allowed to look up *anything?*"

"You got a work file, a federal case number, and an access code?"

"You got a minute to hear me out?"

"Blow on, Mr. Breeze. The meter's running."

I told him about the two deaths. Monty had heard about Mayor Gomez from a former fellow police officer. He remembered Naomi and expressed his dismay. I explained the Akron link and asked him to help locate Naomi's brother, Ernest Bramblett.

He said, "Lemme look into it. I can't promise you a grain of sand."

"Even if you don't give out the information?"

"Right."

I said, "Why did you call?"

"You said an airplane. Where's this so-called job?"

"When did you master the New Jersey accent?"

"I got a surprise vacation," he said. "I got to use it or lose it. Is your house going to be empty this weekend?"

"I now have a roommate. Your successor at city liaison. But I can find you a free condo. I smell a favor in return."

"I wrote down the name. How's your lady friend doing?"

"When you did the media job," I said, "was it sixty hours a week?"

"You need to remind me of my previous life?"

"Well?"

"Maybe once or twice in two years I worked that long. It was yachting nine-to-five, Alex. Months of boredom, moments of panic."

"You didn't have to work late or weekends?"

"Unless I had a situation. Why? Your lady friend doing the grindstone?"

I shortened my story, cried the blues to play a sympathy note. I jokingly asked him to grab background on Whitney Randolph, occupations, legal hassles, addresses. I also told him about Sam Wheeler's trip to Lauderdale and his sister's ID turning up on a mystery woman's body.

He said, "I swear you can't do the fox-trot without stepping in it. Leave a key to the condo and directions with Carmen."

I heard a skid in gravel out front. I knew the squeaks, the rattle when the door thudded shut on Dexter Hayes's toady, city-issue Caprice. He looked grim, and his expression got worse when he saw me on the porch.

"Oh, good, you're here," I said. "You can take me to the airport."

"I heard you were sticking around."

"I left my cameras and a duffel out there."

We stared at each other. I read lines of torment in his forehead. Hammers echoed down Fleming. Scents of fresh pine lumber drifted in the breeze.

I said, "You're at the epicenter for rebuild teams."

Hayes shook his head. "Every nail pounder I've seen in the last hour has been yakking into a cell phone. The grunts are all junior execs."

"Fits their pay scale, if you ask the contractors."

"Thank goodness you and I aren't sawing wood in the hot sun, laying tar strips."

"Speak for yourself."

"You're right," he said. "I might be out of a job. Chief Salesberry's been strange with me. Almost from the day I started working for him, I've felt like a contract employee. Like they'd use me as long as I was useful, then cut me loose."

"Why now, out of a job?"

"When Liska called the chief regarding your Akron, Iowa, discovery, he also told him I might have blown scene details. I'm wondering what brought the sheriff to his opinion."

"You didn't give a shit," I said. "Was I supposed to keep that a secret?"

"Salesberry, in a pure CYA move, asked for my scene notes. To help him, quote, write his report, unquote. One of my men botched his pictures, too. The buck stopped at me."

"Look at it this way," I said. "Your dedication to duty took the afternoon off. Your code of ethics slipped a notch. It happens a lot in Key West. Most of the time it's worse than even you can pull off."

"What is it, you're my ally when I'm my own worst enemy?"

"What else did you do Monday night, Dexter?" I said. "Oh, that's right. You drank beer."

"I never got off the clock. We had a bar fight on Duval. Two boys from Eastern Europe wanted to marry a Chi Omega from Ohio. She was a cutie. She wouldn't pick one over the other. She said she didn't want to be a free pass to a green card."

"Did you defend your Gomez report?" I said.

"I didn't say shit. He had me cold."

"Tell the chief you're going to expand it. Tell him your investigation was correct, you didn't miss a thing. Tell him you've thought about it, you did your job, but the report sucked. Blame fatigue."

"I got nothing more to write."

"Did you note the scrape marks on the concrete seawall?"

Hayes's eyebrows lifted. "You get a picture of that?"

I said that I had. "That's assuming I didn't screw up *my* film."

The gloom lifted from his face. "Give me one more thing."

"Did you mention scrapes on the gun butt? Or a lack of scrapes? How did you explain finding the gun next to the victim? I would have expected to find it halfway to the house."

He stared at me.

"Anything strange about the wife's statement, her manner, her attire?"

Dex exhaled. His forehead unwrinkled. "Okay, say some dork blew off the back of Steve's head. We got no eyewitness, we got zilch. We go to the State's Attorney, we say 'Same hometown'? Where's that take us?"

"Eventually, maybe, to a murderer?"

"Double qualifier, Rutledge. Your tenth-grade English teacher would chop your grade."

"Down the road to a better attitude?" I said.

"Shit. That's not in my job description. Those sweaty carpenters, man, you should think about what they've got."

I didn't know what he meant.

"Quitting time," he said. "You really want a ride?"

I told him no thanks. "I'll leave the bags where they are. I'm out of here tomorrow. I've got a real job waiting."

Before Hayes drove out of the lane, I knocked on his rear fender, got his attention.

"What now?" he said.

"Can you find out the name of a black woman who earned cash to clean Naomi Douglas's house?"

"What am I supposed to do, go house to house?"

"I just thought . . ."

"Wrong."

I opened another beer and called a friend with a guest condo at La Brisa. We had swapped favors for years. He would get pictures of his old boat, his new boat, his new pickup towing his even newer boat. Pictures of his kids for the Christmas card. Once, a shot of an ugly rental duplex he owned on Big Coppitt so he could list it with a broker. I would get all-day fishing trips and dinners on boats.

He remembered Monty, said the condo was open. "Tell him no pets, no smoking, no leftovers in the fridge. Leave a fifty for the maintenance man."

Mission accomplished.

I carried my beer down the lane to warn Carmen Sosa that Monty and his wife would arrive in two days. I wanted to give her a rent check, too. I stored my '66 Shelby Mustang in a garage behind her house. I'd be married to the woman if we had gotten our love life to work out. We're better off as friends.

I found her repotting a rubber tree plant. I said, "I need Grand Cayman for more reasons than work."

"You want to relax?"

"I *need* a hammock, a palm tree, a tall drink with fruit juices, rum and umbrellas. I *want* a topless vacationing sorority girl waving a frond fan, and a club sandwich arriving in four minutes. I want a Chi Omega from Ohio."

"Your idea of paradise?"

"Have I missed anything?"

"You're full of shit," said Carmen.

"How can you, of all people, say such a thing?"

"I know you, Alex. I know you're a closet multitasker who likes to use machines. Paradise for you is downloading your e-mail, making coffee and toast, duplicating a cassette, taking a shower, and talking on the phone, all at the same time. Your secret joy is having that solar trickle-charger, whatever it is, hooked to your car battery."

I said, "Imagine how I get around clocks."

"See?"

"Like you watching TV under a ceiling fan and using your vibrator?"

"You don't know for sure that I do that. You look awful. What did you eat for lunch?"

"Hot air."

"My daddy grilled a mutton snapper last night. I'll make you a sandwich. You want potato salad?"

I said, "You're always trying to save me from myself."

"No different than raising a child. You want another beer? You want me to heat the fish before I put it on the bun?"

"No, thanks, yes, please. I can't believe you haven't found a husband yet. You are more woman than any one man deserves."

Carmen looked at her reflection in the kitchen window. "You want to rephrase that, or do I make this sandwich the knuckle kind?"

I walked back to my house. A dark blue Mercedes sedan was parked out front. Cootie Ortega had made himself at home on my porch. He was stroked out on my lounge chair, jamming his hand into a Burger King bag. I checked out the Benz. I guessed it was a mid-Seventies model. I looked back at Cootie, hoping he had gone away while my eyes were diverted.

He said, "I fell in love by the fast-food window. She got a lucky daddy."

"How does that compute?"

"A man got an ugly daughter, he better get rich so he can marry her off."

Cootie logic.

"You never had kids?" I said.

"One daughter. She lives with her mother in Vero. Come to think, she's no beauty." He caught himself. "I guess I'm an exception to that rule."

I tried to imagine him with a fat bankroll. I gathered that he had as much trouble picturing it as I had.

"What brings you by?" I said.

"Did you tell me you had NASCAR stuff for sale?"

"You brought up NASCAR collectibles, Ortega. I never said the word."

"What'd you say? You said something. Old stock certificates?"

"Okay, okay, I've got a closetful of Barbie Doll outfits."

"No shit?"

I said, "Just kidding."

"You didn't collect when you were a kid?"

"Pine beetles, Action comics, Pez dispensers, lead pennies, baseball cards, and 45 RPM records. I think a few AMT model cars, too."

He munched a wad of fries. "I'll take everything but the bugs."

"My younger brother sold all my stuff when I was in the Navy. He used the loot to buy a Camaro that he totaled in eight days."

"So you don't have anything you want to sell me? Old *Newsweek* or *Time* magazines, from like 1997? Make us both a few bucks."

"Cootie, am I your new best friend because I bought the camera gear? I've got a lot of stuff going on right now."

"Okay, okay, Rutledge. I'm sorry, man. I've been out of my tree since my cousin's husband, you know . . ."

"Shot himself, Cootie?"

My words threw Ortega into an instant funk. His face drooped, his eyes clouded, and he actually pushed the chow bag away from himself. Even for Cootie, I felt sorry. I wanted to dig through my boxes of attic crap, come up with a treasure for the sad man to hawk. I knew I had one or two worthless stocks, reminders of bad moves. One company called

Reliance Insurance. It tanked badly. I had a book of autographs that my aunt had given me after my older cousin was killed in a wreck. Maybe even my lunch box from junior high. It had been baggage when I saved it. I had no use for it now.

On the other hand, helping Cootie would be like feeding a starved dog. He'd be my friend forever, have me up a tree for years, barking at me for scraps.

"I'm sorry I gave you the impression that I had swap-shop booty," I said. "In this house, if I don't touch it inside of a year, it goes into my trash."

Cootie launched himself to his feet, the most energetic move I'd seen him make in ages. He barged through the screen door. The spring on the door whined, the door slapped back into place. He turned to face me. "I don't mess with swap shit, Rutledge. You should keep it in your head that some people take nostalgia serious as hell."

"I get it," I said. "People play futures in the past?"

"You don't need to make fun, bubba."

Cootie moped away like an unfed dog. I had forgotten to ask about the Mercedes. He turned, gave me one more dejected look before he pulled out of the lane.

His face looked like Bobbi Lewis's when she had left Naomi's house.

12

I OPENED MY THIRD beer in an hour, tilted it back, stared off my porch at fluttering shadows in the empty lane. The beer went down cold and easy. I had told Randolph that I wasn't into daytime drinking, but I'd hedged the truth. I dislike socializing with booze braggarts, and I'd had a plane to catch anyway. If I had told him I like beer best when the sun is up, I might inspire a new slosh pal who would stick around and still be here when I returned.

I rationalized this third cold one. I was in my house, but my brain was in Grand Cayman.

I remembered to reconfirm my reservation for the next day at noon. I waited for the agent, a thousand keystrokes, and wondered if I had a job to fly to. Despite what I had said to Carmen, I needed money more than escape. You can't rationalize six-packs and mortgage payments. Or build a career by sitting on the beach. Job or not, I had an aisle seat.

The phone rang as I hung up. Marnie said, "Heard from Sam?"

"No, not since this morning. But it's not time for him to call."

"He asked me for background on a cop up there. I haven't had a chance to do it. Who did you tell about the Akron tie-in?"

"Liska," I said. "He made his token gesture, he sent Bobbi Lewis. I struck out with her, or I should say she waffled. I took her to Naomi's house, she looked at the walls for ten minutes, then boogied. But we confirmed with a neighbor that Mayor Steve Gomez visited Naomi on a regular basis. They were maybe doing nooners."

I knew the instant I said it that I'd made a mistake. I listened to silence for a half minute. My brain came back from Grand Cayman. "Those weren't the neighbor's exact words."

"So that was your golden-tongued paraphrase?"

I had learned my lesson with Bobbi Lewis. I kept my mouth shut tight.

Marnie said, "Love affairs can be beautiful, Alex, for the people having them. Especially if you don't call them nooners. Tomorrow at ten-thirty, First Congregational, William Street. Will you escort me to Steve's funeral?"

No choice, now. "Okay."

"What are you going to do about a memorial for Naomi?"

"I'll let it wait a week," I said.

"You might piss people off, going that long. I talked to Phil. Louie's can do it in the morning, at nine on the deck, but you have to let them know by six-thirty tonight. You want me to make some calls?"

"I want to give people a chance to plan. It'll be hard to say good-bye if we don't know how she left."

She said, "Sometimes you word things weirdly. Did Liska want to look into Gomez?"

"It's a city deal, as far as he's concerned," I said. "And we sure as hell can't go to the cops. They're rock-solid, jammed up with opinion. Have you talked it around, heard any foul-play talk?"

"No and no," she said. "If I talk it up, I lose my scoop. I'm doing what I said I would do. I'm researching the mayor. I found a few things we need to talk about."

"Don't forget the statistics," I said. "Florida leads the nation in murder-suicides."

Another mistake. The big silence.

I said, "Where will you be in an hour?"

"Standing next to you."

"Meet me at the morgue." I checked my watch. "Make it forty minutes."

She said, "I can remember when forensic autopsies were done at funeral homes. Monroe was the last county in the state to get a damn morgue."

"Wasn't that last year?"

In February I'd hired a carpenter to build a shed. We sized it to keep my new motorcycle and a gas can out of the weather. The man anchored it to a thick concrete base, and I spent a bundle on treated lumber and siding. We sloped the roof so runoff went to the mango tree, and placed air vents under the overhang. I owed my classic machine that much. More permanence than I offered myself.

I unlocked the shed door and rolled out the Triumph. I wanted to catch Jack Spottswood walking home from work. Every day at four, you could set your watch by it. If you couldn't get him on the phone, you could stop him on the sidewalk.

I rolled down Eaton. At three fifty-nine, I turned onto Bahama. Bingo.

He said, "Look what rode in on the wind and the tide."

"What's the chance of ordering an autopsy of Naomi Douglas?"

My question stopped him short. It actually pushed him backward. "You had that kind of day?"

"I'm serious." I gave him the condensed version. "Naomi and Steve were from the same hometown in Iowa. They were friends who were never seen together in public. If you ask me, they were dancing the Bone Island mambo. They died on the same day. Am I the only person who thinks that's strange?"

"Who are you?" he said. "Paul Revere? Running around the island yelling, 'The bad boys are coming'? Are you on a mission?"

"Just following Naomi's wishes."

For once I had said the right thing. The skeptical look left his face. He moved in a half circle to get the sun out of his eyes. "Okay, Alex. I'll tell you what you need to know. But leave me out of it."

Jack gave me three names at the county. I knew Larry Riley, the medical examiner, but not the others. He told me how to play each in turn against the other two. If I worked the triangle, didn't say too much, I might succeed. "Don't do it tonight," he added.

"Gomez was on top of things," I said. "I assume he wrote a will."

He thought for a sec. "A long time ago, after he married Yvonne."

"She get it all?"

He shook his head. "Not something I can talk about."

"After a death? I thought wills became public record."

Jack bit his lower lip, then said, "She had family money, and the family made Gomez sign a pre-nup. It was the first one I ever saw. When he wrote his will he turned the tables, for what he was worth. Yvonne would get any house they owned plus proceeds from an insurance policy, so she could have fast cash. The rest went into a trust for some nieces and nephews, a college fund."

"Does that will still stand?"

"He could've gone to another attorney, changed it anytime. I'd have no way to know." Then he said, "Your lifestyle, you don't have to heed many warnings, do you?"

I used my index finger as a squeegee, wiped sweat from my forehead. "I don't own vehicles with seat belt chimes."

Jack cracked a smile. He leaned back, cocked his head as if to regard me with better focus. "Remember, Alex," he said, "a lot of crusaders have come and gone in this town."

I heard it faintly in his voice. His emphasis on the word "gone."

My three beers had trumped Carmen's fish sandwich. The route to Stock Island, through rush hour, required expert skills, and I felt less capable as minutes ticked by. I wove through chaotic traffic, thought about Teresa, the fact that I hadn't heard from her all afternoon. The road maniacs were locals. The tourists were in the bars or headed for sunset. These days the in-town workforce has to rent off-island, in the Lower Keys from Big Coppitt to Big Pine. My guess was that every member of that workforce got off at four and hit the road en masse. I didn't have time to pull over, wait an hour for traffic to settle. Trying to figure out Teresa and the idiots around me, I rationalized again. I joined the club, drove like a maniac to survive. I kept thinking about my tumbling relationship.

Why do we hate boredom and dream of consistency?

Perhaps I'd become a bland dude. Maybe three days in my house had slapped her with the notion that I wasn't the perfect man. Or else she'd been bothered by a no-name problem that Whit Randolph's arrival had helped her define. If that was the case, I would take a hard fall. I had wanted this one to work.

But it wasn't just Whit. Teresa had been pissed for weeks. Her mood had soured during a quiet supper at La Trattoria. We had been celebrating her six-month anniversary with the police department. We had talked about her work politics and the island's politics. There'd been an edge in her voice. Her words sounded cynical, filled with the resignation of a woman trapped. I had tried to ease her pressures, from active encouragement to keeping my distance, showing concern, and minding my business. Nothing had worked. Now that I thought back, she might have begun then to be bored with both her job and me. She had chosen to bottle her discontent, let it further decay and ferment.

I wanted to be out of range when the cap blew.

I survived the fast food strip and got in line to turn up Route 1. Strange area of the island. Palm trees in the sidewalk have always amazed me, but I had seen them in a photo from 1937. They were there long before the liquor stores, car dealerships, motels, and groceries. I waited while the traffic light sequenced four times. A sticker on the Acura ahead of me read, MY KID BEAT UP YOUR HONOR STUDENT. I sucked in smells of fried chicken, a few cubic yards of exhaust fumes and secondhand tobacco smoke. I absorbed head-banger vibes from multiple fuzzy woofers. All part of the tropical dream. I went left, crossed the bridge, and waited two lights to go north on College Road. I wallowed in more oily exhaust, more woof, and a low-tide beach-rot breeze from Cow Key Channel.

What had happened to my sleepy village at road's end?

Finally, one thing went right. I saw two Jeeps in the morgue lot. Marnie's tall Wrangler and Riley's rattletrap, circa post–Korean War. Perfect that he was there. I hadn't called ahead. I wanted to pitch my case face to face.

Larry Riley, Monroe County's medical examiner, had driven the '57 Jeep as long as I had known him. He checked for rust as habit, had repainted the military olive drab several times. He ran it for function over comfort, drove full-tilt around town, and fashion be damned. The Jeep had more style than fifty stereo-driven Acuras.

I had worked several crime scenes alongside Riley. We had the added link of Carmen Sosa as a mutual friend. Larry and Carmen had been high school lovers, but he had gone off to college and she had married a loser named Johnny Sosa. By the time Riley had finished med school, Carmen had ditched her first and second husbands and was the mother of Maria Rolley, now ten, going on fifteen. They had not renewed their old relationship, but both were single and there was always that chance.

I shut down the Triumph.

Marnie said, "Do I just stand there while you harass Doc Riley?"

"You were worried about losing your scoop."

"You make my goal sound less than honorable."

"I want to know what happened to these people," I said. "I don't want a double homicide to be ignored like a branch falling in the forest."

"Are you a cop?"

"No, I take pictures."

"Okay, and I'm a journalist. We're both human. If a crime gets close to us, we'll help solve it. But we can't forget what we always do."

"Sometimes I'd like to."

"Cops want to know 'who,' so they can grab somebody," she said. "They want to know 'why,' so they can prosecute. I do it in the same order, but the 'who' lets me launch a piece and the 'why' lets me dig into it, make it a real story. That's how I tick."

"Are you through?"

"Sam has me worried." She rapped her knuckles against her forehead. "I need to report slippage."

"Let's go dig."

The woman who governed the new morgue's reception desk acted as if we were the building's first visitors of the day. Larry Riley agreed to see us.

He met us in a hallway, and looked surprised to see me there. He smiled but didn't offer to shake hands. Fine with me. Riley was a string bean, maybe five-eleven, no more than 170. I had seen him only once without the ponytail he'd worn for years, but couldn't get used to the sight, or that he showed tinges of gray. He sipped from an old ceramic mug. He wanted to stay in the hall, perhaps to keep our meeting short. I was thrilled not to be ushered into a chilled meat locker.

"I'm doing a double this afternoon," he said. "We had a scuba death by the Western Sambos." He considered his next words, then said, "You're the third amateur detective I've talked to today. One works for the city."

Marnie flicked a glance my way, lifted an eyebrow. The fact snapped into place. Dexter Hayes had run lax procedures at a murder scene three months earlier, had angered Larry Riley. Marnie had told me that Dexter had better watch his step. She knew that Riley's parents lived next door to Chief Salesberry, and Riley had the chief's ear. Dexter's career probably had faltered back then. If he felt unloved in city hall, it was because he was unloved in city hall.

"If I read you right," I said, "that city detective sees a shame where I see a crime. But if he came to see you, he might be picking up momentum."

"Is this your new calling?" said Riley. "Mayor Steve Gomez a friend?"

"Barely knew the man."

"Don't you get a lot of shit when you freelance like this?"

"It's easier to wash off than my conscience. What happened to the open mind of the research scientist?"

He said, "What do you know about that?"

"Squat."

"Why don't you take a cram course? I've got a brochure on my desk, this place in St. Louis gives a medicolegal class six or seven times a year. Hotels, meals, airfare, tuition, you're talking maybe twelve hundred bucks. Invest in your own future, my friend."

Riley wanted to draw me into his profession. He wanted to inspire the bright eyes of a recruit, get me excited about details that stoked his drive. Past years of on-the-job training had taught me that I couldn't detach myself from the real grit. Some people have that power, but repulsive evidence stuck to my senses like dog shit stuck to a sneaker. My wish to solve crimes that got too close to my world fought a constant battle with my aversion to gore, to decay and the dark realm of human action. I wanted to work on a "need to know" basis. If I took any courses, they would stress the memory-erasure techniques that Goodnight Irene Jones had mastered.

My attitude would not please the people who paid my part-time salaries. Tough rats, bubbas. I'm doing favors for friends. I would photograph babies and weddings before I got deeper into blood and crunch.

"Can I ask some general questions?" I said.

Marnie's cell phone buzzed. She glanced to check the caller's name and looked up at me. Her eyes told me it was Sam Wheeler. She excused herself and hurried outside. Riley and I watched her leave the hallway.

Riley said, "Liska's asked me not to talk."

"Just to me?"

He nodded. "Just to you. He said you dreamed up some clues, but you were all bait and no fish."

"I didn't know the sheriff had gag power in your department."

"We cooperate on a lot of things."

"Bullshit. You don't answer to anyone but the people who work for you. They run you around like a frat pledge."

He inhaled, held his breath.

"The reporter's gone," I said.

"You've got ninety seconds."

I said, "Any broken toes?"

"Nope."

"Or lacerated toes?"

"Nope."

"Did anyone find the stick he used to depress the trigger?"

He shook his head. "He didn't use . . . you son of a bitch."

"Does this win me another ninety seconds?"

"Thirty."

"Can you calculate angle of impact, the angle that Gomez held his shotgun?"

"Too much damage," he said.

"Find any scalp or pieces of the skull? Can you be sure the only damage came from the shotgun?"

Dr. Riley stared at me.

"Can you confirm time of death, to match the man's schedule all day?"

His jaw moved forward a fraction of an inch.

I said, "Did that bloodstain on the concrete match the amount Gomez would pump before his heart quit? Or did his blood get pumped into the canal?"

"You're up to forty-five seconds, Alex."

"You sound like you're pissed, Doc. You worried about losing time out of your workday?"

He took a deep breath, then exhaled. "You just asked three questions I'd like to answer, but I can't. You've cost me more than fifteen extra seconds."

"One other small thing," I said.

"No."

"A woman named Naomi Douglas died Monday of old age, unattended."

"No."

"She and Gomez came from the same hometown. There's a good chance they were lovers, in secret."

"Oh, my."

"She's a cremation, on hold," I said. "Who was the third amateur sleuth you talked to today?"

Riley shrugged. "Private eye from Gainesville, named Randy Whitney."

"What did he want to know?"

"His questions weren't as good as yours."

"Was his license issued in Florida, or another state?"

"I don't have time to do my job right. I sure as hell don't have time to check shit like that."

"Thank you for your help," I said.

Riley smiled. "All in a day's work. If the sheriff asks, this didn't happen."

I walked outside to find a dark sky, no breeze, and bugs.

Marnie sat in her Jeep, making notes on a legal pad. She looked defiant, dazed. "I didn't answer in time," she said. "He called from a pay phone. The son of a bitch left a message. He said, 'I'm always there for you, honey. I'm just not there right now.'"

"Doesn't sound like Sam."

She said, "He hasn't acted like Sam since that fucking call two days ago from Lauderdale, pardon my mouth. When Sam gets bold-headed, he doesn't always think straight."

Venus versus Mars.

I came to Sam's defense. "When he goes into combat mode, he calculates all and misses nothing."

"Nice of you to say so," she said. "But don't forget that detail I'm sure you noticed, too. He forgot his Bronco was at the airport."

Good point. He also had left a gas station in Tavernier and driven south instead of north. I needed to keep a close eye on Sam Wheeler, as soon as I could find the chance.

Marnie said, "You'll be happy to know, I fell out of love with my scoop. Steve's gone forever, and Sam's gone for crazy. Maybe I can go to work in a plant store. Grow peace lilies all day long, or work in a flower store and tie cute ribbons on cute bouquets for cute girls and housewives. I could be the Florida distributor for baby's breath."

She waited for me to say something. I was getting smarter with time.

She said, "Sam said he needed to talk to you. You're the lucky guy. I'll see you in the morning."

I rode home in lighter traffic and wondered how my name would sound if I twisted it ass-backward. I'd rather be Alex Rutledge than Rut Alexander. Some names work better in that game. My mother and I once played it about the time I was in junior high. She had turned around Benny Goodman, called him Goony Bedman, and laughed for an entire afternoon.

Randy Whitney, indeed.

13

I LOCKED MY TRIUMPH in its shed, looked for the neighbor's spaniel. No canine company tonight. For all I knew, no human company either. I turned off the yard light, went inside to check messages.

Duffy Lee Hall, about the film he'd processed: "That cop picked up his prints. I had my hand out, he told me to invoice the city. He had a look on his face like, I might get paid someday, but he didn't care. I hate *mañana* money. Rather get it now, like you cough it up. Come get these negs I kept for you. No hurry. They ain't goin' nowhere."

I dialed Duffy Lee. He answered with a mouthful of food. "Cash on the barrelhead," I said. "Run me off another set of prints, only the pix I took, okay?"

"S'pose you want 'em when the sun comes up," he said.

I didn't want to ask a favor, then push the man. "Nine?"

"Eight'll be all right. I didn't see a dead person in your shots. Something you want to explain?"

"The city works in strange ways," I said.

"What's that, a news flash?"

I laughed, polite, and hung up. The phone rang. How did it know?

I could barely hear Teresa on her cell. Her voice blended with noise and chatter, but I made out that she was in the Hog's Breath Saloon.

"I got your message," she shouted, "but I got confused. Why are you here for another day?"

"Long story," I said. "How about dinner?"

"I'm having a drink with my friends."

My friends? We have separate toothbrushes and separate friends?

I said, "I was thinking about dinner."

"With who, Jennifer?"

I heard laughter in the background. Maybe Jennifer was a friend, one of the laughers. Maybe Teresa was on her third or fourth drink, not worried about making sense. I said, "You've lost me."

"That message on your machine. Jennifer . . . She wanted you at her luau in Grand Cayman."

Maybe she was on her fifth drink.

"Teresa, I've never met or spoken to Jennifer. We've never been on the same continent together. Trust me, Jennifer is the least of our worries."

"Come and have a drink?"

I wanted to tell her that her pal Whit Randolph was being nosy about Steve Gomez's death. So nosy and sneaky that he had given an alias to Larry Riley. I couldn't do it on the phone.

"What section are you in?"

"Downstairs, back by the T-shirt shop, under the ceiling fans."

I rode the Cannondale to the Hog's Breath on Front and thanked myself for spending ninety-nine clams on a lock. The bike shop clerk had smirked as he rang the sale, told me space-age materials warranted the price tag. I figured titanium, Kevlar, granules of bulletproof glass. The lock weighed more than my bike. For all I knew, they added Elmer's Glue, fire coral, duct tape, and the coating they put on Stealth aircraft. I locked the frame to the sidewalk bike rack, then used a separate chain to link my wheels together. It takes longer to protect your property than it does to chug four beers. Makes a great argument for a screened porch, bulk purchases, and staying home.

The kid checking IDs made sure I didn't have a drink in my hand. Sure as hell didn't ask me to verify my age. A folk duo on stage near the entrance sang "Southern Cross," the old Crosby, Stills, and Nash song that Buffett had added to his concerts. The patio was jammed. Happy hour was in full force. The best time of day to be handsome, pretty, or clever. I thought of a great line in a James Salter story: "Unknown brilliant faces jammed at the bar."

I found the group, six women and Whit Randolph. He sat next to Teresa and was first to notice me. He grabbed a dripping bottle of cold Fumé Blanc, waved it above the table full of drinks. "Rutledge, my man. Would you care for a breezy somewhat delicate white?"

Teresa's eyes lit up. She thought his words were clever.

"Lovely and charming," I said. "I'll wash it down with gold tequila."

Randolph took me seriously, flagged a server, then pointed to a chair between two women I didn't know. Teresa fumbled her way through first-name introductions, almost spilling glasses, mixing up the names. Then she reached toward an ashtray, picked up a lit cigarette. I'd never seen her smoke before.

Whit sat back, pleased with himself. I looked at him with new eyes. I saw a transparent man, a man who looked hungry, not handsome. I sensed a mismatch of country club clothes and a pool hall face. He'd been buying drinks for a tableful of women, not unlike someone throwing bread crumbs to seagulls, winning them over to human ways rather than their natural direction. The hungry fat cat surrounded by birds.

The server wore matching silver rings in his eyebrow, his ear, his nose, and the side of his lower lip. He carefully placed a napkin, a salt shaker, lime wedges, and two triple shots of tequila in front of me. He held to ceremony amid the craziness, asked if I needed anything else.

Randolph scowled as the young man left. He leaned across the table and said, "How do you deal with all these fags?"

"Gays live here, too," I said. "They're the neighbors."

"They've overrun the place. How do you stand it?"

I shook my head. "It's not something we have to stand."

Disbelief: "You don't see it as a problem?"

I coaxed Randolph to lean closer, so I could keep my voice down. "When I got to town," I said, "it was redneck. Fishermen, the military, conservative Cubans. Cops made life difficult if you wore bell-bottom pants."

"No shit," said Randolph. His eyes had glazed. I could tell I was failing to mesmerize the table. The women had gone to another topic of talk.

"The gays were already here," I said. "They gave a lot of people their first jobs. They reminded a few important people that all newcomers aren't bad. Some of them bailed people out after marijuana busts. Jamie Herlihy, the guy who wrote *Midnight Cowboy*, was always doing that. They blazed the trail, made this town available to my friends and me." I turned, picked up a triple shot, and downed it. "Ask me again if I'm bothered by gays in Key West."

"No," he said. "I have a bitch of a time with people who've got opinions."

I looked up. Teresa waved her cigarette as if scribbling in the air, telling me to chill out. Even in her piss goggles, she had to see shallow water.

I said, "It's not my civic duty to educate dumb shits."

Teresa excused me to Whit and her friends. "Sometimes Alex thinks he's a policeman, social and otherwise."

Randolph said, "Are you one now?"

No, I thought, or we'd be discussing Randy Whitney. "I'm drinking your tequila. Is Teresa giving you a good backstreets tour of the town?"

"She's showing me what tourists don't usually see. I'm really loving it."

"What a guy." I drank the other triple, got up to leave. Almost as second nature, I checked to make sure my wallet was still in my back pocket.

Teresa had a smirk on her lips, a wary touch of sadness in her eye. She didn't say a word. She remained seated.

I caught our server at the drink station, gave him a ten toward the bill. Then I changed my mind. I told him to keep it as a tip, especially if the guy over there paid the tab.

Outside, a man with a huge pair of bolt cutters on his shoulder stared at the line of bikes in the sidewalk rack. For a moment I thought I'd arrived just in time to save the Cannondale, unless the man began to swing the cutters. Then I recognized Charlie Wood, a kayak guide around town for years.

"That red one yours?" Charlie was no bundle of emotion.

I said hello and told him it was.

"Good. You move your fancy ride, I get to mine easier."

"Lost your keys, Charlie?"

He rolled his eyes, looked away. "I went on a toot, late January. I forgot where I left my bike. I forgot I'd been in this bar, or even at this end of town. Hell, I couldn't tell I was on this planet. Anyway, I saw my old cruiser here, the day before yesterday, coming back from lunch. My damned key wouldn't work at all. Welcome to the tropics. The lock rusted shut."

"Nobody looked at you funny, those big claws over your shoulder?"

"Hell. I walked past three cop cars. I could've been Paul Bunyan. I could have been carrying a chain saw the size of a semi. I could've had an AK-47 strapped to my back. They're so thick with gymnasium muscles, they're too stiff to get out of their cars. Or too busy trying to bust open containers and shoplifters."

And they don't care diddly about murder clues.

Two blocks from the Hog's Breath, I saw Whit Randolph's yellow BMW in a slot on Greene. The parking meter had expired. I stopped to have a look, to see if anything on the car, a decal or a license tag frame, would tell me where Randolph had come from, where he'd bought the road rocket. A citation was stuck under his windshield wiper. No biggie for a rich man. I noticed an odd smell about the car, but I couldn't place it. Some kind of natural decay. I saw no decals, no hints beyond the generic Florida plate. The tag read SUNSHINE STATE rather than a county name.

I stair-stepped through Old Town so I could avoid busy streets. As I ran stop signs, avoided blind drivers, my brain sifted the past sixty hours. Odin Marlow, ace Broward detective; Goodnight Irene Jones; the news of Naomi; the call about Gomez; Whitney Randolph's "new kid in town" aura; the link through Akron, Iowa; the postponed trip to Grand Cayman. One fact boomed to first in line. Behind all my pseudo-sleuthing and jealousies, I had forgotten about Ernest Bramblett. I needed to find Naomi's brother, bring him to the Keys so he could inherit a home full of fine art, minus two matted and framed photos that someone had chucked into a garbage can.

That part baffled me, so I stuck with it. Would Naomi Douglas name me her executor, then toss my art photographs? If I began with the commonsense answer that she hadn't thrown them out, I had a clue to the larger problem. Based on what I knew about access to her home, only two people could have done it. The framed photos had been trashed by the woman who cleaned the house or by the person who had murdered Naomi.

I hadn't eaten. I smelled restaurants, clouds of fish and garlic, suppers from a hundred kitchens. I felt tequila corroding my stomach, stress acid hurrying the process. A drunken man staggered up the Grinnell sidewalk. He clutched a string of Styrofoam trap line floats, dodged saplings, trash cans, low-hanging fronds. He sang in a monotone, "Daylight come, me wanna go home." He had turned a work song into a dirge.

I almost offered to sing harmony.

14

I WALKED THROUGH A cloud of sweet night-blooming jasmine, lifted my bike up Naomi's concrete steps, and unlocked her door to stagnant air. My sneeze probably woke the neighbors. Two days battened up, and the mildew had gone berserk. I lifted several letters from the mail basket, stuck them in my shirt pocket, and rolled the bike inside. I wasn't sure why I didn't want to chain it in the yard. I felt watched, spooked by the street.

Think like a pro, I chided myself. The news report of her death had drawn prowlers. I had scared them off. A pro or a plastic hero.

Detective Lewis had warned me not to "foul evidence," so I couldn't open windows again. I wanted to touch as few things as possible. I would have to suffer stuffiness.

I stood in semi-darkness with the door open so I could air out the living room. Give it a try, I thought, listen to the walls, commune with the psychic magnet. Maybe Lewis's mental trick had worked, conjuring spirits, whatever she had done in her silent study of Naomi's home. If a crime had occurred, what were its motives and method? Who had gained revenge or satisfaction or instant income? In the chemical glow of street lamps, I waited for rhythms of knowledge, a pulse of enlightenment.

Two minutes, and I bagged it. I wasn't tuned to receive New Age fuzzies. I saw no flickers down foggy tunnels, felt no insights, heard no guiding truths. The musty room gave me a crappy, hollow sense of gloom. Shadows and odd tints emphasized objects I never had noticed. I had looked carefully at her books nine hours earlier. Why hadn't I seen the small TV built into the white bookshelf? Had I ever checked out the rack full of silver spoons, or read the barometer on the hallway wall?

If I had missed solid objects, and didn't know she had a lover, what else had I missed about the woman? Better question. Did I know anything at all? Did I not know things because she had held back? Or had I idealized her, viewed her myopically, blinded myself to her real world?

One thing I knew for certain. Laughter had thrived in the room only three days ago. The space now felt empty to me, aged like a body hit by disease, a town struck by disaster. Perhaps I discovered what Lewis had felt. Vibrations were frauds that misled or gave no answers. I didn't doubt that my attitude stifled the process. But if spirits were there, they weren't delivering comfort that I recognized. They made me cranky and pushed my ass to confront my mortality.

One death at a time.

I let myself into Naomi's small office, flipped on the gooseneck lamp next to her desk. I was tempted to try again, to sponge up vibes. I finally figured out the problem. Stupid-ass tequila gets me every time. Sends me on mental slaloms, the logic of salt and cacti. I jumped tracks, told the ghosts to take a hike. The big insight: Things I could touch or see would help me more.

The computer brought itself up to speed. I nosed around, switched on her radio. It was tuned to the "smooth jazz" station. She had written phone numbers with a Sharpie pen on her mouse pad. I saw nothing but Key West prefixes, knew most of the numbers. Her grocery and chores list included "heavy trash bags," "half-inch plywood for 1st fl. windows," "Clorox," and "drop dry cleaning."

I opened the antique chest's top drawer. She had stocked typical office supplies. Push pins, a stapler, a plastic bag full of rubber bands.

My Cuervo-addled brain sent out a sidetrack warning. Shopping lists and paper clips fell outside my idea of deciphering crime. Could my investigation get more mundane? Or more dead end?

I closed the middle drawer after finding only a dusty cordless phone, two cookbooks, and an inexpensive Kodak Max camera. Only six frames exposed. I had better luck in the chest's bottom drawer. In a fat manila folder, I found eleven dated envelopes. In each I found color prints. I stacked them according to dates. The most recent was two years old. One blank envelope held enough negatives to have generated all of the prints.

The photos told me nothing new. One packet held group shots, twenty-four permutations of twelve women at a luncheon. Another held a sequence of people mugging at an East Martello party. Another envelope held pictures taken in Naomi's yard, her flowers and plants, bamboo wind chimes, an orchid. Yet another depicted a ceremony that welcomed two women debarking a cruise ship. Odd that she had taken so many photographs and never had asked me about cameras or processing or types of film.

One fact stood out. The prints were sharp, well focused, with good depth and no distortion. These days even point-and-shoot cameras, the small autofocus zoom jobs, capture quality images on 35-millimeter film. The joke was to call them "drunkproof." I had never seen crisp pictures from disposable, plastic-lensed cameras like the Kodak Max. I checked again in the bottom drawer, looked around the office. I didn't see photos that lacked sharpness, didn't see another camera. Maybe she had left one in the purse that I had stashed in my house.

Naomi's computer was as orderly as her home. Her hard-drive files were stacked in alphabetical order. I clicked the window's "Date Modified" box. The files restacked themselves, newest at the top. Her financial folder, the one I'd already found in Microsoft Excel, was most recent. Just below that folder was a Word file named "dear ms. d." Its date showed that Naomi had saved it two weeks earlier. I double-clicked its icon.

Ms. D. was the imaginary recipient of Naomi Douglas's diary. The file held only one short paragraph.

I'm feeling left out. These old men are running around town, acting thirty years younger. They rub stuff on their hair so they don't go bald. They take a pill so they get tent poles instead of bratwurst. Fair is fair. Where is the pill so my titties don't point to Panama? How about a drug to turn my hot flashes into moments of cerebral bliss? Let all the doctors level the playing field, stop these lonely nights.

Her office was also a confessional. Her words sounded rational, angry, frustrated. Not the words of a woman involved in a love affair.

I checked Naomi's phone number file. One complete number for Ernest Bramblett, plus an area code without the last seven digits. I dialed the first one and got a recorded message. No longer in service. I called Information for the other code. A digital voice asked what city I needed to search. I didn't know what part of the country I had called. I said, "Miami Beach," hoping that it might draw a human response. The digital voice told me to try area codes 305 or 786. I dug out the phone book, found the page that listed area codes alphabetically by location. No reverse list, by number. Patience . . .

Noises, outside. I wanted to think that the rapping I heard was a shutter loose in the night breeze. Another knock, this time for certain, the door.

I stuck Naomi's negatives in my shorts pocket, then thought again. Old negs weren't going to tell me a thing if the pictures didn't scream in my ear. I put the envelope in the bottom drawer, went to the second drawer, lifted the Max, and hurried to the foyer.

Detective Lewis looked beat. She wore the same clothing she had worn that afternoon. She said, "What's your deal, Rutledge? Did you have a thing going with the widow lady, too? You working this late, I get the idea you're being more than a dutiful executor."

The pot calling the kettle black? "Nothing but friendship, detective."

"You've been here for twenty-four minutes. Anything to show for it?"

"A shopping list. She wanted plywood to protect her home from weather. It's my assumption that she intended to live through the hurricane season. She had six extra rolls of Scotch tape. Maybe she wanted to live long enough to use it all."

"You're quite the sleuth," said Lewis.

"You left here today, you peeled rubber. You were going snorkeling and yachting, and maybe look me up when this was all over. Now you're out in the dark, peeping and timing."

"I got emotional this afternoon. Once I got away, the place nagged at me. It was too clean. It made me nervous. Did she always keep it spotless?"

"She wasn't a fanatic, but it was never messy."

"I saw spotless," said Lewis. "Too clean, unless she was some kind of neat freak. Also, we got some info from the phone company. What's in your pocket?"

Busted for the Kodak Max? She wasn't that good. I followed her eyes to my shirt. "Naomi's mail," I said. "It arrived after we left."

"Taking it home?"

"That wasn't my plan. They're probably bills, and I have to pay them all, anyway. That's my new job."

"They're all bills?"

"I didn't look. I stuffed them in here while I wrestled my bike inside. The woman trusted her estate to my care. Why are we worried about one day's mail delivery?"

Lewis ignored me, looked at my bike, then around the room.

I said, "You've had a change of heart?"

"Keeps my mind off other things. The sheriff made some calls. Whatever they were doing, Steve and Naomi were great at covering up. They were on committees together, worked civic and charity functions,

129

planning groups, you name it. They spent a lot of time together, and no one thought a thing."

"Maybe he ran for mayor so he could be closer to her."

Lewis swiveled her chin. Her eyes went cold. "Thanks, Rutledge."

I did the mental math. He was running for mayor when he and Lewis had their "fling," as she had called it. I'd done nothing but get crap on my shoes since this all started. Lewis looked like she'd like to crap *in* my shoes.

"Sorry," I said. "My brain's shot. Do you still think Steve took himself out?"

"One thing at a time," she said. "Right now I'm thinking Naomi."

"Okay. Since I'm already in the doghouse, let me ask one thing and not expect an answer. If they were an item, what in their past required that they keep it secret?"

She waved her hand between us. "You care for a stick of gum?"

"Okay, officer. But I've had only one drink. Is it impairing my judgment?"

"He was married, he was mayor, he was twenty years younger. Even in Key West people have reasons for discretion."

"Point taken," I said. "Don't blown secrets become murder motives?"

"For one person, in this case. But Yvonne had already pushed him out of her life. She didn't stand to gain a thing by his death, especially his manner of death. She loved the political power trip. In her little mind, I'm sure, it was better to be the ex-wife of the mayor than the widow of a suicide."

"Speaking of relatives, you said that Naomi's brother, Ernest Bramblett, might make a choice suspect. You thought he was either dead or the killer."

Lewis clammed up. She looked to be summoning thoughts.

I said, "What was Naomi's last incoming call?"

"We had a bitch of a time. Turned out it was some outfit contracted by the Highway Patrol, looking for donations."

"Not a prime clue, then."

Lewis shook her head. "No. But Naomi saved two calls. One from Ernie, the brother, and one we haven't identified. She and the second caller talked money. We traced both originating numbers to pay phones. The timing tells us that her brother couldn't have been in town when she died."

"That doesn't mean he didn't arrange her death."

"That's a leap I haven't taken yet," she said.

"The leap to conspiracy?"

"No. That she died by other-than-natural causes."

"Back to square one."

"Be patient," she said. "And get your ass out of here. It's my turn to sit and think."

"I've got the computer running."

"You can shut it down," she said.

I gave Lewis the two license tag numbers from my wallet, the ones Sam had left in his message. I told her I needed names and addresses. They were unrelated to anything going on in Key West. She sneered, offered no promise that she would help me.

"One last thing," I said. "It's a blow to my ego, but I found my heart and soul in the junkyard."

"Join the fucking club."

I told her about my framed photos in the trash. I gave her content, no emotion, but I caught myself selfishly grieving for the pictures. She thanked me for the info, didn't ask what the photos depicted. She wasn't enthused about their being a clue.

I hadn't gone a hundred yards on my bike before I recalled the smell of Randolph's BMW. I was no expert in island trees, didn't know locations of native and nonnative species, but I knew of an acacia in front of Teresa's old condo in the Shipyard. I had left my Shelby Mustang there for two nights last winter. Acacia buds had fallen into spaces around my hood and trunk, then fallen out of sight, then rotted. It had taken me weeks to clean them all out. Months passed before I rid my car of the smell that I recognized in the BMW.

Okay, I thought. He had leased Teresa's old apartment, paid the month-to-month rip-off fee. Not okay was that Whit had been in town longer than two people were admitting. He probably had spent time, nights, at the condo before she had moved to my house.

Ass backward, my efforts. I was finding evidence where I'd rather not, coming up short where I needed it.

I found Teresa stretched on the porch lounge chair. She had kicked off her shoes, hung her skirt on the back of a chair, and passed out in her work blouse and panties. Before she crashed, she had uncorked a thirty-dollar bottle of Cabernet Sauvignon. Fruit flies had found it and made sure it wasn't going to waste.

I let her sleep. I finished the glass that she had poured for herself, then sat on the porch and stared at her. I asked myself if she was worth all my trouble and pain. I waited for an answer, but my brain went on strike. I shooed the flies, listened to her snore once in a while, and finished half the bottle.

15

DEEP IN SIESTA, I wasn't fooled. I knew the ringing was on videotape, on another sailboat in the marina. Staniel Key's only real phone was in a compact building two hundred yards away. The sounds I wanted were shallow harbor waves, tidal slosh on the hull, slapping halyards, gulls, creaks in the rigging, soft nautical tunes from a cassette player on deck. The television intruded, fouled my midday hammock idyll. I couldn't believe that someone had spent thousands on a yacht to escape to this Bahamas outpost and still need a Betamax. Maybe they would find the irony, pitch it over the side. Sure as hell, and soon, the salty air would melt rubber rollers, corrode play-back heads, pock capstans so that a ringing phone would drag, go vibrato, sound like a water-filled trombone playing taps . . .

A ringing pulled me from my dream.

I woke alone in the queen-size, in my bedroom on Dredgers Lane. Doves cooed from power lines, dawn light played on high crotons. I went barefoot to the kitchen phone. Grit on the floor reminded me to sweep soon. I felt as if I had slept fewer than twenty minutes.

Sam Wheeler said, "I got it from Marnie that you'd hung in town an extra day. You get me my info?"

Beyond slipping the license tag numbers to Carmen and Bobbi Lewis,

I hadn't tried to track them further. I had been minding my problems, but that was a lame excuse.

"No sweat," he said. "I've got plenty to keep me jumping. But don't quit the case. I had a run-in yesterday, hell of a coincidence. Our boy Detective Marlow was riding his bike on the strand where Sunrise hits the ocean."

"A man needs his leisure time."

Sam said, "You should've seen him in his municipal bike helmet. He's got another officer in tow, and this boy's all tricked and buffed out. Elbow pads, knee pads, enough radios to monitor the Space Shuttle. He's probably wired into NATO, filing flight plans for Air Force One. Got arms big around as my legs, but I didn't call you to bad-mouth steroids."

I heard the shower out back, checked the porch. Teresa had undressed where she'd slept and piled her clothing on the lounge chair. I said, "If Odin was exercising, where do his Benson & Hedges fit in?"

"They fit in fine. I walked out of this ratty-ass motel—I'll get to that in a minute—and they're sitting on their bikes, leaning against a post. Marlow's fired one up. The other boy's living clean. He's checking out babes in wedgie bikinis, ogling the jailbait butt cracks. He's resting his tongue on the handlebar. They acted surprised to see me."

"They were waiting for you?"

"Oh, yeah," said Sam. "The odd thing, after his huffy turf speech in the restaurant, he wasn't pissed to find me nosing around."

"He passed the time of day?"

"He spit out questions so fast, he could host an after-dinner quiz show. I was going to ask for prize money."

"Did you get pushed into hiring a private eye?" I said.

"Marlow made his pitch. I pretended to take the bait, to maybe find out who's been following me for thirty hours. I mean, let's make sense, here. Why should I pay some fuckhead to be my shadow?"

"Was that one of those tag numbers?"

"The green Chevy," he said.

"Did you call Captain Turk?"

"That's the best part."

"The ratty-ass motel part?"

"Not what you think. Turk remembered a dude nicknamed Wally Loads. Wally used to run a Midnight Express to the Gulf Stream."

"Sightseeing cruises?"

"You believe that brand name? As if the boat was never supposed to be used in daylight. Anyway, Wally's crew did heavy lifting and very little sightseeing. They'd work a bit, up to no good, and make it into the Dania canals in time for breakfast. Wally hung out in Lauderdale bars all day every day. He didn't sleep much. Who did back then? Turns out Loads did some camp time for Uncle Sam, came back to a halfway house. They turned him into a motel desk clerk here on the beach. I found him in the phone book. You wish every ex-con was Wally Loads. He's got more class than the damn motel, that's for sure."

"Did he help out?"

"Loads watched *The Godfather* once too often. He wanted to play hardnose."

"Let me guess. You broke him down by talking fish."

"How else?" said Sam. "I talked Florida Bay, Blackwater Sound, and the Content Keys. We talked baits, and old guides like Stu Apte and Lefty Kreh, Bob Montgomery and Page Brown. He said Montgomery's in Miami these days, looking good but not fishing much. Anyway, we hashed out legends, then talked newer guides like Cardenas and Becker. After that, he got useful."

"And?"

"He knew Lorie back then. He danced around the fact he probably had a fling with her. Not that I care, but get this: He recognized another girl in the pictures. He said this other girl's brother was going around Lauderdale and Pompano about six weeks ago, looking for her. This brother, an Italian man from South Carolina, thought his sister might be dead."

"Had she been missing . . ."

Sam said, "Seven years since her family had heard from her. Just so happened this guy stayed at the motel."

"Another coincidence. Did Loads lead you to him?"

"Right out of a Ross Macdonald novel," said Sam. "I had to slip him fifty for his help. Anyway, write this down. You ready?"

"Shoot."

Sam gave me an address and phone number for Barry Marcantonio, in Beaufort, South Carolina.

"Shit," he said. "I almost forgot about last night. I went to that saloon Goodnight Irene told me about. The place was packed, but some guy named Lorenzo thought I was hot shit. He likes people from the Keys, so he bought all my drinks. I asked Irene a couple favors. She might call you to leave us a message. I'll hit a few more bars today, then I'm off to Chokoloskee in the morning."

"You need to be watching your step," I said.

"I'm watching my ass. I'm all eyes." He hung up.

I attacked dot-sized ants that had swarmed my kitchen counter. Life in the tropics, and my cave dwellers had come to call. I poured out the wine I had forgotten to cork, opened windows in the kitchen and living room, and turned on the ceiling fans. Carmen, my alternate conscience, had accused me of multitasking. Not true. I do a lot of things, one at a time, early.

I still heard the shower running. If Teresa was trying to wash away sin, my water bill would bust me. Over the years, every time I had fallen asleep on the porch, I had ached for two days and blamed the lounge cushion, not the alcohol.

I doubted that Dr. Lysak would reveal personal data on Naomi's health, but I wanted to try. I dialed his office and told the receptionist I didn't need an appointment. I wanted to chat, and not about my body. She recognized my name and loosened her officious tone. She said that the doctor was having his one-hour workout at the health club on White Street. He would be back to the office at twenty after eight. I checked the wall clock. If Lysak's hour was seven to eight, I could catch him leaving the gym in fifteen minutes.

I heard the shower go off. Somehow I knew Teresa's hangover, the flames pouring from her eyeballs, would hurt me worse than her. I wanted to be on Fleming Street before she entered the house. I found a fresh T-shirt, pulled on shoes and shorts, and squashed a ball cap over my sleep hair. I grabbed Naomi's Kodak Max and my sunglasses, took care not to slam the screen, unlocked my bike, and rolled.

Carmen once told me I had selective communication skills. When I was pissed, my clam-up skills far exceeded my desire to be logical. When I told Carmen I didn't have time to discuss it, she threw a conch shell at me.

The streets were hectic with island locals going to work, mothers taking kids to school. Real life in the hotbed of tropical hedonism. What a concept. I've heard rumors that people even make loan payments and buy household cleaning products. Normal stuff, like up in America.

Duffy Lee came to the door in sweatpants and a Key West Shellfish ball cap. I showed him the Max.

"I've seen them," he said. "You give it to a processor, you get back prints and negatives. The camera goes to the trash, like a Bic lighter. Fifteen years from now, we'll own disposable cars."

"That'll make the island more crowded."

"What'll be different?" he said.

I handed him money. "You say 'processor' like it won't be you."

He winced, looked at the cash in his hand. "I can do it, but it's not my style. If you ever tell anyone I've stooped this low, I'll ruin your negatives for twelve straight months. Let me ask you something. You wanted prints from your negs, but you made a point of telling me not to print extras from the other rolls."

"Why would I want another guy's snaps?"

"You're always curious about one thing or another."

"I'll bite," I said. "Why should I be this time?"

"Two things. The minor thing, you didn't see the corpse, right?"

"They hauled him away right as I got there."

Duffy Lee pulled a five-by-seven from an envelope. He had zoomed into the negative so that only Gomez's arm showed. "See the suntan line where his watch used to be? I checked an old video I kept after I taped a city commission meeting. Long story, why I taped it. Anyway, Mayor Gomez wore a beauty. I'm no expert, but it looked like an old Rolex. You think he took it off before he dusted himself? Who found him?"

The answer took a moment. "The neighbor," I said.

"Will he keep it or pawn it?" said Duffy Lee.

"I say keep."

Duffy Lee shook his head. "Pawn."

"Ten bucks says keep."

"Covered. Now, my other concern, but let me say this first. I always take time with prints. I go for perfection in the darkroom. It's the old-fashioned way I learned all this. I worry about contrast, shadows, and highlights. I never paid attention to content until you started shooting this crime shit. Everything took too long to begin with. Now it's twice as long. I might have to start charging you double." He pulled out another print. I could tell by the grain and contrast that he'd had to compensate for overexposure. The view was from above and behind the body. Gomez had fallen on his side. It was an ugly sight.

I said, "Mush, and a bloody shirt."

He slid the picture back in the envelope, and handed it to me. "Tell me how the shirt got bloody. The blast blew everything away from him, and he fell instantly to that position."

All I could say was, "Damn. You're right."

White Street smelled of Cuban coffee and Laundromat soap. The Conch Train moved so slowly, I passed it without pedaling hard. Two art gallery owners swept sidewalks near their entrances. The moped rush hour was underway. Puffy clouds drifted eastward.

I caught up with Dr. Lysak as he left the gym, walked toward his Nissan Xterra, keys in hand. His T-shirt dripped sweat, and he still breathed heavily from his workout. He had fine-tuned his body language, his defense and quick getaway for people who approached him for off-the-clock health advice. He recognized my face—probably didn't recall meeting me—and tugged on the towel around his neck, as if for security. His frost warmed as he studied my Cannondale. It loosened more when I told him I was a friend of the late Naomi Douglas.

"Wonderful woman." He smoothed out his towel. "Not a strong woman, but her death surprised me."

"She named me her executor. Aside from drawing up a will, I don't think she saw the end this soon."

Lysak waggled his head to one side. "I don't know about that. You must know that the woman had cancer twice."

"Yes," I lied. "But only that much. She wasn't the type to admit to pain. I wouldn't have known if it had come back."

"It was still in remission," he said. "Thank goodness. She told me she hated painkillers more than disease. They made her feel like she was living her life in a fog. Another thing you may not know, and it does no harm now. It amazes me, every time I think about it. She drank. She hit rock bottom in her mid-forties. She took the pledge, then somehow defined her problem as hard liquor. She let herself have two glasses of wine per day. Alcoholics just plain can't do that. No matter how smart or strong they think they are. She broke the rule, and she smoked until after she turned fifty."

"She quit when the cancer hit?" I said.

"Yep. But there were all those years of self-inflicted damage. Are we not supposed to be surprised when her body quits?"

"You have no opinion as to what took her down?"

Lysak resorted to a reserved, pensive expression. The look doctors add to their repertoire in med school. "What we call 'old age' usually means a combination of weaknesses," he said. "With Mrs. Douglas, it probably was multiple organ failure. In physician slang, the 'domino effect' of physiology. Given all I know, I'd play hell to pinpoint a specific cause."

"Does it make sense to think that a body strong enough to quit smoking and curtail drinking, strong enough to whip the Big C twice, was not a body that simply gives up during a bad dream?"

The coldness returned. Lysak tugged his sweat towel with both hands. "What are you suggesting, Mr. Rutledge?"

"A death too soon."

The chill went icy. Dr. Lysak clicked his remote, and the Xterra's locks snapped open. "Do you suggest I had some part in her demise?"

"The exact opposite, sir. I don't think standard medicine, symptoms or cures, had a part in her death."

Lysak sniffed, focused his eyes on the sidewalk. "You think someone did her in?"

"Yep."

"Don't the various agencies have an opinion, here? The Key West Police, the Florida Department of Law Enforcement?"

"The sheriff assigned a detective," I said. "She starts a week's vacation today. The city sees no crime at all."

"The FDLE?"

"A case this small, they wait for cues from the locals."

"Are you getting carried away with your executor duties?"

"Bad habit of mine."

He opened the driver's side door. "You mind if I call the funeral home?"

"Just those words tell me you're as brave as any cop in town, doctor. Her cremation's been delayed. You have carte blanche."

"Does the county medical examiner know your feelings?"

"He complained about a busy schedule."

"Tell me about it." He tossed his towel onto the far seat.

I rode away to give him room to back out.

Duffy Lee Hall's station wagon was gone, but he had hung a Publix bag on his front door. Inside it I found a packet of prints, a hand-written invoice, and the split-open disposable camera.

Funny guy. His invoice said, "For services rendered. U Owe Me."

Someone near Frances and Angela had Iron Butterfly cranked to top volume. On another day, thump rock before nine A.M. would have pissed me off. I had reached the point where nothing fazed me. I was beyond blaming fatigue and last night's wine. I had become the problem, and had slipped into moral mud. I had rapped Bobbi Lewis for taking days off, while I hurried my errands so I could catch a plane.

Marnie Dunwoody's Jeep was in front of my house. She was in the living room, dressed for the funeral, studying a newspaper on my coffee table. She didn't look up when I came in.

I said, "Your right rear tire looks low."

"Sam told me it had a slow leak. He said it needed to get plugged. I told him I did, too, but he left town." She looked up at me, tried to crack a smile, and burst into tears.

I gave her a minute, then said, "Everything okay with you two?"

"If there's a problem, it's mine. I knew what I was getting into, and I never got jealous of the time he spent fishing. It's this new stuff I don't like. I worry like a sonofabitch."

More tears.

Marnie had been priming herself for the service. She had been reading a spread in the *Citizen*'s Paradise section, a tribute to the Steve Gomez years. She had worked herself up. No words would comfort her.

I told her I needed to take a shower.

"Take your time." Tears dripped onto her cheek. "We've got an hour to spare. I went buggy at my house, and I guess I did here, too. I don't usually weep for an audience."

"Have at it," I said. "I'll be ready in twenty."

16

I PRAYED IN THE shower, asked that the minister not open Steve Gomez's funeral to speeches about the deceased. We each grieve in ways that suit us, but a menacing few want the rest of us to validate their sadness. They think that talking longer means they're more sincere. They chat themselves to a dither, forget the gist, run their thought trains off the track. By the time they stop, half the church wants them in the casket, too. Not only would I miss my noon flight, but after ten minutes of blabber I might go for a throat.

After I shaved and dressed, Marnie wanted to show me the Gomez pages in the *Citizen*. She had helped pick the photos and editorial slugs. I wasn't interested, but leaned to look, to help lift her funk. I had seen most of the pictures when the newspaper first printed them. I recognized one of Gomez speaking in a school classroom, one when he posed with the Prime Minister of the Bahamas. I had never seen the group wedding shot, when he stood with six couples on White Street Pier.

In one shot new to me, he spoke to a crowd from behind a tall lectern. From the crowd's point of view, the mayor wore a coat, dress shirt, and tie. The camera angle showed us that he also wore shorts and sneakers. In another, Gomez was on Mangia, Mangia's patio with two men and a woman. Wine bottles and glasses filled the table. I took a closer look. The three other people were former Key West mayors. All four were smiling, pointing steak knives at the camera. Captain Tony smirked. He wasn't holding a steak knife. Someone in the kitchen must have slipped him a ten-inch filleting blade.

Marnie tapped her fingernail. "Our island at its best. One photo is worth a thousand campaigns."

The classic was taken after a city hall employee griped about a dirty rest room. Gomez agreed that the cleaning job was inadequate. He wrote a mayoral order to have it "redone." Sure as hell, his note was misinterpreted. Ten thousand dollars later, he was asked to inspect the remodeled rest room. He turned a fiasco into a fiesta by announcing a "civic upgrade." He invited the media and, grinning, snipped a bow on the toilet seat lid. His ribbon cutting made national news.

I sat in my rocker. "What have you learned about our fine city?"

Marnie leaned back and composed herself. "I checked recent filings and past agendas. Mainly, I asked clerks about upcoming proposals. I wanted to know where Steve's vote might have made a difference. In current business, he was the hot seat for three things sure to split the votes. In each proposal, Steve was the wild card."

"Any of them worth a murder?"

"Not to normal people," she said. "But you know this island . . . One's an old land deal that's been bounced around for twenty-five years. I expect it'll keep bouncing a few more. The other two have drawn the most debate. The BFD and the art museum."

Locals had tagged a Mallory Square project "BFD," for Big Fucking Dome. The idea was crazy, and Gomez had ridiculed it. Most locals were counting on his veto. Two commissioners had refused to "prejudge" the plan. Most of us had read their stand as a vote in favor. We suspected shady dealings.

I had attended the town meeting when a Seattle man had addressed the crowd. He had set up easels with blowups of antique photographs taken on the wharf. Opposite his history shuck were huge, elegant renderings of the proposed dome. Surrounding buildings were made to look large and distant, but Sunset Key and Christmas Tree Island were pulled close and resembled Tahiti.

"Don't let bad weather kill your city's potential," he had bellowed. "Our all-weather dome will have multiscreen projection high on its west wall. Your tourists will see real sunsets on sunny days, filmed sunsets on rainy days. They will use our interactive kiosks to vote on the ten best sunsets of the past ten years. Your local craft vendors will never miss a day's income. Who wouldn't spend a couple bucks to see your performers, your first-rate folk artists, and not get wet? Tourists pay to see the Grand Canyon, Niagara Falls, and the Golden Gate. Why shouldn't Key West and all its citizens make a civic profit from nature?"

The crowd had booed for ten minutes. The commission agreed to delay action so the development group could gather last-minute impact data. The city attorney opined that data was irrelevant. Letters to the *Citizen* asked who was on the take. No one asked who, by name, had let such a bad idea come so close to approval. Marnie learned that a vote could come in the next two weeks. Gomez's death, his lost vote, was a potential disaster.

The other issue was the approval of a Key West Art Museum. This one tweaked my mind. Naomi had chaired the planning group, had done much of the proposal prep work. I hadn't spoken with her about it, but I had read articles in the paper, seen notes in the *Citizen*'s Voice section.

The group proposed that the city collect art that reflected its history and diversity. Three museum sites were offered, including a run-down ex–cigar maker's shop and a brick Civil War–era munitions storage compound. A long list of grants and corporate supporters was offered. A thick book described older artists that might be collected: Granville Perkins, F. Townsend Morgan, photographers Frank Johnson, W. A. Johnson, and Henry J. Mitchell, the linocut artists, the Dudleys. The group stated that the city already had missed buying the early work of

Vaughn Cochran, John Kiraly, A.D. Tinkham, Thom Szuter, Don Beeby, Suzy dePoo, Carolyn Fuller, and John Martini.

A great idea, but two commissioners didn't get it. They wanted to put the money toward making tourists *really* happy. One dimwit had said, "I couldn't believe my eyes when I read that the county was turning Mt. Trashmore into a water sports park. I thought it was the greatest idea I had ever heard. To my dismay, I learned it was an April Fool's joke. How did we miss turning the cemetery into the tourist attraction it deserves to be? Someone is running tours in there. We granted them a license to do it. That could have been our revenue, instead."

The question boomed right to me. Why had Naomi died?

"I want to look into the art museum," I said.

Marnie shook her head. "It's not controversial. It's nonprofit. Once the Arts Council offers a plan for location and parking, the museum will pass no matter who's voting. And that old land deal, with the building moratoriums, nobody's going near land deals, anyway."

I knew the answer: "Which leaves?"

"I say his conscience ruled. He foresaw the Mallory Dome's perpetual cash flow. Every dollar would leave this island. He was going to veto that dome, sure as hell."

"How does that tie in to Naomi Douglas?"

"For all I know, it doesn't. But it rings with everything I know about Steve Gomez."

She had tossed me good argument.

I said, "I'll buy in to your instinct, Ms. Reporter."

"You are a wise man."

I turned the page to another two-page spread. At upper left were reprints of Gomez's letters to the paper. They had formed his platform for election, then his straight-talk, informal statements of city policy. I scanned one called *Protecting our Mental Environment*. He had written, "In 1983, when asked what had changed most on the island since his childhood, Ernest's oldest son, Jack Hemingway, said that the island was greener, with more plants and trees. But old-timers tell me of another big change—the noise." His letter had made suggestions for change, for noise laws. He had closed with the lines, "You think it's loud now? How much louder would it be, if not for all the trees and shrubs that Jack Hemingway noticed?"

He had written about the homeless. "They may look like poop, but if they don't have any on them, and don't smell like urine, I can't kick them off the sidewalks. We can't arrest them any more than we can bust someone for wearing black socks with sandals. If they break our laws, that's different. We will offer them lodging at city expense, after a fair trial, of course. It's the price we pay for having a warm climate. We draw travelers from all over the world. We are a destination. We are Paradise with an open door. Hobos and street people? They are a cost of doing business."

That letter showed his deep regard for both civil rights and private versus public good. It had earned him more flak than any other issue in recent years.

Gomez had left unfinished business, items that meant a lot to him. One more argument against suicide.

"Who runs the city now?" I said.

"The commission has two weeks to appoint a temporary mayor," she said. "That person serves until they hold a special election. Only voters in the mayor's district can vote."

"So any issue where Gomez was swing vote is . . ."

"Up in the air," said Marnie. "And we can't see behind the scenes."

I checked the photos on the next page. I couldn't believe my eyes. I said, "What the fuck is this?"

Marnie looked at the page bottom, the two men with silly expressions. They waved bottles of Key West Lager.

"Maybe they're promoting local beer," she said. "I don't recognize the guy next to Steve. The one in the background is that Polan dude."

I tapped the face of the man next to Gomez. "This is Whit Randolph. He's Teresa's new buddy. I think you saw them lunching."

"Ah, yes, I did," she said. "Your interloper."

"You use too sweet a word, my friend. He's a fucknut."

"He looks like one. Teresa's attracted to this?"

"She claims they're just old friends."

"Can I ask why you like her?"

"Do you *not* like her?" I said.

"I didn't say that. I just wondered what attracts you."

"What am I supposed to say, her eyes?" I said. "She makes love like a madwoman? It's not something I can spout off on short notice."

"You've never told yourself why she's special, why she's the one who won your heart?"

"I've never needed to justify her to myself. I guess I rolled with it."

"So you don't have a ready list of attributes that turn you on? Like she got twelve check marks out of fifteen?"

"She excited me when I met her," I said. "She lives her own life, helps to make my days more enjoyable. The one big fact is, she doesn't wear me out. She's not an energy drain. At least not until this week. Why do you ask?"

"Are you aware of the age difference?"

"Sometimes," I said.

"In what ways?"

"Two that I can think of. Women your age don't like her, and half my record collection died before she was born. Who's this Polan? I know the face, but . . ."

"Nice change of subject. Frank Polan was the guy from Cudjoe with the perfect yard on the bay." Marnie caught herself, looked at me. "What am I saying? You were there."

"That dock where the woman shot her brother last year? I forgot his name, but not his face."

"I interviewed Mr. Polan later," said Marnie. "He told me twenty times how happy he was that nobody had died on his dock. He said it was hard enough to scrub away bird shit, much less scrub blood. He's a fussy man."

"I leaned against his fancy car," I said. "He was waxing smudges as we left."

She looked at her watch. "Speaking of leaving, we need to go."

I waved off her hurry. "We've got a half hour."

"And I'm going to find a place to park? Alex, they're burying the mayor. We'll be lucky to find a seat in the church."

"We're walking?"

"Also, I've got a bad tire."

17

MARNIE AND I STUCK to the side of Fleming shaded by silver button-wood and tall palms. Bougainvillea spilled over fences along the lumpy sidewalk, and yard gardens smelled of wet dirt and evaporating moisture. Except for bike riders and an idiot pack of mopeds, there was no traffic, but that was explained by the jam I saw at William Street, mourners in cars trying to get near the First Congregational. The clouds from earlier had blown away. The day had become one that every Keys resident dreams about. Steve Gomez was missing it.

"I left my Kleenex in the Jeep," said Marnie.

"The Mallory Dome people will be out front selling it," I said.

"Thank you. I'll think about them, stay pissed off, and not cry at all."

Scrawny chickens pecked in a yard near Margaret. Two greasy shirt-less men wrestled an outboard motor on a trailered boat in a No Parking zone. A heavy man in a threadbare undershirt sat in a four-dollar plastic chair on his porch, drank his morning beer. Shades of old Key West, a creature unhurried, oblivious. I hoped that the late mayor would find the same peace on that sunny archipelago upstairs.

Aside from reading about him, hearing talk, I never knew much about Gomez. I hadn't paid attention to the mayors who had preceded him, either. They had generated mild controversies, earned their pay and, in doing so, had bucked tradition. Over the years of my residence, municipal officials had broken more laws than most people knew existed. Corruption had been a way of life, rumors widespread currency. For some reason, the city's mayors had been different, and rare.

The infrequent occasions that I'd seen him around town—lunching at B's Restaurant, shopping in the Waterfront Market, or at a stoplight—Gomez would either say hello or appear not to have recognized me. I doubted he knew my last name, or that I part-timed for the city. He had looked like the people I grew up with in Ohio, European immigrant stock. I recalled pondering his surname, but only once or twice. In Key West, Latin and Anglo families had blended for generations. Mismatches of features and surnames were common. I had become accustomed to dealing with them.

The man had a private side, too, and it hadn't been squeaky clean. He had had an affair with a county detective. He had cultivated an undefined relationship with an "older" woman. The man's wife had cheated on him openly. Perhaps no one knew whose dalliance began first, and which of the two might have reacted to the other's infidelity. But all that was outside the realm of job smarts. Gomez had done a fine job to the moment someone pulled a trigger, not long after he had gone drinking with Whit Randolph.

Motorcycle cops had blocked off William between Fleming and Southard. VIP vehicles were allowed down the street, but only for drop-offs. Dozens more officers and deputies in dress uniform milled about. I watched Yvonne Gomez and two other women in black dresses negotiate the brick steps, enter the red brick building's south door. I could tell by the way they slowed that the church was crowded.

"They weren't too damn steady in those high heels," I said. "The wake must have ended at breakfast."

"Or it's still going on," said Marnie. "I heard someone say yesterday that Yvonne's life has been years of anger broken by brief moments of manic laughter. They said her glass was always two-thirds empty. I don't think they were talking about pessimism."

A pack of smokers stood on the sidewalk opposite the church, toking their last coffin nail before the funeral. A clutch of homeless men stood at the corner of Southard Street. They knew they wouldn't be welcome inside, understood their ongoing odor problem. They were, for a change, embarrassed by their state and content to pay their respect from a distance.

"Stick close," said Marnie. "I don't want to sit with people from work."

"They don't share your feelings toward Steve?"

She blew out a quick puff of air. "Some can barely share a box of Krispy Kremes. Just stay near me."

"You want to go right in?"

"I missed getting a seat at Wright Langley's service," she said. "A packed house on a hot August afternoon. The air conditioner couldn't hack it. I was glad so many came to honor Wright. But standing up wore me out."

We worked through slowpokes, approached the church entrance closest to us. Several local men stood in front of the stained-glass windows, chatted grim-faced, favored the shade of three thin trees. I saw Bobbi Lewis at the same time she noticed me. She stood with a group of detectives, and she was the only one not in uniform. She wagged a finger at hip level to catch my eye, then tapped the shoulder of my least favorite deputy, Billy "No Jokes" Bohner, and gestured for him to follow. They met us on the concrete apron near the church steps.

"Can we talk a minute?" said Lewis. She ignored Marnie.

I checked my watch, then looked at Bohner. His uniform had been fitted thirty pounds ago, but his presence gave an ominous twist to talking "a minute." I glanced at Marnie, then back to Bobbi Lewis. "We're all going inside. It'll wait, right?"

She shook her head and waved her hand at the sanctuary door. "Miss Dunwoody can go on ahead."

Marnie looked stricken, at the same time pissed. A woman's grief and a reporter's gumption. If her lips got a fraction of an inch thinner, her mouth would vanish. She didn't want to enter church alone, sit next to strangers to say good-bye to Gomez.

I refused to budge or react, but I couldn't believe that Bobbi Lewis could be this crass. Maybe she had learned that I had swiped the Kodak Max. But that wouldn't warrant backup, and it wasn't her style.

Lewis set her jaw. "Is this going to be a problem?"

She had gone again to cop lingo. The placating tone, the implied threat.

"It already is a problem," I said. "Are we in a hurry for anything besides a good seat up front?"

Lewis didn't move. We were blocking people who wanted to go inside. Bohner slipped into a bad-ass ready stance, pursed his lips, gave me a drill sergeant look that he had worked up in a mirror.

Someone had to make sense. I began to walk toward Pinder Lane, ten yards distant. "Shall we stand in the shade?" I said. "Make room so people can go to church?"

Marnie took a notepad and pen from her purse. "I thought I could leave work behind for an hour, but no," she said. "Alex, how do you spell 'rinky-dink' and 'roust'? Oh, and 'Bohner,' too? I want to get that one right."

No Jokes didn't back down. He shuffled around to wedge me, to block my escape. He looked like a cutting horse in a muddy corral, snorting from his nose, cornering a cow. He wore his belly like honorable proof of every meal he'd ever eaten. The extra skin on his face forced him to squint, but his shoulders didn't jiggle. Fool that he was, I didn't want to forget he was dangerous. His thick neck was all muscle and bad news. He wanted any excuse to become the loose cannon of the mayor's memorial service.

I said, "You want to ease off, big fellow?"

Marnie didn't trust the moment. She stepped away but stayed close enough to hear.

"What's wrong?" said No Jokes. "You nervous near a Holy Spirit?"

"That's not it, Deputy. You don't sell drugs near schools, and you don't play politics at funerals. They removed your manners before they taught you procedure, didn't they? Tell your trainers I admire their work."

"You got bigger worries than manners, dipshit."

"You think I'm going to run away? Beat you in a sprint to Mallory, leap aboard a cruise ship, sail out of your jurisdiction?"

He grunted, "Won't put it past you."

"Look," I said. "We're making a spectacle here. People are staring. This woman and I are going inside."

"You can forget pew time."

I couldn't imagine what had driven Lewis to suffer his presence. I knew we shared a dislike of Bohner. She must have brought him to help pressure me into a slip, an admission of far-fetched guilt, and it wasn't working. The charade had turned ugly.

"Reduce your stress, Bohner," I said. "You'll live longer."

"Now you're talking my life span?" He palmed his weapon. "I just heard a threat."

Lewis finally turned to him. "Billy, I asked you to stand *by*, not *wide*. Back off a touch."

"Yes, ma'am." He moved three feet.

"More, Deputy."

She waited for him to move two more yards, then turned to me.

A thought hit my mind. "Is this about last night?"

She stared at me, steely-eyed. "Some questions came up."

"Urgent ones?" I said.

"We're talking crimes. Murder and theft, maybe others."

"I was the only one who questioned the deaths."

She bit her lower lip. She looked unfocused, wounded.

Twenty-four hours earlier I had said, *"It's hard to lose friends."*

She had answered, *"It makes you relive history, for a few days at least."*

She had added, *"I didn't think missing him was in the program."*

She had misjudged her emotions, or lied. She was the definition of grief.

Unless she had killed him.

We were surprised by a gas motor and raucous shouts from a nearby construction crew. Someone dispatched a city cop on a Harley to cure the problem. We stood staring at the ground for a minute or so. When the street got quiet, Lewis said, "Did you need the job in Grand Cayman?"

"It's a pretty place. The money'll come in handy."

"What was in that mail in your pocket last night?"

"Naomi's bills, like I said. I'll have to write some checks."

"You're on video. You were taped yesterday morning using a stolen debit card at an ATM on Southard."

Goddammit, Randolph. "You think I stole Naomi's bank plastic?"

"The card wasn't in her name."

"How would a thief know the right PIN?"

"You tell me. Matter of fact, you can come to the county offices and tell a few other people, too."

I looked at Marnie, then said to Lewis, "Who else was in the camera's frame at the ATM?"

"A cabbie."

"You've known me how long? Why would I be that stupid? Why would I draw down bogus plastic right here in Key West?"

Something close to the church caught Lewis's eye. I turned, saw Dexter Hayes leaving his wife, Natalie, at the church door and coming our way. He had read Bohner's body language and wanted in. No one said a word to him.

Hayes motioned toward people getting out of cars, milling around the broad sidewalk. "Packing 'em in," he said. "The whole city payroll, a dozen old county commissioners. The stores must have run out of black dresses. I heard it's the biggest turnout since Blinky Crusoe. They're coming out of the woodwork."

"Like termite dust," said Bohner. "How that schmuck got elected, I don't know."

Dex Hayes ignored him. He checked our faces, saw nothing, then looked back at his wife. "I better go inside," he said. He gave me one last look as if to accuse me of once again ratting him out to the county.

Lewis watched Hayes and his wife walk inside, nod to people we couldn't see. Someone closed the door, and organ music began. The homeless men walked past us, headed for Caroline Street.

Lewis went deep in thought, pointed a finger at Bohner, then aimed it at Fleming Street. He got the message. He hitched up his trousers, wiggled his holster, fiddled with his privates, and walked away.

Why hadn't Lewis told Dexter Hayes about my being caught by a security camera at the ATM? It wasn't that she needed an exclusive bust, or that the city should not be informed. It was more like the whole exchange had not been about the ATM or my being in trouble at all.

The organ stopped. We heard a man's voice, and a moment later the congregation burst into laughter. Only in Key West.

I said, "The bank card was handed to me by a man named Whitney Randolph. I was helping him navigate the machine."

Lewis looked puzzled, as if Randolph's name clicked, but not with this case. I watched her relax slightly. Her tension deflated.

I said, "You talked to the medical examiner?"

"Larry Riley has misgivings," she said. "They're contagious."

"Let's go in the church," I said. "We can stand together, then go to my house, talk this out."

Lewis looked toward Marnie. "The three of us?"

I said, "I don't know why not."

Lewis's face muscles relaxed. "Let's go."

Marnie said nothing but clasped my upper arm as I led her through the door. Just as we feared, standing room only. But the air was cool, and the one-page program mercifully short. It took me a minute to find Teresa. She was in the second row with a group of city employees.

The service went quickly. Someone, wanting to illustrate Steve Gomez's eclectic tastes in art and music, noted that, among his effects, friends found tickets to the New Orleans Jazz and Heritage Festival that was two weeks away. Someone said, "I'll take them," a little too loudly. A round of laughter broke out.

Marnie leaned to my ear. "Give me a nickel for every ounce of perfume in here." I felt relief in her finding a moment of humor, too.

Two men I figured for blatant self-promotion surprised me with heartfelt talks. A city employee spoke about bosses who care for the people who look to them for leadership. A neighbor thanked Gomez for keeping a magnificent yard, for raising property values. The lieutenant governor of Florida spoke to Steve's fighting for state-assisted school funding and his skill in landing grants for civic improvements.

For some reason my thoughts went to Naomi Douglas. It began when an unthinking bastard said, "Only the good die young." Wouldn't Naomi love to hear that one? Had dying old made her a worse person? Who kept score?

The ceremony was ending when Bobbi Lewis checked her watch. She slipped a piece of paper into my shirt pocket and said, "I'll call you later." She nodded good-bye to Marnie, then opened the church door and walked out to the sunshine.

Marnie reached for my hand, gave it a squeeze.

18

WE HAD BEEN LAST to enter, we were first out. I wanted to think that, in reversed circumstances, Steve Gomez would make the same dash. Given the choice, I wouldn't go to my funeral, either.

Marnie looked revived by the speeches and prayers. She saw a city clerk she thought might give her background on the Mallory Dome. She told me to walk home without her. I promised to change her tire if it was flat.

I saw no sign of Lewis or Bohner. My sit-down and quack about the ATM was on hold. I could only point my finger at Randolph, and had no proof but a cabbie without a name. My best hope was that Whit would try the bogus card again, show his smile to the camera.

I walked a few yards up Pinder Lane to check out the slip of paper in my shirt pocket. Lewis had given me the license tag info that Sam had needed. The green Chevy Cavalier didn't belong to a private snoop. It was registered to Odin A. Marlow of Pembroke Pines. Lewis had tagged on additional data. Detective Marlow also owned a new Cadillac Eldorado and a twenty-three-foot Fountain Sportfish CC. Not a bad lifestyle for a cop, though I needed to remember that he had inherited a watch, too. The Toyota belonged to Barry Marcantonio, brother of the other missing woman. Sam had said he was from Beaufort, South Carolina, but the street address for his Florida tag was in Dania Beach.

A second home, or had he moved south to search for his sister?

I hurried out to William Street, got Marnie's attention, gave her the slip of paper, and began to walk home on Fleming. I had thirty-five minutes to make my flight, but I had a strong feeling that Grand Cayman was not in the cards.

Walking to the church, Marnie and I had seen Old Island funky sights. Hurrying back to the house, I faced a new version. A woman in a halter top and spray-on biking shorts waxed a new Acura from Nebraska. A block farther, two men in tennis attire unloaded hanging bags from a Volvo in front of a bed-and-breakfast. Colorado plates on that one. A commuter plane scraped the rooftops of Old Town, inbound with off-season tourists. Someone wanted to widen roads at the top of the Keys. How about one narrow, bumpy lane heading south and three wide smooth ones outbound?

I checked my watch again. In theory, I had time to catch the plane, if a cab showed inside of a minute and I didn't brush my teeth. My cross-lane neighbor, Hector Ayusa, waved from the glider on his shady porch. After all these years, I wasn't sure I would recognize him without his tank top and suit trousers, the unlit cigar in his mouth. Seeing Hector, and having passed the old barber shop with its striped pole a block away, I had returned to old Key West, at least in spirit.

Marnie's tire was flat. My spirits went neutral.

"Yo, bubba," called Hector. "You got a boy come see you. He checking out your house. He check me out checking him, and he go."

"You ever see this boy before, Hector?"

Hector nodded, serious and mean. "Hot rod, color of a school bus. Other day he drove away with your woman."

Randolph had come by during the funeral?

"I'm ready to let him have her," I said.

Hector looked toward Fleming. "Be better off."

I went in, picked up the phone, heard five quick beeps. The introduction to "Gimme Some Lovin'," the old hit by Spencer Davis Group. One message, from Matt, the account executive at the Sarasota ad agency. Matt told me not to worry if I had trouble with my flight. "We found Casey Hample here on Grand Cayman. He can do the first two days' work for us. You can pick up from there."

Casey was a dork and drunk who would ruin the job. I had been fired.

I needed to buy common stock in my premonitions.

The envelope on my kitchen counter yanked me back to current events. It held the prints of my Gomez scene photos, a set of prints from the cop's underwater camera, and another, smaller envelope on which "six exp." was written with a Sharpie. Marnie had been crying when I returned from seeing Duffy Lee Hall and Dr. Lysak. She had distracted me, and I had forgotten to look through the Kodak Max prints. I found six prints in the "six exp." bag, and one clear plastic strip that held their negatives.

The first two depicted a white-flowered stephanotis. The sun's direction made me think that the vine was near Naomi's back door. I didn't recognize that part of Naomi's yard, but I wouldn't know small spaces in my own yard at quick glance. The next picture baffled me. It was a tiny cactus, a miniature of one you might see in *Arizona Highways*. I would have noticed that one in her yard.

What baffled me more was the poor framing, the odd angles. Most of the prints I had seen in Naomi's office had been skillfully shot, close to their subjects, but not too close, and without confusing backgrounds. These failed to use sunlight to best advantage. Highlights were few, contrast was flat.

The final three had been snapped in front of Naomi's house, looking up Grinnell toward the harbor. They were afternoon shots, by the shadows, with purple and gray thunderclouds in the distance. I was surprised by their sharpness. Throw-away cameras use plastic lenses, not famous for crisp images.

So much for clues.

I went to the bathroom for a leak and quality thinking time. Three things came to mind. I wished I had bought the 28-millimeter Olympus lens from Cootie Ortega. I flashed on the hairy look Dexter Hayes had given me on his way into church. And I mentally revisited the small cactus. I sensed that I'd seen it before.

I pulled the prints from the larger envelope, the copies of the boat team cop's and mine. I looked first at Steve Gomez's body slumped with blood on the shirt. I leafed through my shots and finally found one that showed the cactus. The next print showed the stephanotis vine.

Problem solved. The first three from Naomi's Max had been taken in Steve Gomez's yard. Again, I scanned the last three Max shots. They were level and better-composed than the garden photos. A reasonable man would suspect that the Max had belonged to Gomez, that Gomez had been a klutz with a camera, and he had taken the first three images before giving the camera to Naomi. She had done a fine job of framing her photographs. But I couldn't guess what was so damned interesting about Grinnell Street.

I used my four-inch magnifying glass to study the street-scene shots. In the first, a fat orange cat darted between two parked cars. Someone had knocked over a recycling bin. The gas filler door of a Subaru was ajar. That kind of stuff could change the world. The next picture was shot from fifty feet farther north. I could see the front fender of the Subaru and . . . three cars ahead of it, parked at an odd angle, a yellow Z-3 roadster. I looked back at the first shot. I could barely see the Z-3. I checked the third street shot. Clear as hell, and Whit Randolph's car for certain. Had Naomi intentionally aimed her shot to include the BMW's license tag?

I pedaled to Greene Street, locked the bike in front of a small gift shop. The store's display racks were filled with pottery, carvings, custom-glazed tiles, glass sculpture, and porcelain picture frames. A small silver-haired woman tended the counter.

"Let me know if I can help you find something," she said.

"My name is Rutledge. I was a friend of Naomi Douglas."

The woman broke into tears. She was the woman Naomi's neighbor had mentioned, the one with whom Naomi had shared high-priced wine.

I tried to apologize, but scoped her business license while she dried her eyes. Her name was Cristina Alcroft.

She recovered quickly. "I try not to dwell on it," she said. "Naomi was so worried about Steven, and then *she* died."

"Steven?"

She nodded, "The mayor. He told her he felt threatened. Then he died the same day, supposedly by his own hand. You're the photographer friend."

"I am. Did she say why the mayor felt threatened?"

"Bad elements were pushing for certain votes on city legislation. That's not her exact wording, of course."

"Please, I'm not a policeman. But I share your concern about sudden deaths. Let me ask this. Did the Mallory Dome or the art museum worry Mayor Gomez?"

She cracked a sad smile. "The dome worried Naomi. Steven said that was a joke, not a problem. The art museum proposal, Steven had what he called 'hidden support' on that one. No, the proposal that worried him was that island development near the top of Cow Key Channel. He told Naomi that he wasn't old enough to drive when the city first approved it. All these years later, with its value and graft potential, he had bad feelings about it."

"Has anyone from law enforcement come to talk to you?"

"I tried to talk to the police. They weren't interested. I called four times, and nothing. No one would talk to me. At this point, I don't think I could get a parking ticket."

"You say 'police,' you mean the city, right?"

"Of course."

I gave her my phone number and asked her to keep in touch.

"Yes," she said. "I've been meaning . . . But this is not the time."

"For what, ma'am?"

"I would be honored to sell your fine-art photography in this shop. This is something we should talk about another day."

I parked my bike next to the Green Parrot Bar on Whitehead and fought the urge to chug a noon beer. What would I do with a noon beer? Celebrate my lost job, two dead people, or the flat tire I forgot to fix? I wanted to show up unannounced, ask questions faster than he could whip up lies. I wanted to read his face, see how he lived.

I hoofed it two blocks to the condo and knocked. His BMW basked in its spot under the acacia tree. Randolph answered the door quickly. He clasped a Slim Jim in his teeth like a bandito with a cigarillo, held a cell phone tightly to his ear. I thought maybe he was trying to wedge it into his brain. He wore a bleached shark's tooth on a gold chain around his neck, a black Harley T-shirt, and lime-green surfer jams. I noticed for the first time that he was out of proportion, a big head with narrow shoulders. I doubted that he played sports in high school or college. He lifted his hand, motioned that he'd be off the phone soon, and patted the fridge, offered me a noon beer. Celebrate my two trashed art photos, or Sam's dead sister?

Randolph found his remote clicker, pressed the button. His TV flickered on, tuned to the Cartoon Channel. He wandered to a patio, stood just outside the door. I assumed the TV sound was to mask his conversation. Most of his end was grunting anyway. I heard him say, "Look at it from someone else's point of view," and, "Quit jumping to judgment."

I leaned against the hallway wall and looked around. I had walked into a textbook bachelor's pad. On the kitchen counter were a key ring with about ten keys, a mound of coins, crumpled ones and fives, and two bar napkins with scrawled felt-tip notes. In his upside-down ball cap were his wallet, a roll of Tums, and his sunglasses. His kitchen trash bin was full of Styrofoam take-out boxes. Empty bottles lined the sink. Among the dead Heinekens, Randolph's choice, were two empty Miller Lites. Teresa's brand for the rare times she drank beer.

Randolph had scribbled notes on paper scraps, grocery bags, and junk mail. In the scramble of his business day, no surface was safe. There had to be fifteen Post-it notes sticking out of the phone book. I opened up to one in the Key West section. Small world, small island. He'd flagged the listing for Y. Gomez. No street address, no mention of Love Lane, but the phone number was listed.

Whit lived clean. Fresh underwear spilled from a large black plastic bag, probably from the Margaret Truman Launderette. Ten or twelve starched long-sleeved shirts hung in a plastic bag, and loose hangers were strewn about. A lightweight camouflage jacket was tossed over the back of a chair. This was the mess of someone in constant motion, the realm of fast arrivals and exits.

I had expected rent-a-condo furniture and wall art. Teresa had told me that she had rented an air-conditioned storage pod, but her furnishings were right where they'd always been. She had loaned or sold them to Randolph, with the addition of a fifteen-foot sisal runner in the hallway. It was identical in texture to one in Naomi's home. Now that I thought about it, I couldn't recall seeing Naomi's sisal rug since her death. I walked off the length of this one. Too long to fit in Naomi's place, but an odd coincidence.

Newspapers covered the couch. I pushed some aside, sat, and checked them out. It wasn't just today's paper with the Gomez spread, but previous papers going back at least a week, open to photos of local luminaries. Many included a young city commissioner posing with anyone doing anything. Flamboyant as a spring garden, he had become the island's unofficial greeter. Most surprising was the day-old copy of *Investors Business Daily* open to a page that listed IBD's "Ten Secrets to Success." Randolph had placed a check mark beside item three, "Take Action." Next to it, a brochure entitled "Meet . . . Key West" showed pictures of the Prudential real-estate sales force, brokers and realtors. Again Post-it notes, not marking properties, but selected inch-square color portraits. Why was he pinpointing successful people? Why was he in a photograph with the mayor? He had mentioned investors . . .

Randolph hurried inside, tossed his cell phone onto a chair, and waved me into the kitchen. He did a double take on the open Prudential brochure, checked my face for an instant, then kept going. By the time I caught up with him, he had set out a can of Planter's cashew nuts, placed a spoon in an open pint of Häagen-Dazs, opened a cold beer for me, and was pouring beer into a tumbler half-full of tomato juice. Hell, I thought. If this guy wasn't a worm, a probable thief, and a lady stealer, he'd be a wonderful roommate.

"None of that wussy health food for you," I said.

"I do what I like, I eat what I like."

"And, Lord help us if a rule gets in the way."

He nodded. "Alex, you get HBO?"

"Nope."

"You old cheapskate. It only costs a few extra bucks a month."

"Money down the drain. I don't have a TV."

He looked at me like I had just told him my parents had shot each other, my siblings were killed in a car-train wreck on the same day, and my house had burned down.

"No TV?" he said. "How do you get the news?"

"Put my ear to the ground. I overhear talk in bars."

"No movies?"

"Redundant. I live in Key West."

A strange look came over him. "You came by to talk cholesterol, Alex?" He smiled, but I could have cut a diamond on his teeth. "Or have you been worrying? You think I'm going to leave a permanent mark on your girlfriend? You think I'm going to force her to lick my shoe? Do something with her that you haven't tried yet?"

"I never thought I could run her life," I said. "Until a few days ago I was happy to have her be part of mine."

He lifted his beer-juice concoction in mock toast. "So you've come by to punch me in the eye?"

"If I did that, your eye would heal in five days. The broken bones in my hand would never be right."

"That's good, Rutledge. I admire a man who plans his actions, compares upside and downside. Ah, shit." He grabbed a paper towel, poked it at the countertop. "These ants are commandos. They come out of the walls and attack. You don't even see them coming, and I hate the stink of bug bombs." Now he grinned, for real. "It might poison my health food."

"Squirt them with Windex and wipe it up," I said. "Kills the little fuckers, you wind up with a clean kitchen."

"I'll do it. Why'd you come here, Rutledge?"

"You mean come to Key West?"

"No," he said, "but that's good for a start. How did you wind up in this tropical hellhole?"

"I came down for the weekend, twenty-five years ago."

"Clever line, but it's not yours. I heard the dude sing that song the other night."

"It's a line worth repeating," I said. "So why come to our quiet island in the sun? What's your agenda?"

"My pace the last few years, I would describe as hectic. I've come to the tropics for therapeutic boredom."

"You here to stay?"

"You did, didn't you?" he said. "They got visitation rules now, or do you just wish they did?"

"I got to stay because I didn't fuck up. I didn't get my name known to the cops for petty shit. I didn't give anybody an excuse to invite me out of town on short notice."

"That's a good way to play it. You should never crap in your front yard."

The classic motto of the thief, I thought. "I never did that until yesterday, at the ATM."

I could almost see calculations going on in his head, wheels in motion behind his glazed eyes. "What happened?" He forced a straight face. "Your card tilt?"

"No, my image did, in the video monitor. Me and a cab driver, and you weren't in sight. The card you had me run was hot."

He nodded, went pensive. "Are you suggesting I leave town?"

"You need to get your story in order."

Randolph shoved things around on the countertop, found his wallet. He pulled out the card he had handed to me at the bank. "I'm not believing I did this." He put his fingernail on the name. "See? It's my fucking card. I lost it, reported it lost, and the bank sent me a new one. Meanwhile, I found it and I tucked it in here so no one could rip me off." He fiddled around in his wallet, pulled out another with the same graphics. "I grabbed the old one. This is the one I should have used."

"How did the PIN work?"

"Ask the bank. Why should I worry? I used a card that I reported stolen from me?" He walked around, gathered items that he put in his pockets or stacked near the door. "Look, I've got a couple things that need attention." He held up his car keys. "Maybe we could continue this over a beer or two, later today or tomorrow, anytime you like."

"Randy Whitney talked to the county medical examiner yesterday. You know the guy?"

He nodded, quit his quick comebacks. He let his guard down a moment, let me see that he was nursing a hangover. He put his keys and ball cap back on the counter. "I like to play games. Put-on games, play-acting. Harmless, of course, but I've been doing it since high school. Now you know one of my secrets."

"I'm honored."

"I peaked out in Atlanta a few years ago. I forget the name I used. I made it all the way to the CEO's office at NationsBank, before they became Bank of America. I pretended to be a high-priced consultant. I spent a half hour on the top floor talking Lear Jets with the boss."

"Are you interested in the mayor's death?"

He halted, refocused on me. "Your girlfriend thinks it's more complicated than sucking gun barrels. I offered to help ease her mind."

"Your picture's in the paper today, with Gomez."

"So it is. I was in a bar a few days ago, in the early afternoon. The bartender and I were matching coins for drinks. In walked the mayor and a dude with a camera. I guess they were looking for a photo op. The mayor made a joke about us not gambling in front of a city official. I asked for a shot glass, filled it with beer, told him to take his ten percent. It was a Key West payoff for closing his eyes. He loved it, put his arm around me, and knocked back the shot. Right after that, the flash went off."

"You had a new best friend?"

"More or less. Short-term, as it turned out."

"You missed his funeral."

"I don't do funerals," he said. "Especially funerals of suicides."

"So you took a walk."

He finished his drink, to buy time. "Teresa got bad vibes at the man's house. She had her shorts in a knot about bad evidence. Blame it on her criminology courses. I didn't agree with her, but I offered to help, to find out what I could. She asked me not to drag her into it, hence my fake name."

"You drop by my house ninety minutes ago?"

More surprise on his face. "You were leaving town, and she wasn't sure she had the strength to do the funeral. I wanted to come by to offer support. Your house was closed up, so I left."

I pulled the small envelope from my shirt pocket, slid a photo from the sleeve. His Z-3 on Grinnell, from the Kodak Max. "Someone else died the other day. I wonder why Naomi Douglas had a picture of your car."

For an instant he looked like a rat in a corner. He shook his head. "That one hurt. Naomi was hoping to invest in my Fort Myers real estate deal. A storage building on the outskirts of town. Frankly, I was counting on her investment." He looked again at the photo. "I don't know why she took that picture. Maybe her friend took it, the dead mayor. He didn't seem like the jealous type."

"You knew they were friends?"

"Sure," he said. "Didn't everyone?"

"Why didn't you agree with Teresa, murder versus suicide?"

"A pet peeve of mine. Too many people try to read mysteries into everyday events, conspiracy into the mundane. Why does there always have to be a story behind the story? We can thank the media for that. Which takes us back to my asking if you had HBO."

"Your peeve convinced you that the mayor shot himself?"

"He cashed his own check. Gomez was a nice guy, too nice a guy to make a mess. Is there such a thing as a suicide that doesn't leave a mess for loved ones to clean up? From what I've read, bodies leak like crazy. If a guy sails into the sunset, it takes years for families to get him declared legally dead. That's a mess, too, and tougher to clean up. Do me a favor, Alex. Let me know if you ever find a clean way."

"You planning something?"

"No. But I like to keep my options open."

"You've got an answer for everything," I said. "I bet your investors can't wait to get in line."

"Okay, Rutledge. Forget class. Take it down a notch. Let me tell you something you don't realize. A mirror won't tell you this, but you telegraph yourself. If you're working from knowledge, you get this cold look on your face. If you're guessing, you turn to humor. Now, here you are, upset about my diet and pissed because you can't punch me. You've tied me to two dead people, with no possibility that I had a part in their deaths. Why don't you save yourself stress by staying the fuck away?"

"You're right about the stress," I said. "And there's no telling what that tension might make me do."

"You people down here are so insulated. The distance from the mainland may come off as romantic and adventuresome, but I've had better times and squandered more smarts than half this island ever dreamed of having. Can I ask you something?"

"You want permission?" I said. "Why start now?"

"What time did Naomi die?"

"In her sleep, whatever that means."

"So, say, before eight A.M.?"

"Okay," I said.

"And Gomez, what time?"

"Judging by when they called me, in the early to midafternoon."

"So six hours apart, minimum? But they could have died twelve or fifteen hours apart, right?"

"Okay."

"You're suggesting the deaths are linked? That's a far fetch, don't you think?"

I nodded.

"If it's any consolation, Rutledge, I feel bad about Steve Gomez gargling the buckshot, and I feel awful about Naomi Douglas. I have sympathy for anyone that knew them, double sympathy for anyone who knew them both, and that includes you. I will assume your stress explains this visit. No hard feelings."

A rooster crowed in the parking lot. Local color on the hoof.

I looked through the window and glimpsed Teresa's blue scooter racing toward the condo lot's exit gate. I had to guess that she'd made it to Randolph's door, heard us talking inside, and beat it.

Randolph followed my eyes to the window, perhaps sensing what I had seen. He retrieved everything he wanted to take with him. The last thing he grabbed was the plastic water bottle full of vodka. "Now it's time to bid adios."

"You always on the go?" I said.

"I'm a high flyer."

"Don't pack your own chute."

I went east on the walkway, dodged a woman and a dachshund, and tried to assess how Randolph had blocked all my shots. I had arrived with plenty of tricks and had failed to score. With his time-of-death speech, he had slipped past me and dunked one. The security gate began to swing. The BMW squeaked through the instant it could fit, turned left, zipped out of sight. As the gate shut, I hurried out to Thomas Street.

Someone honked at me. Dexter Hayes, in his city car, the stupid-looking Caprice, across the street and five spaces south. I walked up to his window. He was reading a paperback novel of the fist-thick Clancy variety. He turned his head toward me but focused on some point just past my shoulder. He said, "What's up?"

"How you doing?"

He said, "What's going on?"

"You don't want to know."

"What?" said Dexter. "We wait till they write another beer commercial so we can finish our chat?"

"At least we're not frogs who talk."

"Climb in, old buddy."

Old buddy, my ass.

19

DEXTER HAYES'S UNMARKED CRUISER smelled of spilled coffee and stale cologne. The upholstery was worse than smooth. It looked as if someone had cleaned the fabric with Simple Green. A *Car and Driver* lay on the cola-stained passenger-side floor, under several Nestlé Crunch wrappers. A two-inch speaker crackled with police message traffic, codes, acronyms, and slang. I tried to roll down the window. The crank spun around free.

I said, "Did a blue Shimano come out that gate?"

"I didn't see a thing," said Hayes.

"Right," I said. "This street's not paved, and it's pouring rain. People who work together don't rat each other out. Which way did she go?"

Dexter twirled his index finger, which meant anywhere. "What do you think of Mr. Randolph?"

"I think he's an octopus," I said. "His arms go eight directions at once, like his alibis, and dozens of suckers grab his prey. Makes it worse, he's got the brains to keep up with his bullshit."

Hayes nodded his head. "I got him for a jellyfish. Ugly up top and down low he'll sting your butt bad. He's dangerous where you can't see it coming."

"Obviously you know more than I do."

"One or two things," said Hayes. "It's meaningful shit, let's put it that way. He acts like he comes from money. But he looks like he comes from hunger."

"You don't want to reveal your inside information, right?"

"He was bill collecting the other day." Dexter counted his fingers. "Four days ago. We had a solid tip, but we held back on nabbing him. Since then, we've watched him close."

"Bill collecting?"

"He goes out in the morning, after people go to work, and boosts mail. He works it like he's got an address list, full-time locals with big money. He beats the carrier to the outgoing letters."

"And what, of value, would be in that mail?"

"Bill payments. Checks made out to utilities, phone companies, credit card companies. You name it. The guys who run this scam stack up the best checks, for the highest amounts. They open a bank account with a phony driver's license, fake name, and a local address. They use chemicals to blank out the payee's name, and write in the fake name. They deposit the checks early in the bank's statement cycle, then pull the money from ATMs. It takes a few weeks for people to realize that their payments aren't getting where they're supposed to. By the time they complain, the fake account's cleaned out."

"Randolph's doing this?"

Dexter Hayes nodded. "Sure as hell."

I felt questions bouncing in my brain. Why would Whit Randolph let me see all those Post-it notes? What did Deputy "No Jokes" Bohner's stakeout at Camille's three nights ago have to do with city business? I couldn't imagine the county and city coordinating efforts on a fraud case.

"I saw stuff back there in his condo that supports his scam. Can I ask why you don't bust him?" I said.

"Piss on it," said Dexter. "Fraud means paperwork and permanent court cases. The world's insurance companies can deal with that shit. We want to find the bastards making phony licenses, fake IDs, that kind of crap."

"So he skates?"

"Right up to when he cashes one big enough for grand theft. If he stays small potatoes, he can roll. But he'll screw up, you count on it. This time of year, a lot of big checks go to Internal Revenue. If we can hook him to one of those, it's an FBI case, their paperwork, and major camp time."

"A world of shit," I said.

"Right. And I'm glad you understand, because that's what you're in if you can't explain meeting with him in the Hog's Breath Saloon last night. Just now, in our records, you're a 'known associate.'"

He started the engine, eased the shifter down, and cut a U-turn. We drove into the section of town that real-estate brokers and black entrepreneurs call Bahama Village. It was the last repository of island tradition that had not been remodeled and resold. I feared its time would come soon. The first bad sign came three years ago, when city employees tore up pavement and modernized the sewer and water mains. I take that back. The first bad sign was the crack cocaine epidemic, and the second bad sign was sewers.

Why did I feel like I was getting sucked into the business end of a huge Hoover? I was baking in a cop car and could not imagine how the Caprice might fit between all the parked vehicles, cars with their hoods up, or resting on one or two jacks.

Hayes rolled the stop sign where the street names Angela and Thomas were stencil-painted on a utility pole. The bare-wood building on the southwest corner had looked too ruined to stand fifteen years ago. It looked worse now, but still stood. We stopped in front of Blue Heaven, catty-corner from Johnson's Grocery. There was no traffic, so Hayes sat a moment and kept talking. Three men on the corner stared at us.

"You familiar with webcams?" he said.

"Constant movies that run on the Internet?"

"Or still pictures that refresh every five or ten seconds. Like with the cameras mounted in various spots around town. On Mallory Square, or at the Environmental Circus, and inside the Hog's Breath Saloon."

"And there I was . . ."

"Knocking back shots, having a big old talk with Mr. Randolph. Matter of fact, you did most of the talking. Any chance you want to tell me what was so important you had to dominate the discussion?"

"Coexistence," I said.

"Say what?"

"I was explaining how all types of crazies and misfits get along on a three-by-five island. Sort of a modern sermon."

Dexter said, "What'd he do, bad-mouth a gay waiter?"

"You're smart about some things and dumb about others," I said.

"Was that the tone you used with him? Bet you made a lot of mileage on the brotherhood front."

"Whatever I said blew by him like a jet airliner. He'd rather see two men holding guns than two men holding hands."

"Men get set in their ways," said Dexter. "He's one, needs a profit motive to warm up to tolerance."

He cut the wheel, went right down Petronia. People sat on chairs in front of the Swingers Club, eight feet from the car. They stared openly, and I felt like a trespasser. We rolled a half block farther, and I watched money change hands on the corner of Emma, saw the dead end at Fort Street, the old Navy building, the green eight-foot chain-link with barbed wire up top. Dexter veered away from two chickens, turned right onto Emma, then right twice more. We had gone in a tight spiral, wound up on Chapman Lane. We drove past a mess of thin, unspooled cassette tape that had snagged in a busted picket fence and fluttered in the wind. One strand had looped around a large yellow hibiscus blossom. We stopped in front of a small house bordered by a stubby concrete wall. The place needed paint, but its yard was neat and its roof looked new. A chunky, elderly black woman sat on a high-backed rocker on the front porch. She stared at us with no expression.

I said, "I guess we're here, huh?"

Dexter nodded his agreement.

Next door, two middle-aged men sat near the curb in plastic-web lawn chairs. They chewed cigar stubs and drank from paper cups. They refused to acknowledge the city car.

I said, "Why?"

"My father's sister made up for my half-assed upbringing. When you talk to her, take your time. She's never been in a hurry in her life, but she knows more about this island than you and me and ten others put together. Don't be fooled by her walking cane. It's a weapon, not a crutch."

"To hell with catching criminals," I said. "We'll do family visits today."

"Her name is Mary Butler. I call her Auntie Bee, and she'll tell you to call her Miss Mary, so do it. She was Naomi Douglas's cleaning woman."

"Thanks for remembering."

"Get out of the car."

Mrs. Butler didn't resemble her brother, Big Dex Hayes, or her nephew, Dexter Jr. Her broad, fleshy face forced her eyes, nose, and mouth to a tiny group at center. She wore a big print dress and a sun-faded New York Yankees nylon jacket.

Dexter introduced us. She repeated my name, perhaps to run it against her mental roster of old Conch names, and reached out to shake my hand. Her grip was firm. She held on for about ten seconds. I had a feeling that she was sizing me up, or downloading vibes, or whatever wise old women do that lets them see into your soul and know all your secrets.

"I heard your name," she said. "You're the man Miss Douglas wanted to settle her affairs."

How would a cleaning woman know the terms of her employer's will? She held her hands with her fingertips resting against each other as if she was about to start the church-and-steeple child's rhyme. Her fingernails were trimmed short, uniform in length.

I said, "Yes, ma'am, I'm the executor."

"You call me Miss Mary, like she did. And tell me what's so wrong with her affairs you got to come and pester me. And why you got to come with this nephew policeman I got."

Straight talk only, I told myself, and keep it fluid. Dexter would not have brought me here if he didn't think I could learn something. The lightbulb came on. Dexter Hayes was a cop. I was supposed to make a connection with the woman that her nephew couldn't make. I was there to learn something that he couldn't learn on his own.

"We're worried about the way she died," I said.

"She died in private, and asleep. Young man, who could ask better? At my age, my worst fear, I'll fall down and die on Duval Street, in a crowd of strangers. They all in a hurry to get back on that cruise ship, they step over me like a wino lady picked a bad place to sleep."

Back away, I thought.

"Did you clean her house this week?"

"I didn't know they'd took her away. Some days, you know, she goes to Home Depot up in Marathon. She buys her plants, gets her some projects. She kept a good toolbox."

"I didn't know that."

"Now you do." When Miss Mary spoke, she cocked her head as if peering around some obstruction between us. The angle said I don't trust you yet, I'm trying to figure out your angle.

"You went in and cleaned like usual?" I said.

She nodded slowly, and kept nodding. "I go in the house and her bed's stripped, which is how I always found it on my days." Her eyes watered up. "I didn't know they take the bedsheets when they take the dead."

Change of subject. "How do you travel back and forth, from here to her house?"

She pointed at Hayes. "Free taxi. The same way I go groceries, to Fausto's or Eckerd's."

Dexter rolled his eyes, looked away, focused on something down the street. I couldn't think of a better form of graft.

Mary Butler said, "Miss Douglas, she use the same taxi man."

"Was there anything strange about the house?" I said.

"Pretty as ever," said Miss Mary, again tilting her head. "Not much to do. All the plants were watered."

"You said there wasn't much to do. Was that normal?"

"Well . . . That's almost right. She kept it neat, but I kept it clean. I guess that was strange, that morning I went in there. It was neat, but clean, too. As if I'd already been there."

"Did you notice anything changed in her living room?"

Miss Mary's eyes widened. "Now, there you got one. Those big pictures, those artist pictures of railings and gingerbread? They were not on the wall, which I didn't worry until I saw them in that trash. I knew she must've had a big, big problem with that boy who took those pictures. It would have to be a big problem, throw away those pretty frames. There's a thin line between Saturday night and Sunday morning. Sometimes a thin line between love and hate, you know that?"

I looked at Dexter Hayes. He stared straight at his aunt, wouldn't look at me.

Change the subject, I thought. "I like your porch, all the green."

"Those are her plants covering up the chicken shit. When I heard about Miss Douglas, I went back. I couldn't leave them to dry and die, like the lady who bought them. The first thing we ever agreed was the secret to plants in Key West: Put 'em in the ground green side up and add water."

"They look good right where they are," I said. "I like your house."

She bobbed her head, agreeing. "It's all right, but for stray chickens and my troublesome neighbors"—she tilted her head at the men drinking next door—"or some fool down the road turning a paper-thin shack into a quaint home. You make it pretty around here, it draws flies. You see this walking stick? I walk as good as you, young man, but I got to fight off those cherry-vanilla real-estate ladies come down here to tell me I got to stop being happy and contented so I can be rich. You know what I say to them? I say, Ladies, Hewlett-Packard and Intel and Citigroup are all up today, so I can afford my collard greens and a box of fried chicken. Oh, they do not know how to take that. And I got Miss Douglas to thank for that, too."

I wanted to say, "How so?" It was none of my business. I said nothing.

Miss Mary filled the silence. "We help each other in this world, young man. Miss Douglas needed my help with her house, and she give me help with other things."

"With investments," said Dex Hayes. "Auntie sold her mother's home on Green Turtle Key to a wealthy man years ago. Mrs. Douglas kept Auntie in the stock market through the 1990s, then took her to cash before the market went soft."

I said, "You went to her house for friendship. That's what I think."

She cracked a small smile. "Smart old ladies have more fun than you think, young man. We lost husbands. We waved good-bye to our children, if we were lucky. We got nothing left to lose. It depends on approach, don't it?"

"You lived your whole life in Key West?"

She shook her head. "Two years in a city called West Palm. That place smell like cars. It was way too agitated. We never had to rattle our chains on Key West, excuse the expression. Some of the children went away and came back with ideas. They wanted to get ahead in life by using people, not hard work. They sang in small choirs, and they didn't see a twinkling dime from white guilt until the last few years. A few of them got to selling dope, smoking that stuff. A few got the cancer from smoking that dope. They in another choir now, no dope allowed."

"Do you recall a sisal rug that ran down Naomi's hallway?"

"Miss Douglas decided that rug drew dirt. She said next time I came, we would put that dirty old rug at the curb."

"It's not in her house now."

"Maybe she got her boy to haul it off."

"Boy?"

"Her stepson, adopted, whatever he was. Foster child, for all I know. That boy, the mayor."

I looked at Dexter Hayes. His eyes were wide, intense, but he didn't want to interrupt the flow of conversation.

"Naomi Douglas was the mayor's mother?"

"I don't believe she was his natural, but she raised the boy, like I did for this one." She waved the back of her hand at Dexter but didn't look at him. "Miss Douglas worried about that boy more than anything in her life."

"What was to worry about?"

"He treated her different than boys treat their mamas. And I don't mean like better or worse. I believe that was her only bother, and I hated to see that. Worries are better spent on the future than the past."

Yes, but the past holds secrets. "You never had other cause for concern about Mrs. Douglas?"

"One thing." She nodded for about fifteen seconds, then said, "That odd ho-listic bug lady. You cannot meditate bugs away. They too smart. You can't train them. You got to poison those bugs, plain as can be. That's when they understand you mean business. She pay that lady more than Orkin. What'd she get? Flies in her flour, ants in the cereal, cocka-roaches under the house. Why she had a ho-listic bug lady, I don't know."

Dexter jangled his car keys. Miss Mary got the message just as I did. She said, "You go up in town, you find that man that took those broken pictures in the trash can. Ask him what made her angry. Ask that man why she died of stroke or her heart blew out."

One of the men from next door approached me as I reached for the car door handle. He adjusted the napkin around his paper cup. Old Conchs wrap napkins so evaporation delays warming. Fifty years ago it was inspired by a shortage of ice. People still did it in the Seventies, half out of tradition, but almost no one did it anymore.

The man beckoned me toward him. "Hey, brother." It sounded like "Oy ba-rudda."

I looked at Dexter, hoping for telepathic instructions. He stared back, no help at all, almost grinning, waiting to see how it played out.

I said, "How's it going?"

"You don't like me 'cause I'm a poor person. You hate my poverty."

"Nope, that's not it, mister."

"But I was right, right? You don't like me." His breath smelled like an empty saloon in the morning. "Is it 'cause I'm a colored man?"

"Nope. You want to know why I don't like you? I'll tell you. If you came into my life, you'd be a problem, not a joy. I've got enough problems with friends to last me years. I don't need problems from pushy strangers."

The man looked entranced, stupefied by my words. He shrugged, walked away shaking his head.

Dexter popped open the squeaky door on his side of the car. "Well done," he said.

"Thank God I was in a bad mood. I might have let white guilt take over."

"I didn't mean with that man. I meant with my aunt. Ever since I became a cop, she's shut me out. The only thing I can figure is some loyalty to her criminal brother."

I'd never before heard Dexter speak of his father.

We drove over to Whitehead, got stuck creeping behind a Conch Train. A tourist family of four in identical tie-dyed tank tops took up the train's rear-facing backseat. A thirty-year-old German sedan was parked near the Hemingway House. It reminded me of the car that Ortega had parked at my place.

"Can I ask how Cootie came to be driving a vintage Mercedes-Benz?"

"Part of his collectible thing, his fixation."

"Cars?"

"In this case, Princess Diana."

"No."

"You didn't know?" said Hayes. "He's the biggest Di groupie in Florida. People at the city call him Di Guy."

"Oh, bullshit."

"He's got two rooms devoted to her. He told me about it once. Pictures on the wall, a book collection, a piece of fabric from her wedding dress in a walnut box with an etched-glass front and fancy seal. He's got every copy of *People*, a bunch of ski lift passes, a set of earrings, and the veil from a hat she wore to a ceremony in France. He's got three tea sets, a pair of her sunglasses, and five or six scarves in a framed box. I got no idea where he gets it all. The Internet, probably getting his ass fleeced by somebody. Willingly, of course."

Then I remembered. He had asked if I had any *Time* or *Newsweek* issues from 1997. The Paris death.

I dreaded the answer. "Where does the Benz come in?"

"He saw some photo years ago in *National Enquirer*. Princess Di got out of an old Mercedes to fool paparazzi at the rear door of her London athletic club. Cootie saw an identical one for sale by the highway up on Big Pine. He paid peanuts for it, then spent thousands to make it run right and not leak when it rains. I think he put a Cuban mechanic's kids through college just on that car. Somebody down at the city told me he pays three hundred a month to rent a garage for it out on Laird."

"Where does he get that kind of money?" I said.

"Man lives out of his freezer and doesn't drink. He does his own washing and uses coupons at Publix. He's got the secret to being a millionaire in this town."

"I'm amazed by the idea that Cootie might put that much thought into any endeavor."

"For the first time today, I agree with you."

"Thanks. Can I ask two more things?"

"It's not in my self-interest to consent," said Hayes. "You'll ask anyway, so let me ask my question first."

I knew what it was. "The photos were my work," I said. "I didn't trash them, and I hadn't argued with her, or pissed her off. I hadn't seen her in two weeks. I can't believe she would have dumped them. If foul play's confirmed, they could be a big clue."

"Oh, yeah. It's confirmed. Larry Riley got the toxicology results. He told law enforcement, but not the press. She died of an Oxycodone overdose. It's a megawatt painkiller. We're trying to find her personal doctor, ask him if he prescribed it."

"His name's Lysak. I already checked. There was no pain medication. At least not recently. It may have been an outdated prescription."

"Wonderful. Does Dick Tracy need to be put on retainer?"

"Did he say anything about Gomez?"

"He said there wasn't enough left of his head to fill a size-ten shoe."

"But, what time did he die?" I said.

Dexter stared at the windshield.

How many times do you drop the ball before you forfeit the big game?

I said, "If your aunt didn't discover the body and call the city, who did?"

His jaw tightened. "I don't know," he said. "That's the single reason I'm being patient with you and your notions."

"Have you told Teresa that Randolph's under surveillance?"

Dexter looked skyward. "When's your next moment of genius?"

"Why do you ask?" I said. "You need to borrow one?"

"Did I remember that you wanted to find the housekeeper? Did you learn anything in the past half hour?"

"Yes," I said.

"Do I have an obligation to reveal anything to a civilian?"

"No."

"So you don't know how much I know or don't. I could be a slug or a genius."

"I suppose that's correct."

"Did I get this job by being a dunce?" he said.

"Probably not."

"You're more productive, Rutledge, when you're asking good questions and being less of a wise ass."

"Aren't we all?"

"Naomi Douglas left everything to her brother, Ernest Bramblett."

"That's right," I said.

"Why nothing to her foster son?"

20

ALL WE NEEDED WAS the FDLE, the Coast Guard, the ATF, and the DIA. We could have had a quorum on Dredgers Lane. We already had a traffic jam.

I was so inside myself, thinking about Naomi and Gomez, their mother-son relationship, that I'd ignored Dexter Hayes's route. I had wanted to go to the airport to retrieve my cameras and duffel, but forgot to ask. I zoned out during our eastbound run on Truman and didn't notice he'd gone north on White. As he swung onto Dredgers Lane, I remembered that my bike was still locked outside the Green Parrot. My belongings were as scattered as my brain.

The sheriff's SUV that Lewis drove was next to Marnie's Jeep. The Jeep's tire had not fixed itself. Chicken Neck Liska had wedged his Lexus against the Ayusas' hedge. A red Mustang convertible was angled in near Carmen's house, which meant that Monty Aghajanian, my FBI friend, had hit town. A shindig was being forced on me. I suspected someone was about to hand me my ass. At least I would know where my ass was.

Dexter stopped behind the SUV and shut off his car. "Party time, bubba," he said. "I just invited myself."

City and county law officers mix like ditch water and kerosene. "Talk to them about it," I said.

I had spoken too few times in the past year with Monty Aghajanian. He had been a longtime friend and, not long ago, in my backyard, had shot a man about to shoot me. Any other day I would be happy to see him.

Monty had spent eight weeks of the past year in Quantico, Virginia, surviving the FBI's basic-training course. The bureau had posted him to New Jersey to track down stolen Harleys and road-building vehicles, but his job description changed monthly. Now he was back, dressed like a tourist in a luau shirt, milk-white Bermudas, and leather sandals. I sensed distance when we shook hands, as if he wanted to stand away from trouble. I wanted to say that I wasn't trouble, but I felt like a trouble magnet and he was wise to keep a shield in place. Bobbi Lewis was back in her polo-style uniform shirt. Liska, whom I hadn't seen in church, wore a suit and tie. His new gig at the county must be weighing on him. I had never seen him wear conservative clothing. He chewed a plastic straw, looked pensive, nodded hello, but said nothing.

I introduced Monty to Hayes, explained to each the other's job. I could tell by Monty's face that the name threw him off. He knew all about Dexter's father, Big Dex Hayes, and his unsavory reputation. To Monty's credit, he took the introduction at face value, without comment.

Bobbi Lewis sipped a can of Mountain Dew. "Your phone's been ringing."

Sam, I thought. Certainly not Teresa.

No one said a thing. We stood on the porch and stared at one another. I assumed that Liska and Lewis were trying to make Hayes uncomfortable, silently urge him to leave. My ceiling fan spun slowly. Its blades reflected light muted by the screening. I hadn't left the fan on, and I had locked the house.

Lewis followed my gaze. "The air was stifling," she said. "The door was open so I took the liberty."

I shrugged. Teresa had been back, again had left the place unlocked.

"You people want to step inside?" I said. "Cool off?"

"We're fine out here," said Lewis.

Aghajanian looked through the screens. "Nice day, great weather. Sure beats Jersey. We don't see many palm trees up there."

"Real nice," said Dexter Hayes Jr.

Liska looked at the lane, chewed his Burger King coffee straw. He had gone cold turkey, told me in February that quitting cigarettes would save him three grand a year. A deputy at work tipped him to plastic stir sticks, so he fiddled with them like cigarettes, chewed nicotine gum between sticks, and ignored stares.

"I've been away too long," said Monty. "I heard Earl Duncan on the radio, trying to sell Tye-otas and a Mitsu-bitchy. I couldn't understand a word he said, like he had a washrag in his mouth. The man reinvented the Southern accent. Time was, I could decipher it. Hell, I used to work for him."

"Earl's ads have been running since World War One," I said. "He'll be on the air after we're all dead."

"He got me to buy a car," said Hayes.

"Okay," said Bobbi Lewis. "Let's cut the crap."

"Agreed," said Liska.

I braced myself for incoming. They were about to play Pin the Shit on the Scapegoat.

Liska continued. "Monty filled us in on your nosy-business, Rutledge. He told us we'd find a prize when we searched the NCIC. Officially, he can't do it, but he did it anyway, at great risk to his career. So none of this leaves the porch. We all together, here?"

Each of us agreed, but Liska asked again. He looked directly at Dexter Hayes.

"It's your play," said Hayes. "I'm in the balcony."

"All this for Ernest Bramblett?" I said.

"Him too." Monty brushed off a space on my porcelain-top table, boosted himself up, and sat. In his silence, he took command of the porch. I assumed he had learned that move with the Bureau, their basic lesson in dealing with municipal personnel. Liska stood back from the circle, arms crossed and the stir stick wiggling. I wondered how he felt about Aghajanian, once a subordinate at the city, now a federal agent with leverage, resources, and confidence. Maybe he wasn't jealous at all. Maybe he was happy that he could peak his career and not have to leave the Keys.

"First off, Naomi's brother," said Monty. "I found an old ag assault charge on Ernest Bramblett, from South Dakota. He caught a guy humping his wife in the back room of a Sherwin-Williams store. This was in 'eighty-four. He put Sir Stud in critical condition. Standard stuff, no big deal. Even in the Midwest they've got crimes of passion. I searched another database. In the past four months he's made credit card purchases in Bedford, Texas. It's upscale suburbia, between Dallas and Fort Worth. The credit card's billing address is a post office box. A cell phone account is billed to the same box. He doesn't show a permanent address or utility bills, but that's not unusual. Bramblett could be living with a woman or other friends."

Liska glanced at the phone clipped to his belt. He must have had it set for silent buzz. He checked caller ID, pressed a button, ignored it.

"What sort of stuff does Bramblett buy?" I said.

"Groceries, gasoline, everyday bullshit. Forget about it. He's legit. Here's the odd news. When I talked to you, Alex, I wrote notes, which I mixed up. You gave me two names, right? That slick who's chasing your lady? I wrote his name above Bramblett's. The next day, I meant to find Bramblett, but I plugged in the wrong guy."

"Meaning Whitney Randolph?"

"You bet, and talk about a file crammed with data. The National Crime Info Center must have upgraded their computer storage to accommodate him. I thought to myself, I can't afford a house in Old Town, but this dirtbag Randolph's going to inherit one. It took me a few minutes to figure that his age didn't match being the brother of a woman in her sixties. I'd crossed the names, but Randolph looked like too much fun to ignore.

"I found histories under four aliases, two of them now 'deceased.'

Your boy was a child prodigy, a con man, a jack of all trades, and a one-man gypsy band. He's a legend in the world of scams and ripoffs. A summary from the West Coast called him the Tiger Woods of grift. Whatever you think you know about him, throw it away. Including his name."

Aghajanian paused. He looked to the other officers for a reaction.

No one said a thing, but my mind raced. Why had Randolph stuck a Post-it note next to Yvonne Gomez's name in the phone book?

"Keep going," said Liska, but an odd look wrinkled his face. He checked his cell phone, which must have vibrated again. "Go ahead without me." He went outside, found a shady spot, this time took the call.

"One of the old beefs was up in Miami," said Monty. "I saw an old friend's name on the read-out and gave him a call. He said they ran him out of town five years ago. The kid started as a bellhop in a couple of different hotels. Ripping off rooms was minor. His big deal was hooking up with older women, especially married ones looking for strange. He'd take a roll in the sack, then slide out in the wee hours, and a piece of jewelry or a watch would go with him. Married women can't exactly report that kind of theft. After the detectives put out the word in hotels, he got jobs in nursing homes. He was ripping off uppers, downers, and mood pills from the fuzzy brains. They ran him off the Gold Coast, told him that their creep quota was filled. The twit pled poverty, hit up my friend for bus fare to Atlanta."

"Out of your friend's pocket?" I said.

Monty looked at me, eyebrows raised. "There isn't a force in the country that doesn't have a slush fund, Alex. Confiscated cash, for the most part. We cops know that. Randolph knew that. One more little scam."

"If we tried it in Monroe County," said Lewis, "we'd drain the budget to bedrock."

Monty slid off the table. "Can I start my vacation now?"

"You can sure as hell go inside and get a beer," I said.

Monty left the door open while he went to the kitchen.

"This puts a new scope on two of our investigations," said Bobbi Lewis.

"One of mine, as well." Dex Hayes called after Monty. "It's developing into mail fraud, so it could become yours."

Lewis handed me her empty soft drink can. "You recycle?"

"I always obey the law," I said.

"I don't know if you saw," said Lewis to me. "Randolph got his picture in the paper, laughing it up with the mayor."

"I saw."

"You see the man in the background?"

I nodded. "Our old friend Frank Polan, from Cudjoe Key. The guy whose house you might confuse with a Club Med."

"Polan filed a complaint three days ago," said Lewis. "He claimed he was being set up for an investment scam. He said he wasn't born last night. He'd been around the block a few times, and knew a Ponzi scheme a mile away. He paddled his kayak up a canal to the Freeman Substation at Mile Marker 21. He caused quite a stir up there. He walked in wearing a Speedo, a silk tank top, rubber shoes, and a mesh pith helmet. He was smeared with sunblock, and had earphones around his neck, and a cell phone clipped to his bathing suit. I guess he stays connected while he communes with nature."

"It's a lifestyle we all should hope for," I said.

"Now that you mention it . . ." Lewis smiled and shook her head. "Maybe I should check into his hotel. Anyway, Polan gave us Randolph's name, license number, phone number, and a sheet of typewriter paper. It was covered with handwritten six-figure numbers and percentages."

"That was Randolph's prospectus?" I said.

"What's a hundred grand among millionaires?" said Lewis. "Polan must be quite the gentleman. He asked us not to tie him into anything by name. He said that bad publicity might ruin his chances to meet women."

"Was his complaint the reason 'No Jokes' Bohner was following Randolph on Monday night?"

Bobbi Lewis raised her eyebrows. "Not bad, Rutledge. I'll have to inform Billy that his techniques have slipped."

"The slip happened years ago, when the county hired him."

"His report included your name," she said. "You're in the computer for the ATM problem, and now you're a 'known associate.'"

Dexter Hayes coughed softly.

I ignored him. "Teresa's the associate. I'm another scam victim."

Both Aghajanian and Liska rejoined us on the porch. The sheriff had a look on his face. He was full of fresh information.

"You'll like this, Monty," said Bobbi Lewis. "We ID'd two calls on Naomi's message service. The second was from a pay phone, and the caller also phoned his own message service in Redmond, Washington. Sure as hell, Whitney Randolph."

"That's all interesting," Dexter Hayes said to Lewis. "It's the first I've heard of it. Any chance you might tell the city about the ATM problem, too?"

"Oh, yeah," she said. "Sorry to offend you. Maybe you can tell us about mail fraud."

Admonished, Hayes searched his thoughts for a comeback. I didn't want him to kiss up by linking me to Randolph's condo. I broke the news to Lewis myself.

"You paid him a visit, and that surprises me?" she said. "We've already got you as a KA and a coconspirator."

"A few things in his condo matched up to his targeting wealthy people for check washing and investment scams," I said. "He even had Post-it notes in the phone book."

"But why in the first place did you go there?" said Liska. "Or do you have a badge you haven't shown us?"

"He set me up for that ATM bullshit. As a cop, you've got a legal view. But I'm a civilian. I take it personally. I wanted to discuss it with him. Also, my neighbor saw him creeping the lane while I was at the funeral."

"Anything else?" said Lewis. Her eyes told me she already knew.

"He put a full court press on my live-in domestic partner, whatever you want to call her. I think the son of a bitch is laying pipe in my backyard."

No one wished to respond to my admission of being two-timed. Lewis looked ashamed for having brought it up.

"I went for another reason, too," I said. "The ME told me that Randolph had been asking questions about Gomez's autopsy. Riley said that a 'Randy Whitney' queried him . . ."

"One of his dead aliases," said Monty.

"Which I figured out quickly. I wanted to know why he'd used a fake name, maybe get his reaction to a photograph." For the second time in an hour I took out the envelope. This time I didn't show the Kodak Max print. Lewis would zing me for absconding with evidence. Or ruining evidence, because my fingerprints had obscured any others on the Max. I pulled out the bloody-shirt image. "After my chat with Randolph, I decided not to show him this."

Lewis and Hayes stepped closer, looked over my shoulder.

Hayes said, "Messy, and a shit print. I hope you didn't shoot that one, Mister Pro."

"It's a blowup from one of your man's bad ones, Dexter. Duffy Lee Hall noticed something when he salvaged the overexposure. Look closely, since this is your case for now. You told me yourself that the shotgun blast blew everything away from the body. In your words, 'He blew brain salad into the mangroves.' Even Randolph, an hour ago, said, 'bodies leak like crazy.' This picture proves that the bloodstains don't match the gunshot."

Hayes studied the print, then managed to say, "Oh."

Lewis said, "It's my case now, thank you."

"Agreed," said Liska. "It's the power structure at work, Detective Hayes. It's my county-over-city prerogative. The Florida Department of Law Enforcement, our state baby-sitters, can yank it from me just as quickly as I'm lifting it from you. But none of us needs to forget, if we've really got two murders, their connection is thinner than a silk thread. Whitney Randolph made a call to Naomi Douglas's phone, he was in a picture with the mayor, then he got curious about the autopsy. Detective Lewis learned there was a friendship between the two deceased, and Rutledge noticed a common hometown. That's all we have. The skinny thread runs through the man, but it's not proof of squat. Our work has just started. Or the FDLE's work, however it works out."

"It may have been more than friendship, sheriff," I said. "According to Mrs. Butler, the woman who cleaned Naomi's house, Gomez may have been Naomi's step- or foster son."

I heard Lewis inhale deeply, an attempt to calm herself. I did not want to look. I wanted to give her private relief.

"That makes the thread fatter," said Liska.

So would the Kodak Max photo of the Z-3 on Grinnell, but I held back.

"I talked to Naomi's friend," I said, "the woman who owns the gift shop in the six hundred block of Greene. She can't get anyone at the city to return her calls. She said that Naomi told her Gomez thought 'bad elements' were behind that old development project out by the boulevard. The Salt Pond Condos, whatever they're called."

"Who's to say bad elements aren't behind the Mallory Dome?" said Hayes. "Isn't that group from Seattle? Isn't that the same area as Randolph's answering service?"

"Randolph's bubble is about to pop," said Monty.

"It needs to pop now," I said. I opened the door, walked inside. No signs that Teresa had packed her bags. I leaned back out. "Has anybody seen my roommate? She could be in over her head."

"She could be in it with him, too," said Lewis.

I locked eyes with her. I didn't like hearing it, but she was right.

"Lemme make a call." Hayes unclipped his phone and stepped outside.

Lewis said, "We'll contact the airport and Highway Patrol. We'll bluelight every yellow roadster in the Keys."

"If Randolph thinks the fat's in the fire," I said, "that roadster's parked by now."

"Okay," said Lewis. "We'll call the car rental and air charter firms."

"If he rented a car, it was days ago," I said. "He parked it, kept it ready to go."

Monty agreed. "He's that good."

"Shit," said Lewis. "Does he know we're getting close? That's the big question. Maybe he thinks he's skating free."

"One last thing," said Monty. "I've got a friend in the bureau's profiling section, a guy I met in basic. He's already up to speed on a lot of that stuff, personality studies, motivational analysis, and so on. You describe a crime, its details, its timing. Or better yet, a series of crimes. These guys come back and give you the whole ball of wax. They'll tell you the perp's shoe size and year of high school graduation. They'll know ethnic background and number of siblings. They know if the perp ever saw his parents having sex. My buddy told me something that stuck in my head. He said, 'It's rare that grifters kill, and they keep it in the crowd. The vic is almost always another con artist.'"

Hayes came back to the porch. "Teresa didn't go back to work after the funeral." He looked at Lewis. "We've got city cars looking. I'm out of here."

She shrugged, gave no response.

Dexter nodded and went for his car.

"Monty," I said, "can you do me a favor?"

He made a sweeping gesture, talked out the side of his mouth, mocked a nasal New Jersey accent. "What did I just do?"

"I mean unofficial."

"This new job of mine, I don't know that word."

"I need to reach Bramblett. I need to settle Naomi's estate."

"Hire a private eye in Fort Worth."

I looked at Bobbi Lewis. Twenty-four hours earlier, she had suggested that Bramblett might be dead or his sister's killer. She looked back at me, thinking the same thought.

"Thanks, Monty," I said. "The estate can pay to find him. It'll come out of his pocket, not mine."

The porch went to silence, predeparture shufflings. The meeting was over.

Liska said, "What's your pal Sam Wheeler doing in Broward?"

"I'll ask him when I see him."

"Good. You do that," said the sheriff. "You gonna know him in a hospital bed, in an orange jumpsuit?"

Shit. The call to Liska's cell phone. "What did he do, give *your* name?"

"You got it. And I can't recall fronting him any blue chips. You want to think again about his privacy?"

I explained Sam's dawn call, our flight to Lauderdale, the failed ID of the found body. I added the Broward deputy, the private eye, Wally Loads in the motel, and the brother of the other dead woman.

"You and I are driving to the mainland," said Liska. "I'll need to keep a low profile, so we'll take my personal car. Pack a ditty bag."

"Everything I need is at the airport."

He checked his watch. "Let's go."

I had spent four days in passenger seats. Decisions had been made for me, not by me. I had gone from wanting to leave the island to having every reason to stay. I had been in Sam's Bronco, two Lauderdale taxis, Marnie's Jeep, another taxi, Bobbi Lewis's SUV, and Dexter Hayes's city-issue Caprice. Now I faced a long ride in the Lexus.

Questions loomed. Why would Liska want to put himself into a Broward problem? What was his interest in Sam's welfare? Did I need to stay to help find Teresa? A big problem, too. The last thing Sam might want around was one more lawman. A big fact carried the moment. I couldn't learn a thing sitting on my ass in Key West.

With everything I had learned about Randolph, I was glad I lived in an old wood Conch house with fifty places to hide small objects. I was equally happy I hadn't told Teresa about Sam Wheeler's ten thousand dollars. I pocketed the money along with the notes I had scribbled when Sam had called from Broward.

Carmen Sosa stood in the lane. She read my face. She was good at that.

"Back tomorrow," I said. "Keep an eye on the fort, will you?"

She scoped the people around me and gave me a hug. "I'll do that, Alex. You keep an eye on yourself."

One more issue faced me as I walked toward Liska's Lexus.

I hadn't fixed Marnie's flat.

21

"THIS ISN'T THE WAY to the airport."

"We don't have time." Liska waited for a bicyclist, then turned left onto North Roosevelt. "You can buy pit wax at a rest stop. What else you need, a comb, a toothbrush? Put 'em on a credit card. Bill it to your buddy chained to the bed in Jackson Memorial."

"I'm not going to fill your car with luggage, sheriff. I can pull some clean clothes and leave the duffel."

"Idiots up in Florida already think I go to the office dressed like Jimmy Buffett. One attorney in St. Pete heard that my deputies had Hawaiian shirts like turnpike toll collectors. Every call I get from around the state, Orlando, Tallahassee, other sheriffs, they want to know about fishing. Like I ever get time to launch my boat. I got a twenty-one-foot shed queen gathering lizard shit and dust." He waggled his hand between us. "You and me, dressed for a funeral, we never looked better in years. We're not going to a fashion show. Quit your crap."

"I especially like day-old shirts."

"We can buy two up the road," he said.

"My cameras are at the airport, too. They'll be gone if I leave them too long. Georgette can't watch my bags twenty-four hours a day."

Liska relented. He parked in an up-front security zone. I was in and out in two minutes.

"You got time and money for a vacation?"

"A job in the Caymans. I canceled out."

"Tell me another one. 'Work' and 'island' don't compute."

"You live on one."

"I don't care what they used to call it. You don't drive to real islands. This fucking road makes it a peninsula. We live at the end."

I was heading up U.S. 1 with an attitude in the driver's seat and an air conditioner that would shame Alaska. I thanked my stars that he had given up Seventies-era colognes. Also his smoking habit, though the squeaking coffee stirrers drove me nuts.

I made a show of checking the dials on his stereo system.

"I keep my CDs in the glove box and here." He lifted the lid of the center armrest.

I read eight or nine jewel box spines. "I can't tell you how long it's been since I've seen a Barry Manilow record, Sheriff. Maybe not since 1945. What happened to your disco fetish, your clothing collection?"

"It's on hold. I've got a new public image to nurture."

"You're quite the politician."

"No, I'm quite the cop. I use politics as camouflage." Liska whipped his wheel left, went for the center lane to avoid being smacked by a swerving station wagon. A small sticker on the wagon's bumper advertised Jesus. Do unto others, if they're in your way.

People in Conch Cruisers, four-door heaps that locals favor, stared at us. In their minds we were outsiders with bankrolls come to turn islanders into subservient fetchers. None of them noticed the Monroe tags, the Hurricane Reentry Permit on the windshield. They didn't want to know that we were neighbors, part of Cayo Hueso's Human Family.

"Why aren't we flying commercial?" I said. "You're a powerful man these days. Snap your fingers, you could've had two seats bumped for us."

"We got a meeting at the top of the Keys in a restaurant. It doesn't have its own airport."

"Do I get clues, or do I have to guess cold?" I said.

"I don't know any details, but he's charged with assault on a law officer."

I hoped Detective Odin Marlow got the worst of it.

"Half this traffic, it's city cops," he said. "They drive patrol units home to Sugarloaf because they can't afford to live in town. They think they got the right to do fifteen over the limit, and my deputies can't bust them."

"A badge buys certain freedoms," I said.

"You get mixed up in a few more of these, you ought to get that badge I talked about. Sign up for courses at the college. You could be quite the cop, too. Put some stability in your life. You've got a problem on the romance front, I take it."

"Teresa Barga moved in a week ago. It's been downhill since then. We've hit a seasonal change in our relationship. Summer into fall."

"Ah, yes, that psychological trampoline," said Liska. "My wife and I did the big split, once and for all. When they're there, you go through a lot more toilet paper and aspirin. When they're not there, you go through a lot more frozen dinners and alcohol." He toggled his window switch, brought it down three inches, pitched a flattened straw. "On second thought, be glad you're not a cop. Why are some women drawn to losers?"

"I have no idea. Fish to bait, moths to flame. Maybe she's a scam victim, too. A different kind of scam."

We drove in silence across Boca Chica and Rockland Keys, then Liska said, "Off the rock, up here on U.S. 1, they put cute facades on every funky joint. You lose your bearings. You don't know your way around anymore. The old roadside dives, these days, sell eighty foreign beers that after two or three you feel like you drank a box of glazed doughnuts. Mixed drinks have names like Key Breeze and Atom Smasher. The other day I heard a girl downtown order a Buck Naked Belly Flop. It took the kid five minutes and two machines to make her drink. What ever happened to Seven and Seven or gin and tonic? Show me the progress."

I could show him no progress.

He said, "I don't mind tourists, except they drive like tourists. The lead guy won't put his foot in the carb, the next guy won't pass him. What's the plural of 'doofus'?"

I didn't know.

He pulled a fresh coffee straw from his pocket. "My goal is to quit this workaday life in Florida and move north to Canada. I'll spend my leisure hours driving slow in the left lane."

I had heard it before, couldn't muster a laugh. I hoped he was thinking about larger issues and filling the air with words. My thoughts kept returning to Naomi Douglas. She never had filled voids with idle chatter. She had led me to the artistic aspects of photography. Liska, on the other hand, had been the devil to whom I had sold my soul. He had been a city detective when he talked me into part-time police work, the mechanical, mindless side of my craft. Now the man who had dragged me into evidence photography was taking me to Miami. Bad omen.

North of Summerland Key, six fishermen dangled lines into Niles Channel. One angler had rigged a bungee cord to hold his rod so he could gab into a cell phone. Pelicans went nuts in the northerlies, glided low over the road, played gusts, crash landed into waves, lifted moments later with lunch flipping in their beaks.

Liska said, "What do you think about Gomez's death?"

"Let's say he was killed away from his house," I said, "then brought to the seawall. How could a murderer get him into his yard without drawing attention?"

"Good speculation," said Liska. "Keep going."

"The only way is through the garage, with a key or an automatic opener. Someone could unload his body with the door down. With no one across the canal, there'd be little risk carrying him to the seawall."

"More."

"It would have to be a car that the neighbors would know," I said, "like Steve's or Yvonne's."

"His personal car, the Buick Regal, was in the garage, covered in laundry lint. Hadn't been used in a while."

"It's a two-car garage," I said. "How about that white four-door? Was his city car still at the city lot?"

"Yep. Does that leave Yvonne's car transporting the body?"

"You got it," I said.

"We checked. Her Acura was getting repaired at Moore's. Some drunk kid sideswiped her car and two others last Friday afternoon. They were all parked on Southard. She needed a fender, a door, and a repaint."

"Shit."

"We found blood smeared on the vertical face of the seawall. We played with the idea he was brought home in a boat. But that's good, Rutledge. I like the way you're thinking."

"Why are you doing this for Sam?"

"Let me answer that with a question," said Liska. "A few months back, we had a nasty mess on Southard. What the *Citizen* tastelessly described as 'a free-for-all shootout.'"

"I recall." I had been witness to it. I had been in the middle of it, without a weapon.

"The FDLE did their usual crime-scene reconstruction."

"They came and talked to me," I said.

"You were a big help, no doubt."

"I never claimed to be a pro."

"Anyway, with their weapon count, a timeline, a string-and-glue web to re-create shots and trajectories, they came up short. They couldn't account for three projectiles. Almost like another person was there, popping with a gun. Their viewpoint was that some mystery person was working for us. A good guy who dropped out of nowhere, then went back to nowhere. So I've been thinking, maybe you saw someone with a weapon that day. Maybe you saw some person drop into a hole in the ground. Or fly away above the trees."

Wheeler and I had never discussed the incident. Sam had fired a pistol, had saved two lives. He had elected not to "get involved," and split before the confusion ended. He simply walked away. He may as well have flown above the trees.

"You got thirty seconds to answer," he said.

"Oh, a quiz show. Why don't you ask if a mouse lives on a far, distant planet?"

He turned his head. I kept facing forward.

He said, "Is that like you don't know, or it's out of your realm of understanding?"

"I'm thinking, no matter the answer, it'll never change our lives. Or anyone else's."

"You're flinging shit at me."

"You said it yourself. If there was a mystery man, he was a 'good guy.' Don't you have enough 'bad guy' cases to work on?"

Liska reacted with a loud silence, then a straw change. Out with the old, in with the new. He stayed quiet through Marathon traffic, then most of the Upper Keys.

As the sun set, green water and blue sky went to grays, steel-blue, and purple, then red and orange on the tallest clouds. Offshore islands became black worms at the dimming horizon, and distant lights spoke to me as they had to mariners two hundred years ago, as signs of life, possible enemies, navigation hazards. The ocean's surface looked as if someone had spread an immense vinyl mat atop a furrowed field. Closer were modern beacons, the flashing bulbs on microwave towers, reflective mile marker signs, lane lines, road turtles. I couldn't hear wind inside the Lexus, but felt us weave and yaw. The east wind carried mist, scattered leaves and paper scraps across the road. The evening looked cold. I knew it was seventy-five out there.

I rode in luxury, looked south into blackness. Who died first, Naomi or Steve? Did they die for the same or different reasons? Had it been, as I had suggested to Marnie, a murder-suicide?

Liska opened up again. "People in the Upper Keys have a great need to pull into traffic. They don't intend to go anywhere. They just want to grab pavement and slow us down."

I agreed with him. Big mistake. It fueled an elaboration.

"Some older people," he said, "they got nothing left to do in their lives but obey signs. They think they'll go straight to hell when they die if they ever get caught blowing the limit by two miles per hour. They obey to the fucking number. That's their whole program. Not speeding and not making peepee in their pants."

Liska hung a right beyond Mile Marker 94. We parked in a rock-and-shell lot next to Snapper's Waterfront Saloon. I smelled a lagoon and a kitchen. I could already taste beer.

Three thoughts came to mind while I walked into the restaurant. Did Liska really think he owed a favor to Sam for his vigilante act? Or would he try to coerce incriminating info out of Sam in exchange for his freedom? And why, with each passing day, did I feel like I knew less about the world around me?

None of this "Woe is me" crap, I told myself. I hadn't joined the club, hadn't earned the right.

I wasn't pissing my pants. I wasn't dead yet.

22

SNAPPER'S WAS A PERFECT word-of-mouth hangout. Hidden from highway traffic, it had an oval bar and water's-edge deck under five weathered fans and a thatched roof. This year's snowbirds had fled north, so locals ruled and every table was full. Servers scurried, with no time to talk or to steer us in some direction.

Liska grabbed a busboy and asked about a table. The kid pointed at a glass door. We went in, but a greeter turned us around, took us back out, and asked us to wait at the bar. I ordered a Corona, no lime. Chicken Neck said he wanted a Key Breeze. The woman bartender laughed, and Liska laughed with her. He settled for vodka and orange juice.

Five droopy-looking people sat at the bar, apparent leftovers from lunch hour. They had little to discuss except the smoking and drinking of people not present, and the repercussions of those habits. Last night's parties, last week's parties, who got told by the doctor that his liver looked like Swiss cheese, her lungs looked like oil sludge. Liska pulled the straw from his drink, chewed it like the last plastic in the world. Give him three hours in this crowd, he'd flatten his teeth.

I stepped away from the smoke and chatter. The U-shaped dock lined a south-facing cove edged by mangroves. A charter fishing boat bobbed in a slip. Signs promoted jet skis, skiffs, and pontoon boats for rent. I heard fish slap under the dock, saw large ripples and fat, twisting shadows. Tarpon scouting for scraps, I thought, and marveled at the power of french fries, the secret taming snack for the migratory beast.

Away from boozers and diners, my mind retreated. I nursed my beer, looked to Hawk Channel, saw lights beyond the reef, two south-bound ships, a single beacon. My thoughts bounced between Teresa and Naomi. For nine months I had believed that my affair with Teresa might last. We had stumbled into each other, connected, took it day by day. We thought alike, shared humor, swapped books. She knew current music better than I did, but rarely played CDs that I didn't enjoy. She had surprised me with her knowledge of jazz titles and musicians. Once she had shocked me by buying, in the same purchase, Merle Haggard's "Same Train, Different Time" and a Wynton Marsalis classical album. She even knew the names Townes Van Zandt and Gram Parsons.

I'd done my best to introduce her to the pleasures of Keys life. Sam and Marnie had taken us twice to the Snipes and Marvin Keys. We had strapped kayaks onto Sam's skiff so we could explore backcountry flats. The women had gone topless, come home with predictable sunburn. On the second trip we had lucked into a boater who had caught more yellowtail snapper than he needed. We even came across a pod of dolphin, and Sam had played a chase-and-run game with them that lasted ten minutes.

I had shown Teresa the Cuban restaurants, the Jamaican place on Front, the No Name Pub on Big Pine. I had insisted she read *The Young Wrecker on the Florida Reef*, and *Reap the Wild Wind*, Oliver Griswold's *The Florida Keys and the Coral Reef*, and McGuane's *Ninety-two in the Shade*. We never questioned our pasts or worried about our ages. But I was old enough to be her father. If I had to blame one thing for our falling apart, beyond the awful idea that she liked Randolph's company more than mine, I would pick the separation of years.

Yet that was an element that attracted me to Naomi. She may have had twenty-five on me, but it was never an issue. Her knowledge fascinated me. She never had complained of pains or fragility. I felt attracted, never turned off. I loved the life in her eyes, the sparkle and energy, her good cheer and optimism.

Liska rapped me on the shoulder. Someone led us to plastic chairs at a table under a Bud Light umbrella. A large man with styling gel in his crewcut approached us. Hair goo was a fashion stroke I had avoided.

"He called me about your buddy," said Liska.

The man addressed Liska as, "Sheriff, sir," and introduced himself as Denison McKinney. He ordered a virgin piña colada.

Liska winced at the order. "How long you been with Fish and Wildlife, McKinney?"

"I finished the academy three years ago this month."

"You specialized in what?"

"Water rescue, off-road vehicle pursuit, and man-tracking."

"You wrote yourself a ticket to the 'Glades."

"I did exactly that, sir."

Officer McKinney looked to be in great shape, what you see in military men: endurance and muscle without a weight lifter's bulk or the stringy, fat-free look of a distance runner. He was not a smiler, which told us he stayed on the serious side of everything. I blamed the paranoia that law enforcement people often develop, the result of seeing so much scum, of having no time or patience for civility, no room in the brain for the word "relax."

"Why all this for Sam Wheeler?" said Liska.

"Hang with me, sir," said McKinney. "It's a long answer, but I've had a few hours to think it through."

"We're here to listen," the sheriff said.

McKinney looked off to the mangroves. "I know my history," he said. "A century ago the state's game wardens guarded rookeries. They went after bird poachers, bad-ass rednecks harvesting egret plumes. It was a money crop that served the demands of urban fashion. Out in the sticks, for those wardens, it was dangerous. It still is, but it's more complicated today. We've got procedures, regulations, oversight boards and a half-dozen conservation groups hanging over our shoulders. Still, in the swamp, you go on frontier judgment, like the old days. You size up men on first glance. If you're wrong, you die, so you get good at it."

The piña colada arrived. I couldn't peg an age on the guy. Call it thirty, plus or minus six. Early baldness had raised his forehead, unless he was forty-five and fooling us. I wondered if his squint masked his constant study of every person and object around him. He was trained for the Everglades, the skeeter-gator home to bear and panther. He was trained to find more clever predators as well, and deliver them to prosecutors and courts.

"Where we going with this?" said Liska.

McKinney ignored his drink. "I've heard about Sam Wheeler for years. I never heard he was a flake. So when he tells me this and that happened, I want to believe him. I sized up Sam Wheeler, took into account his job, his reputation, the look in his eye, the words he spoke. I compared him to the Broward County weasels I heard on the radio. It was that simple. He said I should call you."

"I'm glad to hear that," said Liska.

"I'm glad I did it," said McKinney. "I called some Lower Keys guides this afternoon, a blind check to see if they'd recommend him for a fishing buddy. Chris Robinson, Andy Brackett, and Rob Reaser. Each said that Wheeler's straight ahead, a fish hawk, and a square dealer. No rage bubbling under his calm."

"What went down?"

"He said his sister was missing, probably dead. He tracked down another guy whose sister was missing, probably dead. Same scenario at the Broward morgue, a misidentified corpse and the same investigator. Right there he saw too big a coincidence. One o'clock today, broad daylight, he's pulled over by a Broward deputy in a road cruiser. No probable cause, every reason to think it's a setup. A motorcycle unit stopped to help, and the first deputy manufactured a bogus, off-the-wall charge.

Wheeler knew he was in danger. I don't know how, but he got on the one officer's motorcycle and ran for the county line. They fired weapons at him."

"Which county line?" said Liska.

"He wanted to go through Miami-Dade and get into Monroe before he was caught. I was on patrol by the immigration prison, out by Krome. I heard an all-frequencies alert on the rolling cycle. Right away I see him, I think I'm on a chase I want no part of. I started at six this morning, I'm ten minutes from quitting time. Next thing you know, he lights his blue flashers, pulls over, and parks it."

"He turned himself over to you?" said Liska.

"Yes, sir. He put his hands behind his neck, and said, 'Listen to me good.' He said his name and, right away, I don't tell him I know his rep, but I'm open to listening. He tells me why he ran, and asks me not to give him up to Broward. I tell him he hasn't broken the law in Miami-Dade. He says, 'How's this?' and comes at me, swings a couple that don't land. I'm thinking, stupid-ass me, I let a motorcycle thief get the jump on my ass. But he stops swinging and says, 'Now can you arrest me?' "

"He gives up, then fakes an assault?" I said.

McKinney's eyes were focused on a laminated menu. His mind was back on the roadside. "I'm thinking, this guy is scared shitless for a good reason. So the next thing, a Highway Patrol is the first unit on scene, like six minutes after first contact. I report the assault on me, the trooper runs the bust, and he's got no choice but to hand him to Miami-Dade."

"Why's he in a hospital?" said Liska.

"Our newfangled rules. I told the highway trooper that I had to whack him upside the head. Mr. Wheeler complained of dizziness, staggered a little. He got a mandatory visit to the emergency room. I wanted to make him more available to you. Eliminate the jailhouse routine."

My turn to speak. "How do we keep Miami-Dade from giving him up to Broward?"

Liska looked to the night sky. "Your friend Aghajanian. If we've got a civil rights complaint, the feds come in and freeze the works. You need to call in your tenth favor of the week."

Liska handed me his cellular.

I walked to the parking lot and ran my options. I didn't know the number in Monty's guest condo at La Brisa, so I tried the friend who had loaned Monty the place but got an answering service. Time to call the person I trusted most. Carmen's drowsy voice told me I'd owe a big payback for this one. I gave her Sam's story, condensed, and asked her to ask Monty if he knew agents in Miami who could look into a possible abuse of police powers.

"You want me to drive over to La Brisa now?" she said. "What if he's not there?"

"Leave him a note, ask him to call you."

"I should warn you," said Carmen. "My after-dark mileage rate for your errands is measured in quantities of Chardonnay."

I thanked her, clicked off, then checked my voice mail. Nothing.

I fought a mental picture of Teresa and Whit Randolph tapping glasses in Camille's.

My sandwich came to the table on a plate that read, COONAMESSETT INN, FALMOUTH, CAPE COD.

Liska said, "I don't know how you do it." He chewed his fish, stared at Denison McKinney.

"What's that?" said the officer.

"Swamp duty."

McKinney shrugged a shoulder, almost broke a grin. "I don't know, the mosquitoes don't bite me. I must be made of bug spray."

"Who do you talk to, the trees?"

"You got a better deal?"

Five minutes later, Liska handed me the tab. "Yours, bubba. You either got a brick or a wad of money in your pocket." He turned to McKinney. "If you drop charges, Broward can grab him."

"I can't drop. They don't let us claim assault, then forget about it. Sets a bad precedent for perps who want to hurt us."

"What am I saying?" said Liska. "I know that. But you can fail to show for a prelim hearing."

"Right. And get a letter of notation in my file."

"Unless you were assigned to my county at the time of the hearing. And you informed me of the hearing date, but it was me who forgot to inform the court. Would I be wrong to guess that Sam offered a few fishing trips?"

"A month's worth," said McKinney.

"Perfect," said Liska. "I need your expertise in . . ."

"Bonefish poaching?"

"Right, for thirty-one days, starting just before the hearing."

"Broward can still take him for arraignment, can't they?"

Liska shrugged. "That's down the road. We'll play the other side's game. We'll post bond, postpone, post whatever."

"If this will help . . ." McKinney worked a folded letter-sized page from his pocket. "I had a deputy friend in Broward fax me the arrest form."

Liska and I walked to the car. "Your job, Rutledge, first thing tomorrow, is to get his ass a lawyer."

"Long drive into Miami, this time of night," I said.

"No lie," said Liska. "We're useless until seven A.M., anyway."

Twelve minutes later I bought two rooms at the Marriott, Key Largo. We live in the age of credit cards. Liska showed his badge so the clerk would take my cash and let me use the phone.

Before we hit the elevator, Liska led me outside to a windy patio. "I don't want to walk into a hornet's nest tomorrow morning. I want every fucking detail in your pea brain right now, on the table."

"That arrest form you got from McKinney? See if Broward's complaining officer is Detective Odin Marlow."

"Shit," said Liska, dumfounded. "Where'd you get him? There can't be two of them."

"He's part of what I'm about to tell."

"Marlow's a born crook. The Key West Police Department fired his ass twenty years ago. He should've gone to Raiford instead of out the door."

Sam had said, *"I think I'll find something, with Marlow attached."*

McKinney had said, *"You size up other men. If you're wrong, you die, so you get good at it."*

Liska held the arrest report up to catch a beam of light. He shook his head. "I don't see his name anywhere. I don't see a detective on here."

I spun the long version for him, for the second time, with more detail. The ME's dawn call, Lorie Wheeler's ID papers held by the dead woman, and our lunch with Odin Marlow. I told him about Marlow's suggesting a private detective and explained about the photo of Lorie, how Wally Loads had tipped Sam to Barry Marcantonio's search for his sister. For the sake of Bobbi Lewis's job security, I said nothing about her matching addresses to license numbers.

Liska digested the story. "Here's how I take it," he said. "Not finding Marlow on the arrest form's a bad sign. If it's dirty deputies, it's bigger than just one asshole. If it's not, then Sam guessed wrong, and he ran from a legit traffic stop."

"You don't think Sam can see a roust from a mile away?" I said.

"You ever sit on a sea grape, and not know it? You're the last one to find out you got a stain on your pants that looks like crap. Don't answer that. I can see I've already stumped you. What I'm saying, they could've pulled him over because of a minor infraction, simple as that."

With a look of doubt and sympathy, I agreed.

He said, "You're in the bars every so often, right?"

"Not like I used to be. You get past your thirties, the hangovers start to climb the Richter scale."

"You ever see Yvonne Gomez out there, chumming up to the boys? Or hanging close to one particular man?"

"Nope," I said. "But I promise you, I wasn't paying attention."

"I didn't think you'd be the type for late-night drunken calls, Alex," said Annie Minnette. "I also can't picture you with a broken heart, or missing me in the slightest."

The clock on the bedside table said eleven-ten. "I've had two beers, total. I could drink eight more and still be sober."

"Uh-oh."

"This isn't about me, Annie. Sam needs a lawyer."

"There aren't enough attorneys in Key West?"

"Miami-Dade and Broward," I said.

"Both?"

"For the moment," I said. "Mostly Broward."

"Why would Sam be north of Marathon?"

I gave her the ninety-second version, during which I heard a man's voice on her end of the line. The voice stopped, shut up by a "mute" button or by her shushing a real human. I was proud of myself. I hadn't stumbled, hadn't reacted to the possibility that Annie had company. Why wouldn't she?

Annie and I had lived together on Dredgers Lane for three years. She had initiated our split, blaming the island atmosphere for her wish to leave. She had worked for Pinder Curry and Sawyer in Key West, and had moved north to start with a firm in Pompano Beach. Beyond that I knew only that she had bought a new car—a lunatic had destroyed her Beetle convertible before she left town—and a new house near Boca Raton.

"I'll meet you at the corrections infirmary," she said. "It's called Ward D, which stands for either detention or disgusting. Better yet, we should meet outside the main entrance. Tell me what time."

"I don't know. We're in Key Largo."

"I've got to make one stop first thing tomorrow. I can't be there until a few minutes after eight."

"It'll be good to see you," I said.

"Yes," she said. "Let's deal with that after we deal with Sam."

She got her money's worth in law school.

I called Sam's house. Marnie was still awake. I told her where I was.

"I'm worried to death, Alex. Bobbi Lewis called tonight. She said Sam's in a jam. Why would she be calling me?"

I gave her a shorter version of the short version I had given Annie. "It's Dinner Party Sam, like you said, doing what he has to do."

"And I can't change him, so I'll never try. At least I've got you to talk to."

"Before I forget," I said, "do you still have those addresses I gave you?"

"I gave them to Sam when he called this afternoon."

"I need them, too."

"Wait a minute. Are you ready to write?"

I copied them, then said, "Get some sleep. Things aren't going to slow down."

"I won't sleep. I worked my ass off on a piece, and the *Citizen* won't let me run it. I mean, Mayor Steve Gomez died. At least *ask* the question . . ."

"It's only part of the story," I said. "Find Teresa, warn her however you can. Randolph may be a key to Steve and Naomi. He may be their killer."

"Yvonne Gomez better watch out, too. I saw them walking down Front Street today."

"Together?"

"Kind of, but more like he was bothering her and she wanted to escape."

"You need to look into him," I said.

"I need more than allegations to write a story."

"How about this? Randolph subscribes to a message service in Redmond, Washington. I think it's a Seattle suburb. That's where those Mallory Square dome developers were from, the ones who pitched the commission."

212

"The BFD people?"

"You want to stir up some shit, see if you can get those people to admit knowing Randolph."

"It's a tangled web, Alex."

"That's how carpetbaggers baffle the locals. Tangle it up, hang it with dollar signs."

"I meant, of course, your imagination," she said.

"Wait and see," I said. "Reality's always more devious."

"I was getting to that. You and Sam bought into a partnership a long time ago."

"Is that a question?"

"Did you?"

"Like, in our grand investor days?" I said. "Throwing out dollars to see if they'd stick? Lighting our cigars with bad checks?"

"Like a shopping center and condominium island near the top of Cow Key Channel? The Borroto Brinas Development Corporation?"

That one hit home. "Was that the thing Sam heard about on the docks, that hot tip?"

"Keep going."

"That thousand bucks that was going to make me a tycoon. I was going to buy a thirty-eight-foot sailboat and cruise to the Virgin Islands. Hell, I kissed that cash good-bye before I bought my house. I remember wishing I had it to add to my down payment."

"Could it have been two thousand dollars? And Sam, four grand, a total of six thousand?"

Oh, crap. "Is this your Gomez research? The old land deal that's coming before the commission?"

"You got it. According to my source, Mayor Gomez held the swing vote. Or he controlled the anti-growth faction, however you want to phrase it."

"Was his vote going to make us rich?"

"Gomez was against it," she said. "You were going to lose the money you already kissed off."

"And now?"

"It'll pass without him there to focus opposition. Even the city attorney thinks that the permits and permissions are legal. He thinks that rejecting the proposal will lead to an endless, expensive court battle."

"Will our names be associated with it?"

"Oh, yes," she said.

"Twenty-year reputations down the tubes?"

"Unless you two can ride in on white horses and save the town from the dragon."

"Can you keep our names out of the paper until we get back?"

"I'll try."

23

A TAP ON THE door, too early for housekeeping. I'd been half-awake for an hour, serenaded by water pipes. Why start your morning while it's still yesterday? I cracked the door, feigned caution, but I knew.

Liska pushed his way in, smelling of Listerine and Right Guard. He looked bald with wet hair. He jammed the *Miami Herald* at me, opened to the Florida Keys section.

A sconce in the hallway lit the headline: GOMEZ MURDERED.

The phone rang. I stumbled to answer it as Liska yanked the curtain cord. A painful reveille, and a dull, cloudy sky.

Marnie, in tears. "I'm quitting this fucking job."

"I haven't read it yet," I said. "Did they link Gomez to Naomi?"

"No."

"Then they can't have the whole story. That part's still yours."

"They wouldn't have shit if somebody wasn't spoon-feeding. I'm going to buy every copy on the island and throw them in my boss's office."

Liska twirled his hand, urging me to hurry.

I said, "Your boss wouldn't feed a story to the competition."

"He wouldn't let me run what I had."

Give her hope, I thought. "Follow up on what I said last night. It's still your scoop, and you'll get it right. Be careful."

"Being right isn't as good as being first," she said.

"Listen to yourself, Marnie."

"Bring Sam home," she said.

Out of my power, but I would try.

I said, "I will," and hung up.

"Let's hit the trail, Mr. Good Guy," barked Liska. "I already checked us out. You owe me eight bucks for two toll calls." He looked like he'd shaved four times. I could see the Sports section reflected on his chin.

I headed for the bathroom. "Do I have time to shower?"

"No. Forty minutes from now I want to be their first customer, bright and shiny. They think cops in the Keys all sleep till noon. I want to take them by surprise."

"This is your advanced course in police tactics?"

"'How to Hurry' is my basic. 'How to Wait' is advanced. You should wet your hair before you comb it. By the way, how did the *Citizen* reporter know you were...? Never mind. I appreciate the irony. That's what makes my job."

"How good for you," I said. "I thrive on sarcasm, myself."

We hit the Eighteen-Mile Stretch. Northbound traffic was frantic and fast. Bumper jumpers, sharks, clueless voyagers baffled by the world's pace. I read the *Herald* while Liska dealt with commuting Key Largo residents and people trying to make midmorning flights out of Miami.

"You're reading some real Shinola," said Liska. "Except for our dedicated medical examiner, it's a thin piece. It's based on a tip, speculation, and that quote from Larry Riley. Read that out loud, where he said about blood."

"'Based on rigidity and lividity, the time of death is consistent with the time frame in which the body was found. Based on bloodstain volume, the location of death is in question.'"

"I will have Dexter's dick on a butcher's block for this," said Liska.

"I know what he did. The schmuck mouthed off because I swiped his case."

"You're sure it's him?"

"You get to the part about Gomez's watch? Read that part to me."

" 'Police sources have confirmed that the owner of Lowry's Island Pawn, in compliance with city theft liaison laws, on Wednesday turned in a gold Rolex watch inscribed on the back, "for SWG with Love." The pawn shop employee who loaned against the watch is being sought for questioning.' "

I owed Duffy Lee Hall ten bucks.

"That's pure city info," said Liska. "If it wasn't Dexter, it was somebody five feet away from him. What did you tell Marnie Dunwoody last night?"

"I suggested the Whit Randolph connection."

"Now she'll get caught in a mess."

"I told her to be careful."

Liska waggled his head. "You forget she's a woman?"

"I'd love to quote you on that one," I said. "How many years were you married?"

Chicken Neck glared at the windshield.

"Sorry, that's personal," I said. "Who's your best detective?"

"I pulled her off the Gomez case this morning."

"Jesus Christ. Lewis was the only one who gave a shit."

"That's part of our problem," said Liska. "We solve this, bust somebody, get it to trial, put her on the stand, and ka-blam. A decent defense attorney could blow our case to Cuba. Don't ask me why. I'm not open to discuss it."

Bobbi Lewis's secret romance was no secret.

"Is she still on Naomi Douglas?" I said.

"At this point, she'd be lucky to get crossing guard duty."

I kept my mouth shut. On the chance that my guess was not correct, and Lewis's affair with Steve Gomez was not the problem, I didn't want to reveal something else that could hurt her.

We hit the top of the Keys, the billboards for auto dealerships, cellular phone services, Seminole airboat swamp rides. Vehicles around us paid no attention to 45 MPH signs coming into Florida City. I tried to read the newspaper, but couldn't focus. I kept thinking ahead to my first face-to-face with Annie Minnette in a year, and the sad irony that I might split with another housemate in days ahead.

When Annie and I had parted, we had assured each other that our three years together had been rich ones. She had taken to island life, to tropical plants and Cuban cooking. She had soaked up nautical atmosphere, the casual approach locals took to dress and dining. She had blended well with the attorneys, courts, and alliances of the Key West legal maze. Yet something behind her spark, her smile, caused turmoil in her mind. She never had shared that part of herself with me. Until she left me.

I had caught myself several times comparing Teresa Barga to Annie. The moments had thoroughly confused me. Smiles are smiles, and smarts are smarts, but attributes and drawbacks can't be tallied on a net basis. Each woman had found another man. When I found time to question reasons, my vanity would blame vagaries of youth. If time allowed, I might consider the comfort I found in Naomi Douglas. I wondered if I would miss her more than two women less than half her age.

Liska knew Miami, the timing and flow of rush hour. He shifted lanes at key moments, chose quick-toll queues, and never got receipts. We did the turnpike to the airport exit, then crept 836 to within six blocks of Jackson Memorial. He knew his way into the hospital complex, didn't hesitate to blow three straight stop signs. He was a man on a mission.

Annie stood at the main entrance. She wore a khaki-colored business suit with a knee-length skirt and low-heeled leather shoes. Her hair looked much shorter, darker, no longer light brown and sun-streaked. Mirrored oval sunglasses rested on her high cheekbones.

Liska rolled to a stop where she stood. His electric locks snapped to the open position, and he used his controls to lower my window. "Get in," he said to her. "We can chat before we do anything."

I reached behind me to open the door.

Annie didn't smile, nodded slightly. "Thanks, no. I'll stay right here. I can make a call or two while I wait for you to park."

"I'll get out," I said.

The locks snapped again. "No," said Liska.

Do we have a controlling nature?

We prowled the lot, searching for a space. Liska wedged us between a PT Cruiser and new Buick. "Defensive parking," he said. "You put it next to four-door cars, you reduce door ding exposure."

His life's structure was low on my list of topics. We had to hike two hundred yards back to Annie. Halfway in I said, "Why did I stay in the car?"

"I'm the coach, and you're the water boy."

"I appreciate your being here, as does Sam, I'm sure. So I'll wait a few days to ask you what the hell that means."

"Yeah, Rutledge, good idea. Wait a year."

Our mood was as lovely as our controlling nature.

Annie closed out a call in time to greet us. She extended her hand to give my knuckles a frat-man crunch. Got to be tough in the mean halls of justice.

"Let's get going," said Liska. He had no time for trivial crap like two old friends saying hello.

"Are you here regarding related charges, sir?" Annie replied. "Or separate charges in Monroe County?"

Liska looked off to the pewter sky, inhaled theatrically, then exhaled out the side of his mouth. "I'm sure you're an honest, ethical attorney, Ms. Minnette. But you need to blow the attitude right out your ass."

"Okay, that's fine," said Annie. "Why don't you put your face down there? Tell me when it's loose."

Liska twisted his head to me, went bug-eyed, then turned back to

Annie. "I didn't drive this goddamn far to work *against* Sam Wheeler, counselor. In Monroe County, he's a solid citizen. I want him on the street as bad as you do. If you go in first, the cops and their bosses won't tell me shit. Right now, if any of us has power at all, I'm the best fucking card you got. Tell me how you want to play."

Annie said, "You better watch your language, or they won't believe your badge. You talk more like an attorney than a cop."

"Is that a yes?"

"It's an apology. I should have worked my brain before my mouth. If you had any charges against him, you'd still be in Key West. You would have sent two deputies and told Alex to take a hike."

"I hope you're an expert on law like you're an expert on me."

"I am," she said.

I felt like I was at a boxing match, counting jabs and uppercuts, pulled punches, hooks, and kidney shots. I said, "If Sam's up to it, see if he can tell you the name of the assistant medical examiner who called him on Monday."

Liska stepped closer, almost to my face. I smelled sour coffee and old Listerine. "I'll do what I can." He dropped his voice so Annie couldn't hear him. "I want to know what went down on Southard three months ago."

Tit for tat was on the table.

He would be pissed when nothing came to him.

He flipped his badge for a security guard and strode into the building.

After about twenty seconds of silence, Annie said, "Guess I blew it."

Her summary was shallow. By slamming Liska, she had accused me of bringing an enemy to the fort. Shut up and keep it positive, I told myself, if only for Sam.

"I called about posting bond," she said.

"I brought money."

She shook her head. "It's a no-go."

I caught cologne that jumped my thoughts back two years, to that exact scent combined with odors of sex, images of Annie shivering and pushing. *Focus, Rutledge. How many more men has she had by now?*

"They can't think he's a flight risk," I said. "He's lived in the same house in Key West for twenty years."

"Miami-Dade has him for assault on a police officer. That's off the scale. Broward's list starts with suspicion of murder, police motor vehicle theft, and resisting arrest. He'll have to face judges in both counties for bond hearings."

"Even for trumped-up charges?"

"That's in the movies, Alex. If, by some chance, they're all phony claims, there's a benefit. The accusing officers have to perjure themselves from the start. The more cops lie, the more chances we have to find cracks in their stories. You need to tell me everything, a timeline with every detail."

So I did. I hurried with the call, the flight, and the failed identity match. I emphasized our lunch with Marlow, and Sam's reaction, his open-ended plan for satisfaction. Annie knew Sam from her years in Key West. She agreed that his mission sounded off-the-wall, agreed with my prediction of no happy ending. I spun it from Odin Marlow to Wally Loads, the tip on Marcantonio, then gave her Denison McKinney's tale about the stolen motorcycle, the chase, the fake assault, and his reaction to Sam's side of things.

I quit talking. Annie fixed her eyes on a distant object. I let her digest the details, watched cars pass, two of them stop to drop off elderly women. A funky old green Cavalier sputtered by, wandered down an aisle in search of a parking slot. I could have told the driver he might find a space in a nearby zip code, but he would have to hitchhike in for his appointment.

Annie said, "You always had good sales pitch, Alex."

"You agree it sounds fishy?"

"Between you and me, it's fishy. We know Sam, and we know he doesn't steal Harleys and he doesn't attack Fish and Wildlife officers. My problem is, I have to peddle this to at least two judges, in one-third as many words."

"He isn't allowed to tell his story?"

"You might say that. This is Miami, Alex."

"With different rules?" I said. "What did they do, ship the Constitution to Haiti with a load of rusty bikes?"

"Crime here is crazy. That's not news to you. What you don't know is that I haven't met a judge who isn't burned out. They're impatient, and they make fast decisions. They look to us for guilty pleas with apologies, and not-guilty pleas with proof. They don't like complicated stories, and they hate defendants who cry 'dirty cop' and 'frame-up.' If I suggest conspiracy, I will have, from that moment onward, the credibility of a shoplifter who forgot a lamp was under my dress. Your story sounds good. You've laid a groundwork that suggests something fishy, which even in Miami isn't a legal term yet. I'm a good lawyer, but I can't be a miracle worker."

"Give me hope," I said.

"I'll bust my ass for Sam Wheeler. But the big word in my little speech was 'proof.' If we don't have it, Sam's fucked."

"Is that a legal term in Miami?"

"You better believe it is."

"You've come a long way from selling Guatemalan blouses on Duval Street," I said.

"I sometimes wonder why I didn't settle for that instead of the rat race. I keep reminding myself, if I can put up with eight years of the grind, I can be set for life. I also could age twenty in eight, and be in a car wreck the day I quit my job. How are you doing, aside from the way you look?"

"Liska dragged me up here on instant notice. These day-old clothes, I'm lucky to have my shoes. In a larger sense, because I know what you meant, I haven't had time to change much. Same town, same lane, same house."

"Are you with someone, or is that topic taboo?"

"Not taboo," I said. "But it's a bad one this week. She ran into an old friend. They had too good a reunion."

"You didn't suspect?" she said.

"She was out of the house a lot, but she works hard. If I suspected one thing, I'd have to suspect everything. That would take all my time. It's easier on my nervous system to trust."

"And then get hurt?"

"Twice in a row my roommates have gone astray."

"Including me, I gather."

I nodded. "Why is that, do you suppose?"

"Women are assholes?"

"Usually it's men," I said. "I guess these days, to be correct, we can give you equal time."

"Oh, no," she laughed. "In the category of assholes, we took our equal time years ago. We caught this disease of trading up. It's one thing to think about better jobs, but people stress over the size of their homes and cars. The next step, they compare their children and spouses, for Christ's sake. They can't exactly trade in their children for next year's model, but so many of them trade up partners . . ."

"Has anyone ever heard of contentment?"

"I'm guilty, too. I thought if I left Key West I'd enjoy my work a lot more. Now I hate West Palm. The whole place smells like cars."

"I've heard that."

"From the first day I drove up U.S. 1, I've missed Key West, but I couldn't come back. First off, I couldn't face you for what I did. That's why you get the rare e-mail and zero harassment."

I hated to think that the word "harassment" applied, but she had broken my heart. I wouldn't have wanted to hear from her too soon after the split. Now it was good to see her. She looked as if she had been taking better care of herself. Many women fail to do that on the island. They don't see the slow damage of sun, late nights in smoky bars, and salt air. They let things slide, cut corners on trying to maintain their health. Some gave up entirely, and the progression of aging warps upward. Except, perhaps, for the sunlight, Annie had not let that happen. Now she looked "big city," with an appealing hairstyle, a touch more makeup, her clothing bought in specialty stores.

Annie said, "Do you think Liska can do any good in there?"

I had no idea what he could do or what he intended. Something steered me in another direction. Hadn't Sam described the Cavalier's color as "puke green," with a license number that began with XSW? I could swear the plate that had just passed us matched up.

Marlow was on the case.

"Can I borrow your phone?" I picked my memory for Liska's cell number.

Before I could bring it up, he walked outside, clenching his teeth. He got into Annie Minnette's face. "Young lady, you'd better be the best goddamned lawyer in this county. You've got a supreme shithead for a client. He'll waste your time bad as he wasted mine."

"In my experience," Annie said calmly, "the time wasters are law officers with narrow minds."

"If I didn't have an open mind," he said, "I'd be a hundred and forty miles from here. I'd be eating ropa vieja at El Siboney, reminding myself to stop at the dry cleaner's on my way back to work. I'll eat lunch there tomorrow, and I'll remind myself that no way does the douchebag captain appreciate my making this trip. He thought I could drop a dime and spring his ass loose, a move simple and stupid like that. Rutledge, here, needs to check his buddy's medicine chest, see if the boy's dropping diet pills or mood-repair tablets."

"This is helpful, Sheriff," said Annie. "What am I supposed to do with it?"

"Do whatever you people do. But imagine a fifty-foot fence across the top of the Keys. I'll be on one side, in my simple, small county down there. All this bullshit will still be up in Florida. We'll be fine neighbors." He began to walk. "Rutledge, you and me, we got one more thing to do."

"Run along," said Annie Minnette, contempt cold on her face. "I'll mop up the mess."

I shrugged my shoulders.

She shook her head.

I looked back from a hundred yards away. She was in the same spot, speaking into her phone.

24

PEOPLE WITH BADGES IN their wallets fear traffic tickets like they fear ants. Liska left the hospital complex the same way he had arrived. He dropped his Lexus to squad car status—all gas pedal, minimal brakes, no concern for tire wear. I scoped people around us, on sidewalks, in other cars. His hot corners and wheel chirps didn't turn a head.

Sad, I thought. In Miami, the word "reckless" had lost its charm.

We were off surface streets, westbound on 836 in four minutes. My mood matched the dirty gray sky. We had wasted a trip, squandered time, blown money, knew nothing, and hadn't helped Sam. I was wedged into the leather, trying to invent a new plan of attack. If I asked our destination, I'd incite a new volley of cynical crap. I was over it.

I figured it out soon enough, anyway. My clue was the LeJeune Road exit. When we turned into Miami International, I knew. After days of wanting that magic flight off the island, my first leg to Grand Cayman, I was about to be dispatched in the opposite direction. Straight back to the rock. Which made no sense. If Liska was going to pack me off, why had he brought me in the first place? He must have known that our mission might not succeed. He had gone into the hospital with a grim outlook, and walked out with worse and me to blame. Something inside had yanked his chain.

I thought fast, trying to evaluate my bind. A short-notice air ticket would cost me a fortune. My best choice was a cab to the Greyhound station, then joyriding the Overseas Highway with a pint of rum, a lime, a bag of Doritos, and a paperback. Hell, I could buy a book with blank pages, kill time writing my diary. Or I could reenact my post-Navy days and thumb down the Keys, catch a tan and count pelicans as I walked the bridges.

We stopped in front of the American check-in booth. Liska double-parked next to a hotel shuttle van, blocking another van that was trying to leave.

I wasn't going to mess with my cameras and duffel. They'd be safe in the trunk. I said, "What time's my flight?"

"That's funny." He popped the locks. "Let me tell you, if I find one stone chip, one hickey in the windshield, a door ding, God forbid . . ."

"You remind me of Detective Lewis two days ago," I said. "Forty-eight hours ago, to the minute."

"Go ahead."

"You dip your toe in the water, then pull your leg back in the boat."

"Your point?" he said.

"I wonder why you did this. Your wild, goddamned hurry, all fact-finding, worried about impressing big-city cops, worried about Sam. Then you rush even worse to get away. Justice goes to the back of the line. You got a hot date in Key West?"

Liska tilted his rearview mirror, checked his teeth for foreign objects. Not that we had seen food since Key Largo. He said, "Did it occur to you that I've got other things on my desk besides a self-important fishing captain and his fucked-up ideas about crooked cops?"

"No, it didn't," I said, "but I know you don't waste time with sub-tlety. And anything I think about you, I should twist it a hundred and eighty. I can warn myself ahead of time about your bullshit."

"My bullshit's all in Key West, thanks to the *Herald*. The murdered mayor is national news, and Simonton Street's a mess with TV trucks and satellite bowls and fucknuts with video gear. So, there you are, Rutledge. This is your best day to commit a publicity-free crime in Miami. Every local station sent their news crew to the end of U.S. 1."

I quit arguing and commanded myself to look at the good side. I wasn't buying an air ticket.

"My pistol's in the glove box. Don't use it, even on yourself. Fill the tank with high test and watch that speed trap in Marathon. Even in my car, I can't get you out of traffic tickets. You ought to hit Stock Island about five-thirty, so come straight to my office. Don't make me wait." He flung open his door without checking for traffic and disappeared into the terminal.

I exited the airport, hurrying to read signs, changing lanes like braiding a camp lanyard. I went right on LeJeune, tried to keep my distance from road hacks and crazies. Three blocks later I pulled into an El Cheapo gas station. I went inside, hurdled the language barrier, and swapped the clerk singles for two pounds of change. Throwing sanitation worries to the winds, I dialed the greasy pay phone on the outside wall between the rest rooms. Five messages waited on my service in Key West.

Monty Aghajanian left his number at the borrowed condo. "Don't wait to call me. I might be at the pool, but I'll have a handset with me."

Jack Spottswood said, "Problems at this end, Alex. Keep it to yourself, but Naomi may have died of a painkiller overdose. One of her life insurance policies is too new to cover suicide. That could screw us up paying estate taxes and expenses. Any luck on finding Ernest Bramblett? Call me as soon as you get back from Grand Cayman. By the way, today's *Herald* says that Steve Gomez might have been murdered."

Marnie Dunwoody, with no surprise: "The county people grabbed Whit Randolph this morning. They found him at Garrison Bight, trying to charter a boat to Ft. Myers. When he saw two marked cars arrive, he chugged his bottle of vodka and dialed out on his phone. They grabbed his phone when they arrested him, and cross directoried the call to a shitbird lawyer in New Orleans who specializes in scam artists. The slime also rises. I'm working three stories at once. I know you would have called me if you had any good news. Call me anyway."

I now understood why Chicken Neck Liska was in a hurry to get back to his office. The dead mayor was a major media splash while a prize prisoner, another headline-maker, was chilling in his Stock Island high-security motel. His circus needed a ringmaster.

Teresa, in tears: "Whitney is under arrest, and I hope you had nothing to do with that. I have to move back into my condo so no one will break in and rip him off while he's in jail. I told Carmen to keep an eye on your house. Did you cancel Grand Cayman? Dexter thought you went up the Keys with the sheriff. If you want to, you can call me at my old number. I want you to."

Duffy Lee Hall: "Our man Dexter Hayes came to the house five minutes ago. He knocked like a storm trooper, almost pushed the door in. He wanted your Gomez negatives. I told him, if I even had them, I couldn't give them away. He threatened a search warrant, told me he'd have my water shut off and my business license revoked. He threatened to bust me for obstruction of justice. I told him he was obstructing my porch, and he could fucking well get a warrant. My whole neg file just went to my neighbor's cigar humidor."

Monty answered the first ring. Even on vacation, his FBI habits never rested. He asked what kind of phone I was on. I told him the pay unit didn't have a logo. He explained that he didn't want me on a cordless or cell unit. He didn't want to chat on an electronic party line.

"So we're cleared to talk, now?" I said.

"Yep. I came inside to take a break. I'm on the wall phone up here," he said. "Where are you right now?"

I told him where I was and that I hadn't seen Sam.

"I called a man in Kendall. He's agreed to help your buddy on the QT. But he said he wouldn't do anything unless you backed off, so stay away."

"Okay," I said, without much hesitation. If the FBI could pull a trick for Sam, I wasn't going to spoil it. I couldn't get into the hospital, anyway.

"What else?" said Monty.

"Marnie Dunwoody left me a message. The county grabbed Randolph, whatever his name really is."

"I heard," said Monty. "I think they screwed up royally. If they had taken time to find an open out-of-state warrant, they could've sat on him for days while he fought extradition. The county would've had time to solidify the murder details. They were in too big a hurry. On the penny-bet charge they put on his ass, a small-time, white-collar snooze, he can bond out tonight. What's with this Bobbi Lewis, anyway?"

"You didn't deal with her in the old days?" I said.

"Damn, you make it sound prehistoric. It was only a year ago. No, I never dealt with her."

"She's the best Liska's got, for my money. But she dropped the ball this time. Liska pulled her from dealing with Gomez. Between you and me, she had a fling with the victim a couple years go."

"Tell me how she dropped the ball."

"Look, I don't have your training," I said. "I was on her elbow some of the time. To me, she was hot-cold, hot-cold. Does that make sense?"

"Can you tell me specifics?"

"She went to Naomi's house, all torqued up, ready to be a prime snoop. Then she stood around absorbing vibrations, taking telepathic statements from the furniture, or ghosts, for all I knew. Then she beat feet, like the place was poison. She said she'd be in touch."

"Keep going."

"That was Wednesday afternoon. That night, nine o'clock, I was back at Naomi's, into her computer, looking for a way to find her brother. He's heir to her house and the money."

"What's it to you?" said Monty.

"Naomi named me her executor."

"You forgot to tell me that detail. What happened that night?"

"She came to the door and wanted in. I figured, nothing to lose, so I vacated. That was the last I heard of it. She never told me what she found, if anything. She didn't say a thing. I asked Liska if she'd filed a report, and he didn't know what I was talking about."

"Where are you going to be?" said Monty.

"Liska had me drop him at the airport. He ordered me to drive his wheels back to the rock, posthaste. There will be no scratches, bugs, or ancillary damage."

"Best news all day," said Monty. "You owe me many beers. Remember my message from that other guy. Capital letters: back off."

"Gotcha."

"Take it easy, Alex."

No way.

I dreaded the drive down the Keys. It was Friday noon, and tourists were filling the funnel. U.S. 1 was a slender spout, an insistent rush complicated by pickups towing huge powerboats, sluggish motor homes, unpassable packs of motorcycles, idiotic stop-and-go.

What waited? My deal with Teresa was history. My old investment in the Borroto Brinas Development Corporation would make me the butthole of environmental correctness. Calculating ahead, I was already late to Liska's office. That promised another barrage of crap.

Four days ago, to the minute, I was climbing out of a ratty taxi. I escaped a bad radio show, a rear seat that had witnessed sex, spilled drinks, and vomit. I had taken refuge in a storm culvert next to a bland morgue. Now I was in a squeaky-clean, climate-controlled luxury boat, free to exercise my choice of not listening to Chicken Neck's pitiful CD collection. The primary change was that four days ago I knew more about the world around me.

I formed a picture of Annie Minnette's face, her cold expression as Liska and I walked away. Not exactly a painless reunion. She was back in her office by now, playing intramural brain tag with the partners and paralegals. I had no idea what she could do, if anything. I also had no confidence in Monty's friend, his agreement to help Sam "on the QT." For some reason, right then, I ran a mental movie of Sam's father, leaving his nine-year-old daughter on a backwater roadside. That did it.

I couldn't leave Miami with Sam still a prisoner, falsified into limbo. Someone, likely Marlow, but perhaps others too, had wanted to stop Sam's snooping. That meant that he was on to something, getting close to answers about dead women with bogus IDs. I needed to grab for threads, for facts that might take me to those answers and might tip me to the depth of Sam's problems.

I went back into El Cheapo and learned that my Spanish sucked. I tried to buy a Ft. Lauderdale street map. The clerk thought I wanted directions to Cartagena, Colombia. We had a wide gap to cross. The guy yelled, "Maria!" as if he was cussing. A dark-skinned, black-haired girl, a six-, maybe seven-year-old, popped her head from behind the counter. She let go a burst of tremolo Spanish then ducked back down. All I caught from her verbal burst was "Broward." Thirty seconds later I had my map.

Back in the car, I shuffled the dwindling ten grand and the notes in my pocket, found the addresses that Marnie had recited to me on the phone.

My list of options. So much for backing off.

25

FIRST STOP, THE OTHER brother of a missing sister. At worst, he could understand Sam's plight. At best, he might offer help in some form I couldn't imagine.

Miami traffic runs at two speeds. A full-stop jam can park you for hours. The map told me to take the Palmetto, but common sense argued a traffic snarl. I went back to 836, then north on I-95, and lucked into a balls-to-the-wall phase at a steady seventy. I kept a watch for Odin's green Cavalier while I clear-sailed to Griffin Road. No one out there but me and ten thousand maniacs, most of them in small Japanese cars that sounded like pissed-off large-winged mosquitoes.

I was northbound, with no sun, a different approach. With my scattered frame of mind, I didn't make the connection. After going west a half-mile on Griffin, I recognized the route our cab had taken on Monday. I was driving the path that Sam and I had taken to the Broward Medical Examiner's Lab.

I pulled over to check the map. Sure as hell, Barry Marcantonio's odd-numbered address backed up to Southwest 31st Avenue. The only way I could reach his place was to drive past the lab. He had moved from South Carolina to a spot fifty yards from the morgue. Coincidence went to hard fact. In his search for his sister, he was ten steps ahead of Sam, but they were hunting the same rat.

The Lockwood Estates mobile home park was all speed bumps, hanging planters, and sprinkler heads. A few trailers had trellises, cute mailboxes, striped awnings. I saw no open doors, humans, or animals. Also, no Camry, license tag MJC-547.

I parked in Barry's short driveway, walked to his door. Fat raindrops hit my face and arms. The wind kicked and shrubs tossed, preludes to a squall. An ominous prelude to my inquiries.

Under the trailer home's corroded aluminum awning, two parched aloe plants sat on a cheap iron rack. His door had a dead bolt and a peephole. He had shut his miniblinds, installed antitheft clamps on his window frames. A fake-looking decal told me the trailer was under constant security watch.

A man's muffled voice came from nearby: "He ain't home."

Not so fake a decal.

I turned, saw no one. I shouted, "What time does he get home?"

The rain fell harder.

"He ain't home!"

Brilliant.

I hustled back to the Lexus, drove around to Southwest 31st. No sign of Marlow's green Chevy, but he could be driving a county car or anything else. I counted the ass-ends of mobile homes until I found Barry's. His west-facing rear window was the only one in the line of trailers not covered by reflective foil. Again, no surprise. He had lucked into a perfect home, with a clear view of the morgue's service road.

What had Goodnight Irene Jones said? *"I saw what came through the back, the messes they offloaded."*

I felt like a detective. I knew that two men were running parallel courses. But if his mission was to watch the morgue, where was Barry? Had he hit the same legal roadblock as Sam? Or illegal roadblock? On second thought, I felt like a failed detective. Every answer led me to more questions. The more I learned the less I knew.

The rain hit harder, the windshield began to fog. The wipers came on automatically, as did the defroster. I was living in luxury.

Odin Marlow's place in Pembroke Pines was in a group of six two-story buildings, six townhouses each, all in need of paint. They wrapped around a paved parking lot and a littered Dumpster plaza. No guard gate, no class, but no speed bumps. Casuarina trees and scrawny olean-der failed to break the monotony. I counted seventeen parked vehicles, two with windows open to drizzling rain.

I angled into the slot nearest Odin's unit, but still had to walk sixty feet to a door with no awning. Like the trailer court a half hour earlier, no animals or people around. I almost pressed the bell, but caught myself. I had no idea what to say if someone opened the door. I could claim I was looking for Sam Wheeler, but why at a private residence instead of the sheriff's department?

Screw it, I thought. Play it as it falls.

I punched the bell, waited a half minute, hit it again. Nothing. I was off the hook for a bullshit story, but doomed again to learning zip. I was already soaking wet. I decided to nose around.

Odin's screen-enclosed patio had no plants or furniture, but it screamed of potential. An exercise machine dripped rust onto faded outdoor carpet. A sliding glass door was wide open, as if Marlow dared anyone to violate his space, dared mildew to come in and take root.

My first thought said to go in. The second suggested that someone had beaten me to it and may still be in there. Or someone besides Odin had left and forgotten to close up. I thought about getting Liska's gun from the Lexus. I thought again. Felony plus weapon possession equals mandatory prison time. I palmed my handkerchief to mask fingerprints, and let myself onto the patio. If I got caught, sure as hell I would be accused of trying to steal his ritzy watch. Worse, they would find Sam's bankroll in my pocket, and Marlow would claim it as his. I had never been fitted for an orange jumpsuit, but I guessed a size forty-four would do it. If I didn't take a forty-five slug beforehand.

Marlow's pad was a study in contrast. His furniture was upscale, his filth downscale. He had a sixty-inch TV, a pocket-sized stereo, and loudspeakers you could camp in. The sofa, recliner, and easy chair were made of matching blond leather. A glass-and-chrome coffee table sat on a huge Persian rug on top of wall-to-wall gray berber. His primary decorations were spindly, iron figurines with that lopsided Picasso look. His pastimes got deluxe treatment. A magnificent glass-front case displayed Odin's collection of beer can insulators. He had swiped them from every hangout in town. Two shelves down I found enough X-rated DVDs to satisfy a prison population for months. None of his fixtures matched the fundamental mess.

I waded through stacks of junk mail and *National Enquirers*, evidence of blended whiskey and Diet Coke, crumpled take-out bags, boxes from pizza deliveries. Odin had left his dirty socks on a chair, skivvies on the kitchen counter. Worse was the garbage smell, stacks of plates caked with residue, and four full plastic bags that he hadn't carried to the Dumpster.

The bedroom carried on the theme. High-end, tasteful furniture, with his white bed sheets gone gray. They matched the carpeting. Two lamps, a pile of jackoff magazines, and a roll of paper towels were next to his bed.

I put my handkerchief away. I wasn't going to touch a thing.

Odin had hung photos in cheap frames, his own little shrine. I couldn't tell if his "ready" stance in jersey 48 was college or high school football. A more recent Odin posed on a yacht stern with a medium-sized tarpon. His fish looked too perfect, as if borrowed from someone's den wall. In a slightly larger picture, Odin was surrounded by four blondes in bikinis. The women pretended to snuggle, but none looked like a friend. In early shots Odin was just another poser with a smile. In newer shots his scowl revealed hatred.

He may have been big in Podunkville, but he was a scrambler on the tide line. Marlow had too much disposable income for a sheriff's detective, even with an inheritance. He was drawn to high life, dragging his anchor through the dregs of a previous existence. Odd that a boy from Greenwich, Connecticut, had picked up his sense of style at the mall.

I had been inside too long. I wasn't even sure what I had wanted to find. When I finally noticed the safe in the bedroom corner, bolted to the floor, I knew I'd find nothing of interest.

On my way out I bumped an end table, disturbed a stack of bills. Under the stack, the corner of a photograph. A picture of Marcantonio's Camry.

I stopped, paid more attention. That morning's *Miami Herald* was spread across a stool. The Gomez murder case got minor coverage on page three of the South Broward section. But the piece was accompanied by a sidebar that hadn't been in the Keys section. Its lead sentence said, "Could people doing business with Key West have harmed the mayor?" The piece listed eight pending commission decisions, including the three that Marnie had told me about on Tuesday. A circle was penciled around the mention of the Borroto Brinas Development Corporation's resort proposal for bay waters adjacent to North Roosevelt Boulevard.

Marnie would be brokenhearted. She had been scooped on the Gomez murder, then double-scooped on background.

I speculated on Odin Marlow's interest in old Keys developments. The project's time frame matched his years in Key West. He wouldn't have circled the Borroto Brinas mention if it hadn't meant something to him. I gazed to the ceiling, searched for guidance. A beacon shone down. It wasn't beaming me insights and truth. I looked closer at the eye above the sliding glass door. I gave the video lens a contrite wave.

I should have guessed. He had cash for leather and sculptures, pretend opulence. Why wouldn't he have it for technology?

I made it to the car and scanned the parking area one last time. Nothing but get-by rides. Beyond those, obscured by a hedge, was a red Eldorado. A new Cadillac, as out of place as a cruise ship.

The last good anomaly.

I hadn't learned a thing, and I'd gone backward in a hurry. Marlow knew my face, my name, and where to find me. He would probably be more bitter about my reactions to his detritus than my trespassing.

I drove back to Southwest 31st Avenue and took another pass at Barry Marcantonio's. No car next to his trailer. A quarter-mile away, on the corner of Griffin Road, I found a phone on the front wall of a convenience store. I had one last chance and only one way to reach her. I called Cozy Cab for a pickup at the morgue. I asked them to send Goodnight Irene.

I went in and got a PayDay, a Coke, a small bag of Fritos. Jazzy nutrition to make up for no breakfast or lunch. The rain had quit, so I went back out to wait. When Irene Jones drove by, I would follow, meet her in the medical examiner's lot. I would ask about the Broward ME, see what she knew about Odin Marlow, maybe find myself at another dead end.

I waited twenty minutes before the shit storm hit.

A black Dodge Intrepid turned off Griffin and sped down Southwest 31st. It went about seventy-five yards, hit the brakes, then hit reverse. It backed until it reached the convenience store driveway, stopped, whipped into the lot, and drove straight for me. Its bumper stopped ten feet from my knees. I saw three men in the car.

The front passenger got out, crouched behind his door, and pointed a pistol. All I could see was a crew cut and a gun muzzle.

He bellowed, "Face down, fuckhead."

I dropped my Coke and took his suggestion. My clothes absorbed greasy water from the blacktop. I struggled to keep my face off the ground. The man was on me fast. He put a knee to my shoulders, cuffed my right wrist, yanked it to my spine.

"The other arm nice, or you like pain?" he said.

Another man thrust an ugly weapon at my nose. The muzzle's black eye stared me down. I moved my left arm to the restraint.

Crew Cut stripped my watch, snapped the second cuff. "What's your name, boy?"

"You don't know?" I said, from the side of my mouth.

"Believe me," he said, "you want to cooperate."

"I'm Jack Shit. Tell your friends you know me."

He pulled my arms upward, wrenched my shoulders and elbows. Pain shot down to my toes. "Cute, dickweed," he barked at the back of my head. "We just changed it to Deep Shit."

26

THE GUNNER WITH SHORT white hair tongue-fired thin saliva squirts through his teeth. Expelling hatred or the childhood demons that led him to his line of work. He stood back while the driver, a five-five mouth-breather, did his macho act. The bastard flipped and gut-poked me, tore open my pockets, and hoisted me like a sugar sack. No witnesses came to my rescue. A kid gassing his tricked-out pickup watched it go down like street theater.

I peered into the market. The good Samaritans were grabbing their asses back by the milk and yogurt. To a passerby, I was a drunk being helped by friends. No one on the road had time or the guts to butt in.

Where's a cop when you need one?

Macho heaved me into the backseat. He secured my feet to manacles on the floor, then latched my cuffs to a clip behind me. You don't see that many sedans customized for abduction. Before he slammed the door, he hooked my shoulder strap. Only the best kidnappers are safety-conscious. Macho smelled like baby powder. I didn't mention it.

The third man, a sullen, pock-faced tough with massive shoulders, drove east in Liska's Lexus. Macho turned his sled into a Dodge Teflon, boogied out of the C-store lot, then west on Griffin. He oozed through traffic, lane hopping, a contender in the urban derby. I've never suffered motion sickness, even at sea, but my snacks wanted freedom. My shoulders ached, and my pits reminded me that I hadn't showered. Odor was the least of my worries. I wasn't being judged on hygiene. Goodnight Irene had set me up. I had called for a cab, but I was getting a different ride. My brain, for once aligned with common sense, told me to stay in high gear.

I could bank on only one fact. I wasn't dead yet. I might, some day, drink beer with Monty Aghajanian. On second thought, he had told me to back off. I had done the opposite. Monty would be unsociable the next time I saw him.

Crew Cut, up front, huffing for breath, kept dialing, canceling, redialing. I sensed a frantic soul under his scalding veneer. They had grabbed me like pros, but had lost their way. Why didn't he call Irene Jones? Driving a hack, she had to be an ace with directions. I absorbed like a son of a bitch. Crew Cut wore a wedding band, my first good sign. I had to think that married men make poor hit men.

Fit the ugly pieces. How had I wound up shackled to a floorpan? She had quit the morgue, drove a cab, but Irene was moonlighting the dark side. She was working with Odin and my hosts in the Dodge. Sam had stumbled into the web and I, like a lemming, had followed him in. Our bad luck, because the machine would grind us up and keep chugging. Where would these boys throw me my private party? First guess: an empty industrial park.

We barreled through light traffic. A vision of mile-long beach in Grand Cayman flashed through my head. Lounges, umbrella drinks, no dead people. Then I clicked to an image of Naomi, laughing at Louie's. Next came the real world. I peered out at gunpowder sky, ashen clouds, thrashing palms, bus stop benches, angry people with wet hair.

West of Flamingo, my prediction hit home. Macho eased the Dodge over a curb, into a shut-down construction site. We rode the washboard, stopped between chain-link and a concrete block shed. My stomach was everywhere. Why stifle it? I should mess up their car before they whacked me. Barf acid would corrode the D-rings, give the next guy a fighting chance.

Crew Cut got out, spit a few times, kicked a couple clods of dirt. He kept dialing. Macho hummed an eight-bar melody. "All we are is dust in the wind." My mind flipped around, refused to focus. Was the song part of his execution ritual? How could I postpone the inevitable? Beg them to let me die in the Keys?

Macho checked his side mirror. A Broward cruiser passed, going west. I beamed a psychic message, asked the deputy why a clean car was parked in a mud field. Ninety seconds later a black and gold FHP unit rolled the other direction. We didn't rate a head twitch. The boys were clocking out. Their minds were on beer-thirty and lounge chairs, worried less about suspicious activity than asteroid collisions.

I checked Crew Cut. He'd connected, looked relieved, hearing what he wanted to hear. He glanced back at me as he talked, listened, talked again. He nodded vehemently, said about four words, and clicked off. He had been told where to dump my body. I waited for him to high-five himself.

He got in. "Seventy-five, south. They want us at the Ops Box."

Macho had it in gear. He weaved through a dozen fifty-five-gallon drums and bounced us to the curbing. He looked left and said, "Fuck."

Blue lights flashed.

He said, "Sit tight."

I had no choice but to take his advice.

The Highway Patrol trooper aimed his black push bumpers at Macho's door. The cop's eyes went frantic. He was seeing ten things at once. I counted love-bug splats on his grille. Everything froze except Crew Cut's right arm, below the trooper's line of sight.

I couldn't duck in a firelight. I was high target in a shooting gallery. Blame my stupid psychic message. I began to shake my head, bob it around, trying to warn the officer. I could have spun it like in *The Exorcist* and still gotten no attention. Crew Cut put his cell phone to his right ear, hidden from the trooper's view. At least it wasn't his weapon. But Macho moved his right arm, too, below window level. Each movement lit a fuse. I waited to see which bomb blew first. Why had I thought that married men can't be hit men? They can't go home like everyone else, bitch to the wife about workload?

The blue lights intensified, mixed with reds and whites. I looked right. The Broward deputy angled his Crown Vic, stopped six inches from the Dodge's headlight. The deputy yanked his riot gun from its dash mount, slid low in his seat.

Under his breath, Macho said, "We got a nervous one. Don't lock eyes with him." It was the first time I'd heard his gravel voice.

Everyone waited for the other guy to move. The tension inside the Dodge smelled of nervous sweat and baby powder. The two up front were a psychic act, not speaking, but coordinated, in tune. I had chided myself for being along for the ride. My pattern was holding, descending.

Crew Cut spoke into his phone. "Dick Tracy, eight one eight, eight two three, state and county. Hard nose." Then, monotone: "Right you are. We're from the bank."

The lights were tough on my eyes, reflected wet surfaces, but I saw the trooper speak into his radio mike. He tossed his eyes, deputy to Dodge. I looked back to the deputy. He keyed an epaulette-mounted mike, did the eye dance, too. His mirrors, the trooper, the Dodge's front seat. Why hadn't one cop or the other taken command? Were they waiting for backup? Was I caught in a silent standoff, a test of first move and forced move?

Someone burst the balloon. Both units cut their flashers. The deputy secured his riot gun, sat higher, began typing on a console keyboard. The trooper whipped a circus turn in reverse, spent a few taxpayer dollars on tire rubber. He was out of sight in thirty seconds. By that time the deputy had moved back to make room. Macho had never taken the Dodge out of gear. He lifted his brake pedal, crept slowly over the curb, then gunned it westward. Crew Cut kept his eyes forward. Neither looked at the deputy.

The lightbulb clicked in my head. I deciphered Crew Cut's code numbers. We were on State Route 818. Flamingo Road probably was 823. He had given our location, and his office had told the trooper and deputy, via their bosses, to keep their distance. I was riding with the big bad boys, the Florida Department of Law Enforcement, the heavies who made the rules. I was chained into a car doing seventy-five on rain-wet I-75 in northwest Miami-Dade during rush hour on a Friday.

Stupid me had asked, Where's a cop when you need one? Stupid me had found renegades, probably in cahoots with Marlow. All it would take is one jalopy with a blown-out tire, or one dickhead to drop his cell phone, spill his beer when he grabbed for the phone, slide into the next lane for a crushing instant of metal-to-metal. I would survive the collision but not the fire.

Worse, I might live to wish I was dead.

Why I chilled in knowing that Macho and Crew Cut were FDLE agents is beyond me. My knowing who wrote their paychecks didn't lift the chance that they could be underbelly fuzz, like Marlow, who intended to add me to their victim list. Still, that single piece of knowledge gave me a toehold outside of confusion, a sense of order, and allowed me to think on other questions.

Five topics, for starters. I needed Ernest Bramblett's location and story. I wanted to learn about Naomi Douglas's use of Oxycodone. Why had Odin Marlow penciled a circle around the BBDC mention in the *Herald*? What had Marcantonio learned from watching the Broward Medical Examiner facility? Who dumped my black-and-white art photos in Naomi's garbage can?

Four more, to keep my energy flowing. How did Randolph's money scams tie in to two murders? Who called the city to report Naomi's death? Why had Monty Aghajanian been so curious about Bobbi Lewis? Who was the tipster who had undercut Marnie's prize investigative piece?

Three bonus shots: Did Teresa know in advance that Randolph was coming to Key West? Did she have any part in drawing him there? What was her state of mind when she agreed to move into my home?

Screw that last one. I'd visit ego questions only if they helped me answer the first eleven.

"How long you been with FDLE?" I said, directing my voice toward Crew Cut.

He said, "An hour too long."

"A ditchdigger might say the same thing," I said. "You must like it, the badge, the power, a car with air."

"The power, you got that right," he said.

Oh, Mister Tough Guy.

"You come up through a county job, or straight from the military?"

Crew Cut turned, went eye to eye with me. "My partner sees things. A lot of times dogs run in front of the car. Or ghosts of dogs. His reaction time would make you jump out of your seat, even with those bracelets on your wrists. Funny how a stray mutt can jerk your arms out of their sockets."

"In other words, you want me to shut up?"

"Nine words ago."

"You boys are good," I said. "You should've been in intelligence."

Macho tapped the brakes, and the Dodge went squirrely on the damp road. We drifted sideways, returned to our lane, and never lost pace. Macho wanted to make a point, but I missed his exact message.

I went back to my nine questions. One fact begged for attention. Broward Detective Odin Marlow, former Key West cop, was a double link. Lauderdale and Key West. Liska had said, "*Marlow's a born crook. We fired him twenty years ago. He should've gone to Raiford instead of out the door.*"

Two other questions came to mind, but they hadn't come from me. Whit Randolph had said, "*They could have died twelve or fifteen hours apart, right?*" When I had agreed, he said, "*You're suggesting the deaths are linked?*"

He'd had a good point. Maybe I'd been chugging down the wrong track for the past forty-eight hours.

We took I-75 to the Palmetto. Thirty minutes later we were on

LeJeune at the airport entrance. In five hours I had come full circle, but we weren't catching a flight. Macho passed MIA and turned right on Northwest 25th. We entered a chuck-holed maze pocked by corroded metal buildings and enclosures full of semis and heavy equipment. Someone had made a killing in mansard overhangs. I suspected that all of the structures had been built after Hurricane Andrew in the early Nineties. Their owners were waiting for the next open door to insurance money. Aside from simplistic black-paint gang markings, the ubiquitous graffiti, with its flowing letters and tropical colors, improved the district. Two writers—Raven and Oiler—had signed their work.

The "Ops Box" was a long, narrow building fifty yards west of the Miami River. Except for one small mirrored rectangle, no doubt bulletproof glass, every window was bricked shut. The concertina wire that lined its flat roof barely disguised a cluster of antennas and dishes. I saw no company name or address numbers on the building. One piece of graffiti, the stylized initials "FA," adorned its front wall.

I wanted to assume it stood for Federal Assholes.

Macho keyed a remote transmitter. A garage door lifted on the building's east end. It had barely cleared five feet when he drove under the still-rising door and parked next to Sheriff Liska's burgundy Lexus. Before he put it in park, he zapped the remote again. The last thing I saw outside, reflected in an outside rearview mirror, was the orange sun breaking through a hole in late-day clouds. The Intrepid's headlights illuminated the garage. Another Dodge and two black Ford SportTracs lined the far wall.

Crew Cut opened my door. He began to unhook my manacles and belts. "Sorry about this hardware, bubba. It was for your own safety."

"My kidnapping was a safety move, too?"

"We kept you from certain death." He elbowed my gut, where Macho had nailed me at the C-store. The Fritos and Coke rose. He jerked me out, and almost got to wear Technicolor chunks.

"That was for your 'intelligence' remark."

Don't say it, I told myself. *Don't say, "Duh."*

Macho shielded his hand, punched code into a keypad. A man in a polo shirt and dress trousers opened a metal door. Fluorescent light shone out, the yellow-green that fills a room with mouthwash mist, makes everyone look like a hangover. I was pushed up a single stair. The door was locked behind me. I smelled instant office, installed within the past week: portable walls, cheap carpet and chairs, metal desks, organizers. The air was cranked down to sixty. A veneer-topped table held a coffeemaker and radio gear set to low volume.

A young clerky-looking fellow at a metal desk said, "How ya doin'?" Two more the same flavor studied a corkboard that displayed a satellite photo of Miami-Dade and two city street maps. One map had sectors outlined in blue. Each man said, "How you doin'?"

I was walking through another beer ad.

Crew Cut led me to the building's west end. At the last office, we went right. Sam Wheeler, in his own clothes rather than jailhouse duds, sat next to the far wall. His eyes flicked my way, then resumed their stare. Sam's stoic face meant that he had legal problems, or knew that his sister was dead, or one crooked cop was just the start of our headaches. At least he wasn't chained to a bed or locked away. He said nothing, kept his lips pressed together.

I took his cue.

27

THE FIFTEEN-BY-FIFTEEN OFFICE WALLS were bare but for a poster of the Miami skyline. No windows, no proof of the outside world.

Crew Cut pushed me into the room. "Prize for you, Red."

Red, long ago, could have changed it to Whitey. "Leave him with me," he said. "We called every air charter company in a fifty-mile radius. It's been an hour, Marv. Expand it to a hundred and fifty, and e-mail each a photo."

Marv?

I was just getting used to Crew Cut. He went from tough guy to champ buttkisser in a flash. He praised his boss's idea, then strode out. I heard him delegate the task to a weasel out front.

Red stood behind a wood-grain desk that held file stacks and phones. He was a tall, broad-faced man, probably in his fifties, and wore a lavender shirt open at the collar and tan cotton slacks. A pager and a small empty holster were clipped to his belt. In another setting, minus the holster, he was a small business owner in a bad mood. In this room he could be anything he wanted, from dictator to chief puppeteer. He looked at me like I was snot on his wall, and pointed to an empty chair.

Circulation was returning to my feet and hands. The last thing I wanted was a seat. "I'd rather stand," I said.

Red called out, "Yo, Marv?"

I heard his hard heels in the hall. Call it self-destructive, but I wanted to see how far these idiots would go to force the seating arrangement. Bad mistake. Marv kicked the back of my right leg, slugged my right shoulder blade. I went sprawling.

Sam started out of his chair.

Red said, "Don't even think . . ."

I looked. Red was fast. He pointed a small pistol at Sam's chest. "We sprung your ass from the hoosegow hospital. This is your thanks?"

"Where with this one?" said Marv.

"Leave him there," said Red. "He wants to play wise fuck so let him eat rug. Leave his head turned like it is. I can watch him sweat. I want to know why he went knocking on those two men's doors."

Marv dug his heel into my spine. He'd been trained to target vulnerable disks and nerves. "Maybe he can tell us why, as of an hour ago, one man was critical and one was a fugitive."

"Ah, yes," said Red. "We're in the middle of doing you right, Mr. Wheeler, and your so-called pal here steps in shit. You probably think he was trying to help you. We think he was trying to squeeze the deal."

Marv said, "But he ran good camouflage, driving that dweeb sheriff's car. Chicken Lick Fresca, out of Monroe."

"You people are fucked," said Sam. "Take me back to jail."

Red said, "Why waste your money? We can keep it in this room. We got an undercover operation down the tubes, you follow? You reimburse us for the cost of a four-month sting, as the media calls it, you can bargain all your problems down to a jaywalking ticket. Isn't that cheaper than attorneys?"

"You're forgetting I was a victim twice," said Sam. "A death scam and my civil rights."

Red was unimpressed. "Your point?"

"I'll be rich when I get through with Broward. I'll buy lawyers."

"You forget you're in Miami right now?" said Marv.

Sam's voice went low. "I don't forget anything."

"Great," said Red. "The world's going to beat a path to your door so you can bitch about injustice. Obviously, you boys don't think we can cornhole your civil rights. You could wind up sweeping a barber shop in Haiti and be happy for the opportunity."

"Let Rutledge up before I make you use the gun," said Sam. "You pop a hole in me, the paperwork and hearings will last you more than four fucking months."

"You tried to escape, Mr. Wheeler."

"Like I'm some shitbird running from a road gang? Give the civilian world a little credit for smarts, Mr. Whatever."

"My name is Simmons, sir." Red shook his head, let things settle, then gave a silent command.

"You want him sitting, or a pile of skin?" Marv yanked my belt, jerked me to the empty chair, then moved back against the door frame. He checked his view of the hallway. You can't be too secure. He probably wore his weapon in the bathroom. Spent his nights watching Bruce Willis flicks.

Red placed his gun in a drawer, plopped his butt on the corner of his desk. "We got us an issue with an assistant state attorney, Mr. Wheeler. His happy ass has been on the line for our investigation. He okayed the funding, fronted us to judges for search warrants. We were going to pull our sting next Monday, bust the scam open, headlines and all. Mind you, this is an ASA with political aspirations. He wanted headlines more than we did. Your meddling squashed it all."

"I went looking for my sister," said Sam. "No more than that. I got told not to look by a Broward detective, which is a red flag. I broke no laws until I got mugged by a bad deputy, so I'm not your problem. What happened was you didn't fail-safe your sting. It got blown by innocent victims."

Red's eyes went to slits, focused on nothing. "What did Marlow want from you, Wheeler? How much did he ask for?"

"The whole ball of wax. Anything with my sister's name on it, old photos, old phone numbers, canceled checks, financial records, club memberships."

"Would I be correct to assume that you gave him none of that?"

"One old phone number," said Sam.

"And he asked you not to butt into his investigation?"

Sam nodded yes.

"Let me guess. You saw him following you."

Another nod.

"You doubled back, followed him to Marcantonio's mobile home, but he knew you were there. He turned around on your ass. You tried to evade him and got blue-lighted."

Sam's teeth clenched. "You're not guessing. You knew."

"Ever heard of LoJack?" said Red. "We've got our own version."

"On my rental car?" said Sam.

"On every car we've mentioned."

A female voice said, "Including mine."

Goodnight Irene Jones stood next to Marv. She looked like a cab-driver, but a leather badge wallet was clipped to her belt.

Sam said, "So you shits used me to bait your trap? You dangled my ass out there to make your work easier?"

No one spoke.

Sam thought a moment. "You hung Marcantonio's ass out to burn like mine, didn't you?"

Red stared ahead. "He was one of us. He was found alongside I-595, bleeding from face and arm wounds. He was incoherent. We think he was blue-lighted, beaten up, and his car was stolen."

"You've got a good tally going here, Simmons. You sanctioned a muscle job on Rutledge here on your carpet. You talk hot-shit satellite tracking units, but they didn't keep me or Marcantonio out of jams. You probably know that my sister's dead, too. Let's call that assistant state attorney right now."

Red, to his credit, held back his repartee. "I assure you, Mr. Wheeler, the department is sympathetic to—"

"Odin Marlow wanted me to hire a private eye. He offered to rec-ommend one. Was he running a scam to pad the pockets of a scumbag gumshoe?"

Red shook his head. "No, that wasn't it."

Red's intercom made a crackling noise. A voice said, "We're into mop-up, Major. We popped the doc and a uniformed deputy. The other bird ditched his car at a Roadhouse Grill by Federal and Hillsboro."

"I want evidence techs on that vehicle before it gets towed."

"I'll make it happen." The intercom went silent.

"Was the doc inside the morgue?" said Sam.

Irene Jones looked him in the eye. "Yep, but never again."

Sam turned to Red. "What the hell were they doing?"

"Selling new identities. You wouldn't believe what foreign nationals will pay to stay in this country. They come over here, they see the good life, they put their green card expiration in the same category as early death."

"Okay," said Sam. "You asked if I had given them details on my sis-ter's finances and so on . . ."

"You were their worst nightmare, because you were wise enough not to fall for it. Most of the other victims gave them truckloads. They wanted to do everything possible to find their loved ones."

"How did they pick me?"

"Unfortunately, you were next in line," said Red Simmons. "This started eleven months ago. A woman was found dead in a stolen car. She had no ID, no fingerprints on file, no labels in her clothing. Mar-low found her. We can't prove it, but we think he stole her IDs before he called in the coroner's investigators."

"She remained a Jane Doe to her grave," said Irene Jones.

"Seventy days later," continued Simmons, "another woman's body was found on the beach right at the end of Sunrise. Marlow contacted the first woman's family. Those people came down here from Atlanta and looked at the corpse. It wasn't their daughter. Marlow feigned compassion and stonewalled. We know that an illegal immigrant from

Poland is now using the first dead woman's identity, but she'll be in Gdansk by the first of June. Anyway, that started a cycle of four deaths and failed ID sessions. We now think that the conspirators got impatient with their process, tired of waiting for more bodies to be found."

Sam said, "Sounds like a lot of trouble . . ."

"Someone paid forty thousand for the Polish woman's package," said Red, "and that was a low-end price. So, do the math, figure these IDs go to the highest bidder, you get an idea. Their little industry had the potential to pull down millions. Again, we can't prove this, or we would have made arrests by now. Hence, the sting. We think they murdered your sister."

"How long ago?"

"Four months ago, sir. Please accept our condolences."

Sam ignored the sympathy shot and jerked his thumb in my direction. "You beat on him, push us around like cops out of control. Bottom line, your top secret operation had a hole in it. I walked through, then Rutledge did, and now your bad guy did, too, going the other direction. You need to drop the drama and go to work. It's time for us to go home."

"Believe me, Mr. Wheeler, our job description is not drama."

"Bullshit. You ask questions, you already know the answers. You select your beefs and edit fuckups. Now you're desperate to find a fugitive, but it sounds like he read your mail and blew town."

"Mr. Wheeler, you may be right. Being right's real important to you, isn't it? Say we botched a sting. Our fuckup will be noted in Tallahassee and it'll boomerang back to this desk. If I don't charge you both with obstruction, my career gets it in the ass." He peered at Irene Jones. "Pardon the metaphor, Detective Sergeant."

Goodnight Irene said, "What's wrong? You want to say your career gets porked in the rectum? Either way, you lose your retirement health benefits."

"Thank you, Irene," said Red.

Sam sat back in his chair, crossed his ankles. "You're a powerful man. That's what's important to you, isn't it? Power?"

"Glad you recognize that, sir."

"So let me explain another source of energy. The woman who shares my house is a *Key West Citizen* reporter. She knows a hot story when she sees one, and she's placed her stories all over Florida and the Southeast states. She knows I've been here three days. She'll compare that to your task force and methods and the four months you've pissed away. I'm a victim of con men and you're treating me like I've acted in bad faith. I swiped a deputy's motorcycle to save my life, to escape from a scam and a sting that danced each other out of control. She'll tell how long your operation's been sucking on the state's tit, and how many women died while you jacked around. How long have you known that my sister was dead?"

Red put a less wise-ass expression on his face and looked Sam in the eye. "We didn't know who she was until you arrived at the Broward ME's office."

"Your trail is getting cold. You've got grunt work to do, and I have two sisters who need to know about the death of Lorie Wheeler."

The intercom again. "Red, an attorney named Minnette on the horn. A lady lawyer."

"Get a number."

"It's about those two . . ."

"Get a number."

I said, "Right now, where's Marlow's Cadillac Eldorado?"

Sam looked right at me. His eyes perked.

Red looked at Irene and Marv. Both shrugged their shoulders.

Sam said, "Where did Odin Marlow keep his boat?"

More looks, more shrugs.

I said, "You didn't know about his twenty-three-foot Fountain Sport-fish CC?"

Simmons flashed a grim glare at his people.

"Runs a 225-horse Yamaha," said Sam. "That boat's a major investment. People get attached to their boats."

Irene Jones said, "That Roadhouse Grill is right next to a marina. They share the same parking entrance."

"Bingo," said Sam. "It's my ass to your lunch money that Marlow's in Nassau right now, slugging down Chivas, tipping blackjack dealers with fifties."

I looked at Marv. Hatred and shame in his eyes. I shifted over to Irene. She was staring at Sam with a touch of admiration in hers.

Red Simmons focused on nothing as he formed his response. "Bahamas Immigration has been asked to bust on sight."

"Then we got him," said Marv, but he knew he'd messed up.

I thought about the penciled circle around the Borroto Brinas mention in Marlow's *Herald*. "That boat could make Key West in time for supper," I said. "Liska told me that Marlow used to be a cop down there, but he got fired. He said he was a born crook who should have gone to Raiford."

Sam grinned. "Won't Liska be glad to hear that Odin's on his way back?"

"We can tell him when we drop off his car," I said.

Simmons moved his jaw as if he was cleaning sirloin scraps out of his teeth. His eyes went to Marv and Irene. "Mr. Wheeler has reminded us that there is grunt work to do. He and his friend have given me more sleuthing sense in a half hour than you two in the past ten days." He turned to Sam. "You know the waters down there, right?"

"And boats. I can tell from a mile who's robbing traps, who's a tourist from upstate, who should be there, and who shouldn't be."

"You're going back to work when you get back there?"

"I've got some catching up to do out on the water," said Sam.

"If you find Marlow, what will you do first?" said Simmons.

"I could give your chopper a GPS location."

Red asked Irene Jones if Sam's belongings were in the building.

"In the trunk of the car, sir."

Red turned to me. "When my men requested that you accompany them, over on Griffin Road, was there any force involved?"

I said, "None that I recall."

"Are we going to have problems down the road?"

I wanted them to pay for my trousers. I wanted out. "No problems."

Sam said, "You never answered my question, Simmons."

Shut up, I thought. The door's open. Don't make it slam shut.

"Which of your questions was that?"

"Do you dangle innocent people to make your job easier?"

Simmons's eyes contracted. He gazed at the wall, then moved his eyes back to Sam. "Yes, Mr. Wheeler. Not all the time, but when I must. It's a cold approach, yet one fact comforts me. When I catch criminals and they are punished, my sins are absolved."

Sam's face showed no reaction. "God bless you, sir. Where's my fucking rental car?"

"We turned it in."

"Great. Thanks."

28

SAM ASKED TO DRIVE down the Keys. His mind was a war zone of revenge and memories. He needed escape. My head still was full of questions, anyway. I didn't trust myself with the Lexus. The FDLE had hung out Sam to bait their trap. In a sense, Chicken Neck Liska had joined their club. He must have known when he handed me his keys that I wouldn't go straight home with Sam still in limbo. He had opened the gates for me to be grabbed, pounded, threatened with jail, and lucky there wasn't more. I wasn't in the mood to guard for gravel dings.

We traveled in silence until Sam stopped for gas at the Snapper Creek Turnpike Plaza. We stood on the fuel island, watched the pump do its thing. After the Ops Box, anything was entertainment.

"We're twenty miles down the road," I said. "You got a perspective on Red Simmons and his Bully Pranksters?"

Sam looked across the parking area. "The world of assholes is divided into two groups," he said. "Half will buy you a beer, then punch you in the nose. The other half, the Simmons type, will punch you first, then buy you a beer. Do we make calls now or wait?"

"You want to tell Marnie you're alive?"

"Ten bucks says Liska already told her. Let me think for a minute or two. You feel like buying us two clean shirts?"

Inside, I ruled out Coke, Fritos, and PayDay. I found a T-shirt for

Sam that read, DO NOT TALK UNLESS YOU CAN IMPROVE THE SILENCE. I almost bought myself a beauty with a pastel grouper, but chose instead a patriotic statement. Above an American flag were the words MÁS UNIDOS QUE NUNCA. I grabbed soft drinks, a bag of chips, and four Hershey bars, got in line to pay, and stared out a window.

Something in the parking area for northbound vehicles caught my eye. Sam stood behind a freight truck, then went under the trailer. I looked away so no one around me would notice my stare. When I came back out, Sam was shirtless, leaning against the Lexus. Two welts stood out on his chest.

I said, "Am I allowed to ask . . ."

He shrugged. "One dumb cop. The price of an education."

"Not the welts," I said. "The semi across the way."

"Those super cops were too proud of their satellite tracking devices. They couldn't let us go scot-free."

He had found a transmitter on the Lexus, and sent it in a different direction.

"Where will they be looking for us?"

"The license tag was Virginia." He pointed at the candy. "Why did you buy all that shit?"

"Self-esteem," I said. "The joy of making my own decisions."

Sam pulled on his new shirt, then went in to phone Marnie. A rented Mustang convertible pulled up next to the Lexus. Two couples, sunburned, partying their way to Margaritaville. They did a piss-poor job of hiding their open beers. I waved a five and offered to relieve them of two unopened.

Sam opened his the instant he got back in the car. "Wonderful," he said. "The sheriff's own ride, we can go to the edge. Follow our FDLE session with an open container charge. I quiver in fear." He chugged it.

We started down the Eighteen-Mile Stretch. Sam spun me what Marnie had told him. "Whit Randolph's attorney is no slouch. This is the guy who got famous by a television news exposé of the Travelers, the scam artists who work out of the Carolinas. He's their attorney du jour, always rushing to small towns where they've been snagged in fraud. He chartered a jet out of New Orleans and got to the Monroe County jail before the deputies finished the booking process. He brought along a goofball lawyer from Whitehead Street and a bail bondsman. When he got Randolph set to hit the street, he called a news conference. Our naive local stringers took the bait."

"Did he offer any legal brilliance?"

"He claimed that he can prove that his client had not committed a single crime. He also said that, within forty-eight hours, he and his client would deliver the mayor's murderer to justice. His real words were something like, 'My client will let these rube cops know who really did it.'"

"The scam bust was a delay tactic so the police could build up murder evidence. Why would the lawyer want to go there?"

"Fire with fire?" said Sam. "Maybe to let the fuzz know that he was wise to their tactic?"

"Make you glad you're a fisherman?"

"I've never doubted my choice. But everybody wants to be like me. This guy is busted, then bonded out in five hours. The cops have their own catch-and-release policy."

"We should hope they left the hook in his mouth."

Our timing down U.S. 1 was perfect. The sun dropped below the horizon as we rounded the bend into Key Largo. I said, "Two hours earlier, we'd have had it in our eyes for a hundred miles."

"Still a bunch of shit," said Sam. "Friday night, the Upper Keys, you get drunken pull-outs from bar lots. Those end-of-the-week brews make people forget to turn on their headlights."

"You think Marlow's down here?"

"If it were me, I'd have gone thirty or forty miles north and put into a marina where no one knew me. Marlow's smart enough not to go to Bimini. He knows the easiest place to hide. He's got an 'FL' hull registration number, so his boat will blend in anywhere in the state. His first goal is to hit money machines close to home, because he knows they'll track him. After that, if he's got a cash stash, he can take his time, go anywhere."

I said, "He was in the fake-identity business."

"Bingo," said Sam. "He can be anybody and go anywhere. For that matter, his boat could be registered to a fake identity, which makes him a free man indefinitely. What the hell. He could have a car, a home, and a new job, but I doubt it. Marlow was a cocky bastard. He wouldn't have looked ahead to possible failure."

"Can you think back twenty-five years?" I said.

"No."

"Who sold us those shares in that development project?"

"Some dock jockey at the yacht club."

"Where were our brains?"

"We must've thought we were flush," said Sam. "I remember those men on the fuel dock, Norman Wood, his friend Foster, the can-opener tycoon, and the dockmaster, Jabe. They looked at us like we were nuts. Of course, we thought Norman was crazy for investing in Treasure Salvors. What the hell did we know?"

"What'd we give them, two grand apiece?"

"You did, but I doubled-up. I never told you that."

"I remember thinking for about a year and a half, I was going to make a killing. I was going to pay off my mortgage twenty-seven years ahead of time. I finally, mentally, wrote off my riches. I hadn't thought of it in fifteen years."

"I don't even know if that company still exists."

"I was getting to that." I told him about the issue coming before the city commission. I explained Marnie's heads-up regarding our names appearing on the list of owners, the circled BBDC mention in Marlow's newspaper.

"I don't remember Marlow the bad cop."

"Me either," I said. "If he was on the take—what cop wasn't back then?—he had money to burn. If the stock was sold before he got fired, maybe he invested cash he needed to hide."

"You or Marnie would've seen his name on that list."

"He could've used a corporate name. You recall any more about the guy who sold us those shares? Wasn't he a townie?"

"A blip in the back of my head says he was a Cuban Conch who left town for a while, then came back. He knew a lot of locals, but he was connected to Miami money."

"Miami money came in funny flavors back then," I said. "Maybe some of the investors would rather forget their involvement."

"You better believe just as many are hoping for that big payoff in the sky. Once again, I'm glad I fish."

"You could write a book about your past five days."

"I'd have to think about things I would rather forget," said Sam. "I tried to write a book in the early Seventies. On active duty."

"How did you find time?"

"I did my last two years at a desk in Fort Knox. I was supposed to train recruits, but some lieutenant colonel thought I was too extreme, too over-the-top. They put me in charge of filing psychological profiles. I supervised a civilian, a widow with three young kids. She did all the work. She was great. I didn't have to do squat, but I turned into a slug. I reached a point where my eyelids were tired, my legs were tired, and my brain was in overdrive. It was making me loopy, so I wrote to save my sanity."

"A book about what?"

"My best friend in Vietnam. Boy who didn't get out."

"Did you write a whole book?" I said.

"I didn't finish. I made it fiction, because I didn't want to tell stories and name names. I can't remember, but I think Crumley's *One to Count Cadence* was the only fiction out there. This was before *Going After Cacciato* and *Dog Soldiers* and *Fields of Fire*. Anyway, I got my discharge papers when it was half done."

"You never thought about going back to it?"

"I came to Key West, and one of my first charters was two men from Elyria, Ohio. After the first day's fishing they invited me to join them for a beer at Cow Key Marina. One of them began to shoot pool, and I got into telling the other guy about my book. I think he brought up the subject. Anyway, I gave him background, a few combat details. The man says, 'You're talking about the Foster boy, aren't you?' He pointed to the pool shooter. 'You're talking about his son.' I didn't see that one coming. The man playing pool was my friend's father."

"Small world we live in."

"I thought for a few days that meeting his father would inspire me to get back into it. It worked the opposite. The father was an asshole. He got drunk and begged me to find him a hooker. I decided my friend died to escape his old man. I took my manuscript to the far end of the Northwest Channel and gave it the float test."

"And?"

"It failed. Sank like sledge. Come to think of it, I taped it to a sledge."

"Your friend in Nam was a hero?" I said.

"No more than fifty-eight thousand others. He was just another story."

"What's a hero's secret?"

"You take abject fear, fight it back with a death wish, and people think you're courageous."

"In other words . . ."

Sam said, "In other words, you fight crazy people with crazy logic, you force the other guy to share the fear. It's all they respect, and if you're lucky it takes them by surprise." He changed the subject. "Christ, look at the price of gas."

"Every ten miles it goes up a nickel a gallon."

"And the closer you get to Key West," said Sam, "the more people live for today and to hell with tomorrow."

Full circle. He was back to memories and revenge.

I called Liska's office from Murray's Food Mart on Summerland Key.

"Gone for the day," said the dispatcher. "He left you a message, bubba. 'Keep the car. See you A.M.' I also got another for you, ten minutes ago."

"What's that?"

"From Agent Simmons, Miami FDLE. He said, 'Very funny.' I assume you know what that means. He wasn't laughing."

I went into the market, bought a six-pack. It was gone before we reached Searstown. Key West was oddly quiet for a Friday night. Elizabeth Street smelled like a valley of frangipani.

Sam's house was dark. "Marnie's cashed it in for the night," he said. "Teresa going to be waiting?"

"You've been in Lauderdale, you missed the soap opera. I should have bought a T-shirt that said, IF YOU LIVED HERE YOU'D BE HOME BY NOW."

"Didn't she just move in?"

"Remember, 'If you love somebody, set them free'? It's a crock of shit."

"Ask her to wear a zapper collar. You can install an Invisible Fence."

"Too late. The best I can do is call Animal Control."

"Looks like it's back to Annie Minnette," said Sam.

"Jesus. I forgot about her."

"Ah, subconscious smarts. By the way, your meddling saved my ass. Thanks."

"Blew their sting to shit, though."

"Flatter yourself, bubba. We don't have that kind of power. No matter what they say, they blew it themselves. Can you imagine trying to catch a fish from inside my house? They thought having an Ops Box would cause bad people to wave white flags. That's what smart people call caca."

"I almost forgot to ask you," I said. "What went down between you and Liska when he came to the hospital this morning?"

"Never saw him. They yanked me out of the hospital at dawn. When you got to the Ops Box, I'd been sitting there eight hours."

My house was dark, too. I went in, locked the door behind me. Teresa's packed bags were next to the door, her squash racquet and snorkeling gear stacked on top. She had taken two prints from the bedroom wall, cheap prints unworthy of their frames. Also the Isabelle Gros painting, which I would miss. Two boxes of books were there, too, mysteries she had kept to reread. Right on top was one named *Love for Sale*.

Honey, you could write the sequel.

I blew off my messages and opened the only beer in the fridge. I would learn in the morning that I drank maybe two sips before I passed out fully clothed.

29

WOODPECKERS AND A BAR fight. Roofers' hammers, brass gongs, a hardball through a window. Twenty people shuffled on my porch. The cast of *River Dance* had decided I wasn't supposed to sleep late. Why couldn't I live on a peaceful dead-end lane on a tropical island where everyone slept late? I had wasted my money on an alarm clock.

Empty space on the dressing table. Her knickknacks were gone, her eaux de toilette, ceramic alligators packed in boxes, ready to roll. They had been there only a few days, but they had added a secure touch to the room. Safe to assume that Teresa would move back to her old condo and Whit Randolph would gain a roommate. Or vice versa, depending on their arrangement. She preferred to be on top. I didn't know if that position applied to her business deals.

Good morning and look at the bright side, I thought.

You are not manacled to floorboards.

Someone peered through a pane in the French door. I hit the bathroom. My hair looked like an explosion in a wire factory. I would have to wear a ball cap to greet visitors. My face looked like a topological chart of northern Montana. They would have to suffer that. I brushed my teeth—for myself, so my jaw wouldn't stick shut. Baking soda toothpastes make your mouth feel like you've chewed a handful of sand, though there are times when that can be an improvement.

I walked outside. No one spoke.

Marnie, Monty, and Liska had made themselves at home. Coffee for the men, a Sprite for Marnie, nothing for me. The porch air smelled wet and warm. Birds sang, late-season gray catbirds, tree swallows. Fat April foliage blocked traffic noise on Fleming. Monty's ketchup-red rental convertible was snugged behind the Lexus. Marnie's Jeep was parked behind the ragtop.

Chicken Neck resembled a tourist in a yellow mesh T-shirt and tan shorts with fifteen pockets. He chewed his coffee stirrer, appeared taciturn, almost smug. Had he forgotten that he'd set me up for an FDLE beating? And why would he be with Monty on a Saturday morning?

Monty looked grim. He had succeeded in getting a deep tan, had slicked his hair back to expose a balding pattern I never had noticed. The style did him no favor. He looked like a junior Soviet diplomat in a Cold War newsreel.

Marnie stared at Liska as if he was a crazy man who could go berserk without warning. She wasn't too placid, herself. She looked like she hadn't slept in days.

I wanted to stare at my magenta bougainvillea, ignore them all. I felt like a fat mango, ripe to pick. I hoped that Marnie didn't want to discuss the Borroto Brinas Development Corporation in front of the sheriff. I didn't want to explain my part ownership that early in the morning.

Liska said, "Nice pants."

I had slept in the trousers that Macho had torn apart in the C-store parking lot in Dania Beach.

"Bad dreams last night," I said.

Liska nodded. "Saw your name in the paper this morning."

So much for keeping my BBDC investment under wraps.

"The *Citizen* or the *Herald*?"

"Does it matter? They spelled your name right."

"Top of the day to you, too," I said. "I just woke up, recovering from a long day yesterday. If you came for snappy chatter . . ."

Monty said, "Why don't we let Marnie take care of her business first?"

"Good," I said. "The tank's full. I'll get Liska's keys for you."

Monty shook his head. "We have much to discuss."

"Okay," I said. "Your slot's in fifteen minutes. You're better off that way, because I'm barely awake right now. Maybe you could run to the Sunshine Market, buy me a newspaper and a greasy glazed doughnut."

Liska appeared frightened at the prospect of exercise. Monty sneered. He led the way out the door.

I caught myself staring at Marnie's Jeep. "Sorry about the tire."

"Why? You didn't poke a hole in it. But I like your sense of duty. Make your coffee while you can, and I'll tell you what I've found out."

She followed me to the kitchen, glanced for a moment at Teresa Barga's belongings inside the door. "Shouldn't that go to the curb?"

"If she doesn't come back, I'll auction it to benefit the homeless. Have you recovered from getting scooped?"

"I buried myself in work. I dug into old newspapers, county tax records, and state corporate papers. I spent eleven hours online. I've done fifteen telephone interviews. It's like untangling a hair ball."

"Because time has passed, or people made it complicated?"

"Both," she said. "I learned yesterday that Borroto Brinas was started by a Miami architect, Manuel Reyes Silveria. He came up with a concept, then brought in advisors and investors."

"I know there's a chapter two."

She pulled a Spiral notepad from her back pocket. "From the October seventh, 1983, *Miami Herald*: 'Reyes took his life with a shotgun yesterday at the canal edge behind his Coral Gables home. A friend said he had been despondent, "embroiled in a war of lawyers and financiers for control of his company." A BBDC spokesman, Artemio Fernandez, expressed his colleagues' "infinite grief and sense of loss." He noted that the company's projects in Dade and Monroe counties would move ahead "in keeping with our founder's dreams." ' "

"Jesus," I said. "Identical suicides, a generation apart, under the dark cloud of BBDC. Do we know anything about the company's other projects?"

"Nope," she said. "Just that island. They wanted condos and gift shops within swimming distance of North Roosevelt. I can't find the corporate name attached to anything else. It was a one-pony circus."

I said, "Why didn't they build back then? Or do we know that?"

"They had everything in place by 1978. They got a hundred-year lease from the city, hired marine engineers, got all the permits, all the financing. Then Florida threw a wrench in the works. The state said the land was bay bottom. It wasn't attached to the main island, so it didn't belong to the city in the first place. It belonged to Florida, so all those permits were useless. Everything stopped in early 'seventy-nine."

"Let me guess. That land is part of the big parcel the feds made the state give back to the city. When, two years ago?"

"Right," said Marnie. "The district court said that the state's land policy back then was illegal."

"Should I be foolish enough to ask about environment?" I said.

"Our city attorney thinks that the project's grandfathered in. Even if it screws the water and kills baby birds, there's no way to stop it."

"When the dreamer died by his canal, who inherited BBDC?"

Marnie checked her notepad. "His fifty-one percent went to a nephew and two nieces. They all live in Coral Gables, and the nephew's an attorney. He campaigned for years to get the feds to declare the land grab void, and won. He's the one who's been pushing this deal into the city commission's face. You want to guess his name?"

"The spokesman who bubbled over with grief?" I said.

"You got it. Artemio Fernandez."

"Maybe Artie's our expert in neat suicides. Who owns the rest of it?"

"Forty-four percent is held by Remigio Partners. Either the partners went by fake names, or they're all dead. I found one reference to Remigio in the archives. It was an old DEA district court filing. The government wanted the company's bank records during a big drug sweep called Operation Grouper. That was when the cops busted a hundred people, then the cops got busted, too. They got greedy with confiscated cash."

"What you've told me adds up to ninety-five percent."

"BBDC's last five percent was sold to people in Key West prior to 1979. People who might have helped promote the project. Even quarter shares were sold on the docks and in bars. That's where you and Sam and eighteen others came in, including five dead ones on that list, too."

"Who were Borroto and Brinas?"

"I couldn't find them in the corporate records, or anywhere else," she said. "They may have been ancestors honored by the company name."

I carried my coffee to the porch. Marnie followed, sat across from me.

"You said the other night that Gomez's vote would've cost Sam and me our investments. Let's say it passes now. Where's that leave us?"

"I can only begin to guess," she said. "With current land values, growth restrictions that this project could ignore, and future rents, we're talking hundreds of millions. Even with your fractional ownership, you could be into the high five-, low six-figure range. Sam, twice as much. Who knows? It could be triple that. You two could sit back and take dividends and be set for life."

"I had no idea . . ."

My phone rang. At the crack of dawn on Saturday?

Marnie said, "Don't answer it. The *Herald* is running down that list of BBDC names. There's nothing you can say that will sound good."

"How is that different from the way I look and feel?"

"Let's talk about your pity problem."

I decided not to mention her bemoaning the *Miami Herald*'s scoop. "All this research, and we still don't know who murdered Steve Gomez."

"If we knew that, we could celebrate. Spend the day in the Snipe Keys."

"We should do it anyway," I said.

"On whose boat?" said Marnie. "Sam blew out the door at six-thirty. He took his skiff keys, but not his fly kit. He rolled his gun into a raincoat. It's not going to rain today."

Two possibilities. If he found Marlow, Sam would call the FDLE, give precision coordinates to a SWAT helo. Or else no one would ever again see that Fountain with its Yamaha motor.

"He needed to escape," I said. "What does he call it, hydrotherapy? A trip to the backcountry and home by noon."

"Too fast an answer, Alex. He doesn't have a charter. He didn't get any calls from friends in broken-down boats who needed to be towed in. What's he doing?"

"I don't know, for sure."

"You're holding back."

I wanted to sip an endless coffee so I wouldn't have to speak. It was too hot to put near my mouth. "I try not to be a gossip or a tattletale."

"I just handed you three days of research, you bastard. Talk."

"The man who probably killed Lorie Wheeler is a fugitive. He could be anywhere in America, but he ditched his car and owns a boat. Sam knows what the boat looks like . . ."

"Searching the ocean? That fucker. Is that why he took his gun?"

"We're talking about a heartbroken man, Marnie."

"You are so full of shit. He's my partner and he's shutting me out."

The phone rang again.

I began to get up. "You going to advise me not to answer it?"

Marnie went for the door. "Kiss my ass. I'm not saying another word."

I let it ring.

Marnie spun her tires in gravel as she hurried out of the lane. A guest at the Eden House pool played Dire Straits' "Sultans of Swing" for the dozen homes within earshot. I couldn't hear the guitar solo because a twin-engine airplane flew low overhead.

Liska said, "We're chasing our tails, here. The media's watching. You know what happens when you chase your tail a thousand miles an hour? You look like a blurry circle, a hairy doughnut. You look like a tropical storm on the Weather Channel. You look like a poorly focused asshole."

I put the glazed doughnut back in its bag. "Good similes," I said. "Bad for the appetite. I watch the Weather Channel more than I look up assholes."

"Obviously you and I don't work in the same building."

I warned myself to watch out. Aghajanian and Liska were more than just an out-of-town FBI guy and a rookie sheriff. They'd worked as a team at the city and were known for grabbing hardcore thugs. They had gone beyond good-cop–bad-cop routines, had taken their Q-and-As to free-form, abstract levels. Their act was more pester-and-comfort than maim-and-reprieve. They had puzzled criminals, confused them, coaxed accomplices' names, street tips, and confessions. What they'd saved on rubber hoses they could have spent on Kleenex.

"Everyone's looking for Odin Marlow," I said to break the ice. "I saw him drive by the hospital in Miami when you were inside."

Liska owed me an apology for his hospital tirade about Sam. He had called him a douchebag, a time waster. He'd insinuated that diet pills or mood drugs were behind Sam's craziness.

He was going to save the apology. He inspected a spider's web on my screening. "Marlow was my supervisor twenty-five years ago. He was taking payoffs to avoid certain docks at three A.M., so bales could be moved from speedboats to vans. He was a rare one, never let the money show. They had to shitcan him for snagging free pussy off teenage whores. They got long-lens black-and-whites of a young girl squeezing his dick at four A.M. in the alley next to the Swizzle Stick on Duval. I say, 'they,' I mean, 'me.' I had to hide on the roof of the bank building and take his picture myself."

"Bottom line, Marlow's a Broward problem," I said. "Has anyone made progress with the alleged murders of Naomi Douglas and Steve Gomez?"

"Have you talked to Bobbi Lewis?" said Liska.

I shook my head.

"You know about her relationship with Steve Gomez?"

"She mentioned they'd been friends."

Liska faced me. "Or more than that?"

"I got that impression."

"You know who ended it?"

"Don't those things stop by mutual agreement?"

"Never," said Liska. "Or should I say 'always' and ask how your personal life is doing?"

I turned my head to Monty. He looked impassive, patient. The FBI gives out its own annual Oscar awards.

"Lewis ended it," I said. "He wouldn't leave his wife for her."

"Now we're getting closer. A year ago his wife turned the table. She left him. We might assume that he didn't resume his affair with Lewis."

"We don't know that," I said.

"If he had, there would have been nothing wrong with making it public."

"I'd have to be a dunce not to see where this is going."

Liska went back to the spider. His eyes traced the web strands to where they connected with the screen framing. "Did you get the idea that Lewis had counted on that split with Yvonne?"

"When she talked the other day, the first I heard about it, she sounded like she had come to grips. It was over and done."

Monty said, "You told me her investigation was 'on again, off again,' or something to that effect."

"But that was her approach to Naomi, not to Gomez."

"Right," said Monty. "But you told us Thursday that Naomi had raised Steve Gomez. I sensed that Lewis learned that fact as you spoke it."

"I did, too."

"How do you think that affected her?"

"She might have felt a certain relief," I said. "I was with her when Naomi's neighbor told her that Gomez was a regular midday visitor.

Both our minds, right then, went straight to nooners. That was one of the times when she went flaky."

"What were the others?"

"Can I suggest you ask Lewis instead of me?"

"Since our last meeting here," said Liska, "no one has seen or heard from her."

I added up forty hours. "Has she missed work assignments?"

"She doesn't punch a time clock," said Liska. "She's expected to call in so we can find her when we need her. She hasn't called, she's not answering."

"Anyone knock on her door? Where does she live?"

Liska nodded. "She owns a canal house on Aquamarine, on Big Coppitt. We checked. Her Celica wasn't there. One of our female dispatchers picked a lock on a sliding glass door early this morning. We were afraid she was in there, maybe done something to herself. Nobody home."

"I've never heard her talk about friends," I said.

Monty butted in. "We think she left town."

In other words, they thought she was a valid suspect in the murder of her ex-lover.

"I was standing right where I'm standing now," I said. "I showed Dexter a scene photo. The bloodstain on Steve Gomez's shirt. He reacted by saying, 'Oh.'"

"You betcha," said Liska. "Right then I took the case away from the city."

"No, you didn't."

"Bullshit. I assigned the case to Lewis."

"Wrong. She said, 'It's my case now,' and you said, 'Agreed.' She took the initiative. Did she take the case file, too?"

Liska looked at Aghajanian. They both knew I was right.

"Fuck," said Liska.

"I take it the FDLE didn't swoop in and lift the case from your hands."

Liska shook his head.

"Back to square one?" I said. "You're not sold on Whit Randolph?"

"You ever see Randolph and Lewis together?" said Monty.

"No," I said. "But let's start from the beginning. Why don't we go over to Steve Gomez's yard and get a feel for his last moments? Do some down-and-dirty detective work? Maybe a bright lightbulb will appear in one of our heads."

"Monty and I can go alone," said Liska. "You stick around, do laundry, maybe take a few pictures in the yard."

"You two will look at the yard like cops," I said. "I'll see it my way. Did anyone else notice the Akron, Iowa, connection? Wasn't it me who showed Dexter how the blood on Gomez's shirt didn't match the shotgun wound?"

Liska looked at Aghajanian.

Monty said, "Change your pants first."

The phone rang as I locked the house to leave. Its ring sounded ominous. I took Marnie's warning and let it go.

Monty drove his red convertible. The top was already down. Liska sat in back and I could swear he scrunched down so no one would recognize him.

Once again, I was riding shotgun. People on White looked at us like the last three stragglers from spring break. If they had looked closer, they'd have guessed three guys on the rock for a funeral in the only rental car they could get.

30

MONTY STOPPED THE RED Mustang across from Gomez's house on Riviera. The wind had gone still and smells of salt rot from the canal wafted out to the road. A spindly egret stood on the roof of a Dodge Ram pickup three houses down. Four houses away in the other direction, a maniac blew dust off his driveway with a screaming machine.

Gomez's next-door neighbor probably went 260, but didn't have the height to carry it. He was trimming fronds from a six-foot pygmy date palm near his front door. His broad Panama hat, if real, had cost hundreds. The Bermuda shorts wouldn't bring fifty cents at a Goodwill.

"That's who found the body Monday morning," I said.

"Shit," said Liska. "His name's Darling, and he's good for a letter a week to the *Citizen*. He started that push for a Law Enforcement Review Board."

"If he shuts you out, go away," I said. "Let me talk to him."

"Okay, Mister Pro. What will he confess?"

"Forget it. I'll stay in the car."

"Come on," said Monty. "You can be our civilian oversight committee."

Liska didn't like it. "Don't say one fucking word until I walk away."

Liska had the sense to introduce the three of us by name, not by title. The man knew, of course, that he was speaking to the county sheriff, and he may have recognized Monty's name. But he didn't know me and probably could see by looking that I wasn't a municipal employee.

Liska asked if he could ask questions.

"I mind my own business."

"You found the body, sir. That's very much my business."

The man lifted his hat, used his index finger to swipe sweat from his forehead, then replaced the hat. The humidity on his face suggested he had been at work for some time. Only six or seven brown fronds lay at his feet. "What about these two?"

Liska looked at Monty. "These men are plain citizens, like you."

Darling had teardrops at the corners of his eyes and a mucus drip. He probably sprayed saliva when he talked about popping popcorn. He held small pruning clippers, but stuck close to the ten-inch hedge shears on the ground. He said, "I ain't plain. You are."

Liska scoped the green plaid shorts. "I agree, sir. I think you know what I meant."

"I don't know what you meant. I flunked mind reading."

Liska said, "To your knowledge, sir, did anyone else in the neighborhood hear the gunshot?"

"Never nobody home. Boy down here works at Manley-DeBoer. Lady two houses over runs a fabric store by Sears. Across the street, they sleep past noon. They're party people with bad taste in music. Even worse taste in the lowlifes they invite to party."

"Did you call 911 from your home phone?"

"What kind of stupid-ass question is that? You're the sheriff. You got the ultimate caller ID, and you don't know I used the dead man's dock phone?"

"Did you touch the body, or in any way move it?"

"I took his pulse. The way he looked, I hoped the poor bastard was dead. I sure as hell didn't want to do mouth-to-mouth. You would've thought the same way."

"I'm sure I would, sir. Did you see any vehicles come or go on Monday morning?" said Liska.

"I thought about that after I found him, you know. Nothing registered, not to say it didn't happen."

"No police cars or city vehicles?"

"I would've noticed police cars," said Darling.

"How about boats in the canal?"

"I saw two go by—folks live up the way about eight, ten houses. I thought they was crazy, the way the wind blew."

Liska shifted topics. "Are you familiar with Yvonne Gomez?"

"I never laid a hand on that slut."

"Sorry about my phrasing. You see her coming and going lately?"

"You think I hang around cheap motels? She ain't been here."

Liska said, "Sorry to bother you." He elbow-nudged Monty, looked at me, and walked away.

I hung back, locked eyes with Mr. Darling.

His right toe touched his hedge clippers. "You got a problem?"

"A question."

"Fuck off."

"I'm a threat, too?" I said. "I've never carried a badge in my life."

"I don't give a shit what you never did. You're with them, and they got the badges. You're part of their club, I want you gone."

"So I ask you a question, or I ask the sheriff a different one. You want to know what I'll ask him?"

"I said I don't give a shit."

"I'm going to remind him of that item in the *Herald* about Gomez's watch showing up in a pawn shop."

"What's your question?"

"Then I'll ask him if anyone's checked the store's videotape."

Darling bit his lower lip, thought about it. "What's your name?"

"Rutledge."

"What were you going to ask me?"

"Did you see any cars pull into that garage before you heard the loud boom?"

Darling fixed his gaze on Monty's convertible. "I saw the mayor's city car. But not just before the shotgun. I saw him come home about the time he usually went to work, twenty of eight that morning. They never change the oil in that hooptie. It smells up the neighborhood something godawful."

"He was driving it?"

"Who else?"

"Did you see his face?" I said.

"No, I didn't see his face. Sunlight off the windshield glass that time of morning? You couldn't see a fucking elephant in that car."

"And you never saw him leave again?"

"Nope. But it's not like I don't get a haircut and go to the post office every Monday. Come to think of it," he said, "I smelled that car again. Right when I was calling 911."

"How much did you get for the watch?"

"Not nearly enough. If I ever find out you tipped the heat, you'll never own a stereo more than ten days. You follow me?"

"You talk like that, I wonder if you shot the man. Just to get his watch."

"Anything's possible, except I didn't. He was a good neighbor. Now I'll get more party people or minorities, if you know what I mean. Meanwhile, what is it you got? A jukebox CD player with two hundred discs?"

"I've got a Cuban neighbor," I said, "a retired man who keeps an eye on our lane. He spends his time hiding Spanish brandy from his wife and cleaning his gun collection. The last guy who tried to break into my house needs to be in therapy, to regain the use of his arm. It's a shame the prison system has trouble hiring therapists. It's a goddamned scandal."

Darling bit the other side of his lower lip. He studied his pygmy palm. More liquid appeared on his face.

I said, "With the Gomez place locked up, we need to get to his backyard through your property. I need you to invite the sheriff to walk down the side of your house, use your canal bulkhead."

"You take him back there. I ain't talking to that shitbird no more."

I walked out to the street. Monty and Liska sat in the two front seats. I told them we had Darling's permission to access the Gomez yard.

"I can only hope his first name's Dick," said Monty.

"We going back there?" I said.

"This was your idea," said the sheriff. "It was a bad one. I can't figure out what we'd learn standing in the sun looking at a dead man's dead flowers."

"He saw the mayor's city car drive in at seven-forty that morning. He thought it might have left about the time he was dialing that dock phone."

"Was that the only bone he threw you?"

"It raises a question or two, wouldn't you say?"

"Good, Rutledge. Maybe the car shot him, then escaped. But you know what's shitty? It'll rust to death before it gets convicted. You believe what you want. Me, I'll go back to reality. You walking, or you want to get in?"

Something or someone, like Bobbi Lewis, had Liska's motor running at the red line. I climbed over the side. My turn to scrunch down in the backseat. My turn to wonder about Lewis. She had picked me up at the airport Wednesday at noon. Within thirty minutes she had told me that she and Gomez had been lovers. She had brought up the subject. Almost as if she had wanted to become a suspect, as if guilt was driving her to confession.

Dredgers Lane was quiet and empty. The sun had lifted above the trees high enough to heat the pavement. Barely midmorning and shrubs already looked defeated. I knew how they felt. I was tempted to close up the house, turn on the air conditioner, and hibernate all day.

Before Monty drove away, I said, "Any more on Ernest Bramblett?"

"I don't know. Just for a while, stop asking me for anything."

"I can't ask you out for a beer?"

"I'm out of here at two. My next vacation's in Cabo San Lucas."

"We didn't have a chance to bond."

"Right. Maybe I'll see you in a couple years."

The FBI had taught him an attitude, too. His front wheel chirped as he turned left onto Fleming. Marnie, now Monty. The neighbors were going to complain about reckless cars leaving the lane.

I dialed my access number. Five messages.

Annie Minnette. "I would very much like to know what the hell is going on. You came within an orange hair of embarrassing me in court. Whatever happened, and I don't really want to know, I got all charges dropped. When I went to secure Sam's release, he'd been gone for hours. I feel used. By doing what you did, you effectively turned me into a law officer. You made me part of a sting, and I don't even know whose it was. I don't like being lied to. I don't like being used. I don't—"

The message was cut off after thirty seconds.

The next was Matt, the underpaid account executive from the Sarasota ad agency. "Sorry to call on the weekend, Alex, especially from the scene of a disaster. Casey Hample discovered over-the-counter downers, which he mixed with Appleton rum and hashish. Yesterday's shoot was more like a rampage. One girl went to the airport in tears. My boss won't come out of her hotel room. If you could be here by Monday, or Tuesday at the latest, I'll reinstate your day rate and throw in a bonus disguised as per diem. Call my cell number. Save my life."

Then, from Teresa. "Sorry about those boxes. The person who loaned me her truck had a Cayo Hueso problem. She forgot that she loaned me her truck. New topic. I won't get much sympathy, but Whit's out on bond and he says he's being followed and it's not paranoia. This unmarked car is for real. He goes to lunch the same time each day. Who would follow him to the Turtle Kraals every single trip? Also, this didn't come from Dexter, who's depressed, but it came from him: Keep your distance from Bobbi Lewis. Something's going down. I shouldn't have said this to a tape recorder. I miss you. I really want to—"

The message was cut off.

Teresa, criminology major, was portraying Randolph, grift champion, as a victim. Did she know that he was a murder suspect? Or had she forgotten that detail?

Annie's voice, again: "And I hate people who don't have call waiting. I don't have the energy to go through all the paperwork to find Sam's home address, so the package and the bill will arrive on Dredgers Lane no later than Tuesday morning. I would appreciate your attention to the invoice. My company closely tracks our billings." She hung up.

If law school taught her anything, it taught her how to use adverbs.

Teresa, again: "Funny, I've never left you a message long enough to find out there was a time limit. I forgot what I was going to say, anyway. Did you hear me say that Bobbi Lewis is being watched by the county's internal affairs group? I know you trust her, but be careful. Call me soon. Really."

Forgot what she wanted to say? She was going to suggest a hand-holding session so she could explain why cheating is a symptom of growth. Perhaps she would call a third time to warn me about Lewis. Were the calls meant to deflect suspicion from Whitney Randolph? Was his long criminal past being glossed and sugar-coated and minimized? Was I the only person around who wanted Lewis to be innocent?

The phone rang while I still held it. Jack Spottswood said, "You were going out of town. Why am I catching you at the house?"

"Your first chance in three days," I said.

"I just got a call from Mrs. Douglas's brother, one Ernest Bramblett."

"From Texas?"

"From Grinnell Street. Somehow the FBI got word to him that his sister had died. He just called me from Naomi's front porch. He wanted me to tell the neighbor lady to give him a house key."

"You want me to go over and . . ."

"Please," he said.

"I don't want to get tied down with this guy all day."

"I can open a slot for Monday. Put him off until then."

I put down the phone. It rang. How did it know? I capped my desire to chuck it in the yard.

Sam said, "I'll pick you up for lunch. We need home cooking away from home."

"Save yourself running circles on one-way streets," I said. "I need to walk that way, anyway. I'll meet you there. Give me a ten-minute head start."

Bramblett looked to be in his sixties, and harried by travel as opposed to grief stricken. "The neighbor let me in," he said. "I assume the house is mine now. I'd feel foolish wasting money on a hotel room."

Was that my thanks for showing up? This stuffy fucker needed my permission to stay in the house. I clammed up. I needed his help to settle the estate.

Bobbi Lewis had said, "He's dead, too. Or the killer."

By his attire and manner, Ernest Bramblett looked out of place. He wore dress trousers, faint pinstripes on charcoal gray, and held his suit coat over his arm. His starched pink dress shirt had collar tips sharp enough to draw fingertip blood. He'd loosened his Repp tie. His face was smooth as a baby's ass, and showed the blush of someone fighting blood pressure. Bramblett probably had not lost much hair since his youth, but it had turned brilliant white.

His cell phone, a briefcase, and a business envelope rested on a chair cushion. A note was scrawled on the envelope. On another cushion was a stack of magazines, mailers, junk offers, flyers.

"You're the executor, Mr. Rutledge?"

"Yes." My stomach growled.

"You might have held her mail, for security reasons. So the home did not look unoccupied."

"You're right. My mistake. This has been a hectic few days. That detail slipped past me."

"You're the fine-art photographer?"

"Naomi appreciated my work," I said.

"I hear the past tense, sir. Did she change her mind?"

"Not that I know of."

"Perhaps she grew tired of your pestering her?"

"Pestering? About . . ."

"About managing the new civic art museum. She said on the telephone that you'd become a nuisance."

"I never discussed the museum with your sister," I said.

"Never?"

"Not one time."

"I must have the wrong man. Have you time for a walk-through?"

"I need to spend time with you, sir, but I didn't expect you to arrive today. Can we talk Monday morning at the lawyer's office?"

He scanned his new yard and porch furniture. I saw the neighbor doing a surreptitious check. Her face read, "Don't look at me, I'm ignoring you."

"If that's what works for you, Mr. Rutledge, that'll be fine. This grubby damned town is not my idea of paradise." He laughed without smiling, without a trace of humor. "I'll spend tomorrow finding a real-estate broker."

31

I WALKED GRINNELL, TURNED west on Caroline. The new ferry terminal made me ashamed of the island. The shrimp boats were gone forever, their rigging and spidery masts banished to low-rent wharves on Stock Island. That was a function of real-estate prices, but the bulldozing of tradition was greed. The island's history was being edited for family consumption, was now a cheap commodity like T-shirts and keychains made in China. A dome over Mallory Square? Hell, turn the lighthouse into a Bungee-jump concession. Put a water slide on Solares Hill. There were too few of us left to fight. Attrition had been house by house for thirty years, and Key West had soaked up new money. We citizens hadn't stepped back, grasped the picture, put up a united effort to stop it. So many old Conchs had migrated to Ocala that parts of that landlocked city were bilingual. If they painted the new Conch Harbor to match that cookie-cutter strip mall on Simonton, we'd know it was time to take to the boats.

Sam pulled into a metered spot in front of PT's. His Bronco had reached a stage of decay that worried me. I feared that it soon would be put down like a loyal pet, sent to the crusher in a shower of prayers and tears. Maybe he could donate it to an artificial reef. He saw me staring at the rusted rear bumper and taillight housing.

"Marnie hinted in March," he said. "She gave me a brochure for a VW Passat station wagon. Have I gotten fuddy-duddy?"

"Maybe she's trying to force-molt the crab. Hard-shell to soft-shell."

"Can you see me in a cute car?"

"You could wear a palm-frond hat. Tie a coon tail to your antenna."

Sam said, "Blow yourself. It'd be dying an early death."

Inside PT's a drunk approached us. He wanted to whine about his stolen bicycle. "Now I got to shell out money I ain't got to buy another bike 'cause I didn't have money for a lock, and still don't. Is this American fair play, I ask you? Is this why I fought in Nam?"

The dude wanted a handout, knew his game well. We would have to buy our privacy, but we refused to play. I forced myself not to rush the kitchen where I would grab anything nonhuman, nonmetallic and stuff it down my gullet. Chain-drinker's quacking lasted until our food arrived.

Sam deadpanned, "You didn't go to Nam."

"Whatever," said the drunk. He caught the steel in Sam's eyes. "I *thought* about going there. I'm not a nice person, but I think nice thoughts."

"Think about distance," said Sam.

The man had just enough sense to follow instructions.

I said, "Even the hustlers are victims."

"Especially the hustlers," said Sam.

We set to packing in chow and didn't speak until we paid the check. We stayed in the booth and nursed our third beers.

"I got a call from Goodnight Irene," said Sam. "Eight-fifteen this morning."

"She want to meet you at Cheers?"

"That first invitation, I think, was a freelance move on her part. Like she wanted to tip me off to the sting before I got my ass in a jam. Anyway, she said you bought our butts out of that Ops Box when you described Marlow's boat. Up till then, they were going to mess with us, hold us a few days to yank our chains."

"I was grabbing at straws," I said.

"I guessed right, too. She said Marlow withdrew two hundred from an ATM in Deerfield Beach, about the time Simmons cut us loose. He tried a machine an hour later in West Palm, outside a marine supply store. The bank told him he'd maxed his daily limit. Their next stop going north could be Jax or Savannah."

"Don't forget he took interest in that company we bought into. We could run into him at Captain Tony's. Or we could see Macho and Marv in there, for that matter. Maybe Irene was calling from a booth on Duval."

We left PT's and crossed the street. Sam pushed five quarters into the meter so he could leave his Bronco in the parking slot. He wanted to walk to the Sea Store on Greene. Bill Ford has sold nautical artifacts for thirty years, a perfect coda to his Navy career. He'd been through phases of binnacles, wooden blocks, glass bottles, brass portholes, and exotic driftwood. During the past fifteen years he'd pushed Patrick O'Brian novels and conversation. He was holding an antique chart for Sam.

We hit the waterfront boardwalk, walked past Schooner Wharf. "The air tastes like twenty percent seawater," said Sam. "A month ago we had hot sun and cold north wind. Turk bitched when he had to heat his house and air-condition his car."

"People claim we don't have seasons."

Sam grunted. "We got changes up the wazoo. The island used to smell of shrimp heads, diesel, and barnacles. Now it reeks of garlic, hotel soap, and moped tailpipes."

"When I got here, nobody had heat in their house or air in a car," I said. "The only carryover is cigars."

"Still, two things are different about them, too."

"The price?"

"And the number of women smoking them."

"What you just said is politically incorrect."

"So is smoking, but it's our last tradition." Sam stopped and offered to help two people find their way.

"I thought you hated tourists."

"As a species, I do," he said. "Those were just lost people."

"You think Odin Marlow stuck around town after he was fired by the Key West police?"

"Back in the Seventies? If he was a crook, he had two choices. He could hang in, cash blue chips, and chase poontang. Or he could go far away and spend his dirty profits without raising eyebrows."

"Maybe this time his 'far away' is right here."

Sam shook his head. "I was running down the front side, and I started thinking about those guys from the Seventies—Buzzy Burch, Tazzy Gucci, and the boys. They ran their marijuana wherever they wanted. The whole Coast Guard was looking for them, radars and what all. Nine boats made the beach for every one that got caught. Here I am, one guy looking for one boat. How fucked up is that?"

"It's a big ocean," I said. "A boat like his, if he had the fuel, he could hide out there for days."

"But he doesn't have the fuel, and that's his weakness. That boat has to come ashore sooner or later."

I told Sam about Liska's fresh suspicions of Bobbi Lewis's actions.

"How do you read it?" he said.

"The short bridge between a crime fighter and a criminal."

"So you buy the possibility?"

"Everything I know about her says it's impossible. Everything she did on Wednesday and Thursday was off the wall. The coin's heads or tails. No middle ground."

"Sounds like you and me," said Sam. "You got a theory that might play better?"

"My theory holds massive bias."

"Why would Randolph want to kill?"

"Frustration. He may have seen this island as his masterpiece scam in the making. Who's to say he didn't set up Naomi one day, Gomez the next, then learn they'd put their heads together and shared their misgivings? If so, he saw the goose drying up and his golden eggs turning black. Maybe they told him to leave town, threatened to expose him. Maybe he killed them so he could stay in business."

"Assuming they were sharp enough to spot a scam . . ."

"Naomi was a careful investor," I said.

"Sounds about perfect."

"Meanwhile," I said, "a character on Cudjoe complained to the sheriff. The guy spotted Randolph for a hustler." I saw a sudden mental picture of Frank Polan in his kayaking outfit and sun oil, and a gruff substation desk sergeant trying to keep a straight face.

"That guy's not dead, too?" said Sam.

"Not yet."

Something nagged at me, a detail I was supposed to remember.

Bill Ford's shop was closed. No surprise. His schedule worked as a function of season, grandparenting duties, and nap time. I walked another fifty feet, then motioned Sam into the gift shop. Cristina Alcroft saw Sam first and openly regarded him as a potential shoplifter. Then she recognized me.

"You won't believe this," she said. "A woman from the sheriff's office came by yesterday. Funny attitude she had. She was dressed like she was going to a resort, but at least she came and asked questions."

"Do you recall what she asked?" I said. "Were the questions as odd as her uniform?"

"She couldn't have been nicer. You wish they all could be like that. She asked what I guess were usual police questions. How long I'd known Naomi, visitors lately, mood changes. I'm afraid I wasn't much help. Everything had been fine. Whenever we got together, Naomi and I would always laugh and say, 'Ain't life grand?'"

"Did the deputy bring up the death of Mayor Gomez?"

"Well, that was quite strange. She asked if Steven could have harmed Naomi. I told her the notion was ridiculous. He was wonderful to Naomi, devoted to her."

"So that was it?" I said.

"The woman asked if Naomi ever had mentioned two or three Cuban-sounding names."

"Borroto or Brinas?"

"Yes, Brinas for sure," she said. "It sounded to me like Bina's. That used to be the name of that small grocery on Fleming."

"Did she mention a Manuel Reyes Silveria?"

"No. I would have remembered that one. I have a friend named Manuel, an elderly man who's not well. One other thing she asked, she wanted to know if Naomi had employed a financial advisor."

"Was that something you could answer?" I said.

"No, it was none of my business."

"When you say this deputy was dressed in resort wear . . ."

"Oh, that's too fancy a term, Mr. Rutledge. These days, 'resort wear' means expensive. This woman looked like she intended to spend the rest of the day out boating. She had those wrap-around sunglasses that fishermen wear. They hung from her neck on a fluorescent strap."

"I still share your worries about these deaths," I said. "What you've said might help the detectives."

"I hope so," she said. "And, again, this may not be the best time, but I still want to talk about putting you in my store."

"Why my photos?"

"I admired the two in Naomi's home. She spoke highly of you, and said you had a chest full of Key West pictures that you've been taking for years. I want that in here. History and craft and a feel for island light." She handed me a small business card. "Will you please call me when we're in a better frame of mind?"

I agreed, and managed a smile.

Sam and I stood on Simonton and looked north. Only one cloud in the sky, but the haze a block away was a rain shower. If it drifted with the wind, we'd be soaked in three minutes.

I said, "Captain Tony's?"

"Forget Macho and Marv," said Sam. "Let's head for the Bronco. I'll drop you at the house."

"I just figured out what's been bugging me for forty-eight hours. I left my bike chained outside the Green Parrot. That drunk's speech about his stolen bicycle didn't do my nerves any favors."

"You go that way, I'll go this way."

"We never discussed our investment," I said. "Our exit strategies."

Sam started toward Duval. "I'm in no hurry. Let's hike."

We made it around Sloppy Joe's, the Saturday-afternoon crowd listening to a guitar player with a sound system better than his voice. He did an old folk song and substituted off-color lyrics to cheer the high-noon drunks. They loved him.

"I can take cute trash cans and brand-new old-style lamp posts," said Sam. "I accept the fact that people who walk the slowest take up the most sidewalk. But the fucking pigeons."

"They're living the good life," I said. "Gourmet droppings from tourists' fast food bags."

"When doves are too fat to fly, are they pigeons or rats?"

"Which brings us back to our investment," I said.

"I don't know how, but here's my thinking. We were young, foolish, in it for the money. Now we're older, and in it for the write-off. I don't even know if we got documents. We don't have canceled checks, right?"

"I used cash tips from bartending," I said.

"I did a cash thing, too. Weren't we the brilliant ones? Did we get some kind of receipt?"

"I'll have to think about that. I've got boxes in my attic, but it gets hot up there. My rule is to visit the attic only in December and January."

"I'll talk to you later." Sam started up Eaton Street. "Marnie requested a reunion before the sun goes down."

"Remember that gun you loaned me awhile back?"

He nodded. "The Walther? It's still in some evidence locker."

"I should pay you for it. It saved my life. You may never see it again."

"We'll get square one way or another."

"It doesn't have a brother, does it?" I said.

"You're thinking, if we found Odin . . ."

"He's been a cop half his life, lately gone to murder."

"If I put one at your house, where would I hide it?"

"My outdoor shower, there's a hook," I said. "Behind the soap dish, between the house and slat wall. Reach through the croton bush."

I passed the La Concha's ground-floor bar. Carolyn Ferguson waved, got off her barstool, and came to the door. "Did you hear all those sirens?"

I hadn't noticed them.

"I think there was a bad wreck on Whitehead. I'm not going to go gawk. I don't gawk at accidents. I don't gawk, I really don't."

The first bad sign was Wayne the Lemonade Man shutting down for the day. His Dalmatian looked worried by the schedule change. The next bad sign was the quiet on Fleming between the old Kress building and the hotel. No exhaust echoes, no traffic at all. The police had closed the intersection. I walked in the shade of the hotel's ancient arcade. The closer I got to Whitehead, the less it looked like an accident.

I saw yellow crime tape, then started to check faces. Dexter Hayes with two other detectives. Cootie Ortega with his camera satchel. The action was between the First State Bank on the northwest corner and the county courthouse annex just south. That made three choices: a jailbreak, a robbery, or funky action in the post office. Pedestrians were being pushed from the corner, back toward me. Motorcycle cops were redirecting traffic the wrong way through the post office lot.

A uniformed patrolman tried to stop me as I caught Dexter's eye.

Hayes called out, "That man stays where he is, Calametti, but no closer."

The cop still wanted me back ten feet. I acquiesced to his power huff, moved backward. I still couldn't see the problem, and the confusing crowd now consisted entirely of law officers.

I heard the blip of a siren closer to Duval, then commotion from behind me. Two motorcycles escorted three vehicles the wrong way down Fleming. The county's new medical examiner van carried Larry Riley and an assistant. That confirmed that someone had died. The van was followed by a Dodge Intrepid, then the beat-up, windowless Dodge Ram van that belonged to the local FDLE office.

As the crowd of cops and detectives made space for the arriving vehicles, I got my first clear view of the scene. Whit Randolph's yellow BMW roadster sat at an odd angle, halfway into the intersection. Its windshield was shattered and the driver's-side headrest was shredded. I saw the top of Whit's head, the dripping copper stains on the driver's-side door.

I fixed my eyes on Hayes. He turned. I raised my hands and mouthed, "How many?"

He held up one finger.

Whitney Randolph's criminal past was history.

He had reached his dead end at Mile Zero.

32

SIRENS FILLED KEY WEST. You would have thought the crime had happened two minutes ago, across the island, many dead in a stadium or mall. I tracked emergency vehicles going every direction but straight to the dead hustler.

Crime-scene analysts and supervisors blocked my view. A quick glimpse told me that a headlight had burst. I saw no other damage besides the windshield and headrest.

Dexter Hayes approached me. "Someone poked him a third eye."

"Was anyone else in the car?" I said.

"A young woman with a bloody face ran from the scene. We think she got hit by broken glass. I'll get a call from the hospital the minute she walks in. We put a civilian car on Fleming to scope the lane."

"You're wasting your time there. Check her place in the Shipyard."

"We sealed it eight minutes ago."

"Her mother's house?" I said.

"Shit," said Dexter. He made a fifteen-second call on his cell phone.

"She left me a message last night. She said Randolph was spooked by a car on his butt. The term he used was 'unmarked,' and it followed him to lunch, the same time every day. Maybe right about now."

"It wasn't us. I'll ask my friend Liska. He wanted that bird to him-

293

self. Lewis wanted him even worse." Dexter glanced at the murder scene. "Why a message, if you don't mind my asking?"

"I haven't seen her since the funeral," I said. "I saw the back of her head in church."

"She got militant yesterday when the county picked up her friend. We had to send her home. I wrote it up as admin leave."

"How did she take that?"

"She whined like cheap tires on the Seven-Mile Bridge. Told me I'd proclaimed her guilty by association."

"To which you said . . ."

"Look, Rutledge," said Hayes. "There's a little more to it—"

"A municipal secret?"

"Thursday night, after Lewis told us on your porch about Randolph calling Naomi Douglas, I wanted to ignore the county and pop him on suspicion of murder. I had me a sit-down with Teresa, told her what I was going to do. You said yourself, he had eight arms, all dealing excuses. For all the hours from Sunday midnight until Monday morning, during the time Naomi died, your octopus had an alibi."

"Do I want to know?"

"No, but I'll tell you. Teresa Barga swore he was elsewhere when the crimes went down."

"How would she know? She was in my bed from eleven o'clock on."

"That's our little problem," said Hayes.

"So he doesn't have an alibi at all?"

"She got up to use the bathroom?"

"Is that a question?" I said.

"He was in his car, parked on Fleming. They went to the Ramada."

"Horsecrap. If they went anywhere, it'd be back to her old condo."

"Well, for some reason, they didn't. She snuck out, they did their thing, she came back to your place at sunup and went straight to the shower out back. When she got out of the shower, you and Sam Wheeler were leaving for Lauderdale."

"Too complicated," I said. "It's horseshit."

"She still had the motel receipt."

"You called him a jellyfish?"

"Yep," said Hayes.

"Bingo. Add slime."

"It gets worse. You flew to Lauderdale, and she took a long lunch."

"They did a double?" I said.

"So he's got his alibi running well into our best guess at Gomez's time of death. Unless we want to think that she's an accomplice. In that case, they did a double, but it was murder."

I pointed at the yellow car. "Any suspects?"

"Only you," said Hayes. "That's why I told the uniform to let you stick around."

"Give me a minute. I'll figure out how that makes sense."

"Your girlfriend couldn't make up her mind, right? Rutledge or Randolph. You wanted to help with her decision?"

"Not my style, Dexito. I would've spray-painted WASH ME on the trunk of his car. I would've short-sheeted his bed."

His eyes wandered a moment, then came back to me hard. "You admit that revenge entered your mind?"

I pictured myself shackled into another backseat. My Cannondale would fuse to the bike rack before I ever got to the Green Parrot. "The last six days, what hasn't entered my mind?"

"Must be crowded in there. Do you sift turds to find lost jewels?"

"The victim was doing me a favor," I said. "My deal with Teresa had run its useful life. The way it went down, she split. I wasn't the bad guy."

"You were ready to rotate the stock?"

"No, I got dumped on. The way she did it told me she wasn't the perfect package I'd hoped for. Not classy, not truthful."

"Can we do a chemical test on your hands and clothing?"

"Don't waste your time," I said. "The past hour, lunch with Sam at PT's, ten minutes in a gift shop on Greene talking with a friend of Naomi's. I've got witnesses, receipts, beer breath, and a letter from my mom."

"The bullet that put the third eye in Randolph's forehead was a big one." Dex pointed at the Florida Keys Publishing building. "We found a Winchester .270 hunting gun on the roof. If we've got an assassination here, it probably got set up by a phone call. Teresa might have facts we need quickly."

"I can't believe the shooter didn't draw attention, climbing up there with a weapon."

"Who looks at anything in this town? If he was dressed like a worker, it's for sure nobody would pay him their mind."

"Like a City Electric shirt?"

"Or a roofing company. Or no shirt at all, like he was going up there to fucking sunbathe."

"That building's open to a street view on three sides," I said. "Shot-guns aren't quiet. How did he get down in a hurry?"

"You want to quit the snoop act, Rutledge?"

"You accused me. I have to prove myself innocent."

Dexter pointed. "The men who own that house run a shop at the south end of Duval. They weren't home. We think the shooter climbed down in that narrow alley, went out to the La Concha parking lot, and walked. Two dudes back there run the scooter and bike rental conces-sion. They didn't see shit. We questioned the parking valet. He sees fif-teen or twenty people an hour cut through to Duval. He said they all look like freaks, one type or another."

"So the shooter was a local?"

"How did we jump to that?"

"The shooter knew the place was empty during the day. He knew how to walk away without attracting attention."

Dexter Hayes stared at the house. "He had to get around those elec-trical wires. We might pull a shoe print off the top of the AC wall unit back there."

"Anyone inside the print shop hear noises?"

"Saturday. It's empty, too," he said.

"So, a local put the weapon up there last night. Then he climbed up in daylight, looking official, like you said."

"Want to be a detective? Go to school and take the exam."

"My life's dream, Dexter. Maybe you'll have a real suspect by the next commercial. You ever heard of Artemio Fernandez?"

"Nope," he said, uninterested. "But I saw your name in the *Herald* this morning. Anything you need to talk about?"

"Marnie turned up a beauty. If I told you, it'd make the *Herald* before she got her *Citizen* story into print."

"Bullshit, Rutledge. I don't talk to the press, and I never have. You play that crap in my business, your stairway to success gets fragile. I saw that paragraph about the pawn shop. I knew the minute I saw it, only the man at the top of the stairs could've let that one slip. Chief Salesberry."

"Assuming a story develops, will she get it?"

"I'll do what I can. I'm not going to gift wrap it, take it to her doorstep."

I moved into the shade of a scrawny gumbo-limbo. "That condo development in the *Herald*? Its founder killed himself with a shotgun in 1983. He was standing next to his canal in Coral Gables."

"That's her scoop?" he said. "Two points close to Mayor Gomez, and it's a four-star fucking coincidence? We live in Florida, Rutledge. The whole state is canal homes, permits to carry, and elderly suicides. Park it with your expertise on fluid dynamics. Put it with your theory about bloodstains not matching a shotgun blast."

"I also had a theory about the same hometown."

"It wasn't a theory, Rutledge. It was an observation. So far it's gotten us nowhere."

"Do yourself a favor, Dex. That gun you found on the roof? See if it came from Gomez's storage case. He must have had a purchase record, or listed it on his homeowner's. Ask his old hunting buddies, Bruce Noe or Doc Wicker. They'll know his gear. If you don't find a match, you can bad-mouth coincidence all you want. And me, too."

Hayes got a steely look in his eye. "You through?"

"You bet. That was my last good guess. I see you're wearing your open mind today."

"Where would it get me?" he said.

"Why would someone shoot Randolph? Did he already rip off a mark for big cash? Or did someone stand to gain by his death?"

"He can thank his redneck lawyer. That speech he made when he bonded him out. He said that Randolph would make fools of the police."

"That riff about identifying the mayor's murderer?"

"Right, and now he can't."

"Where's that slick attorney from New Orleans?" I said.

"He checked out of the Casa this morning."

"They come and they go, Detective. Naomi's brother rolled into town this morning."

"Great. We should all get together for lunch."

His radio chirped. Someone barked a numeric code. "We need to clear the block," he said. "Look at the good side, Rutledge. No one's ever accused you of minding your own business. Take a hike, and be thankful you're not taking pictures. Cootie's here to bless us with his wizardry. Adios."

"He's Johnny-on-the-spot for a Saturday, isn't he?"

"He was at the city, watching a stock car race with the desk sergeant when the call came in." Dexter turned, hurried toward the mop-up.

I followed as if I belonged. Uniformed cops assumed I was tagging along with Dexter's permission. The medical examiner's people had seen me at crime scenes, so my presence wasn't questioned, and Dexter didn't hear me behind him. I accomplished my goal, saved myself the long-way walk to the Green Parrot via Duval Street. I ducked under the yellow tape, dodged two gophers pulling a body bag from Riley's new van, and started down Whitehead.

Thirty feet away, Marnie sat on the steps of a gentrified Conch house, now an attorney's office. I stood and said nothing while she wrote on her steno pad. She looked up at me with frazzled eyes, focused, and thought through her words. "I've stopped being pissed," she said.

"I just had lunch with him."

"I know." She tapped her cell phone, then flipped through her notepad. "The City of Key West fired Odin Marlow in February 1978. Within a week he was chief of security for the Borroto Brinas Development Corporation."

"He must know some wonderful old secrets. Was he a shareholder?"

"No," she said. "We would've noticed when the *Herald* printed the list."

"Borroto Brinas didn't need security," I said. "They had nothing to guard but one man's dream and a bunch of lawyers' briefcases."

"Now it's one lawyer's briefcase," she said.

"Artemio Fernandez, in Coral Gables?"

"He's had a mega-buck dream for over twenty years. Wouldn't he kill for the payoff?"

"Wouldn't we all?"

Marnie shook her head. "No."

"I don't know where that came from," I said. "But I just blasted Dex Hayes for not having an open mind."

"Would you kill for big money?" she said.

"No, and neither would you. And I have to wonder about Artemio. For all these years he went after it through the courts, the legal process. He took it this far the right way. Would he risk screwing it now?"

"He might," she said. "Where does an open mind come in?"

"You said this morning that Remigio Partners might have been formed using fake names, and the partners could've invested tainted cash. Maybe Borroto Brinas was the righteous side, and Remigio was the dark."

Marnie gazed at the action beyond the crime-scene tape. Her

expression showed defiance and pride in doing a fine job. "Am I getting closer to a good story, or farther away?"

"Your story is coming right to you."

Trust the Green Parrot. My bike was right where I had left it. A crust of beer residue never hurt anyone. Before I unlocked it, I walked to Jeanna's Deli, bought two bananas and a box of crackers, and asked for a damp napkin. I freed the Cannondale, wiped the seat clean, then coasted back down Whitehead to deliver food to Marnie.

"Sam called me back," she said. "He'd contacted friends, told them what he wanted to find. One of the guides got right back to him. Marlow's boat is docked at Oceanside."

"Like I said, your story's coming to you."

"What happens now?" she said.

"I don't know. He used his boat to get here, but he won't use it to leave."

Carmen heard me in the garage that I rented behind her house. Prepping my old Shelby Mustang for the road is a ten-minute process of wires, cables, switches, pressure checks, and airing out. I use it once or twice a month, and only for trips off the island.

"God, you look rough," she said.

"I've had a disgusting week. You?"

"Do I have to apologize?" she said. "This year it's been perfect."

"A new gentleman friend?"

"No," she said. "It's my favorite week of the year, every year."

"I'm listening."

"My body is past its adjustments for Daylight Savings Time, so I'm not dinged out. Tourists are gone, so my town becomes my town again. The streets are calm, Publix isn't a zoo, my plants know that summer's coming, and mosquitoes are two weeks away. Everybody in town acts different, like they aren't sure why, but they love this week, too. All you have to do is sit back and enjoy it. It's pretty much a no-fuckin'-brainer."

"Quaint." I snapped the clips on my distributor cap.

"I'm sorry," she said. "I know your thing with Teresa's gone sour. I wish I could help."

"Your mind is a steel trap. The name Remigio mean anything to you?"

"The trap's a little rusty. I've seen that name, but I don't know . . . How far back do I have to think?"

"You were a teenager," I said.

"Like when I just started at the post office? My job then was sorting mail for the house-to-house carriers."

"If any connection comes to mind . . ."

Carmen squeezed my arm. "I'll let you know in person."

The Shelby started on my second try, with six quick pumps on the gas pedal. It blew stinky smoke into Carmen's yard, then ran fine. I backed out, locked up behind me.

As I reached the stop sign, it clicked. I backed up, shut it down, walked to my backyard. The neighbor's springer spaniel yelped at me. I reached behind the pinewood shower enclosure. Sam had hung a Para-Companion, a small .45, on the hook. I checked out the safety, found seven rounds in its stubby magazine. I wrapped it in my ball cap, took a minute to swap secrets with the dog.

33

KEY WEST IS PACKED to the seawalls with people dodging their previous lives. It's an okay place to hide from old lovers and the laws of other
states, but the island gets dime-small when local cops are after you.
Dexter Hayes would find Teresa quickly.

I hadn't offered to join his search. She wasn't in danger, or she'd
have been shot alongside Randolph. She wasn't in trouble, either.
Hayes had made his "accomplice" remark for impact. All I could do
was hope that her injuries were minor. A doctor would patch her up
and detectives would browbeat her, to a point. The turmoil would be
light duty, her solutions post-Rutledge, and they might let her keep her
job. Wounds pull sympathy, and to people in law enforcement they sig-
nify paid dues.

There were two speed traps on Boca Chica. Seven maniacs were
running fifteen over, tailgating, showing me they were slick, but they
stabbed their brakes when they sighted the FHP Camaro. Two hundred
yards along they were back to the gas pedals, lane hopping, inside passing. Then, a county cruiser on the shoulder. Another mass whoa,
macho-merging for the Rockland Channel Bridge. The sun cooked the
roof, forced heat to my *Gumbo Limbo* ball cap. Shelby Mustangs
weren't built with AC, but I didn't live in South Florida for chilly
winds. East of Shark Key, thin mist kicked off wave tops. An inshore

chop darkened the grassy shallows and, to the south, sea and sky blended in cool pale gray.

I was cruising when I passed Baby's Coffee at Bay Point. There was no way to drive and be along for the ride at the same time. For once, it was my game. I had a passenger, though. Naomi sat close, urged me to explore, told me that most things I did were right. She began to fade, but gave me a stingy smile and said I was going in the right direction.

A real estate sign on Sugarloaf yanked me back. I pictured a similar sign, soon to be on Grinnell. I hated the thought that Bramblett would sell, and Naomi's home would go to strangers. But who was Ernest Bramblett if not a stranger? I wouldn't be his drinking pal if he stuck around.

Bobbi Lewis had bemoaned the fact that Sam couldn't take her fishing. On Wednesday she'd said, "Maybe I can find a place up the Keys to veg a few days." On Thursday, speaking of Frank Polan, with his mesh pith helmet and a cell phone clipped to his bathing suit, I'd said, "It's a lifestyle we all should hope for." Lewis had said, "Maybe I could check into his hotel." Cristina Alcroft, the gift shop owner, had described Lewis's Friday attire. "Like she intended to spend the rest of the day out boating."

Spanish Main is a straight one-mile shot from the Overseas High-way to the Straits of Florida. To the east is Kemp Channel, its constant changing colors. Across the land spit, fat and shallow as a hubcap, is Cudjoe Bay. Polan's home on stilts faced northwest. His sunset views had to be worth a fortune. Under his house, I found a two-seat paddle pontoon, an electric bicycle, a new F-150 pickup, a Mercedes C-Class coupe, and an outdoor shower. Call it Club Polan: a dozen palm trees, kayaks on the boat ramp, a wooden dock, a jet ski on a floating mini-dock, a catamaran on twin slings.

No Celica. If Bobbi Lewis was there, she had caught a ride.

I wedged Sam's Para-Companion into my belt, covered it with my shirt. On the second-level veranda, I stood ready, knocked on a sliding glass door. No one answered. I opened the door a crack and called inside. No response.

Out on Cudjoe Bay two sailboards ran crossing patterns. By the suits, one male, one female. By their moves, expert windsurfers. A flat-decked pontoon boat was anchored midbay. One of the boards stopped alongside it, and the woman tilted a beverage. I saw her in a new perspective, a new depth.

I went back to my car, stashed the pistol under the passenger seat, then snooped the outside shower. A blue mesh carryall hung from a teak post. Cute soaps, pink disposable razors, hair elastics. Bobbi Lewis on vacation.

Back on the high porch, the hammock looked perfect, but I would shut my eyes and go out like a light. I plopped my butt on a plastic chair, gave my brain a break, watched water sports. After ten minutes I got nosy in an Igloo cooler. Frank would've offered the beer, anyway. I could pay him back with a six-pack.

"You found the missing deputy, Rutledge. You win the prize. You get to trade jobs." She looked great, dripping wet, a blush of sun on her face.

"I'm leaning more toward basket weaving." I stood on the dock, watched them off-load the pontoon boat. Polan, as advertised, in his Speedo, rubber Birkenstocks, and pith helmet. Finally Lewis took a breather. She came over to beg a sip from my beer.

"You're sharp on the sailboard," I said.

"You've got nice legs."

"Where the hell did that come from?"

"Many years ago, I was an instructor," she said. "Off the deck at Louie's, when the restaurant was closed those couple of years."

"I probably have pictures of you."

"I'll buy them all." She laughed to herself, gazed across the water.

"Good day off?"

"Rutledge, I was ready to start my vacation on Tuesday. Way too ready, two days too early. I got drunk at the Turtle Kraals. Someone gave me a ride home, I don't even know who. I woke up Wednesday at ten, fully clothed, thank goodness, and got a cab to my car. I shouldn't have waited to call the office."

"Still slurring your speech?"

"I could barely hold down dry toast and Clamato."

"Punishment?"

"You." She stared, bored holes to the back of my skull. "I got sent to the airport, detailed to follow up your Naomi suspicions."

I had thought she'd been pensive. She'd been queasy.

"You had a broken heart and a hangover?"

She bit her lip and looked back at the pontoon boat. "You make it sound too majestic. I was too hung over that day to feel any emotion. But yes, the broken heart has eaten up my last seventy-two hours."

"I got it from Teresa that the deputies are looking for you. She mentioned Internal Affairs."

Lewis shrugged and shook her head. "I'm a good cop, Rutledge. I did my years in a road cruiser, stood up to idiots. No black marks. I got promoted, stayed clean. I write the best scene summaries in the department. My case rate is always top-three. All I've ever wanted to do was keep doing what I did. I would do it for free, if I didn't have a mortgage. Now all this, but it's out of my control. In the end, they're going to fuck with me or they're not."

"Someone shot Randolph ninety minutes ago. In his car, on Whitehead."

"They're going to fuck with me less," she said.

"First they have to find out that you couldn't have done it." I pointed at the magenta skin on her chest. "That sunburn is your best alibi."

"You want to see the merchandise, just ask. They're nipples and boobs, like a hundred million other women in the lower forty-eight. I'll peel down and we can have it settled."

"I would've thought you'd be more relaxed, after all that exercise."

"I needed this, so I got it while I could. I knew they'd suspect me sooner or later. You didn't answer my question."

"If you're aching to show off, I won't look away. Or we could take a rain check, maybe ramp down the tension."

"Good idea." Lewis smiled a moment, then went back to being serious. "Wednesday night, you were leaving Naomi's?"

Polan called down from his open porch. "Can I offer you two a nice Pinot Grigio?"

We said yes, to get rid of him.

"Stay on those concrete circles," he said. "Don't walk on the pea rock."

We said okay. He disappeared again.

I said, "Wednesday night?"

"I brought in two friends," said Lewis. "They work for Larry Riley. We found evidence of cleaned-up blood in the hallway."

"You kept it a secret?"

She twisted my arm to read my watch. "I can phone Tampa for results in twenty minutes. My bet says the blood matches Gomez."

"He was killed in her house, and she was killed to eliminate a witness?"

"Too easy. I have it the other way around. She called him for some kind of help. He was injured when he got there. She died first. He may have died there or somewhere else."

"Do you even have to call Tampa?" I said.

She shook her head. "You think Randolph killed them?"

"I had him for it until Monty told us about that grifter profile. That bit about their victims always being other con artists."

She walked to the shower, peeled down her bikini bottom. She turned, dared me to comment, then unhooked her top and hung it on a hook. She swung the door shut and latched it.

"Great," said Polan. He stood next to me, holding two plastic wineglasses. He looked stricken. He knew the show hadn't been for him.

His deal was growing wings. "I wasn't really attracted to her in the first place."

I asked if I could use his phone.

"You like my bay view?"

"Pretty as a Hawaiian shirt."

"The phone's upstairs. Don't walk in my kitchen with wet shoes."

I called Sam's home and dock. No answer, twice.

I dialed Marnie's cell phone. She said, "No one's found Odin Marlow, but they're looking for a dune buggy stolen from Oceanside. A mate from one of the yachts left his keys on the floor mat."

I thanked her and dialed my answering service. Two messages.

Ernest Bramblett said, "Please call." He gave me Naomi's number, one of the few I had memorized. No hurry there.

Carmen Sosa: "That name, Remigio? My daddy says it rings a bell, and my mother might know. She went to Winn-Dixie for rice pudding and frozen arroz con pollo. Can you believe frozen? She'll be home soon, so call me back."

Bobbi Lewis came upstairs in shorts and a baggy T, toweling her hair.

"You want to go into town?" I said. "Resume your vacation tomorrow?"

"What makes you think there's anything I need to do?"

"My clues from eight directions at once."

She said, "You're going to explain, right?"

I strung the tale of Marlow's history on the Key West police force, his Borroto Brinas security job, his job in Broward, and his false-identity scam. "Sam pegged the scam, and we ran smack into an FDLE sting. Marlow got spooked on Friday, so the sting deflated. But that day's *Herald* tipped him to the link between Borroto Brinas and the mayor's murder. Marlow got a new agenda. Now he's a fugitive and his boat's parked at Oceanside."

"You lost me on the agenda," she said.

"A corporation called Remigio Partners invested dirty money in

Borroto Brinas and wound up with forty-four percent of the Key West condo project. If the principals used dirty money, why not dirty tactics, like murder? It's my guess that Marlow knew about Remigio when he was here in Key West."

"Take it farther."

"Let's say someone from Remigio killed Steve Gomez to make sure the condo project would pass."

"This is new territory," said Lewis. "It sounds damn logical so far."

"Marlow sees a chance to muscle into Remigio, or his boat wouldn't be here. Find him, find the profit center. Find Remigio, find Gomez's killer. We're not solving shit standing right here. Downtown?"

"We?"

"Allow me the honor of delivering you."

"To where?"

"Closer to where you can do your job. Yes or no?"

"My service pistol is locked up at my place, and I know they're watching the house." She turned to Polan. "Frank, you got a weapon I can borrow?"

Polan loaned her a new .40 caliber Smith & Wesson SW99. "Try not to use it near saltwater," he said. He took a special cloth from a Ziploc bag, pretended to clean the piece, then handed the gun to Lewis. He'd rubbed off his fingerprints. "And don't fire it if you don't have to."

Southbound traffic was a zoo. It took us two minutes to exit Spanish Main and hook up with the flow.

"Unique fellow," I said. "More money than one man needs?"

Lewis checked out Polan's pistol, practiced the safety, reloaded the clip. "He's a generous host, but he guards his privacy. He wanted me to stay in that room under the house."

"Makes it hard to get lucky."

"He wasn't really my type."

The Pro-Realty office at Sugarloaf bugged me again, property for sale, and Bramblett's instant decision to take his money and run. He might want to hurry. Blood on the walls hurts resale value. I flashed on a vicious attack in the hallway, and on Lewis's remark Wednesday night that the place looked "too clean." Mary Butler had said, "It was . . . as if I had already been there."

The photographs in Naomi's garbage were calling to me.

What else?

We crossed the Saddlebunch Keys. Lewis said, "This'd be a great patrol car if it wasn't so smelly." She began to talk louder to be heard above the exhaust roar. "I love the fact that it doesn't have air-conditioning. Gives it character."

"It's a Shelby GT-350H," I said. "The 'H' stands for Hertz."

"As in 'hurts your ass'? You're more in touch when you feel each bump?"

"It's a racing suspension."

"So why the hell do you own it? You ought to—"

A hot-dogging Navy F-18 swooped above us as we hit the slow-down zone on Big Coppitt. Her words were lost to afterburner roar. How can a pilot describe the feeling of a ninety-degree bank at ten times the speed of a fast car?

Without slowing I whipped the steering wheel hard left. The Shelby cut the corner without sliding. In two seconds we'd turned from U.S. 1 onto 941, and our forward speed hadn't dropped five miles per hour. I slowed, pulled to the side of the road.

The aircraft noise faded. Lewis's eyes had a look of fear that gave way to glee. I was sure she admired the vehicle more than my stunt. We remained silent. We both knew the problem. We had great intentions, but no destination. Any speck of information would help.

I drove a quarter mile back to the Circle K on the corner. I fished under my seat and found a film canister full of quarters and dimes. I always keep a stash for phones, newspaper boxes, and parking meters. The pay box next to the entrance stairs was vacant. Any speck of info . . . I dialed Naomi's number.

Ernest Bramblett said, "This place has a certain charm."

"I agree with you, sir."

"So I was thinking, I'd use my sister's equipment, walk around town, take a few photos. Maybe even learn a little about my surroundings."

"Great way to spend a Saturday afternoon."

"Where's her camera?"

"I found a cheap point-and-shoot," I said. "The police have the negs and prints."

"I'm referring to the bodies, lenses, and flashes I gave her years ago. By any chance did she loan them to you? I can't imagine she gave them away."

I thought about the prints I'd found in her office, the envelopes full of sharply focused pictures. "Was it thirty-five-millimeter gear, Mr. Bramblett?"

"All of it, Olympus brand."

I cut the connection, dialed Duffy Lee Hall. I heard him answer, then drop the phone. He said, "Fuck, fuck . . . hold on . . . hello?"

"Duffy Lee . . ."

"Sorry, I'm in the darkroom. I dropped—"

"Stop talking, Duff. I'm in a hurry. I need an address, maybe from an old invoice." I told him what I needed.

"Shit, Alex. I know I have it, but it'll take me a couple minutes to close down and open up."

"I'll call you right back."

I dialed Carmen's number.

"My mama's spacy these days," she said, "but she has a perfect memory. Remigio was a gambler, ran bolita for years. His real name wasn't Remigio. They called him that because that name was on his building, on Whitehead. He died years ago, and the building was torn down in the early Nineties. My mother never knew his name."

I asked Carmen to look up Mary Butler in the phone book.

"Alex," she said, "an FDLE agent was in the lane. I dated him four years ago. He told me you'd been charged with Obstruction of Justice."

"Call Sam and warn him, okay?"

"Got it. Mary Butler on Chapman Lane." She gave me the number.

Another call. Patience, I thought, she's not too spry.

Eight rings later, Mrs. Butler picked up.

"This is Alex Rutledge."

"Now you want stock tips, and you can't have any. Or you want to buy my house."

"I need to know about a man called Remigio."

"That man, yes," she said. "He was not a bad man, as Conchs went. He gambled like they all did that, but that man was true to his blessed wife."

Grab for straws. "Do you recall anything about business associates, or his family?"

"They adopted a boy, raised him like I raised that Dexter. One morning that man Remigio's wife didn't wake up. One day after they bury that poor lady, old Remigio put a gun to his head. That odd one, that boy they raised, he wasn't a smart boy. Now he works with my cop nephew, Dexter."

"In what way?"

"He takes all them messy pictures."

"Thank you."

The greedhead got tired of messing with trivia, speculating on NASCAR collectibles. He had inherited the Remigio Partners shares and wanted his big payday. He had asked if I had worthless stock certificates for sale, then sold me Naomi's photo gear. The stupid shit had tossed my art prints into Naomi's trash.

A modus operandi echo: Cootie had snuffed his adoptive parents. Take it one step further. He'd have been in his early twenties when he'd debuted his canalside shotgun routine. He had killed Manuel Reyes Silveria, the Borroto Brinas founder and dreamer. Cootie had been planning this for half his life.

I dropped two more coins, punched up Duffy Lee's number. He read an address. He was still talking when I dropped the receiver.

34

I TOLD LEWIS TO snug her seat belt, then tighten it more. I hauled ass over Big Coppitt, saw daylight, passed three cars in the double yellow, and hoped no one pulled out of the Mobil station. A life-sized Marilyn Monroe waved from Fred's Beds and gave us a flash of blown-up skirt.

Let it hang out, Marilyn. It's all the rage.

Finally, something in my favor. No Boca Chica speed traps. As I ran eighty-five on the four-lane around the Naval Air Station, I checked my dials. Water temp too high, oil pressure low. Bad time to grenade my engine. Pavement dips tried to launch the Shelby. I had a license to fly, I could chase F-18s in the touch-and-go pattern, climb to ten thousand and scope out Cuba.

I cranked up my window to cut wind noise. I still had to shout, condense my story. I spun the list of calls, spiraled the blame down to Cootie Ortega.

Bobbi Lewis went two thumbs up. "No holes," she said. "I'll buy it."

I said, "How do we do this?"

"We don't," she shouted back. "Miss Mary Butler's already called Dexter Hayes. He needs to salvage his rep. He's on his way to Cootie's right now. We hope he doesn't go in alone. He'll get his butt shot to Big Pine."

"Mary didn't like Dexter the cop. I say she won't call, it's just us."

"Us? Fuck that. You don't have a gun."

I reached behind her seat, pulled out Sam's .45, handed it over. I slowed for the bridge to Key Haven. Sun glare turned my windshield into a white wall. I checked the rearview. Still cool.

Lewis released the Para-Companion's magazine. "Seven plus one," she said. "You ever fire this?"

"I saw it the first time an hour ago. I think I hold tight and squeeze that skinny piece of metal."

"You want to bet your life on it?"

Only if I have to.

Traffic forced me to slow on Stock Island. It's hard to boogie on Saturday evening. My Shelby doesn't do curbs and off-road excursions.

"You came up with a shitload," said Lewis.

"Marnie did it, not me. If a story comes out, she gets it."

"She can do my paperwork, too. First things first."

I crossed Cow Key Channel Bridge, hit the left lane, found a hole. I blew the red light to a horn chorus and went south. The curb lane approach to Flagler is the worst pavement in America. I ran the fast lane until the instant I cut off a taxi and hung a right.

"We're there in twenty seconds," I said. "Plan?"

"We go in, shoot it out," she said. "You got a hero hat in the car? Two Kevlars and a riot gun in the trunk?"

Sarcasm for a reason. I shut my mouth.

"I'd lose my badge if I took you in. I'd lose it if I went in without calling for backup."

"What badge?"

"The one I might get back, if I do this right. Pull over."

I slowed, skidded in next to a hydrant. Antifreeze steam filled the car.

"If I call before I'm on scene, they'll order me off," she said. "They'll bust me before I can log the collar."

"Who's looking to salvage rep, now?"

She looked me in the eye. "Why do you want this?"

"For Naomi. So I don't feel useless."

"So die, then ask about useless."

"Call it," I said.

"We could be pissing into a thimble. Let's drive by, look for his car, see if he's home."

I pictured the old Benz gleaming under a palm tree. I pictured Cootie force-feeding pills to Naomi, beating the life out of Steve Gomez.

"Maybe Dexter'll show," said Lewis. "I can go in with him. We can earn back our stripes together."

My hot-dog driving had blitzed my brain. I'd forgotten Cootie's house number, but I didn't admit it to Lewis. Duffy Lee had said 1593 or 1953.

I turned onto Twentieth, went left on Eagle Avenue. A residential strip, well-kept homes, a few behind tall fences. The block was a long stretch. No number 1953. Next choice.

I slid the stop sign, dodged three kids on Razor scooters, then saw the dune buggy wedged between two tall trash containers.

I pointed. "Marnie told me that buggy was stolen from Oceanside."

"Two against two changes our nonplan," said Lewis. "I hate even odds."

"Shit," I said.

"My hero has second thoughts?"

"Look."

"It's a cluster fuck," said Lewis. "Take a right and park."

I turned, rolled a half block, and found a slot behind a boat trailer.

"Go find out," she said. "Don't take that weapon!"

The same gear, the cast of characters from the Whit Randolph ambush on Whitehead. Yellow streamers bordered by the FDLE van, Riley's ME wagon, and county patrol cars up the ying-yang.

Liska stood next to his Lexus with a uniformed deputy and "No Jokes" Bohner in civvies. He watched me approach, regarded me like a town punk come to take abuse so I could hang with the cool guys.

Cootie's place was the ugliest house on the street. Two spindly palms, a scrabble of dry grass and gravel, cracked Cuban tile front steps. An antique AC box cut into the lowest eight panes of a jalousie front window.

Airtight, like Cootie's alibi.

Liska had sweated through his striped polo shirt. He had been enjoying his day off. I smelled liquor behind the chewing gum.

"What brings you by?" he said. "It ain't hit the news yet."

How did he know that? The man had never been news sensitive before.

"I figured out that Cootie killed Gomez and probably Naomi, too."

"Oh," said Liska. "So you were coming by to talk it over with him?"

No answer would work.

"We got two down in there," he said. "Lead poisoning, one shot apiece. One in a La-Z-Boy and one on a couch. You've been working with a freak all these years, Rutledge. Cootie had a Princess Di museum in a locked room. Boxes, books, and fifty pictures of her on the wall. Six are muff shots, obviously not legit."

"Marlow the other victim?" I said.

"Oh, you're well-informed. He was still wearing his red Broward County Sheriff Department shirt, and now it's perforated. I would ask how you knew, but I don't want to be disingenuous."

"Marnie Dunwoody . . ."

"Right, and this time your buddy's not going to skate. We found him on his porch, tying flies, chilled out like he had no problems in his world. We're searching his house for a pistol with a silencer. He's my guest at the county as we speak."

They'd pegged Sam for revenge. What were the odds? "Does that make sense? Sam in there, and those men were sitting down?"

Liska studied the pavement, sniffed, exercised his Doublemint.

"How, in your mind, does a fishing guide turn into a murderer?"

"It's not so big a leap, Rutledge," said Liska. "The guide's an old macho warrior, combat vet, slayer of sea life. He falls in love with his vigilante self-image. The vigilante on crusade doesn't see his terminal actions as murder, but society does. I'm not high society, sir, but I represent its high interests."

"You tell a good story," I said. "Almost as if you were writing the news."

"The public wants justice, and that's my job description."

"Does this mean you stop looking for anyone else?" I said. "Did you test Sam's skin for gunpowder?"

He looked up, tapped his forehead. "I do it the old-fashioned way. Cranial forensics. Don't hurry off to post bond. I'll make sure he rides the metal bed straight to indictment. That tan jumpsuit looks just like his old fishing outfit."

"Where's Dexter Hayes?"

"Drinking beer. Or back at work, trying to diminish his father's crimes by logging successes. He found them and called it in. At least he didn't try to cowboy. He brought his SWAT boys for backup, but he got here too late. None of the neighbors heard shit. Dexter took his city people home when FDLE grabbed command."

"No one saw your perp?"

"Good use of lingo, Rutledge. It doesn't matter that no one saw the perp."

"Cootie killed Gomez and Douglas," I said.

"Elvis had lunch at Blue Heaven," said Liska. "Stay in town awhile. We definitely need to chat."

"Chatting's good," I said. "Almost like getting mugged by state agents."

"Push me," he said. "Go ahead."

"I can't, Liska. You're towing too much baggage. Maybe you should quit the sauce and start smoking again. You used to be a good detective. Now you're a politician. Why fuck with the truth when headlines are waiting?"

Billy Bohner started for me, but Liska held him back.

I headed for my car.

Liska said, "Your chum's gonna ride the upstate chemical sled in about four years. Maybe they'll let you take pictures."

I got back in the Shelby. Bobbi Lewis was soaked in sweat. I started the engine, began driving toward North Roosevelt. "Cootie and Marlow," I said. "They grabbed Sam Wheeler for it."

"How do you see it?"

"Cootie got mad and shot Marlow. Before he died, Odin got Cootie."

"That's not what I meant."

I thought it through, to convince myself. Sam was my best friend, flaws and all, but bumping off criminals is over the edge. I finally hit the snag in Liska's logic.

"He didn't do it," I said. "Sam's no splash artist. He had no reason to kill Cootie. His beef was with Marlow. Even with his head warped, it'd be some other way, like out at sea. But Cootie, too? No damn way."

"Okay," said Lewis. "I'll buy that. Common sense wins the war."

"Where to?"

"Your house," she said. "The balloon's deflated, and nothing's solved. I need to use the toilet and the shower."

"Where's your Celica?"

"Back at Frank Polan's. He owns a rental house four doors down from his place. It's in the carport. Did Liska connect Cootie to the mayor?"

"I suggested it," I said. "He wised back."

"I could be Sam's detention facility roommate by morning. I trust you have beer."

I cut north on White. Our mission had deflated, but my mind was still doing eighty-five in a fifty-five. A double murder was a small mind's revenge, and the puzzle still had pieces that didn't fit. With the tension drop, the pieces, one by one, fell into place. Cootie had been watching a stock car race in the police station, so he couldn't have shot Whit Randolph. His alibi was golden. To a rational person, it was too golden, too solid.

For five days Dexter had fumbled. He had picked his battles poorly, been hot and cold like Bobbi Lewis had been. But Dexter was not a stupid man, as evidenced by his bringing the city SWAT group to Cootie's.

Why hadn't he thought beyond the obvious?

Lewis said, "Your face looks like a boat propeller."

"Sam didn't shoot them," I said. "Cootie and Marlow didn't take turns shooting each other in the head. Someone else was there."

"Expand."

"Follow the money," I said. "Who benefits with Cootie gone?"

"Other shareholders, Cootie's relatives . . . Oh, shit. Do you know where she lives?"

"Love Lane. Marnie came through with that, too."

I hurried down Southard, in the poor visibility of dusk. Just past William Street, Lewis pointed. Dexter's Caprice, illegally parked. Dexter had thought a step further, had figured it out, too.

"We go in guns drawn," said Lewis. "Assume Dexter's not in there. We explain about Cootie and say we're there to protect her. Make no big deal, but keep your piece in your hand. Keep looking around, as if at any moment a bad man could jump out of a closet. Because a bad man might."

I pulled into Love Lane. A heavy man blocked us. "No parking."

Lewis showed her badge. "It's Saturday," she said. "I don't have a radio. Do us a favor, call 911."

The man looked thrilled, as if deputized, put on a mission.

We hurried around Yvonne's Acura, hit the porch. The door was half-open. Dylan's "Like a Rolling Stone" played softly next door.

"One last thing," said Lewis. "This is nut cutting. Caution's a bad bet."

She pushed the door. We could see straight through the house, out the French doors, into a tiny backyard. Yvonne was raking leaves with frantic motions and crying.

I scanned the yard, a tropical paradise in spite of itself. Deep burgundy crotons, overgrown yellow hibiscus, unkempt magenta bougainvillea. A garden by mistake, awash in dead sea grape leaves. A four-foot chain-link fence drooped around it all, pulled down by vines. A broad tarpaulin was spread open, with raked leaves piled on it. I saw sudden movement to my left. A blue-green lizard prowled the top grate of an AC fan unit. Careful, buddy.

No Dexter.

Yvonne looked up, quit scratching at the bricked patio. Her eyes were bloodshot. Her upper lip gleamed with snot and sweat. She had pulled back her hair with an elastic terry-cloth band, but ran her hand across her head to push back imagined loose strands. She didn't react to our being huffed up, guns in hand. She began to converse as if she'd expected us all along.

"My girlfriend lives on Eagle," she said. "She called me. Cootie's dead."

Yvonne dropped her rake, bent down, clutched a wad of dead leaves, and dropped them on the open tarp. She took the rake again in hand, and picked at clutter behind two rocks.

"We heard about Cootie," said Lewis. "Please accept our sympathy. Did you know that your cousin had inherited Remigio Partners' stock?"

"Cootie was such a groveler, messing with his trivia. He dreamed he could live like a prince. That stock was worthless."

"It was," said Lewis, "as long as your husband was there to vote down the Borroto Brinas project."

I heard a sharp clicking noise behind me. I leveled my pistol. The lizard had tumbled into the fan, had been chopped to bits. Another hunter lost to the hunt.

Where was Dexter?

Yvonne raked a small stack of leaves toward a larger pile. Deliberate, dutiful in working off energy, sublimating her grief.

"When did you come out of shock?" said Lewis. "When did you realize that your cousin killed your husband?"

Yvonne glanced up. "I don't think I heard you right. Cootie Ortega lived in a dream world. He sat in his ugly house and stared at pictures of the dead princess and jacked off, for all I know. He wanted the big time, being rich and important, but he could barely cook a microwave supper. What makes you think he killed Steven?"

"Cootie wanted to run the new art museum," I said. "He was a very bad blackmailer, but he was good at murder."

"Blackmail who?" said Yvonne.

"Here's one possibility. He went to Naomi Douglas and your husband. He threatened to expose their affair if he didn't get the museum job and a vote in favor of Borroto Brinas. It's my guess they laughed in his face, which was worse than not getting rich and not getting that job. So he got even. However it happened, greed drove him to murder."

The air-conditioning unit cycled off. The neighbor's music had stopped, and quiet filled the yard except for a faint, pulsing, whistling noise that I couldn't place.

"You figured it for Cootie the day it happened," I said. "Maybe you didn't want your husband dead, but there was no going back. You also knew how cousin Cootie would benefit, and those millions would come to you if he was dead, too. But Whit Randolph screwed it up, didn't he?"

"Who?"

They'd been seen walking together, arguing.

"Exact wrong answer, lady. Randolph talked to Teresa Barga," I said. "With enough facts, he guessed your deal, or came close enough to do his own blackmail, didn't he? You had to remove his complications by removing him. You had Cootie follow him for a few days to learn his schedule. Today was your big day, and Randolph never made it to lunch at the Turtle Kraals."

"Fuck off. I'm tired of your face."

"Take a good look," I said. "Maybe it'll bore you to death. It'd be a less messy way to die than how you snuffed Randolph. And once you

320

did that, there was no reason not to shoot your cousin and a Broward cop you didn't even know."

Yvonne scowled but almost smiled.

Shit, I thought. Everyone was drawn to the riches. Odin Marlow had worked for Borroto Brinas, had come to town to squeeze big cash out of Cootie, and Yvonne probably knew him from years ago. Finding Marlow at Cootie's house was pure convenience. Killing him had fit perfectly into her plan.

The faint whistle pulsed again.

Lewis looked for it. "We've got a snake in here somewhere."

Yvonne reached down to the pile of leaves. She raised a weapon, swung it toward the tarp.

Lewis and I shot Yvonne Gomez at the same time. The bullets knocked the woman into an Adirondack chair, killing her instantly. Her gun clanked to the bricks.

Lewis yanked the tarp off Dexter Hayes. His face was ashen, his eyes rolled back. The hole in his shirt explained the whistle. Bobbi rolled him to check his back. No exit wound. She jammed her thumb into his chest to keep air in his lung.

Sirens filled the island, all inbound.

"Don't assume those are for us," said Lewis. "Call 911. Say 'Officer down,' and 'Trauma-Star Helo.'" She bent to begin CPR.

I had to dial Yvonne's phone with my left hand. I wanted to like hell, but I couldn't let go of the gun.

35

AT 5:45 A.M. THE next morning, I got a call to pick up Sam on Stock Island. The island was asleep. No hint of sunup, no other cars on the road, four on-duty cop cruisers gathered around a camper in Albertson's parking lot.

I had left my Shelby Mustang outdoors all night, a bad slip, the first time ever. I had remembered it as I fell onto my bed, but had been drained from hours of interviews and let it slide. Car theft ranked low on my impact scale after having pulled that trigger.

Sam was standing in the detention center parking lot, chatting with a female deputy, airing jail stink out of his clothing. I knew the outprocessing had begun at four A.M., but he looked rested. I suspected he had slept more than I had.

"Couldn't face another taxi." He shut the car door and settled in.

That was all the conversation we needed.

Before I could find reverse, Chicken Neck Liska stopped his Lexus next to us. He'd lowered his passenger-side window. His raised index finger asked us to wait a minute.

"Fuck him," whispered Sam. "Let's go."

Almost as if Liska could read our minds, or hear my transmission go into gear, he backed the Lexus in a quarter circle to block my departure. He got out, walked to my window, and peered across at Sam. "I owe you something of an apology," he said.

"Sounds tentative," said Sam. "Like you either don't mean it, or you got other ammunition."

"Every piece of paper with your name on it will hit the shredder by eight A.M. The past is history, and history doesn't excite me."

"What does?" I asked.

Liska took a moment, during which I figured he judged the consequences of punching out my lights. Then he surprised us both. "I'm excited by being a better cop and a piss-poor politician. I may have to start smoking again."

"Hold on to your gains," said Sam. "You can buy votes but not health."

Liska cracked a grin. "Am I one percent forgiven?"

Sam said, "You're a hundred percent right about history."

I took Sam home and drove to the lane. I found Bobbi Lewis sitting on my porch.

"I couldn't sleep," she said. "I came into town for breakfast at Harpoon Harry's, but I knew I'd blow lunch in public if I tried to eat."

I got a towel from the house, marched her to the shower, then left her alone. I searched the kitchen until I found a peppermint candy to toss on the pillow, turned back my bed, and made my second trip to Stock Island.

Teresa appeared to know that I was there as a friend, as an ex-lover. She still wanted me to hold her hand, to look in her eyes and not at the bubble of gauze that ran from her forehead to her left shoulder. Neither of us knew what to say, so we sat silently until nurses came in to make checks. One offered a tray of food that wouldn't satisfy a small bird. When Teresa's mother arrived, I left. At the information booth I was told that Dexter Hayes, in the ICU, couldn't have visitors. He'd been upgraded to serious condition, so I should check back in two or three days.

I needed more sleep, but Bobbi was out solid on my bed, in the sleep of the weary, the victorious. She had found one of my bed-only T-shirts, one that said GET YOUR STUFF TOGETHER.

I gathered up Naomi's camera gear, delivered it to Ernest Bramblett, and escaped after minimal conversation. From there I went to Harpoon Harry's where I saw no one I knew.

Sipping coffee, waiting for my omelet, I overheard two people talking about Bloody Saturday, as the *Herald* had tagged it. One man said, "Screw that big-city crap. For once the *Citizen* got it right. That black cop is gonna survive, and the city's better off with the bloodsuckers dead."

On Monday morning, Jack Spottswood called the Miami FDLE to discuss our surrender procedure. The call was passed to Red Simmons. He informed us that, as promised, so long as Sam and I minded our own business, all charges were dropped. Simmons had seen the initial FDLE Crime Analysis on Mayor Gomez's murder. Motives still were hazy, but they confirmed what we already knew. Cootie's city-owned Taurus, which was a year newer than the mayor's identical Taurus, was missing its trunk mat. Blood had dripped into the rear fender wells. The investigators felt that Gomez had died of head injuries while being transported in Cootie's trunk.

I went home to a waiting phone message from Detective Bobbi Lewis. She had called from Grand Cayman Island.

"Liska rewrote my vacation request," she said. "He predated it to last Wednesday, and gave me a four-day bonus. I just arrived down here and it's beautiful, so on a whim I tried to make you a reservation. They said you were already booked for tomorrow noon. It'll be great to see you, away from all the mess. This place is really alive."